STRANGE TRICKS

SYD MOORE

A Point Blank Book

First published by Point Blank,
an imprint of Oneworld Publications, 2021

A CIP record for this title is available from the British Library

ISBN 978-1-78607-548-2
ISBN 978-1-78607-549-9 (ebook)

Typeset by Fakenham Prepress Solutions, Fakenham, Norfolk NR21 8NL
Printed and bound in Great Britain by Clays Ltd, Elcograf S.p.A.

Oneworld Publications
10 Bloomsbury Street
London WC1B 3SR
England

For Ciara Phipps whose awesomeness does not go unappreciated.

Strange /streɪn(d)ʒ/

Adjective: strange

1. Unusual or surprising; difficult to understand or explain.

Comparative adjective: stranger; *Superlative adjective*: strangest

Synonyms: Odd, curious, peculiar, funny, bizarre, weird, uncanny, queer, unexpected, unfamiliar, abnormal, atypical, anomalous, different, out of the ordinary, out of the way, extraordinary, remarkable, puzzling, mystifying, mysterious, perplexing, baffling, unaccountable, inexplicable, incongruous, uncommon, irregular, singular, deviant, aberrant, freak, freakish, surreal, alien.

PROLOGUE

The door banged.

This time it didn't stay shut.

Nor was there the turn of the metallic key or the clunk of the padlock dropping back on its chain and knocking against the wood.

A shard of light slanted across the floor. Not much. If he'd have been at school and Mrs Green had told him to measure it, he reckoned it would only be up to two centimetres on his wooden ruler. Maybe even less – millimetres.

The Boy let a breath of frustration escape his lips. What wouldn't he give to be back at school? Instead of here in the dark. It wasn't fair. Even though The Washing Up Man brought him sweets and chocolate and jam sandwiches and a drink which tasted like Tizer but had a medicine in it, he knew he shouldn't stay.

Despite his years, The Boy had an understanding that his stepdad would be worried about him. Not necessarily out of affection, but he'd be aware of the stares of the neighbours and the judgement in their eyes if The Boy wasn't seen at home. Indeed, when Brian sobered up, after his latest four-day binge, and realised The Boy wasn't there, then The Boy would be in trouble, heaps of it, when he got home.

Brian's anger scared him. Though it was less frightening than The Washing Up Man. His stepdad's fury was physical – a couple of slaps here and there and it was over and done. You just had to grit your teeth, fingers crossed they didn't get smashed, and put up with it.

But The Washing Up Man was way different. He didn't show his anger out front, but it was there. You could feel the heat of it coming off him, bubbling under the surface like a volcano. Almost ready to blow. Sure, The Washing Up Man acted nice to The Boy, but there was something that was not okay: The Boy had complained to The Man that he needed to go home, that his stepdad, Brian, would blow a gasket. Not that he was sure what a 'gasket' was, but he'd heard Brian say it often enough and knew it warned of violence. But The Washing Up Man had kept him. Told The Boy that he couldn't leave until he had played with his brother. But so far this brother hadn't come.

The Boy had persisted though and mentioned it again last night. 'I ought to get off now. Dad will be wondering …'

The word 'Dad' had sounded peculiar on The Boy's tongue. He had never used that term for Brian before, but it sounded more convincing. And, so as to be polite, like his mum used to instruct him, The Boy thanked The Man for the game and he thanked The Man for the sweets and thanked The Man for having him and he told The Man that he would definitely come back to play with his brother. Probably tomorrow. He promised. Honest.

But The Washing Up Man said, 'Just one more day.'

And click-clunked the door outside.

And locked him in.

With the cake and red drink that was tasty but made him sleep.

So this morning when The Man came with Kellogg's and milk and the drink and then, later with the burger and coke, The Boy pretended to eat them but he didn't really. He went and buried the food in a hole under the mattress at the side of the room. And left only crumbs on the plates.

Which meant now he wasn't tired.

He pretended he was.

And crawled under the dirty sheet.

And, although his tummy rumbled, The Boy could feel that his sacrifice was paying off: he was staying awake.

As the light outside dimmed, The Man came back to collect his plates.

The Boy heard the dragging slouchy footsteps cross the floor. They stopped near his corner. The Man's breaths carried on, heavy and hard.

Underneath the sheet The Boy tried not to move.

The Man grunted, satisfied, turned and picked up the plates. Then he went out the door. But this time The Man did not lock it.

Slowly The Boy got up and padded over, putting his eye to the gap. The outside made him blink. He had been so long in the darkness that even the dull white-clouded sky hurt his head at the front.

There was no one there in the yard.

The Man had gone inside.

The Boy took a breath and moved the door. It creaked. Whoops.

Better go now, he thought. Before he hears me or remembers the lock.

And so gently, gently, quietly, quietly The Boy squeezed out into the yard and skipped down towards the field at the end.

It didn't take him long to slip through the hedge and then he was running, fast, over the stiff grass, joyful in his freedom.

There were trees up ahead. He knew them.

But – a shout. From behind him. 'Hey you!'

The Man was running, chasing after him.

But The Boy was lighter, quicker and he knew this place.

'Come back!' yelled The Man, gaining ground.

The Boy made it into the shade of the trees. A few more metres and he would be lost in the thicket. A few more leaps …

And then he was inside the snug darkness of the wood.

He crouched down and slunk through the twigs and bracken. The Boy didn't care about the scratches on his legs or the bashes on his knees. On and on he went trying to find a place to hide.

Behind him he could hear The Man, and his loud breaths, stopping, calling his name, asking him to go back, but The Boy would not. The Boy knew it wasn't the right thing to do.

And soon The Man's shouts grew fainter. He was losing him. Only a little further now and The Boy would be free.

Free, he thought and let himself enjoy the word for a bit. Free, he smiled and allowed himself to stretch and stand up and jog a few paces on.

Ah, ha! Here he was. Nearly at the edge.

But as he was thinking this, something hefty hit him. It was sharp, and metal, and came into the back of his head. The impact sent him spinning unsteadily. He staggered on a few more paces. The sounds of the wood were lost, muffled in the undergrowth, drowned out by the silent scream inside his brain. The dizziness unrelenting, disorientating, buckled his legs and he hit the ground.

The Man was near and The Boy knew it. He crawled like a soldier through the scrub, twisting, turning, elbowing his way under the bushes.

Another crack.

Beneath him.

Not *in* him this time.

The forest floor was giving way.

He felt for a moment as if he were flying, then he landed with a thud.

The world spun briefly and finally calmed. There was no pain, only that in his skull which had come before.

Underneath the tips of his fingers The Boy could feel mulch and dead leaves, and when he breathed through his nose there came the dark smell of the soil and its woody tendrils.

Everything was brown.

Ah yes, he thought. *One of our traps.*

Good. I am here.

And through slitty eyes he realised he was in a hollow with walls of smooth mud. His friends had often covered it with sticks and leaves and twigs, hoping to catch a poacher or a crocodile or something infinitely more interesting. Now it had caught him. But The Boy was glad.

He wriggled out of the light coming down between the tree branches and scrambled underneath where the hairy roots grew together in a strange earthy lace. This was the Root Cave, the most excellent and secret place for hide and seek.

And it was working. It was hiding him good and proper: because The Boy could hear The Man swearing.

'I can see you,' The Man called, breathless and panting. 'I can see you now. Come out. Don't make me come and get you.'

The Boy pressed himself up against the side of the Root Cave knowing The Man was fibbing. If he could *see* him, he would have come and got him. Which meant all The Boy had to do was be quiet and try not to fall asleep in the thickening gloom.

But The Boy was tired and his head hurt.

And just as he was about to drift off he heard a woman's voice, unfamiliar, but soft and kind. She was near him in the dark.

'Where are you?' she said. 'Tell us where you are.'

CHAPTER ONE

I am looking into those dark, dark eyes and wondering if they might conceal the secrets of the universe. So old, so deep, so velvety. Soft? No. There is hardness there. Around the pupil a green ring is tinged with gold. Its edges have the look of exquisite tracery, an intricate pattern, hardening larva. Something wants to spill out of them. Fire burns there.

And then he touches my hand.

I feel it like a trail of sparks across the skin.

And gasp with pleasure.

And he says …

And he says, 'How much is it to get in?'

Then withdraws his hand and coughs. 'You all right?'

'Er, yes. Sorry, I was thinking about something,' I said.

Goodness knew how that vision had managed to wriggle its way into my thoughts.

'Yes.' The customer grinned displaying strong white teeth with a pair of sharp canines. 'I could see that.'

Stop it, I cautioned my naughty imagination. *Still thyself, damn harlot brain.* There are certain limitations to customer service that must respectfully be observed. Imaginary shagging was probably one of them.

But then again, this bloke was exceptionally endowed in the handsome department and, to be honest, I'd been a bit bored in the ticket kiosk.

'It's Rosie, isn't it?' he said, leaning onto the counter. A musky aftershave pooled in the air. It smelt of antique leather and classical music. Beyond that, a rich coconutty perfume, that must have been radiating from his hair, as black as midnight and shining like the moon. Soft and thick. Something to hold on to … *Stop that.*

'Rosie, yes,' I managed, grateful Auntie Babs had done me a spray tan at the weekend.

The bloke nodded, then dazzled me with an ultra-bright, honest-to-God super-sly sizzlingly sensual, smile. And I was visited by a series of images – wind picking up in the north, the boom of a cannon, hard-tipped boots, feathers stroking my skin, a haven of shadows concealing lovers' sultry embraces.

Jeez. What was the matter with me? Usually I could command these sorts of impulses, but my imagination had gone all loopy, hijacked my mind and slung me over the back of its horse so it could gallop off and do its worst.

'Oooohhh,' I said as I framed his features into context: clean-shaven, pale-skinned, silk shirt, stiff double-breasted military coat. Ting! The bell in my head finally rang. 'Oh, yes! It's Dorcus, isn't it?'

Now I'd got his name I was surprised at myself for not recognising him immediately. Really really. Because he was dead fit and sexy. Although, to be honest, the last time we'd met, or I thought we *might* have met, I'd been in a forest tripping off my nut with belladonna poisoning, convinced that this slightly gothy but definitely fit-looking bloke was a vampire, or possibly a stag, potentially a shape-shifting goat-footed god with powers over the forces of nature and the underworld.

If indeed he had been there at all and wasn't a symptom of the atropine ingestion.

I used to be a Benefit Fraud inspector.

In an attempt to repress this sudden unbidden release of lust, I directed my internal focus to the next job I had on my list, once the museum was shut – cleaning the men's toilets. Not a chore I would be relishing.

The prospect of such life-enriching activity worked my ardour down for a moment, which was long enough for Dorcus to lift his face, and let his hair fall away to reveal those slanting cheekbones, and say, 'You remembered! I wasn't sure if you would. The last time we met, it was er …' His smile lit up my ticket booth (not a euphemism. Well, maybe. A bit).

I didn't want to come out and ask him if he was referring to the goat-foot god episode for obvious reasons, so I went with a neutral, 'How could I forget?' Plus, he'd also found my phone in a graveyard during a storm on a previous occasion when we had been investigating reanimated stone knights, so there was a possibility he might have been referring to that.

My life one year ago = simple, despite numerous attempts by persons living in or around Leytonstone to claim unsanctionable benefits.

My life now = complex. The role of proprietor of the Essex Witch Museum brought along much weirdery. If that wasn't a word before I arrived in Adder's Fork, it was now.

It had its perks, though. I was looking at one. 'Of course, I remember you.' I decided to avoid all reference to drugs, embalmed knights and poison and keep it light. 'You found my phone. Thanks again for that!'

'Correct,' he said and spread his lips so I could see his strong teeth. The action unleashed a flush of hot chemicals into the pit of my stomach.

'Are you still staying in Damebury?' he asked.

'No,' I said, and pointed to the ceiling of the ticket office. 'I live above the museum. There's an apartment.'

'Oh, I thought that you maybe … oh it doesn't matter. Well, that must be very convenient.' Dorcus straightened up and took a step towards the 'Abandon Hope' door.

'Are you still staying in Damebury?' I tried to keep my gaze away from his chest.

'No.' His eyes were hypnotic. 'My place,' he shrugged. 'It got, er, disrupted.'

I nodded. I'd had that before. 'Flat share?'

'Sort of. Other people moved in and it became too noisy.'

'I hear you,' I said. 'That would annoy me.'

The corners of his mouth tucked up. Adorable. Actually no, I corrected myself, this man wasn't adorable, that was the totally wrong word for Dorcus. He was powerful and attractive, not adorable and cute.

'I've not gone far,' he was saying. 'Rented a place just up the road, in the village of Haven. Do you know it?'

'Not really,' I said, doing my best to be agreeable and conversational. 'Heard of it. Never been there. Properties are quite cheap. Thought it must be a dump.'

'Well, there are some very nice bits to it,' he said and stepped back. 'I'll show you around if you fancy it?'

Blimey.

Really?

Was this pale-skinned lothario fluttering his eyes at me?

I did fancy it. 'Maybe,' I said, wondering (very briefly) if this might contravene any unknown rules about mixing with visitors.

Dorcus fished something out of his breast pocket. 'Here's my card,' he said and slid it across the brass counter with his index finger. 'My mobile's on it. Text me, then I'll have your number.'

The little cardboard rectangle was inscribed with gold lettering and a picture of a feathered quill. 'Dorcus Beval, Writer, Archaeologist, Historian'. Underneath was his mobile number. Nothing else. No email or address. It was immaculate apart from the top left corner which was curling back to reveal gold underneath. I rubbed it but the card's surface was even, not flawed.

'It's a trompe l'oeil,' Dorcus grinned.

'A what?'

'A trick. Optical illusion. Makes it look 3D.'

'Oh right,' I said and grinned. 'Clever.' But I wasn't really interested in that part of it. 'What do you write about?'

'This and that. I'm involved in military history.' His eyebrows lifted. The skin on his forehead remained smooth like marble.

I felt the impulse to put my fingers there and feel it to make sure it wasn't cold. With great effort I resisted and said, 'Fascinating,' which was a lie.

'Yes,' he brightened. 'This area of Essex has seen quite a lot of action in that regard. The Battle of Assundan for instance, in 1016, you know,' he looked at me with expectation, 'King Canute? Mentioned in the *Knýtlinga saga*: "brown was the flesh of bodies / served to the blood-bird in the slaughter—"'

Oh God, I thought. 'Yes, well Dorcus,' I interjected, heading off the Boy's Own concise history of East Sax's bestest bash-ups. He was fit, but he weren't *that* fit. 'I have to tell you. Time isn't quite on your side. If you want to be admitted into the museum, then you should go in now. We close in an hour.'

An older couple, to whom I'd sold tickets but half an hour ago, emerged into the lobby looking flustered. I waved at them pleasantly but they scowled and scuttled out the front door. Some people don't get that the stuff in here is genuinely disturbing. I don't know what they imagine might be in a witch museum, but the history of witches in Essex ain't all ruby slippers and green face-paint.

'Oh right.' Dorcus took a deep breath and turned his head away from the door through which the visitors had charged. 'Yes. Sorry, forgot myself.' He looked embarrassed though didn't flush.

'Or you could come back another day and I could show you round?' I said to compensate. Nothing wrong with a little one-to-one customer service, was there? According to Sam, I needed to work on my personal skills. There had been some negative reviews on Tripadvisor. Personally, I thought it was more likely to be Vanessa's mum, Trace. She didn't suffer fools gladly and, I can tell you, a lot of them turned up at the Witch Museum.

Dorcus puffed out his oh-so-manly chest. 'That'd be great.'

'I have to man the ticket booth this arvo. Can't take you around myself. There's no one else available. But another time ...?'

He sort of chuckled and began, 'That sounds like an offer I can't refuse ...'

A clatter of Cuban heels and some muffled cussing summoned our attention to the porch and in bundled my curator, shaking raindrops from his hair and a broken umbrella with baboons printed across it.

'Bloody hell!' Sam tried to collapse the spines. 'It's cats and dogs out there and this brolly from the Pound Shop is useless.'

'Can't think why,' I muttered.

'You bought it!'

'Pay peanuts, get monkeys.' I gestured to the print and laughed at my excellent joke.

'Exactly!'

'Why you blaming me?' I said. 'You're the one who borrowed it.'

'I would have liked to have borrowed a better—'

'Or, as you didn't actually ask me, then I think that might constitute half-inching my umbrella.'

'Half-inching?'

'Pinching.' I rolled my eyes. Posh blokes – honestly.

'Okay, then I would have liked to have half-inched a better-quality waterproofing device which worked on more than just one outing.'

'I always lose umbrellas. That's why I buy the cheapos.' I was tiring of this conversation. 'And denim jackets, black cardigans, sunglasses. Always the same. Now stop sniping and let me introduce you to Dorcus.'

I gestured to the ledge of the counter, where the dark one had been standing, and leaning and lingering, and smiling and … but there was no one there. The 'Abandon Hope' door was swinging very slightly so I guessed he must have gone through. 'Oh bugger. You scared him, Sam.'

'Who?' he said, squelching his way to the ticket booth. 'Scared someone *into* the Witch Museum. That's a new one.'

I concurred. 'Dorcus. He was just here. I met him in Damebury. After you bashed your head on that tombstone and went all weird.'

He smelt of damp and hair product. 'I didn't go weird. I was considering the possibilities of life after death and the non-linear potential of time.'

'Yeah,' I said. 'Weird. Anyway, don't start harking on about that old chestnut now.'

'What particular chestnut are you referring to here?'

'The ghost chestnut. There was that name on the tombstone – same as yours, then we went to the pub and you were going on about the possibility that you'd seen a ghost on the film talking to me – remember?'

Sam leant on the counter. He was taller than me by about half a foot, so I had to look up at him. Sometimes I liked this.

Sometimes I didn't. Today I was favouring the latter. 'Yes, yes. Of course I remember.'

'We both know very well just how many strange tricks the mind can play,' I told him. 'Not on purpose necessarily but because it thinks it's doing you a favour. Like with Mary at La Fleur and her sight condition – her brain thought it was helping her out, filling in the blanks her eyes couldn't see. But it wasn't, right?'

'And yet it was. It is possible for there to be two truths in play at the same time …'

I ignored him because he had a point. 'Other times it's been about denial – we know it's easier for folks to think witches did it than admit they might have a murderer in their midst. Other times it's just bizarre – remember when Matilda said she'd seen the White Lady do a poo in her garden?'

'Yes, well she was a child of only seven then and that was more likely to do with an over-active imagination and all the hysteria occurring in the village at that time.'

I agreed with him privately but couldn't be bothered to say so. 'Anyway,' I carried on, driving the point home. 'I'm basically reminding you that the mind is a remarkable thing. The lengths it will go to keep the body alive and functioning are extraordinary. Self-preservation is an exceptionally powerful impulse.' I'd just been reading about it in a magazine at my Auntie Bab's salon. There had been an article about some bloke who got his leg stuck under a rock and had to eat it off or something.

My curator nodded. 'I'll not disagree with you there, but the film …'

'Monty said the film was inconclusive,' I said, marvelling at how I was coming across as ultra-rational. Almost as logical as the curator himself.

'Yes, I know.' He blinked. Deep within his eyes golden flints began to whirl and shine, catching the light of his excitement. Sometimes Sam's intellectual curiosity was so intense it made him glow like a Chernobyl engineer. 'Our dear friend's inconclusion,' he said, 'is therefore open-ended. This means there are several possibilities demanding serious consideration. Shall I list them?'

I was unable to stifle a yawn. 'No, you're all right.'

'You know, for aeons, people believed that if a ghost was present it turned flames blue.'

I thought about gas, then the oven, then wondered what we were having for dinner. I didn't want pasta again. All Sam's meals were so predictable. Maybe I could do a green curry and try to keep it low fat with some seafood. Or perhaps we should just throw caution to the wind and eat at the Stars. After all, it was probably wise for us to turn in early. We had a big day tomorrow. Montgomery Walker, the agent from the Occult Bureau in MI5 or 6 or 7 or whatever, Monty, who called upon our services quite regularly now, had decided to take us in hand and sort us out a bit. Unofficially, though somehow using official resources. In the morning we were off to a secret location in Middlesex where we were to undertake some basic training. I was looking forward to it.

'Rosie! Rosie, pay attention!'

'What?' I'd forgotten he was here.

'You said "prawns".'

'No, I didn't.'

'Yes you did. And, more to the point, you started this.'

'I didn't do that either.'

'Yes you did – you said I went all "weird".'

'Oh yeah,' I said. 'I did. Fair cop.'

'Now listen, talking of serious consideration, which I was, before you tactfully zoned out, I'd like you to come into the office?'

'Okay. Don't forget we've got that training tomorrow.'

'I haven't, but I want to discuss something I just heard: there's witchcraft abroad.'

I groaned.

'Witchcraft-slash-Satanism,' Sam finished and looked on with a similar expression of expectation as Dorcus had just used. Like he wanted me to jump up and down or something.

This time I supplied a fitting response. 'Oh here we go … wonder what that's covering up then? Teenagers frightening the locals? Waitresses executing their dastardly machinations? Hunters lopping off animal heads for interior designers?' We were both very familiar with elements of 'witchcraft' being used to mask and camouflage other insalubrious goings on. The world wasn't done with scapegoating poor women despite, or maybe *in spite of*, the Enlightenment, education, technological progress, Brexit …

'Not sure what's behind it,' he said. 'Seems to have started recently.'

'Who told you? Monty? Did he get out his tom toms and send smoke signals through the secret MI5 grapevine?' I punctuated my question with a snigger.

'Will you stop mixing your metaphors? That was a sentence worthy of George Bush. But no. Nothing like that.' Sam screwed his face and rubbed his hand through his hair. It was a habit. But this time his fingers came out quickly: he had recently submitted to my Auntie Bab's nifty snippers. She had cut him a style that worked well on his auburn locks. Textured with a bit of a quiff at the front. Not bad at all.

'Steve had a Haven parish magazine in the shop,' he said, inspecting his fingers which had dislodged something from his hair that he appeared to find surprising. 'He showed me.' Sam waved his other hand, which I now saw contained a pale-green-coloured leaflet. From this distance it looked like someone had photocopied pages and stapled it together by hand. Totally old skool.

'Hang on, did you say the Haven parish magazine? Funny,' I said. 'That's where Dorcus has moved to.' I pointed to the 'Abandon Hope' door. 'The bloke who's just gone in. I think.' Or transformed into a bat and flown out of here.

Don't be silly Rosie, I told myself.

That was another thing that had changed since I had landed in this little corner of Essex – my imagination had stretched and grown with staggering speed. It must be all the fresh air.

'Oh, all right,' Sam said. He was vague and partially absent – his mind already turning over the news about Haven. 'Well,' he pushed through the 'Staff Only' door into the ticket office, then opened the next one which led into our office/diner/kitchenette and disappeared. 'See if you can find him in there.' The door closed. His voice muffled. 'The fellow might have heard a thing or two about it. Then shut up shop.'

It irked me to follow commands from blokes. Especially when they were, if not on equal footing, then due to me being the owner and he being the curator, certainly command-*able* (if that was another word). However, Sam did, as blimmin' usual, have a point. Dorcus could well have picked up some important intel regarding the shenanigans going down in his village. He would probably be more familiar with the layout of the area too. Which would be helpful. If we needed to investigate. Plus really, I wasn't too put out about sloping into the museum in pursuit of a tall dark stranger. Well, not that he was a stranger any more. We were on first name turns and that made us acquaintances. It was a step in the right direction.

I took his business card out of my pocket and looked once more at the corner, designed as if it were turned back. A trompe l'oeil. Strange. I found it a tad fussy. Dorcus must be the type of bloke who liked little details. And then suddenly there I was again wondering what he was like, what kind of things he did to pass his day. I'd have to try and keep a lid on this. My imagination will be the death of me, I thought as I entered the 'Abandon Hope' door.

But there were those who would counter it was actually quite the opposite.

CHAPTER TWO

No longer in the presence of an attractive man, I found it much easier to keep my thoughts clean as I hummed my way through the Witch Museum. The engraving of the Judas Cradle on our 'Instruments of Torture' wall always helped in this regard, it being literally sphincter-splittingly alarming. Seriously, the bloke who came up with that device should have been locked up. Allegedly it was one Ippolito Marsili, who thought that it was a humane, yes humane, alternative to smashing up bones and burning flesh. Fifteenth-century Italians did my head in sometimes.

I pounded past the pyramid with speed. As always, it was a relief to get round the corner to the Blackly Be display, with our freshly moulded Black Anne – a much-wronged local lass tried for witchcraft in 1621. Her mortal remains were buried outside by our memorial garden, along with those of Bartholomew Elke, who we learnt through various tests, was actually her dad. That investigation had been quite a mammoth one for us. Reaped all sorts of surprises, including the fact that the aforementioned Black Anne Hewghes had actually been black. Yep. Who'd've thought. Anyway, this was why we now had a new model of her. To reflect that. It was much needed. Pricey, though. Sam had been too busy with the rest of the exhibit, so I had been charged with getting the waxwork of Anne sorted. Turns out Madame Tussauds are well expensive. But they did a damn fine job.

I muttered a greeting to the tableau in which a local nobleman consulted a very lifelike Anne. On the table in front of her was spread a map, some alchemical instruments and a compass. If you asked me, which no one did these days, the scene looked intriguing and it was, for sure, one mega-interesting story. If you hit a button located at the side of the exhibit, the lights would go on and you would be treated to an audio of our friend, Carmen, recounting the tale of Anne, Bartholomew and the Howlett hoard. That's treasure to you and me. I'd also decided to do something with smell to make it a little more immersive. So now we had a diffuser that worked with mossy earth, cedarwood and frankincense. It emitted bursts of the different fragrances throughout the day. The designer had told me that smell was one of the most powerful senses. It touched parts of your psyche that nothing else did. They actually called it 'psychic'. To say that I totally dig that now is something of an understatement. Anyway, apparently each perfume we selected was designed to touch something deep inside your brain – memories or experiences – walking through woods and forests, picnics. Mossy earth and cedarwood reminded me of the Sitting Pool in Adder's Fork, a strange, fairy-like dell where time stood still. Sometimes. As well as memories the smells conjured wishes – frankincense was packed full of spice and wonder. It was a fragrance that touched your heart and filled it with optimism and joy. Well, that's what it said on the label. Cool, right?

But there was so much more to tell of this legendary Adder's Fork tale – we were currently awaiting the trial of the current Lord and Lady of the Manor, descendants of those who murdered Anne Hewghes. And they'd also tried to kill me. I know. It is, as our European relatives say, 'compliqué'. For my mother's story was wound up with it too. And my grandmother's. The whole episode had caused a sensation locally and nationally. And personally.

However, never one to look a gift horse in the mouth, I could see that it presented a good opportunity for us at the Witch Museum. Obvs, because part of it was autobiographical, I had dibs on the story. And I was definitely going to large it up here and make the most of my connection. But we had to go to court first. So we'd put a sign up explaining some of that and adding 'Watch This Space'. Which we meant literally – we'd already cleared out another exhibit to make room for a 'De Vere' tableau. That bloke was going to get his comeuppance very publicly indeed.

I walked on, trying to shake all these thoughts from my head. If I didn't, I'd never sleep.

The more 'standard' museum sections were always a joy to meander around. The next room displayed various items used in folk medicine. It was light and airy on account of the large skylights. In the corner our little waxwork hedgewitch cackled in her rocking chair, keeping an eye on anyone who might want to half-inch the exhibits. I usually found Hecate, our museum cat, curled up in her lap, but she was absent today. As was Dorcus.

'Is there anybody there?' I called out and unexpectedly felt a shudder run down my spine. The air-con must still be on.

There was no answer so I turned out the lights.

Before turning back I carried out a quick check on the talks area. Sometimes you found lurkers there having a sit and a chat, occasionally chomping a packed lunch. But it was quiet and dark. I shut the door and trundled through to the Hall of Divination, one of my favourite places in the museum and definitely one of the lightest. Instead of rebuilding part of the leaky roof in the Cadence wing, we'd gone for more skylights down the middle. As a whole cartload of magic mirrors adorned the walls, it meant that when the sun was out this was one of the brightest, most dazzling spots in Essex. Of course, the upshot of that was that we had to rotate the exhibits on a regular basis to prevent sun damage and fading, but that wasn't difficult.

Divination was one of the most amply supplied areas in terms of artefacts. Every culture across the globe had a different method of telling the future. We were proud of our collection, which illustrated everything from Abacomancy – the interpretation of patterns of dust or dirt or sand which some of the county's 'sea-witches' used to have a pop at – to Zygomancy, which is prophecy with weights. Not the gym kind but pendulums and stones and that. One of the villagers had recently donated such an item. It was polished well and had a leather braid threaded through a natural hole. Martin, the donor, told Sam that his grandma used to use it to predict the future. She'd hold it up and then ask it a question. If it moved to the left, the answer was yes. If it moved to the right, then that was a definite no-no. I thought this was brilliant and began to look for stones with holes in that we could clean up, thread with string and then flog in the gift shop (ticket office) for twenty quid or something like that. But Sam said 'no' and that it was unethical.

Sometimes he was a bit of a killjoy.

Anyway, it wasn't the collection or the light that drew me to the Hall of Divination. It was the fact that we'd recently popped a few of my family's bits and bobs into the collection. Namely, my mother's tarot cards. One pack figured quite centrally. They were steeped in a new kind of knowledge for me, as she'd sketched them in the journal I'd found. It was hard to look at them, fanned into a semi-circle, knowing what I did now. But at other times the awareness that she had handled each one, the fact that her DNA was on them, well, it made me feel closer to her. That was priceless really, as I had no real memories to go on – she'd died when I was only weeks old. And when I say 'died' I also mean *was possibly murdered.*

But that was another story.

My grandmother's personal items were exhibited in here too. The fortune-telling cup she had received from her aunt was presented and labelled meticulously in the Methods of Western Divination section. Though Sam said that my grandfather told him Ethel-Rose used any old cup. Any old cup however would not wow the visitors. This one had symbols and signs etched inside it which bestowed an air of mystique.

It comforted me to know that people were looking at these items, intrigued, fascinated, respectful.

I still had boxes and boxes of Celeste and Ethel-Rose's belongings to go through up in the loft so there was a possibility I might find more artefacts to extend the collection. Plus, we'd also uncovered a few more of my Great-Aunt Rozalie's bit and pieces. Carmen had found her witch bottle and hamsa buried under the floorboards of her cottage. We'd arranged them in one of the vitrines in 'Magic'.

Here, in 'Divination', were laid out a selection of oddly shaped rune stones that I discovered in a hat box inscribed with Rozalie's initials. Sam thought they might have been handmade. Perhaps by her, perhaps by someone else who she knew. They were shiny and smooth like pebbles but some of them had been carved. Beside them were two of her astrological charts and a little black scrying mirror made of obsidian.

Further along we had a pair of dowsing rods that once belonged to my grandfather, Septimus. Sam told me he hadn't been convinced by the methodology despite uncovering several water sources about the village.

It was nice to have them here – these fragments of my family's past, these people who I had never known but was now becoming more familiar with.

I realised I was staring at a shamanic headdress from Iceland. How had I ended up here? These days I always seemed to be setting off in one direction and ending up somewhere completely different. It was the story of my new life. I shook my head – the headdress was lopsided. Opening the case, I took it out and stroked the feathers and tiny teeth embedded into its headbands. The piece really was intricate and quite, quite amazing. I think my grandfather acquired it before he died. Sam said it reminded him of something that happened back in the war. I rearranged it next to a drum and shut the case.

There, everything was fine again. Time to switch off the Divination lights and move on to 'Necromancy' (communicating with the Dearly Departed).

I had every intention of passing through briefly just to see if Dorcus was lurking. Somehow I thought he might find this section more compelling – don't ask me why – it was a hunch. However, it was empty. Talking of hunches, as I passed a rather unflattering illustration of the Witch of Endor, I thought I saw something move in the neighbouring vitrine. When I approached and peered down into the display, everything was perfectly still. It must have been my imagination. Although the Ouija board's planchette had been jogged off-centre. The heart-shaped pointer was quite a pretty item, I'd always thought. 'Hello' and 'Goodbye' were carved above and below the 'eye'. It was, however, signalling towards 'YES' now.

'Is there anyone there?' I called out and then giggled.

The planchette didn't move.

Nobody of living breathing flesh in the vicinity, for sure. Not that I could see anyway.

I decided to check in our new cinema area. We'd roped it off due to the fact it wasn't finished yet but some people ignored the KEEP OUT sign. I wanted to change it to

DANGER. Sam got stroppy and insisted it was too melodramatic and might frighten visitors. So I was like – 'Have you noticed where we work?' He won the argument anyway.

Unfortunately, the contracted workmen who, to be frank, seemed to spend most of their time in the kitchenette making tea, had been called back to another job. One that had previously 'fallen through'. Their wording didn't inspire much confidence. They had promised to return in the new year. That was fine by us – the Christmas holidays were coming up, and that was always a very busy time. That and Halloween.

To stop me whining, Sam hung a sign on one of the blue display boards from the Talks Area. It read 'No Entry – Work under Construction. Exciting new feature coming soon!' We argued over the exclamation mark, but I won that round.

I didn't know Dorcus well enough to guess whether he was the type to flout instructions, so I poked my head in just in case.

There wasn't much apart from an assortment of planks, two metal workbenches, various builders' tools and a vacuum cleaner which I had been looking for, for over a week. I wasn't a domestic goddess in that regard. But nor was Sam. Luckily Trace managed to put the duster about a bit when it wasn't busy. If we did all right over the Christmas period then we might be able to employ a cleaner. Sam had suggested we got a volunteer to do it, but funnily enough scrubbing public toilets does not come up high on the list of responsibilities people are prepared to do for free.

I gave the cinema space a quick sniff to see if there was a whiff of any expensive aftershave in the vicinity, but just got damp and stale air.

He wasn't in the Ursula Cadence wing either. Just Ursula brewing her cures and humming in the glow of the artificial fire. I went over and switched her off.

'Nighty night, Ursey. You take care, all right?'

Sometimes I wondered if I'd ever hear an answer in the darkness.

But I hadn't.

Not at that point.

It hadn't spoken to me yet.

CHAPTER THREE

So, Mr Tall-Dark-Fit-But-Possibly-Boring was not in the building. Perhaps he'd slipped out whilst I was looking for him. I felt a snag of disappointment.

Switching the 'Open' sign to 'Closed', I proceeded to lock the front door. Not because we had any bother with people breaking in and stealing stuff. It was more about them breaking in and *leaving* things for us: strange floral bouquets, weird coded messages, meat with teeth in it or artefacts like corn dollies and such that they wanted to get rid of. All part of the colourful tapestry that was life at the Witch Museum. I was learning, adapting, becoming comfortable with it all. It was amazing really: a year ago I'd never heard of the place. Now look at me.

Sam was hunched over his laptop on our long dining table when I reached the office. There was a fresh cup of tea at the place opposite.

'At last,' he said, as I sat down. 'So – skinned cats.'

'Couldn't manage a whole one, thanks.' I glanced at the kitchen. 'Though I am definitely getting peckish.'

Sam ignored me.

'Sorry,' I said. 'That was a dad joke.'

His eyebrows rose. I knew what he was thinking.

'No, not one of *my* dad's.' I added a reference to my current fixation – 'whoever he is' – and continued, 'It was a "generic dad" joke.'

Sam's lips wrinkled. He looked like he was smelling something bad.

I shut up.

'There's been two. So far.' He stretched his shoulders and straightened into his chair then returned his eyes to the laptop.

I picked up the tea and sipped it. Yum, strong and dark. Just the way I liked my … stop that … like nothing. I snapped my thoughts back to skinned cats. 'Why would anyone want to do that to a pussycat?

'I doubt it's about the cat. Not with the way the body was positioned. Whoever did it expected a reaction.'

'What's that? Disgust?'

'Certainly revulsion. And they would have known they'd provoke extreme feelings. Especially when you hear about the site where one of them was found,' he said and looked over, waiting for me to ask where that was.

I didn't, not just yet. I returned his gaze and wondered if he was as tall as Dorcus. I hadn't seen them together but I was thinking now that the darker man might have an advantage over him in the height department. Sam was somewhere around six feet. Although maybe Dorcus looked bigger because of the hats he wore. He had such a firmly established style – sort of Byron-meets-Edwardian sea captain.

I liked that. On the other hand, Sam's mode of dress was kind of haphazard. Schizophrenic some might say. At times he'd look cool in T-shirt and jeans. But the next day he'd go all preppy with chinos, shirt and formal jacket. Neither was unappealing. Especially when you could see under those clothes a well-worked-out body with toned muscles and a six-pack. Which was pretty amazing as he spent a lot of time at the desk upstairs. I had seen him creep off from time to time for a gym-and-swim in Chelmsford, but mostly I think he kept in shape running in the woods. He didn't tell me what he did when he crept out of the museum in the morning and some evenings, but he had jogging bottoms on and trainers. It was his private time. And I had no desire to ask. I liked that we still didn't know everything about each other. It kept things exciting.

He was still looking at me.

'What?'

'Considering the context,' he repeated, a verbal nudge.

'Oh yes. Okay, what's the context?'

'Interesting you should ask,' he said, satisfied, ready to unfurl his knowledge like a flag. 'Right, well, yes – the first one was nailed to St Olave's.'

'Ooh,' I said. 'A church door. That's a statement and a half. What's it all about? What does it mean?'

Sam's eyes didn't leave the screen. 'As far as I'm aware there's not a phrasebook or manual on how to decode symbolic gestures with skinned cats.'

'Really? Someone's missing a trick. There's a certain kind of person who would buy it.' I meant it.

'Well, us for a start,' he said and smiled wryly. Then he folded his arms and sat back. 'Let's see – there's a lot of elements here. Church for one. What does it symbolise?'

'Establishment. Christianity. God. Christmas. Baby Jesus, choir boys, paedophilia …' I tried to conjure more associations, but my family had never been particularly religious. At least, the side that had brought me up and posed as my mum and dad for thirty-odd years. 'Um, that's all I can manage – I'm spent.'

Sam was happy to expand. 'Yes, well to many other people the church also represents sanctity, tradition, love, benevolence and spirituality, peace. I'd say the act of nailing poor skinless Kitty to the door is certainly indicative of violence, anger. And you could be right about it signifying the establishment too. In which case the act also poses a challenge to the status quo. It's provocative and sacrilegious. Designed to shock and horrify. Not to mention desecrate …'

'Deconsecration,' I said. 'Such a powerful word. Reminds me of *The Omen*.'

'Actually,' Sam said. I could feel a lecture coming on. 'I think the correct term in this instance would be desecration.'

'What's the difference?'

'Deconsecration is about the process of removing blessing from a church or sacred site because it is going to be used for something else – another function.'

'Like flats?' I said and rolled my eyes. Everywhere in South Essex was being flogged off to developers eager to cram as many people as possible into tiny tiny spaces – sectioned-off parts of churches, shops, post offices, community centres, garages, ruins, bakeries, pillar boxes, manholes – you name it. If you could squeeze, push or coax someone into it then some fat cat called John was going to shamelessly do just that. And make their victim pay excessively for the privilege too. Oh God, and there were so many cowboy builders out there. None of them gave a toss about the neighbourhoods and communities that they affected, impacted, inconvenienced, ruined. Because really they were all, 'I'm all right, John/Jack.' My Auntie Babs had had to deal with a couple lately – they'd 'accidentally' demolished her garden wall while she'd been on holiday, 'accidentally' killed the birds nesting in the ivy there and 'accidentally' built their roof on it, which was basically a land grab. She'd consulted solicitors but they'd told her to let it go. Even though she was in the right and would probably win her case in court. It was likely to cost her about £10K and the developers could appeal to the Home Office and they'd overturn the decision as there was a shortage of homes in the South East. You can't win, can you. Then, as a parting gift, they cut off her electricity and smashed their equipment into the side of her house. When Babs filmed this for the insurers, the yee-haws came over and intimidated her. Some blokes do that, I've found. When they know they're in the wrong. They loom over you and shout and use their larger physicality to make you back down. Not all of them, but certainly those cretins did. Luckily Babs has friends like Ray Boundersby who paid them a visit to see if they still needed their kneecaps, or could he perhaps develop them?

'Like flats,' confirmed Sam and brought me back to the subject at hand. Which was good because whenever I thought about those builders my anger began to build. I didn't want to be angry all the time. Too exhausting. 'Desecration,' he confirmed, 'is an act that deprives a place of sanctity. It is contemptuous. Destructive.'

'So someone's angry?' I said, thinking about developers.

'I'd say.' Sam nodded. 'Or perhaps they have an issue with the church. Or want to appear as if they do.'

'Mmmm,' I said. Thinking it over. Sam was right. One had to be so careful when assuming motivations. We'd learnt over the year, that things were never exactly what they appeared to be. 'So where's the second cat?' I asked.

'Outside the library.'

'Bloody hell!' I said at a volume that surprised even myself. 'That's crazy!'

'Exactly,' said Sam and shook his head with great sadness. 'Who'd have a go at books? Although it could be another statement. Perhaps one about the current state of literacy?'

'No, I meant it's crazy that they've still got a library. How did they manage that?'

'Oh, right. Well quite.' Sam fussed over the laptop. 'They are rather an endangered species these days.'

'Yep,' I said. 'Which means there's – like other rare breeds – there's a bunch of austerity-mad hoorays hunting them down and killing them. It's a blood sport.'

'Is that what you call the ministers for culture these days?'

'No. Actually I think the collective noun is a "Bullingdon".'

Sam raised his eyebrows. 'Very good. Well, this library has been saved by a philanthropist. And it's staffed by volunteers.'

'Oh what? So he or she is not an austerity-mad hooray?'

Sam began tapping the keys of his laptop, switching his eyes to the keyboard. His aesthetically pleasing broad shoulders hunched a little. I wondered if he'd object to me pulling them back and straightening them? 'No one knows who it is,' he said. 'He or she wishes to remain anonymous. But there's funding put aside for a part-time manager.'

Interesting. 'How do you know all of this?'

He stopped typing and waved the pamphlet. 'Parish magazine. And this trendy new thing called t'internet.'

'Mmm,' I said, processing. 'But the question remains – why would anybody want to hang a skinned cat outside a library? One that obviously means a lot to the local community. And the patron.'

Sam opened his mouth to reply just as we heard a meow from the corner.

Hecate must have snuck into the office, unnoticed, but was now staring at us with accusation in her green eyes. We both froze.

'Oh dear,' said Sam. Colour began to flush his face. 'Didn't see you come in, old girl.'

The museum cat meowed again. It sounded like 'Whaaa?' Definitely a question.

'Nothing,' I told her. 'We weren't talking about anything.'

Sam began to whistle absently. Hecate tilted her head and speared me with a gaze. Clearly unconvinced by my pathetic lie, she blinked three times, then tossed her head as if in despair – 'Humans!' With a dismissive twitch of her tail she padded off into the kitchen from whence issued a series of increasingly outraged meows.

'Dinner time,' said Sam. 'You don't think she heard, do you?'

'Who knows?' Our museum cat acted like she knew what we were thinking before we even thought it. It was unnerving. 'I'll prepare the evening meal for the mistress. What are we lesser beings having?'

'There's some of Bronson's paella left in the fridge.' Bronson, our erstwhile museum caretaker/handyman/guardian/bouncer/pillar of support/sentinel etc., had surprised us when he announced he was taking a course in Mediterranean cuisine. He thought it might help him get out of the village more. The poor bloke had quite a hard time in the summer when it was revealed that the Lord of the Manor, Edward de Vere, who had been his friend, in a kind of cap-doffing come-and-play-chess-with-me-oh-serf manner, had murdered his good friend's wife, who also happened to have been my grandmother. Not to mention that De Vere's daughter, Araminta, with whom Bronson had also been acquainted, may have bumped off my mum.

And then the Lord and Lady tried for a hat trick and attempted to murder me.

Bronson cut off all contact.

That kind of thing can strain a friendship apparently.

I fed the mistress of the Witch Museum then returned to the table with two steaming bowls of paella. And very tasty they were too. Bronson had done good.

'So,' I said, sliding my empty bowl into the middle of the table. 'Going back to Haven for a minute. Do you have any theories brewing?'

Sam hadn't finished. He ate like a man whose mind was not focussed on the taste, to Bronson's dismay – dinner was just a pit stop to refuel.

'Well,' he said, stretching over for his PC. 'Am I allowed to have this at the dinner table?'

I'd banned electronic devices at the table when we were eating. Otherwise it was pointless having physical company. But on this occasion Sam was clearly absent anyway. The laptop might bring him back. 'Go on then.'

'There's been a resurgence of big cat sightings.'

'Big cat?' I said imagining a giant Hecate sitting on top of the museum licking her paws.

'Yes. They're usually rarer than big dogs.'

'Big dogs?' I was baffled.

'Black Shuck?' Sam ventured.

'Black Shuck?' I repeated.

'Oh for God's sake! If you carry on like a parrot, I'll get Hecate to eat you. You must have heard of Black Shuck?'

'Picture, if you will,' I said, 'an alternative reality where people don't grow up in a cabinet of curiosities designed to illuminate diverse aspects of supernature, challenge perceptions of witches and the bigotry that surrounded the historic Essex witch hunts. Where lives are lived out hanging around parks, playing Knock Down Ginger, watching *Grange Hill* or obsessing over *Fame Academy*. Hard to imagine, I know.'

'Point taken.' Sam inclined his head to the screen. He spun it round to show me.

The page on the screen was the front of a popular tabloid newspaper. The headline read 'Alien Big Cat Theory Returns.'

'Black Shuck is allegedly a ghostly black dog said to roam the countryside of East Anglia,' Sam explained.

'Okay,' I said, holding my hand up to stem his flow. I knew what he was like – he could go on for ages and I'd forget the original point. 'But that's a dog. Not a cat.'

'Yes,' he said and nodded as if calming the enthusiasm of a young child. 'You're right. But the myths are similar. And they both might be cryptids.'

I opened my mouth to ask what a cryptid was when it was at home, but he had foreseen the question.

'Disputed beasts that no one's sure about – the Yeti, Abominable Snowman, Beast of Exmoor, Nessie, Chupacabra, the Kraken etc.'

'Okay. Thank you Mr Witchipedia.'

He continued, ignoring my little jibe. 'Black Shuck is local to our area. Said to be a harbinger, a foreteller, of doom, death and bad luck. He is a large black dog, sometimes described as having one eye.'

Ah, poor thing, I thought. 'Sounds like he just needs some TLC.'

'There have been sightings of big cats in these parts too. They are ascribed the same terrible qualities. No one sees them for very long. And no one knows where they come from.'

'Not even the local zoo?' I said and raised my brows. We'd had some experience of escaped snakes on our last case.

'I knew you would say that.'

I dismissed this with a waft of my hand. 'You can't be suggesting that this Black Shuck is skinning cats and hanging them on libraries and church doors? They haven't got the required, er, digits and manual dexterity, have they?'

'No, of course I'm not saying that. I'm just pointing out that there have been sightings of such beasts and I'm simply wondering if there might be a connection?'

'Oh,' I said, then stopped abruptly. Someone was banging loudly on the front door.

Sam frowned.

Two more hard raps. Or booms really. They had an explosive echoing quality to them when the entrance hall was empty. We used to have some exhibits in there which soaked up the sound, but since we'd replaced them with panels explaining the link between the stereotype of the witch and that of the Essex Girl, there was more space, ergo more reverb and echo. Yep, and I'd started saying 'ergo'. No guesses who I picked that up from.

'Oh bloody hell,' I said. 'That might be Dorcus. I hope I haven't locked him in.'

'Your turn then,' said Sam and tugged the laptop fully in front of him.

I was happy to take myself off to the lobby, expecting to see my tall dark friend there. However, the hall was empty. Must have come from the outside.

I drew back the bolts on the large wooden door and hauled it open.

There was no one out there. But it had started to snow. When I looked down at the thin white carpet I saw it was unblemished. No footprints.

A few months ago, this sort of thing might have unnerved

me. A lot. But I'd been living here long enough now to know that the museum had a mind of its own.

Noises like this were quite common. The knocks and bumps and lights and creaks presaged things or people on their way to us, travelling through the aether.

Except of course they didn't. Not really. They were quirky, abstract, random groans to be expected from such an old building. Aches from the fabric of the place, the materials, contracting or expanding according to temperature changes, air pressure in the pipes, the central heating etc. These ordinary functions were often interpreted by the human brain as meaningful, significant indicators. And that was Apophenia. Sam told me about it a while back. I'd just about got to grips with Pareidolia, so wrestled a bit with Apophenia. Luckily, it's the same sort of thing – the universal human tendency to seek patterns in random information. Gamblers get it. As do people who are paranoid and think they are being followed. Or, as Sam said, people who think they are being haunted and hearing noises. You can tell if it usually happens at night when it's quiet. Usually during the day such sounds are simply drowned out by the hustle and bustle of everyday life.

It's an error in perception.

I did not err in my perceptions.

I knew that buildings were not sentient.

It was just nicer to think sometimes that the place had a mind of its own, rather than that it was simply falling down around us and grumbling as it crumbled.

So those bangs we'd heard were probably the central

heating going at it full pelt, it being cold and dark outside and now snowing.

Anyway, there I was standing on the doorstep in my feathery mules, watching the snowflakes waft down, my 'internal mum voice' chastising me, insisting I would catch my death of cold.

I remember shivering as I closed the door. 'Got you, Apophenia.'

How smug I must have sounded.

How stubbornly deaf and blind.

The museum was trying to warn me: something horrendous was on its way. And I think there was a part of me that did pick up on that.

For as I looked into the darkness it wasn't the cold that made me shiver.

The repressed sentient part of me was quivering with fear.

CHAPTER FOUR

The day had been odd-ish, that talk of Haven a smidgen unsettling, the knock on the door – strange.

A nagging sense of unease that I had carried with me from the lobby still hung over my shoulders as I climbed into bed. I couldn't shift it. It was like a physical weight. I tried rubbing some tiger balm into my neck but it didn't do much to relax my muscles.

It was old-school comfort I was desiring. So in the end I took out my mother's journal.

I'd read it a hundred times or more. Though some of it was too poignant to bear, a large chunk was zippy and light. Well, the first part anyway.

Sometimes when I read her musings I could almost hear her enunciating the words in a clear, feminine voice with a firmness at the edges and a softness in their centre.

And who doesn't want to listen to the soothing words of their mother when they've had a hard day?

How like me she was. Or how like her I am.

In some ways at least.

Not all, though. She was different enough to still be a stranger.

I let the notebook fall open at the beginning. My eyes roamed across the picture she had painted upon the page. A tarot card.

There was the date scrawled in her handwriting.

'*15th of December 1982*' it read.

The Fool

The cards were right! They always are. I don't know why I doubted them. Perhaps I was thinking of a real living human being when I consulted my dear friend, Tarot. Of course The Fool cannot be tied down to such literal interpretation. A person, indeed. How dull my senses are sometimes. The Fool can signify a concept: the beginning of an adventure. And I believe it is so.

Really I do.

I have my secret hopes. And I could do with something like that. Something exciting. Not that living here in this deliciously barmy museum with Daddy isn't full of its own consolations. It is only that I am ready for something more now.

And now the cards foretell – something new is on its way.

By the pricking of my thumbs …

I wonder what this way do come.

Oh, I love The Fool. I do, I do. It annoys me that so many think it a bad card. Simply reductive is what that is.

True – a superficial reading of the first card in the major arcana may give the impression it is a warning. For there depicted is The Fool, one foot angled over the cliff top, eyes not on the edge, but on the heavens above. Staring into the celestial realms. Some of us do that all the time – we fix our eyes upon the stars and our feet upon the ground. But The Fool, though he appears to be approaching a precipice, about to topple off the edge of the cliff to imminent disaster, he only feels the sun on his neck. He is alive. Look at him! He smells the dainty fragrance of the rose he holds in his fingers. Coloured like my mother's rose – yellow for bliss, pink for love and gentleness, magenta threads for majesty. I wish I had known her. Sometimes I am jealous of Ted for the years he had with Mother.

Of course sometimes I am not jealous at all. Because the loss of her is not so bad for me. I cannot remember Ethel-Rose. Ted, he does. And that pains him. It has made him go inside a brittle and hard shell. He hides his true nature within and will counter nothing of her gifts. It is why he ran from the museum, Daddy's tribute to his wife. A commitment to what she believed – that we cannot think to know everything. There are unknowable mysteries out there – always have been, always will be.

And why shouldn't there be?

Life would be so dull if we knew everything.

Ted runs from us and all that is 'Strange' and strange. He buries himself in the solidity of numbers and money. I do not like this way of his but I cannot blame him for the denial. We must do what we must do to survive our lives.

However, many we may have. It's all part of the plan.

But I digress.

The Fool, dear Diary, to The Fool!

Behind him undulates a line of mountains. Or are they clouds? I suppose it's a matter of opinion. Or perception. Oh yes, that shifting sand – Perception. The cards are open to interpretation.

In my world, if anyone cares to know it (and I expect there will be none but thee little diary), in my deck The Fool is up high on a mountain. I think it is the perceived height here that causes those who are perhaps glass half-empty, to assume the card presents a caution of sorts – be careful, look before you leap. But to me – for whom all glasses are almost always half-full, the card is joyous, brimming with sunshine, innocence, youth. It is optimism. The Fool takes a leap, yes, but it is a leap of faith – he does not fall off the ledge. Instead, he discovers he can fly! Yes! Because he is the holy fool, the sacred child, the gentle idealist protected by the King. His number is zero, the beginning of all possibilities. The eternal continuous cycle of life, birth and death.

Rebirth.

He was there from the beginning, when I dealt the cards, tucked between the Chariot and the Queen of Cups. When The Fool announces his presence he advises the questioner to let go, take a risk, not to worry about silly things like gravity because they will be protected. A miracle will happen so they will not crash down upon the rocks below. They will find their wings.

Much as it might seem crazy to others, this idea, the leap of faith, the encouragement to embrace spontaneity, well, it was this thought that made me run out after the dark stranger.

I suppose it was naughty of me to have eavesdropped on his conversation with Daddy. Not that I could hear it with distinction. It's a false rumour that a glass held against a wall will amplify the sounds within. I came away with a soggy ear and only a notion that, on the other side of the wall, in the office, voices had been raised.

It was intriguing. He *was intriguing.*

I had been upstairs in Ted's old room when he arrived earlier. I was looking for a book and heard the loud slam of a car door, then French swearing. That was what made me stand up and peer out of the museum's left eye – its window on the first floor. That's what I call it anyway. And there I saw him striding with purpose across the grass, attaché case in hand. That's why I knew he wasn't a customer. Who turns up to the Witch Museum with an attaché case? An attaché, I suppose. But it's been a while since we had any of them sniffing round here.

As far as I'm aware.

'Course I've been away, playing house with James in London, so I wouldn't really have a clue about the exact comings and goings of the Witch Museum over the past few years.

Eek. James.

Just thinking about him makes me shudder.

I should have left him long before I did. The signs were there. And in the end he turned out just like his father. Such a shame. He'd been so different at the beginning. Back then, when we first clapped eyes on each other, he was full of wildness, passion and Romance with a distinctly capital R. There was magic in his soul. As long as he stayed out of the parental sightlines.

Then as soon as he moves back south, to the family fold, and re-enters their orbit, he shows his true colours. 'It's time to grow up now, Celeste,' he told me. The cheek of it! Like he knew it all. Understood the exact passage of life. Like he had experienced accelerated growth and developed innate knowledge and insight. He knew what was expected of him. But he professed to dictate what was expected of me! *Pah! What a dickhead. My father has never presumed to preach at me. He has only said that I should remain true to myself and be happy.*

Grow up indeed! James was always narrow. Square. And actually he hadn't grown up, he'd sold out. Sold his soul for an easy life. I could see very clearly how happily he made his way down the road to Conformity. He felt safe there. And he anticipated me falling in line behind him. Several steps behind him, if his mother had her way. As if!

God knows, if I wanted a conventional man who would have me play conventional wife or girlfriend then I would have gone for a rich one.

But enough of that. I'm making myself mad talking about James and he is not the point! The point is the dark stranger had arrived. And there he was, in the drive, attaché case in hand, striding with purpose across the garden.

Attaché. That sounds rather exotic, I must admit. Perhaps he is a diplomat?

Though we didn't speak much, I did hear an accent. French perhaps. That's always persuasive. Sultry. Sexy. I might be inclined to go for an attaché I suspect.

Which makes it more confusing as to why Daddy had a fight with him. An attaché. A foreign one too. He usually gets on well with those types. He's worked with them often enough.

Daddy doesn't raise his voice very often. Even when some visitors are rather horrible and cross about our little museum and the exhibits we have. Think them unholy and satanic. Which is so stupid it makes me want to shout. Though Daddy manages them well, soothes and calms. He is better than me at keeping his temper. I have a feeling the argument between him and the dark man had nothing to do with the museum. I know this because when I pressed my ear against the wall between the ticket booth and the office I heard the words 'mother', 'sister', 'daughter'. He said them – the dark stranger. But Daddy said, 'There are none to be had.' Then the door opened which forced me to run and hide. But then it slammed. The dark stranger stormed out. Daddy didn't even see him to the door. Which was quite rude. And another reason why I went after him. It wasn't just the impulsive nature of The Fool that inspired me – I didn't want him to think badly of us and our manners. Not a man like that. And I am Daddy's daughter, aren't I? I deserved to know what was said.

He was striding again. Marching back to the car. His gait more hurried than that he had used to get here. His attaché case firm in hand.

Maybe he is *with MI6. An agent perhaps? Daddy worked with them yonks ago, though I'm not meant to know that. Uncle Sixus told me when he was drunk. So, I'll ask him. The stranger, that is. Though I suppose he wouldn't tell me anyway. But I will try when he comes back tomorrow.*

See, I touched his sleeve by the car and apologised. Then quickly, in a whisper, I told him Daddy was going north in the morning. He is examining a petrified boot from Mother Skipton's cave. Oh, the glamour! Then visiting his cousin in Harrogate. Won't be returning till Monday so I've got the place to myself for four nights. I told the dark man he could come back and talk to me. Maybe I could help?

And, do you know what? He said he would indeed. That it would be 'a pleasure'. And he had a look in his eyes when he said it. For the first time in ages I felt a spark.

I can hardly wait.

So begins my adventure.

CHAPTER FIVE

My curator was wearing a tight-fitting tracksuit, which I did not object to, for on display was a network of muscles which were neither too flabby nor too large but, à la Goldilocks, just right. This was topped off with a camouflage print T-shirt and good trainers. Lord knows how he could afford them on the pittance I paid him from the takings. Perhaps I'd look into that.

Myself, I'd got on trainers and a black jumpsuit, limited edition, a bit Purdey from *The Avengers* circa 1971. Joanna Lumley. My dad (not biological) always had a thing about her and, yes I could see the glamour there. She was fit, aloof and stylish. Not unlike my good self.

I'd gone for a sleek outline with a bit of a leopardskin frill on the shoulder, inspired by our convo about big cats last night. Two pairs of Spanx were batting down my stomach so there was only a small mound to indicate where this morning's sausages, egg and beans were digesting.

Might as well have not bothered in the end, because the first thing I had to do was take the bloody thing off.

'This cost £69.99,' I told the soldier waiting to give me some soiled jogging bottoms and matching T-shirt.

'Well,' said a voice from behind. 'You probably want to save it then.'

I spun round and found a grey-suited man standing there, watching me. He smiled.

I didn't recognise him at first but then Sam said, 'Agent Green, isn't it?'

And I remembered him from a cellar in Damebury. Though, to be honest, all those agents looked the same with their short back and sides and nondescript suits. I think that was on purpose – they were meant to fade into the background.

Agent Green nodded.

'Ah, yes,' I said. 'You work with Monty, don't you?'

'Work FOR him, is the correct wording,' Agent Green smiled. I don't think I'd seen him do that before. 'Commander Walker has entrusted me with letting you know he will try very hard to see you if he has time.' Sam nodded. I looked at him and wondered if he was going to mention the skinned cats in Haven, but he just shrugged.

Agent Green passed on Monty's expressions of delight that we had finally decided to acquire more skills befitting consultants to his 'department'. Then we were ushered through into what looked disappointingly like a bog-standard classroom. Agent Green introduced us to Sergeant Trooper (not her real name) who was the soldier I had more or less dismissed as a valet when we'd come in.

Cloakroom assistant, however, she was most definitely not.

And she was going to prove it.

As soon as Agent Green said his goodbyes and left the

room, Trooper asserted herself as very much as the boss, explaining that we would be going through some basic rapid-fire training techniques. Which sounded more exciting than the reality.

If I told you everything that we did then obvs I would have to kill you, so suffice it to say that in the morning we mostly learnt valuable 'running away' skills. There was some 'keeping quiet and hiding' tactics thrown in, along with some 'how to phone Monty silently' info sprinkled on too. All of which we'd been doing anyway, but nonetheless, these exercises would help in terms of smoother execution.

I was hoping for some proper James Bond-type training (cocktails, martinis, seduction techniques, arms training, yacht identification, gadgets, poker coaching etc.) but Trooper kept rolling her eyes and tutting, repeating ad nauseum that we were moving on to basic threat recognition and self-defence.

Threat recognition comprised two videos narrated by robot voices. The situational awareness suggested we shouldn't use our phones much and take more notice of our environment. Like – duh.

However, there was a lot more information on the second video, which gave techniques on how to be calm and make effective judgement calls when your body wanted to go down the fight or flight response. That was interesting. We learnt breathing techniques and a weirdly named process which helped you order your thoughts into action.

Self-defence classes, at least, meant a change of scene. I was thinking mirrored studios with sexy men in martial arts outfits. But it was Trooper in a gym that smelt of socks and vom. There was a bucket in the corner to catch the sleety rain.

The sergeant roughed us up and threw us around, then showed us a couple of moves. I got to throw Sam over my shoulder and then straddle him. It was both embarrassing and yet nice. Overall, I couldn't really work out what the more dominant emotion really was. I don't think he could either because it was a bit awkward in the car on the way home.

We muttered a lot about the scenery. I'd allowed Sam to drive on this occasion and as we re-entered the county he pointed out an area of forest where a woman had found a half-eaten deer surrounded by big paw prints. We slowed down a bit. There was little traffic on the road, conditions being pretty rubbish. But Essex was in no mood to be trifled with. Dark and brooding and pent-up, the land was keeping its cards close to its chest and obfuscating this particular stretch of trees with a thin mist of sleet. The forest about it looked threatening – all dark and jagged and feathered like a wall of angry Morris men. Not the kind that waved hankies and wore bells and straw hats, but those terrifying pagan types who blackened their faces and went after each other with massive sticks. And scared the shit out of children.

It was decided we should return tomorrow and inspect the 'kill site' after finishing our chores at the museum. Daylight allowing. The mid-winter solstice was approaching fast and the sun was making increasingly rare appearances. It was getting dark by four. So we'd have to see.

We were talking this through whilst rounding one of the sharp bends that cut through the tangled woods. And as we took that curve something caught in the headlights: a flash of tan, the leathery colour of the rug on the living-room floor. It darted out then galloped across the road.

I took a shot of adrenaline straight to my stomach.

'Woah!' said Sam and slammed on the brakes. 'What was that?'

'I don't know.' I'd unconsciously gripped the dashboard and braced. 'A fox?'

'No,' said Sam. We had slowed to a crawl but not stopped. 'No way. It looked much bigger than that. Bent over though, fleeing, lolloping.'

'But it wasn't big enough to be human,' I said.

'Maybe a child.'

'Out here? In the middle of nowhere? Why would a child be running through the woods at night? On their own?'

He returned his foot to the accelerator and incrementally increased his speed to ten miles an hour. I looked back at the road, into the roots of the trees and bracken, uncertain now, wondering if we should stop. Have a look? Were we shirking our civic duty? 'Do you think we should check, Sam?'

The curator paused. And swallowed. 'We didn't hit it.'

'What if it was a kid?'

Little beads of sweat had popped out across Sam's forehead. 'No. You're right. It must have been a fox.'

I nodded, completely unconvinced, and peered through the rear window. The trunks of the scrawny trees nearest the car glowed a demonic red, reflecting the brake lights. Whatever had scuttled across our path had gone to ground in the woods. The wind rustled the leaves and uppermost branches. There was no movement beneath. Though I couldn't see very clearly.

'Yes,' I said to Sam, trying to persuade myself. 'A big fox.' That was probably it. I turned back to face him. 'We've wound ourselves up with those stories. It might have been a deer.'

'Oh yes,' Sam returned, relief loosening his vocal cords. 'A deer! Of course. They can disappear into the shadows in seconds. That'll be it.'

I waited a moment then asked, 'And are there deer in Essex?'

'Oh yes.' His tone was more jovial. He was recovering himself. 'There's deer here everywhere, dear.' When he laughed, it sounded like a release. 'Deer, big cats and big dogs. They seem to be the theme of the week!'

'They do indeed,' I said, speculating how long it might be till we paid a visit to Haven.

I could see exactly where this investigation was going.

Except, I couldn't. I had no idea of what lay in wait.

Not then.

In a way, I'm glad I didn't. I wouldn't have gone through with it if I'd known.

CHAPTER SIX

The museum was closed when we parked up. Trace and Vanessa had already left. I suggested we go round the side to let ourselves in via the office rather than struggle with the front door and all its bolts.

As we crunched up alongside the wall, a memory of the summer wafted across my brain. We had a bonfire here back then. I had chopped a witchfinder's head off and Sam had removed his shirt. Good times.

I was surprised to see the great circular window illuminated. The office lights danced through its red, amber and blue stained-glass pattern. Sam had told me he thought it might have been brought over from a church in France. Though I could never see anything particularly religious in it. It lacked saints and virgins and babies. However, it was totally out of place as an office window – too grand and far too large. But there you go, that was the Witch Museum – full of grandiose gestures and occult idiosyncrasies.

And people, I thought, as I approached the door, and voices.

One of them was definitely Bronson's. His low regular bass punctuated another voice I didn't recognise at all.

'Someone's here,' I said to Sam. My powers of deduction are profound, I tell you.

'So it seems,' he said, only half engaged. His mind was elsewhere. Probably back on the road where we had encountered the deer. 'I didn't see another car outside. Perhaps a visitor from the village?'

'Well it's got to be someone we want to see or he wouldn't have admitted them,' I said.

'Let's go in, then,' Sam said. 'It's cold out here, Rosie.'

We fell through the door and shook dew off our coats. The warmth of the room immediately embraced us, wafting over an aroma of hot chocolate and freshly brewed coffee.

'Oh, that smells good,' I said, recognising the bulky form of Bronson. He had his yellow sou'wester off. It was hanging off the back of the seat next to him, which was pretty extraordinary.

Mr Montgomery Walker, our erstwhile *X-Files* contact, sat opposite with a smile arranged across his chops that spoke of years of manicured grooming. I liked him. He was a lovely bloke, despite his unfortunate background of privilege and wealth. Whenever he grinned I couldn't help but smile back. 'Monty!' I said and skipped round the table and threw my arms around his neck.

He accepted my embrace then peeled me away. 'Lovely to see you, as always Rosie.'

Sam came round and shook his hand. 'I'd forgotten Agent Green mentioned you might be popping in.'

'Ah, yes,' I said. 'I thought he meant you'd come to the centre.'

'Got waylaid,' he said simply while we sat down.

Bronson made a grunting noise and said, 'I was just telling Montgomery that I'd been doing a course. Anybody object to herbed lamb cutlets with roasted vegetables? Almost ready now and there's enough for four.'

No one was going to argue with that, so Bronson went off to serve up while Sam and I dressed the table.

'I think,' I said as I shook the tablecloth out, 'we know why you're here.'

But Monty's face contracted. 'Really?' He lowered his eyebrows and checked out Sam's face, but he was busying himself with the cutlery.

'Haven,' I said and gestured for Monty to grab the other end of the cloth.

He took the hint and together we let it fall over the table like a fresh sail.

Monty returned to his place. 'Haven?'

I squatted down by the old oak sideboard and took out the Wedgewood plates. Well, it was an occasion wasn't it – having Monty to supper.

'Skinned cats,' I explained, placing the crockery at the places Sam was laying.

It was only when he had placed the final fork that my curator looked into Monty's face. 'Oh!' I heard him say. 'It's not about Haven, is it?'

The agent shook his head. 'Not yet, but naturally I shall investigate in due course. Thank you for the tip-off.'

'So where is it you want us to go?' I pulled out a chair and sat down: Bronson was on his way in with a platter full of steaming roasted vegetables – red, yellow, green peppers, purple aubergines, and herbs. Those colours were just what you needed on a cold winter's night.

'How do you know I want you to go somewhere?' Monty bent his head towards the platter. 'Smells wonderful, Bronson. Thank you.'

Bronson nodded without expression, but the tell-tale tips of his ears started to blush.

Sam and I added our own compliments and began spooning out portions onto our plates. Bronson went back to get more dishes.

I picked up on Monty's question and said, 'You wouldn't come here unless you wanted us to do something for you, would you?'

He considered this for a moment. 'Fair enough. And yes, I would like you to pay a visit down south.'

Sam's ears pricked up. 'South? We are south.'

For a second I saw Monty squint as if he was trying to peer inside Sam's brain. But it was momentary. 'Well,' he said, completely in control of his expressions once more. 'I want you to go and see this woman, Pearl. Quite a character, I'm told.'

Sam's teeth crept out over his bottom lip. 'What's she then? Tarot reader? Clairvoyant? Medium? Psychic healer?'

Bronson returned with a silver server. 'La pièce de resistance,' he said. With an uncharacteristically flamboyant flourish, he set it down in the middle of the table and lifted the lid.

The herbed cutlets did, indeed, look delicious underneath.

'Tremendous, Bronson,' I applauded. 'I do think it important that single men learn how to cook,' I said in my best Jane Austen voice. 'It makes one so much more marriageable.'

Sam's eyebrows picked up. 'Did you say manageable?'

I looked at him and said, 'No, not yet.'

Monty wasn't sure what was going on with the banter but assumed it best to head off any potential brawl and picked up the tongs. 'May I do the honours?' he gestured to Bronson who had taken his place at the table.

'Please do,' said Bronson and held his plate out.

'Bravo,' said Monty. 'La présentation est magnifique!'

Sam and I muttered our approval once more.

We stopped talking temporarily so we could shovel forkfuls of the roasted meat into our mouths.

Then I said, 'She's not a fortune teller, is she?' I was thinking about Celeste.

'Who?' asked Sam, as if all of the last few minutes' convo prior to the lamb tasting had dropped entirely out of his head.

I rolled my eyes. 'Keep up. This woman Pearl.'

'Oh yes,' he said. 'Writer?'

'No. You're both wrong. None of those,' Monty replied. 'She suffers from something called Near Death Syndrome.'

Oh, so *this* was where our next investigation was going – not to Haven but Heaven. A destination I could no way have predicted.

'Intriguing,' Sam said and popped a large roast potato in his mouth.

I glanced at Bronson. 'Never a dull moment at the Witch Museum, is there?'

Monty went on, 'Her full name is Pearl White.'

I sniggered.

'She lives in Surrey. Near Woking.'

Bronson slurped and said, 'I had a cousin there once. Builder. Said he built a wall for Paul Weller.'

Monty was completely nonplussed by that (slightly out of character, but nevertheless well-clunky) name drop, and continued. 'As I mentioned, she suffers from Near Death Syndrome.'

'So what does that mean exactly?' Sam asked.

Monty coughed and laid his knife and fork down to one side. 'It's a very strange condition. Near-death experience occurs, usually, with impending death. People who have experienced it say that they move through a variety of sensations, often in sequence, and feel themselves detach from their physical body.'

'Oh, right,' I said, aware we'd all stopped chewing and started listening. And intently so.

'Some of them,' Monty continued, 'return with the impression that they have levitated and moved towards a bright and vibrant light. In "near-death" situations the event is interrupted, and they are pulled down again. Back into their physical body and this material world. However, they allege that sometimes they see people in their visions. People who have died.'

'Near Death Syndrome,' Sam repeated and took out his phone.

I nodded. 'I think I've heard about that. There was this bloke in Waste and Fly-tipping ...'

Monty's face clouded. Bronson tried to rescue him with 'Council,' which didn't really seem to clear matters up.

I couldn't be bothered to explain that because it wasn't the point anyway, so barged on, 'Steve or Colin or Mike or something, you know – boring name, and fat – well massive, like Cyril Smith-massive. Beer I reckon. All red in the face. That's right,' I nodded to myself. 'I recall it now – his name was Fat Mick. Always bragging about himself – "The Big I Am". Showing off about winning down the casino. But you can't gamble down the casino if you're on a council salary, right?'

No one reacted. Didn't matter. I was on a roll. 'Backhanders, I reckon. That's what they said. Anyway, one night he's down Southend, does all right on the poker table. Quids in, and Fat Mike, well he's as happy as Larry. Goes outside to celebrate with a thick Cuban.' I turned to Monty. 'That's a cigar, not a person.' Shifted back to Sam and Bronson. 'So, he's on the steps, puffing away and wham! Massive heart attack, right there, outside the casino. Everyone thinks it's "Game Over", literally, but somehow he pulls through.'

Monty and Bronson seemed to be keeping up, but Sam was squinting at me weirdly. I ignored him and carried on – I was getting to the point. 'So he comes back to work three months later and he's like a different bloke. Well, still fat, still balding, still red in the face. But *nicer*. Like, makes coffees for everyone even though he's given it up. Doesn't blah blah about himself any more. Asks people about *themselves*. A bit kind of modest. So one day I'm next to him in the canteen and it's raining and really grotty outside. Everyone's moaning about their jobs as there'd been a staff meeting that went on for years – redundancies. Anyway, when we get to the mains up at the server, it's sausages or salad. And I was like, "At least that's cheered me up." But then I realise, queue-wise, I was *behind* Fat Mick and there weren't many left. Sausages. And they look well tasty. Not like Tesco stringy ones, these are nice and juicy. Though there he is, *in front of me*, all big and blobby and hungry and that. But guess what?'

'Don't tell me,' said Sam, trying very badly to conceal his irritation. 'He goes for the salad?'

'Yes,' I said, with amplified amazement. 'And I'm gobsmacked because, well you know, you don't get a belly like that *just* from the odd beer, you've got to put some effort in with the saturated fat. And old habits, they die hard, right?' Bronson nodded at me with enthusiasm. 'So, I said to him, trying to be subtle, "You've changed, Big Boy." And he says, "That's right."

'And so I said "I suppose it was the brush with death, was it?" And he goes, "How long have you got?" I was kind of interested to find out, so I sat down with him and he told me about how, when they reckoned his heart had stopped, he found himself floating upwards towards this light, and he felt good and he felt loved. But he said before he could go into the light, a voice boomed out "No. You've got to go back. You have more to do, Fat Mick." Although I don't know if they used that name. The voice, that is. Anyway, next thing, he wakes up in hospital. Been pronounced dead but he came back to *life*!'

Monty pointed his right finger up in the air 'Yes, yes. I have it on good authority that is a very common experience, as far as these experiences can be termed "common".'

Bronson wiped his mouth with the only napkin on the table. 'Who did Fat Mick think was talking to him?'

I spluttered through a mouthful of roasted veg, 'God.' Swallowed down the herby loveliness. 'And that's why he changed. Because he realised what was important and what was not.'

Sam smirked.

I added, 'Allegedly,' to quell his smug expression. 'He reckoned God sent him back because he had to spread the word about the Meaning of Life.'

Sam made a 'pfft' sound and then crossed his arms. 'Which is?'

I frowned at him. 'Love, obviously.'

'What do you mean, "obviously"?' Sam snapped.

'Why are you so antsy?' I asked.

Monty came back with, 'It would be true to say that the concept of love in all its variations – spiritual, altruistic, platonic, fraternal, familial, romantic etc. – is at the centre of most major religions. Many tend to believe that it's what gives meaning to life.'

Sam tapped the table with his fork and asked, 'But THE meaning of life?'

'Why not?' I said and, as Eros was in the vicinity, or at least being spoken of, I threw in a flutter of my lashes and hoped he didn't notice the drizzle of oil on my chin.

Over the other side of the table Bronson fidgeted in his chair and put the napkin next to his plate. 'Seconds?'

Sam looked like he was going to say something, but the notion of more food distracted him. 'Yes please.' He held out his plate then turned to me. 'It's likely that in near-death situations the, er, victim I suppose you'd call it, may undergo random but intense experiences and feelings triggered by the brain shutting down. Only later when they are trying to make sense of it, they find meaning in them. We, as human beings, are constantly seeking purpose.

'That doesn't suggest it's *not* the meaning of life. Aristotle proposed that happiness was the true goal and that the function of human life was to achieve that.' It's amazing what you could learn browsing magazines in Auntie Bab's salon.

Sam's eyebrows hoisted briefly. Then he sighed. 'There you go – Apophenia.'

Bronson wrinkled his forehead. 'What's that when it's at home, Sam?' He grinned at Monty and shook his head in a show of exasperation along the lines of 'these silly young people with their made-up words'.

Monty offered a semi-nod back, clearly puzzled by Bronson's inclusion of him in the old fellow's age group. The agent was only in his early forties but his black hair was receding around the sides and temples, which made him look a tad older despite the glint in his eyes and the supple way in which he moved.

Sam cleared his throat. 'Apophenia: abnormal meaningfulness.'

I added, 'The tendency to make connections in unrelated or random things.' Then for clarity, I added, 'Mistakenly.'

'Oh I see,' Bronson nodded slowly. 'Like Granddad did with the Blackly Be boulder.'

Granddad was an ancient member of the Adder's Fork community. No one could recall his real name any more.

'Yes!' said Sam. 'Granddad remembered all the things that had happened when the boulder was moved back in the forties.'

'Or remembered people talking about 'em,' Bronson offered. 'Don't think he's had his telegraph from the queen yet.' Then he scrunched his face up with doubt. 'Or maybe he has.'

'Well, anyway,' Sam continued, 'he connected them to the disturbances in the village when the developers charged in and tried to move the Blackly Be ...'

'True enough. He said there were trouble over at the Bridgewaters'. Warned us, he did, that things weren't going to end well,' said Bronson. 'And he were right – things did 'appen. Bad things.'

Sam opened his mouth to challenge him, then thought better of it and gave up.

I said nothing for a minute. There was something in Celeste's journal about the Bridgewaters. The mention of their name made me shudder.

Then Monty, who the rest of us had forgotten about, said, 'Jolly good then. Shall I assume that's an acceptance?'

'Of what?' I said. My mind was still getting over the shudder.

'That you'll visit Pearl White and investigate her? She's had a couple of hits lately.'

'Hits?' I said.

Sam stared at Monty as he spoke. 'Accurate predictions?'

'Correct,' said the agent. 'And one of our …' he hesitated. His eyes left Sam's and cast around the table for another focus. 'Sources. Yes, one of our sources believes she's on to something at the moment.'

'So we'll meet them down there?' said Sam trying to make eye contact with his friend.

Monty brought his gaze back to the table. There was something guarded in his expression. His grin, however, wiped it clean away. 'Yes. I'll give you Pearl's address.'

'And when do you want us to start?' I enquired, already knowing the answer. 'Yesterday?'

'Also correct,' Monty beamed. 'Details of the hotel.' He passed a printout over the table to me. He had booked us rooms already. 'And, of course, I can promise a small fee and a blind eye on the expenses. As usual.'

Monty lived in another world. His 'small' fees regularly propped up the finances of the Witch Museum. They were getting harder and harder to say no to.

'Great,' said Sam and got up to clear the plates. 'Bronson, you all right to rule the roost for a bit?'

Our caretaker agreed. 'But right now, if you don't need me, I'll be off. I've a date at the Stars.'

Which was just as unexpected as Monty's appearance had been. Although I'd looked at Bronson with new eyes since I'd read about him recently.

'Well, Rosie, if you want to start packing I'll see Monty out,' Sam said and looked at his watch. He knew me well. 'How will we find this contact?' he asked.

Monty got to his feet and straightened his tie. 'Oh, you'll know him when you see him,' he said to Sam.

He wasn't wrong about that.

CHAPTER SEVEN

The following morning was cold. One of those days that can't make up its mind as to whether it wants to have a personality or just be dull. In my head I expected a certain amount of pathetic fallacy whenever we embarked on a new adventure. I mean – a new case. A bit of blazing sunshine or glowering ominous clouds. But the reality was that regularly we packed the car up and set off under an ordinary English sky, which started off grey and stayed that way till sundown.

Sam settled himself on his phone so I turned on the radio. We stayed this way for a while.

It was when we slowed to a crawl over the Queen Elizabeth Bridge that I got bored and decided I wanted some attention. The clouds were low and the banks of the Thames beneath us spectacularly uninteresting. Even the water had deserted the riverbed leaving it naked for all to see its dirty mud.

'And this also has been one of the dark places of the earth,' I quoted as we crossed what remained of the Thames.

'*Heart of Darkness*,' Sam guessed. Correctly.

'I did it for English,' I told him. 'Did you know Conrad

wrote it near here. Stanford-le-Hope. My class went there and had a look around.'

'And what was it like?'

'I thought it might be a bit French, maybe have a chateau or three. What with the name and that. But it didn't. It was like this.'

Sam grunted and looked over his shoulder back at Essex. 'On a day like today you can see how Conrad developed an obsession with darkness.'

I glanced quickly out the window. 'And rivers.' It would look so much better if the water was in. Made such a difference.

As a rule, you see, I liked Essex waterscapes. Which was lucky, as you couldn't get away from them: the whole county was fringed with waterways. I got off on the way the marsh spread out into glistening flatlands; and the birdlife that hovered on the edges of the tidal waters eyeing up ragworms in the mud. Yeah, yeah there were those who complained about the lack of contours in the landscape but I found the flatness enabled you to see far far away. Over the seas. All the way to the curve of the world and back. I agree that sounds a bit flowery, but that's just how the landscape moves me. I have my moments, you know.

But, like I said, today the landscape had been drained of water.

Minging.

The dominant colour was grey. It stained everything – mud, banks, industrial plots, cranes, shopping centres, hair, faces, eyes, skin, blood, souls. And it wasn't a chic kind of dove grey, nor a shade that might feature in an Ikea woollen throw. It was the variation that you saw on broken-down railings and smeared electric casings and polluted roadside dirt. The kind that stained your fingers and came out of your nose when you sneezed.

Grim wasn't the word.

Depressing wasn't the word either.

Miserable was getting a bit closer but it didn't hit the jackpot.

The traffic slowed to a stop.

'Have you found anything about Pearly Gates, then?' I asked Sam.

He looked blank.

I sighed. 'Pearl White. The woman. Who we're on our way to see.'

'Oh,' he said, and looked up from his phone. 'Yes. Not a huge amount. She had a hit a few years ago with a little girl lost. Said she was wandering where the land met the water.'

'That old chestnut,' I said. In our experience cons were usually vague. Their predictions weren't ever specific enough to prove or disprove. Water often featured. Fortuitous, as it was everywhere.

'Yes, but she described the shape of it. Said it was like a jigsaw and brought in a piece that she thought resembled the body of water. The police seemed to think it did too. When you viewed it from above. Despatched a search party to the local reservoir, a few miles from where she was last spotted, and there she was by a jetty, waiting to be found.'

'Alive?'

'Yes.'

Well, that was a positive outcome at least.

'Did the girl say that she'd seen the woman, Pearl?'

'No links between them were ever detected.'

'So how does that relate to Near Death Syndrome?'

'Allegedly Mrs White often communes with spirits during her near-death episodes. She had one. Saw various spirits during the episode. They told her where to find the girl.'

I thought about the aerial view of the reservoir. 'Did she get paid or a reward?' That was another indication of authenticity or lack thereof. It wasn't unknown for people to fake children's abductions or deliver sightings dressed up in psychic prediction in order to receive money.

'No cash exchanged hands.'

'Really?'

'Yep.'

Unusual.

A car blared its horn at me. I had veered into the middle of the road during the conversation.

'Careful now.' Sam's vocal cords constricted.

For once, I obeyed and focussed on the road.

The traffic thinned.

Then thickened again.

Minutes ticked by.

The day progressed.

At mid-morning a gap in the clouds occasioned a brief break in the gloom. For a moment, light beams poured down out of the hole and splashed around the London Orbital.

God rays, I thought. That was what my mum used to call

them, which was kind of odd as neither she nor my dad were religious. But I could see where she was coming from. If you had just a modicum of imagination you might be fooled into thinking that the shafts of light were coming from an amazing, glorious but distant realm. Certainly somewhere a little bit more enchanting and magical than the M25. Though let's face it, anywhere was more enchanting than the M25. Even our little patch of Essex.

I gave up trying to conjure places that were remotely less boring and let my eyes flit over to the panels of sunshine. They weren't doing anything to raise the temperature, though I think that their beauty certainly lifted my mood.

Slightly.

Light glittered on the smooth frost-kissed trees growing at the sides of the motorway. There was something slimmed down and elegant about them: the black branches like arms – graceful, uncluttered and bare – reaching up into the winter sky. Here was a simplicity which was refreshing. Or perhaps it was just the contrast of them there and still and silent, to us here, skidding, indicating, weaving, speeding, honking.

Then the clouds shifted and the god rays withdrew.

Sam, I remembered now, had called them something different. I thought about asking him but he was looking out the window, trying to avoid eye contact. Ah yes, that was it – 'crepuscular rays' which were, if I recall rightly, apparently just 'sunlit air'. Now it was coming back – he had been quite adamant that each ray was separate and parallel and that the idea they were all coming from one source was just a trick of perspective which might account for the ladder in Jacob's famous dream. As ever, my colleague, curator, tantalising love-interest and deeply unknowable friend, had been there at the ready, to challenge, myth-bust and generally stamp down on any spiritual tomfoolery or fanciful romanticism.

The satnav told me to turn off. It was one of the few things that got away with barking instructions at me. It was lucky.

I brought my speed right down as we came off the M25 and then slowed more as we turned into a narrow B-road. It was a relief from the relentless uniformity of the motorway. The byroad was pretty. Ish. With trees and farms either side, in the distance the sweeping Surrey Hills rose, brown-topped and balding.

Presently we came into little villages, much more photogenic than Adder's Fork. And rather more grand. Stockbroker-land, no doubt. Except Surrey stockbrokers not Essex ones. For some reason they seemed to be posher.

I sighted the hotel on the outskirts of town, an old Edwardian block, and followed the signs to the car park at the back that had taken the place of the garden.

Sam, who had buried his head back in his mobile, stirred in his seat, then unfastened the seatbelt and got out.

We unpacked our luggage, picked up our keys and agreed to meet in twenty minutes in the lounge. Both of us were keen to get going. It was always like this at the beginning.

Once I'd got into my room I quickly set out my heated curlers, straighteners, small portable make-up bag, large unportable make-up bag, toiletries, shower cap, silk kimono, jeans, trainers, heels, cowboy boots for various occasions (rough purple for cross-country, black for formal and gold with sharp tips for everyday wear), slippers, day dress, nightdress, lift-and-separate jeans, relax-and-veg-out loungewear, T-shirts, vest tops, shirt (satin), bras (push-up, hold-down, balcony), knickers (no VPL and reinforced Spanx for stomach-taming), tights, stockings, woolly socks, bed socks, and cocktail dress (just in case).

Out of habit I touched up my make-up, wondering if I should change my lipstick. What shade said 'Near Death Syndrome'? Difficult to tell really. *Candy-yes-yes* was a no-no – too pink and devil may care. *Red Ruby Velvet* – too bright. *Too Faced* was too boring. In the end I went for *D is for Dagger*, as it was bloody but not gory, and toned it down with a subtle smudge of toffee-coloured lipstick. I thought it symbolised a kind of muted respect and gravity. If toffee could do actually do that.

Then I put on my black cowboy boots (formal) and went downstairs.

Sam had clearly been waiting for me for a while and rolled his eyes when I got to the bar. I decided to rise above it and even let him drive us to Pearl's house. The satnav took us out of town into the outskirts through the woods and thickets of Surrey, a thin strip of flat land with what looked like playing fields on one side and farmland on the other. Soon we turned off and came into a housing estate that consisted mainly of bungalows. Most of them were functional rather than aesthetic, so could only have been built in the 1960s.

Eventually we pulled into a cul-de-sac. My mum would have called this a 'close'.

Pearl White's house was at the far end next to a narrow alley. The windows had white PVC frames and scalloped lace curtains. On the sill of the largest stood a small Christmas tree made of tinsel, a china wheelbarrow bearing a bouquet of artificial flowers and a lamp that was fashioned to appear Victorian but looked more seventies in terms of manufacturing.

As we dutifully scrambled up the garden path Sam nudged my elbow and pointed to a small gnome holding a wheelbarrow.

I sniggered, but Sam said, 'Fanciful, d'you think? An indication of the occupant?'

'Nah,' I told him. 'You want to see what Dad's allotment gang have in their patches and they aren't the types to entertain flights of fancy. I think it's more of an "age thing" than a "belief thing".'

'But,' he whispered, 'some people are of the opinion that they protect from evil and bring good luck.'

'Do they?' I said, genuinely surprised. 'I thought they were just decorative, made for people who were naff. Or German.'

Sam frowned. 'What?'

'Didn't the Germans start the trend?'

'How do you know that?'

'Dad. Ted.'

'Sometimes I'm amazed by what you come out with.'

Well, that was rich. 'Excuse me Mr Pot, have you met Ms Kettle?'

'Fair point.' He took a step closer to me. 'Audrey has taken up destroying the gnomes in Terry Bridgewaters' garden. Were you aware?'

Audrey was our resident protestor. Well, not quite resident as there was an injunction keeping her off the property. She had however taken up an alternative pitch on the pavement outside. Daughter of a long-dead fire-and-brimstone type of preacher, the woman was bat-shit, although, in her favour, she had recently provided a significant clue which had led to the solution of a very important murder. It would have all come out years earlier however if she'd not conflated the words 'de Vere' and 'devil'. But she had the latter on her mind. A lot.

'That's a bit harsh,' I said.

'Smashed old Ash Bridgewaters' gnomes and fairy statues. He used to collect them apparently.'

'Oh no,' I said. 'Bet Terry wasn't happy about that.'

'It was Tone that they had to stop going round her cottage and giving her a piece of his mind.'

'And something else too,' I said, remembering the young man had been lithe and agile enough to break our kitchen window in the summer, and crawl through with a large bouquet of flowers.

'Indeed,' Sam agreed.

'Why did she do that then? Audrey? What's she got against gnomes and fairies?'

'Worshipping of false idols.' He reduced his voice to a whisper. 'Plus, they are pagan, and possibly the servants of Satan sent to infiltrate our domestic spheres.'

'Oh right,' I said and sighed. 'That woman needs a holiday.'

'She can't,' said Sam. 'She's announced she's a Watchman.'

I was going to say, à la Bronson, 'What's a Watchman when she's at home?' But I got all tongue-tied and burbled, 'Whatchawhatchmanome?'

Sam darted me a glance to check I wasn't having a stroke. 'She thinks there be demons in Adder's Fork,' he said and for emphasis added in a theatrical side whisper with his hands held floppily like a B-movie Dracula, 'Demons at the door!'

At which point the door of the bungalow was thrown open.

If there *had* been a demon at the door it might have explained Sam's reaction. For he stood stock still, his mouth lolling open, and stared, eyes wide, at the man in the doorway. His breath iced the air.

I'd never seen him like this before. What was going on?

I tore my eyes from him and looked back at the bloke. There was nothing particularly distinctive about him apart from his face, which was wearing an expression of what I would describe as meek hopefulness – his head thrust forward, away from his neck, eyebrows raised; he stuck out a hand, but with trepidation.

I took it and shook it and said, 'Hi I'm Rosie.'

He paid me no attention but kept his eyes fixed on Sam, who was still goggling at him.

It was all rather perplexing.

I searched the stranger for clues. Attractive for a bloke in his sixties, he was tanned but pale behind it. Salt-and-pepper hair was brushed back into a classic style – short, neat. He had chinos on and a stay-press shirt with a lot of creases in it, which suggested he'd been sitting in one position for a length of time. Plus there were bags under his eyes.

Suddenly he stepped out of the door, with both arms extended, and grabbed Sam in a bear hug.

There was a strained and taut quality to the embrace. Something akin to desperation.

Sam responded to the tight squeeze but discomfort pinched his smile. And something else was there, that worried his eyebrows.

When the older man released him, my friend managed to compose himself, skin brightly flushing, and then took a wobbly step back. 'What are on earth are you doing here, Dad?' he asked.

CHAPTER EIGHT

'Bloody hell.' I said. 'Dad?' Though it was more of an exclamation than a question.

Come to mention it, there *was* a resemblance. 'Oh right. I thought he ...' I mumbled to myself, as neither of them were paying any attention to me. 'I thought he, you, lived in America ...'

'I do,' said Sam's dad.

'Then what ...' I asked, stuttering, still processing his appearance. 'What are you doing here? In Godalming? With a Near Death Syndrome ...' I gave up.

Sam's dad nodded. 'Didn't Monty tell you? I had the impression he would.'

'Ohhh,' I said, penny dropping. 'Are *you* our contact? Yes, that's right – he said Sam would know him when he saw him.'

I looked at Sam for confirmation, but he was still agog.

'But why are you here?' I asked.

Mr Stone senior dispensed with the middleman (me) and directed his gaze straight at Sam. 'Son,' he said. 'There's been a development.'

'A development?' Sam's voice was weak. He was starting to thaw out from shock. Though it was very cold out here. My nose was going a deep scarlet, borderline *Ruby Red Velvet.*

The older man nodded gravely. 'It's Jazz.'

The effect of this sent Sam reeling. Literally. He lost his footing and careered around, almost stumbling, and headed back to the car.

I watched him, turned back to the man on the doorstep, whose face was all creased with worry, then decided my loyalties were with Sam so also headed to the car and got in the passenger seat.

I didn't think I should look at Sam, it felt intrusive. So I stared straight ahead at a strip of garages. The handle was dangling from one of them. Another had a broken-down caravan parked out the front. It had orange curtains and was for sale. There were places like this everywhere across the UK. It said something about the national character. I wasn't sure what, but I had a hunch if I was to dwell on it I might find myself depressed by the conclusion.

Out of the corner of my eye I saw Sam's dad open the back door of the car and get in behind us.

None of us said anything.

The air thickened and flexed.

Traffic and street sounds receded.

Sam breathed out through his nose.

I heard Mr Stone senior swallow noisily. His mouth was dry.

The tension in the car was stifling, pressing against my

temples and becoming oppressive. I didn't like it. I'd have to break it.

Allowing my mind to mull over what his dad had said, I concluded I had no idea why Sam would react so violently to the mention of an African American musical genre that originated in New Orleans.

It was bizarre.

But clearly affecting everyone.

I sucked down a breath then took the bull by the horns. 'I know we lag behind America in some new developments, Mr Dad-of-Sam,' I said. 'But we've been doing jazz this side of the pond for nigh on a century.' I thought I conveyed a lightness of tone with my words, a little gift to diffuse the icy atmosphere that had frozen the car.

It didn't work.

The temperature continued to plummet.

'Shut up, Rosie,' said Sam. Which was, it had to be said, rather startling. This went way, way beyond his usual irritation. The bloke was bossy with me, yes, but never openly hostile. My well-tuned ears detected fire in his words – powerful emotions flickered within him – lots of them. I'd not experienced that before. Then he went, 'Oh for God's sake, Dad!' and this time his voice was layered with acid. The force with which he expelled his next words was almost brutal: 'Jazz is dead. Why can't you get that?'

It seemed a rather too impassioned denouncement. Quite over the top really. And I thought there would be plenty of advocates to suggest that, contrary to Sam's statement, jazz was experiencing a bit of a renaissance. Certainly, at the

Seven Stars when they had their monthly 'curated' jazz nights the pub would fill up with old people who didn't drink much but applauded often. There were always some youngsters in there too, lowering their voices to order half pints of shandy in monster voices that they thought made them sound over eighteen years of age.

Dad-of-Sam emitted a hoarse breath from the back seat as if he were going to say something, but his son wasn't finished. 'No. He's dead, Dad.'

Which kind of shocked me – Jazz was a person.

I turned in my seat and tried to gauge Mr Stone. His son's words seemed to have barely registered.

Mr Stone senior stood firm. 'This one's good, son. A promising lead. I wouldn't be here if it wasn't.'

I was beginning to wonder when someone was going to let me know what the bloody hell was going on.

Sam sighed at volume then he also turned in his seat. 'How many times have you said that, Dad? You've done so well for the past couple of years.' His voice softened. 'I thought you'd sorted yourself out.'

Mr Stone's shoulders dropped. He ran his fingers through his hair. The execution of the mannerism was exactly his son's. Leaning forward he spread his hands across the fabric covering of Sam's seat. His face took on a collapsed, caved-in look which made me instantly feel sorry for him. 'Just give Pearl a chance, son. She's good.'

Sam let a snort find its way out of his nose.

I nudged him. 'Monty wants us to check her out and we said we would.' I didn't wait for a response but turned to Sam's dad and held out my hand. 'I'm Rosie, by the way.'

I'd said it before, but he'd ignored me. Weirdly this time it seemed to rouse Sam out of his dark slump.

'Sorry,' he said, shaking his head. 'I forget my manners. Dad this is Rosie, Septimus's granddaughter. She is the new owner of the museum.'

Sam's dad shook my hand and smiled weakly. He looked grateful.

Sam went on, 'Rosie, this is, as you've probably worked out, my dad – Michael.'

'Good.' I said. 'Now I can stop calling you Sam's dad. You've come an awfully long way, haven't you?'

'Well, yes …'

'Staying at the George?'

He nodded, but was prevented from confirming verbally by a loud rap on the window which drew all our attention.

A heavy-set man was bent over, peering in at us. He motioned for Sam to wind his window down, which he did.

The chunky bloke stuck his head through the window. 'Are you coming in or what?'

To which Michael replied, 'Yes, yes. Apologies for the delay, Donny. This is my son, Sam, and his friend, Rosie.'

I didn't buckle at the use of friend. In fact I enjoyed it.

The bloke nodded. 'All right?' Then he stood up.

He didn't look like a Donny. Somehow the name conjured up images of Mr Osmond in his coat of many colours and a soulful-looking Jake Gyllenhaal brooding in the eighties.

They were both slim and dark and good-looking. This Donny was dark but that's where the similarities ended.

I realised, as I got out of the car and he straightened to his full length that he had a bit of height on him but he wasn't attractive. His skin was in dire need of a good tone and cleanse.

I made my way round the outside of the car and plonked myself next to him. Then I opened Sam's door. 'Come on,' I told the curator. 'Out. We've got work to do.'

We had, it was true. We couldn't let Monty down, even if he had set us up to collide with Sam's (possibly estranged) dad. The former hadn't ever told me much about him. You didn't have to be a detective to know there was some kind of conflict going on between father and son. I guess I'd find out more as we went along. And to do that I needed to coax Sam out of the car. I think Michael got that too, as he turned round and headed for the bungalow.

'See you inside,' he called, over his shoulder.

Donny took the lead and bent forward, nudging me gently out of the way, hand sliding down his thighs onto his knees. He ran his tongue over his teeth and lowered his head to Sam's window again. There was a cluster of pronounced blackheads on his nose that my Auntie Babs would have paid to get her hands on. His face was so greasy and shiny that even from a yard away I could see the poor lad suffered from a surfeit of excreted sebum. If I was him I'd start with a gentle micellar water and work my way up to an acid peel. But it was probably best to mention this further down the line once I'd got to know Donny better.

'She don't bite, my mum,' he told Sam. His voice was surprisingly gentle and warm. 'We're friendly, honest.'

Which was quite generous – all things considered. In my experience people like his mum tended to attract all kinds of attention, some of which was not just undesirable, but openly antagonistic.

Anyway, it did the trick. Sam sized up Donny, looked back at the steering wheel, then must have decided there was no getting out of it and humphed himself out of the car. I took the keys off him and locked it, then the three of us returned to the porch.

Donny opened the door, which was on the latch, and went in. Pressing himself against one side of the hall he politely bade us enter. But the poor bloke was so large and the hall so narrow we had to breathe in to squeeze past him. My boobs touched his boobs as I shimmied down the corridor. He smiled, embarrassed.

I sent one of my 'oh well, never mind' grins back and popped out the other side of him. We were instructed to take the first door on the left, which I duly turned in to.

And boy, what a sight it was. Pearl was clearly chintz-mad. For there were chintz curtains, chintz armchairs, a large overstuffed chintz sofa, chintz lampshades and chintz cushions. Thank God the walls weren't covered in chintz paper or else there would have been an infinite number of shades and hues producing an infinite amount of clashes.

Sam fell silent at the sight. I was thinking that if I stayed here for a very long time the surfeit of flower forms and colours could well trigger a psychotic episode. There was a lot of them. I mean, a LOT.

It did cross my mind that the decoration might have something to do with Pearl's condition, but there was no time to externalise the thought, as a whirring sound started up from the adjoining dining room. I looked over to find the source and spotted a woman gliding forwards upon a gigantic electric wheelchair that looked very much like a portable throne. Someone had sprayed it gold and upholstered it with a large velvet cushion trimmed with extravagant purple fringing.

'I call it The Flower Room,' the queen within said. There was a smidgen of an American accent though I was unable to detect anything more specific, no regional variations.

'It's an interesting look,' I said back. It was as polite as I was prepared to go.

'We're putting up the Christmas decorations tomorrow. You know,' the woman I presumed to be Pearl responded, 'to sass it up a little.' She sent the three of us a collective and very disarming smile. 'I do so love this time of year, you know. Now it's real sweet to make your acquaintance.' Pushing a control stick on the right arm of the throne she wheeled into the room fully, like a regal and better-looking Davros, and stopped by the fireplace. I noticed that the carpet (giant tropical flowers and ferns) threads were bare, and understood immediately that this was 'her place'.

'You've met Donny, I see,' she cooed. 'I, of course, am Pearl.'

Donny rolled into a depressed sofa and beckoned the three of us to take a seat.

Sam and I looked for places to perch. Michael had already bagsied the only other armchair. There was a large olive green pouffe in the middle of the room, so I went and plonked myself down on it. Sam took one end of Donny's sofa.

Michael, who appeared to already be acquainted with Pearl and Donny, introduced us – Sam his son, then me, his son's 'friend'.

Pearl instructed Donny to sort out a tray of teas, coffees and squash. He smiled weakly then rolled himself back off the sofa, onto his knees, feet and then waddled off to the kitchen.

We made small talk while we waited for him to return. Pearl asked us if we had far to come. I told her not far – not as far as Michael – and looked at him to see if he'd pick up the baton, but he was watching Sam with great concentration. Pearl, gracious and silky in her responses, talked about the terrible congestion on the M25.

For someone so large and incapacitated I was noticing that she had an amazing aura of glamour about her. Not the 'glamour' you get from fairy magic, some of which I may, or may not, have been subjected to by persons who may, or may not, have been of the fairy heritage back in the summer. The interpretation of that pretty much depended on how you approached these sort of things, and it appeared I was approaching these things in a much more open way these days. True, I'd been sceptical when I first met Sam. But now I had seriously loosened up in that department. I mean, I'd had a thought about vampires earlier which just shows you how far I'd trodden down the road from Ye Olde Blind Cynic

Inn. That's not an actual pub by the way. More of a metaphor created by Sam and me on one very drunken night out. He thought that my intuition was strengthening and was toying with the notion that I might have inherited something from the women in my line. Laugh? I nearly did. I may have waved goodbye to Ye Olde Blind Cynic but I hadn't yet disappeared behind the 'Abandon All Doubt' door.

ANYWAY, back to the psychotic Flower Room and the Queen that ruled it. The glamour that Pearl radiated, I thought, was amplified by sensual cosmetic enhancement, luxury and charm. She did her make-up very well, and her face was perfectly moisturised. In fact she shone with a dewy glow. Though in her late sixties, her allure remained strong. I imagined she would have a certain amount of sex appeal to some.

While I was concluding my admiration for Pearl, Sam joined in the conversation. He was folding his legs and saying, 'No, not like TOWIE, thank you very much!'

Pearl took this in without as much as a raised eyebrow. If she was offended by his tone, she didn't show it.

Donny trundled through the archway with a hostess trolley. It bumped over the intensely patterned carpet making the collection of crockery and vessels on its uppermost shelf tremble: a cafetière (which I was happily surprised to see), five cups and saucers, a teapot and a large plate full of Wagon Wheels and Jammie Dodgers. I edged towards it.

Pearl smiled gratefully at Donny then turned back to Sam and commented, 'You don't have no accent. Nor does your father. Not so much.'

Michael began to explain that he was an ex-pat.

Without getting up I swivelled the pouffe, one way and then the other, with my bum and feet, zigzagging it out of the centre, so I was out of the path of the trolley (but near to its predicted destination point). Sam, oddly, seemed nervous. I could tell. His behaviour was well off baseline. They'd used that expression yesterday, during training. Couldn't be sure what it actually meant but I had an idea it was agent-speak for something like 'normal'. Sounded good anyway.

He was trying to keep his hands folded across his lap, but one kept straying up to scratch his nose. Then it came down again, stayed with the other hand for a minute. Next it was sloping up to rub his eye, check his nostrils were obstacle-free, smooth his hair, poke his ear etc.

Although I was still curious about the Jazz conundrum (that sounded like the name of a terrible band), I knew this wasn't the right time. Things would become clear, I suspected, when we got down to business. Presumably Michael would lead on that. Out of us all, he alone appeared to have the strongest idea about what he was doing. As far as I was concerned, I was down here to check Pearl out and report back to Monty.

As the conversation about accent had come quietly to an end, and Donny divvied up the refreshments, I decided to progress my personal investigation and asked, 'So how long have you been doing this sort of thing then, Pearl?

In retrospect it might not have been the most tactful way of phrasing an enquiry into a life-threatening disability. Donny made a sound that was almost a growl. Michael pursed his lips. Sam obviously didn't hear it properly as he had his hyperactive finger wedged in his inner ear. But Pearl was graceful.

'Ah, doll,' she said, glowing with benevolence, 'too long.' Then she shook her beautifully coiffed hair. As it moved, silver-grey and purple shades glistened like her namesake jewel-of-the-sea. It must be quite a feat styling that barnet every day, I thought. A lot of time and energy had gone into teasing and spraying it into a globe, about the same size as a goldfish bowl. Quite clever really for it reflected the different colours of the furnishings. There were so many in here that, at certain angles, Pearl's hair was positively iridescent. I wondered, fleetingly, what Auntie Babs would make of it and concluded she'd probably be impressed.

But I was stupidly distracted. I took myself back to the matter in hand – death. Or rather near-death and my clumsy opener.

'Sorry,' I said. 'That's probably a really rubbish way of asking.'

'No,' she waved a long nail at me. 'That's fine. I got nothing to hide. You can ask me what you will.'

To my surprise it was Sam that piped up next.

'So,' he said and grasped his hands round his knee. He tossed his head so his hair fell off his face. It must have picked up some of the moisture in the air outside when we had come in from the car, because it was starting to kink. 'You believe you have Near Death Syndrome.'

'That's right,' Pearl returned. She whirred forwards to readjust the position of the chair.

Sam watched the wheels straighten themselves and still. 'How does that work?'

I wondered briefly if he was asking about the wheelchair, but then Donny started to speak. 'Mum, are you all right to continue? Just say when you get tired.'

His mother winked back then turned to Sam and silenced him with a frown. 'Work?' she said, as if she had just heard the word for the first time. Then murmured to herself, 'I suppose "work" is what it is.'

Sam's eyes narrowed. 'Do you charge for your messages?'

Michael, who was wiping his forehead with a hanky, started. 'Sorry, Pearl. Sam, that's impertinent. I didn't bring you here to be rude.'

'*You* brought *me* here?' said Sam. 'No, it was Monty who directed us to visit the south and investi … oh,' he said, realising the collusion that must have taken place. Monty had been in communication with Michael. Or vice versa.

There was a possibility, I was thinking, that it could well have been Michael who had alerted Monty to Pearl. Had he then asked the agent to request our services? So he could see his son? After all, I knew that Monty was very well aware of Sam's background. He'd hinted at a family issue a few months back. Plus, Monty had been vague about his 'sources'. This was no doubt why. Would Sam have accepted the job if he'd known that his father was involved?

Right now, if I was a betting woman, I'd put a fiver on Donny having contacted Michael and kicking the whole process off.

Sam, however, was still working these connections through and had fallen into a state of mild bafflement.

His father lurched forward as if he was going to touch his son, but Pearl stopped him by wafting her hand in the space in between. I noticed her skin was quite wrinkle-free.

'I have been having these episodes for a while,' she said and bowed her head, keeping it there so that, for a second, I thought she might be praying, but then she raised it. I got a good view of her face; her eyes were light grey and bright, spinning into the past. There was no confrontation in them. I was sure of her conviction. 'A few years ago,' she said, 'I got knocked over, while crossing the road. Hit and run. Just back there,' she jerked her head. 'In Godalming. Unusual really. People here tend to have good manners. You know, we observe rules. Polite. That sort of thing. But anyways,' she thumbed the wheelchair. 'Ended me up here.' Our dismay registered. She didn't react. You could tell she'd done this speech a few times.

Nodding as if she were agreeing to an unheard question, Pearl went on. 'Oh yes, indeedy, this incarnation has certainly been a helluva journey.'

I snuck a glance at Sam. He looked completely blank, but I knew his bullshit-detector would be springing into action. The word 'incarnation' tended to set it off.

'I believe, however,' Pearl went on, forming her features into a charming smile, 'that the good Lord, in his most mysterious of ways, used this great calamity to lead me to my true purpose.' She stopped for a moment and swept the room with her gaze, touching on each of us individually. There was a lot of the preacher in her delivery.

'Which is?' Sam asked with evident impatience: he had started patting his kneecaps in a regular pattern, like a drumbeat. If he didn't stop soon, I was going to have to get down there and grab them.

Pearl stroked the outside of her palm down between her breasts to her plentiful belly. 'I am a guide, Samuel,' she said, as if she were explaining something obvious to a child. I also noted her use of his full name, though he hadn't been introduced like that.

My friend's eyebrows furrowed. 'A guide?'

'Why, yes. When I died and went to heaven I brought back a li'l of Jesus's light inside me. This, I use, to help poor souls. Souls that are lost, that need to find their way. I am the lantern, the torch in the darkness, when our Lord and Saviour can't be around.'

'You died?' I said. She was definitely there, in that golden wheelchair, breathing and smiling. I could see her boobs going up and down as her lungs inflated and deflated, and smell her perfume, which was something full and heady like Opium.

Her lips parted and a slice of serenity detached itself from her core and washed all over us. 'That's right, baby. But I came back again. It wasn't my time.'

Her presence – aura or atmosphere or whatever you liked to call it – was improbably serene, even as she described these traumatic events.

Michael leant forwards clasping his hands loosely together then letting them fall between his knees, making him look a lot more louche than I reckoned he was feeling. 'Do you mind me asking what that was like? I know you started describing the experience earlier, before …' he glanced at us and shrugged. 'Before we got interrupted. Could you recap for the benefit of our new guests?'

'Oh sure,' said Pearl and buzzed the chair clockwise towards us.

Michael gestured to the wheels on the chair and added. 'As long as it doesn't upset you.'

'No, honey. It's a wonderful memory. Why would it?'

I thought that if I were to kick the bucket, or nearly kick it or kick it then come back again it was doubtful I'd find the experience 'wonderful'. But I wasn't Pearl, was I? We were definitely different types of people.

Taking a cup and saucer I sipped my tea and waited for her to tell her story.

The clock on the mantelpiece ticked. We all quietened down and made ourselves comfortable as if it were *Jackanory*. When we'd settled she began.

'It was similar to what other folk do say,' Pearl sighed. 'Those who have faced near-death. But mine, in many ways, is unique. Individual. Though I 'spect we all think that. Each one of us imagines the whole world, the universe, that God himself at that moment, was concentrating on them. Just them.'

Which I was thinking was a very insightful comment to make.

A beatific smile beamed out of her round face. 'But that's just how the Lord Jesus Christ makes you feel. Special. We all agree.'

Sam coughed angrily – well, I could tell it was angrily. To an outsider it must have appeared he had a stubborn old frog in his throat. I didn't know what was going on with him. 'You *all*?' he said. 'You talk to others who have been through the same?'

'Oh, there's a survivors support group. We meet once a year. When we can.'

Sam took out his notebook and began writing. I was glad to see him more focussed. His brain was getting over the shock of seeing Michael so unexpectedly.

'Don't remember much of the physical collapse,' Pearl said, watching Sam's fingers on the pages. 'One minute I was watching *Countdown* on the TV, the next I was coming to in a hospital ward. But it's the in-between which is most colourful.'

'Don't tell,' Sam ordered. 'Let me guess – there was darkness. All around. Then you found yourself floating?'

'As a matter of fact, I did,' said Pearl. 'But it was not the floating that came first. It was the light. *That* was the first thing I remember seeing – a blinding bright light. White, though I could see in it the spectrum of colours, like a neon rainbow – blue, yella, violet – in amongst them sparkles of green – a metallic glitter – silver, gold. I think it was as if all life on this plane …'

'We don't live on a plane,' muttered Sam.

I shook my head at him and said, 'Sorry Pearl. We know what you mean. Do go on.' Then I sent him a look full of daggers, reflecting briefly on how dramatically our roles had reversed: a few months ago, it was far more likely to have been Sam apologising for me.

With impeccable manners she took the olive branch and fastened her eyes on Michael who was utterly absorbed. 'It was like all the elements in this physical world were represented by colour – minerals, fire, water, air. And *then*, after I had noted this, after The Power had *seen* me note this, I felt my body rise up into it. Into the colours. My, I was so pleased because I was free, not shackled to a heavy shell. I could move without limitation. It felt good. When I looked down I could see myself asleep in the chair, here,' she glanced at the fireplace. 'But I had no fear. And because I felt no fear, no dread, my astral body was able to ascend through the colour plane and into the stars.' She took a deep breath into her stomach and then exhaled. 'There was a passageway, a tunnel of light, and it drew me to it.'

Sam coughed and muttered, 'Lack of oxygen and fear has been known to cause tunnel vision.'

Michael hushed him but Pearl did not even acknowledge his comment.

'I passed through the tunnel,' she said, keeping her voice dramatic and whispery. 'Out the other side everything was calm.' She spread her hands as if smoothing out the wrinkles on an invisible sheet. 'There were clouds and lights and a gate. They swung open with no noise. And there I saw Jesus, in all His glorious splendour.'

Sam tutted. 'And he said it's not your time. Go back?'

Donny glowered at him.

But Pearl cruised on, filled with the warmth of her recollection. 'That's right. And, I don't remember what happened next, but within seconds, or less than seconds, I was back here. But not in the chair, on the floor. I had fallen. Donny was at my head shouting something. And the good doctor was here.'

'Her heart had stopped,' said Donny matter-of-factly. 'Doctor Frank had to perform CPR.'

But Michael was impatient. 'So you came back to life? Go on ...'

'That experience will never leave me.' She smiled, weirdly, at the memory.

'But you have Near Death *Syndrome*?' I said to clarify, because it sounded like she was talking about one episode in the past.

'That is so, honey.'

'Like – you *still* have it?' I pushed on.

'Oh sure,' she said. 'I get these attacks now, where I ...'

Again, Sam tutted and sighed. 'You have to go through that whole process again? Every time? See yourself, floaty float float up through the ceiling, tunnel, Pearly Gates, Morning Peter, How's your father ...' he could not keep crude sarcasm from his voice. It was starting to annoy me.

Pearl rose above it. Metaphorically speaking. 'No, not any more. I'm there so much I have my own shortcut now. Kind of like a frequent flyer pass, I guess you could say.' She chuckled. Donny lifted his head and curled his lips with appreciation.

'Now and then when I go, which is often, I don't find Peter at the Pearlies as you suggest. There is another place. Just outside the gates.'

Sam folded his arms like a stroppy teenager. I pinged him

an angry glance which he heeded. Though he couldn't stop himself communicating his disapproval, and rolled his eyes in a silent yet very obvious manner. Donny squinted at him. A shade of menace darkened his face.

There was something going on inside his head. This wasn't just about his scepticism in the face of Pearl's testimony. He was profoundly upset and doing a bad job of trying to mask it with disdain.

Pearl breezed on, oblivious to the tension invading the room. 'This place – it is for the souls who can't, or won't, enter the Kingdom of Light.'

'Aren't they meant to go downstairs?' I asked. 'You know, to have a chat with Lucifer?'

Pearl's head fell back and she trilled out a laugh. 'No. It's not like that, hon. These guys have got unfinished business on earth, something that ties them to the physical plane, which makes them reluctant to pass through the gates.'

I gritted my teeth and waited for a loud huff to come from the other side of the room, but Sam had got tired of doing that and was staring at Pearl.

Michael leant forward, still paying keen attention. 'So, who are they? These "guys".'

'Well, I don't see them, as such. They flit like shades. Mothwings, shadows against a flame. I receive "impressions" of what they were like in their earthly incarnations. I'm not sure they can see me neither. But they sense me, and they sense my connection to the earth. Which is why they talk, whisper little messages that I can take back down to the living.'

Donny glanced meaningfully at Michael, who extended his neck even more. One push from behind and he'd topple over.

'So these "shades" outside the gate …' I asked for clarification. 'They aren't part of the living? Are you saying you hear messages from the dead?'

'That is what I believe,' said Pearl.

I saw Michael's Adam's apple yo-yo in his throat. He looked under his eyebrows at Sam. It was a furtive gesture. Evidently not finding what he sought, he locked back on to Pearl's eyes and faltered, 'And Jazz was there?' His voice cracked on the last word. 'Amongst these things you mention, gathered outside the gates?'

She paused and screwed her face up. Then she swung the chair over to Michael. Her eyes softened when she saw the pain on his face. 'I cannot say for sure, you understand. There is a group detached from the crowd. I call them the Spirit Boys for there are no girls amongst them. And they have been removed from our earthly plane.'

Sam moved now, very slightly. He raised one eyebrow in contempt. 'And you've told my father that Jazz is there?'

Pearl didn't answer that question directly. 'He wasn't the one who spoke to me. It was another lad, Dylan.'

'Sorry – Dylan?' Michael repeated.

'Yes. There are a few there, with him.' She frowned. 'All boys. Jack, David, Elliot. Ray, Nick … some I can't hear too well. Cunar? Frett? Maybe Fred. I don't know.'

Michael and Sam swallowed simultaneously.

'They, or at least he, Dylan, he owns the voice that is the

clearest. There's another that's joined them recently, Tuey. I can tell he's a newcomer because sometimes I hear him panting, breathing heavily. He don't realise there is no need for that any more. He hasn't adjusted.'

Odd, I thought. 'Tuey. Funny name.'

'Well, that's what I could make out. Sometimes names get lost in translation. Sometimes those in limbo speak in the language of angels. It's a bit like baby language – goo goo gah gah and so on. That's what we all speak before we are incarnated, you see.'

My buttocks tensed in anticipation of a snarky comeback from the Sam corner.

But he said, 'Tuey. Like Chewy? Chewbacca?' Then rolled his eyes. 'What's his message, then?' he asked as if the whole thing were boring him.

Pearl's face creased. She sucked in her lower lip and regarded us gravely. I'd seen that look before on people we'd talked to: there was something she didn't want to reveal. 'He is still unsure of where he is. I feel he's trying to lead me to a place.'

'What place?' Sam asked, evidently less bored.

Again, she hesitated.

Michael leant forwards and, this time, almost toppled off his chair.

'I'm not sure,' she said, dropping her eyes, 'that he is fully aware of his position.'

I didn't really understand what she meant by that. Did she mean that he was dead, or that he was outside the Kingdom, or that he was sitting weirdly? And was it relevant?

'I have been asking him to tell me where he is.'

'But why are they together?' Sam interrupted before I could ask Pearl to spell it out. 'Him and these other boys.'

There was that flicker of worry across Pearl's forehead again. 'They seem to have a common thread. That is, they talk about the same man. In different guises.'

Sam opened his mouth to speak but then went quiet.

'Dylan talks about the Lord of the Flies.'

I darted Sam a glance and mouthed 'Devil'. We had come across him in our last escapade. That was another name for the goat-foot god.

Sam shook his head minutely and put a finger on his lips.

'I think it's a bit like shorthand for the Bogeyman,' said Pearl, going full Southern belle on the last word. 'But some of them, the faintest, who have been there a long time, agree with those who are new. They're worried he's back again, this man that keeps them. That's what I think they are saying. This guy, the Lord of the Flies, he lives on his own but keeps his family near, I think. That's what I'm getting from them. I don't really understand what they mean all the time. I try to ask about where he takes them.'

She paused and looked up at the ceiling, trying to recall her exchange. 'One of them said, "Out there by the hill. Away." I heard that clearly.'

She sighed. 'Tuey talks about the Washing Up Man, or something that sounds like the Washing Up Man.'

I shivered. For some reason, that freaked me more than Lord of the Flies.

'Dylan,' she continued. 'Says he's the same. He's, er ...' she folded her hands together on her lap and framed her features so that she looked resolved. 'This man talks to them. Gives them a lift, or something, then takes them home.'

'Keeps them?' said Sam and knitted his brows. 'Takes them?'

Pearl nodded sadly. 'Yes. In his van, apparently.'

My throat had gone rather dry. I could feel the palms of my hands getting moist.

'Family means everything, they say. But he's not right, not normal, in that way. Then again he wouldn't be, would he? If he were taking the boys and …' Pearl glanced guiltily at Michael and sucked the rest of her words in.

Mr Stone senior seemed to block out those unsaid words. 'And?' he motioned with his hand. 'And Jazz …?' He couldn't get the words out.

'Yes. Dylan mentioned a Jazz who had been with him. I couldn't work it out first of all. I thought it was Jackson. Then it became clearer. Jazz. Then Stone.'

'Was that when you googled him?' Sam's words came out sharp and loud like a cannon.

Michael coughed back the seer's attention. 'Pearl, Pearl – did he have a message?'

Her gaze changed when she looked at him. Her eyebrows bent and lowered. She bowed her head. Her voice was gentle when she said, 'He wants you to know that he's okay. He's safe now. And he's happy.'

Sam's fists clenched. His knuckles were turning white.

Michael nodded. 'Did he say *where* he was?'

In heaven obvs, I thought but didn't say. Thank goodness.

Because Sam grimaced and I realised that Michael wasn't talking about his spirit form or whatever it was. He was talking about his body.

Pearl shook her head. 'No. Dylan has mentioned trees. A wood.'

'How wonderfully generic,' Sam interjected, back to being cross again. 'I do hope you are not expecting access to the reward based on that: trees and a wood! Really!'

Ah, right. So Michael had put up a reward. Now I was beginning to see why his son was so stroppily protective. This was indeed an incentive for all sorts of charlatans to crawl out of the woodwork. And yet, Pearl didn't appear to be in it for the money. But then you never knew about these things, did you? People, I was learning, even the ones you trusted and lived with for thirty-odd years, were rarely what they seemed. Everyone has secrets.

Michael disregarded Sam's disparaging comment and pressed on with continued urgency in his voice. It was clear there was an intensity of feeling welling up in the man. 'But what can you tell us about where he might be?' His voice faltered. 'I … I …' His forehead was another grid of lines. Desperation rose into his voice. 'I have no closure. It … I can't rest until …'

I was beginning to get an idea about what was going on.

If I was right, then it was horrible.

'I'm sorry,' said Pearl and manoeuvred her chair over to Michael where she placed her hand on his. 'Really. But, like I told you, I believe he is linked to Tuey. I need to speak to the little lad again. He's the freshest.'

I winced at the term.

She caught me flinching and explained. 'His memories will be the most accessible.'

'Pearl,' Sam said in a scarily controlled voice. 'What did you tell my dad to make him fly all the way over here?'

Michael spun round. 'That he was or had been with these Spirit Boys, once. And she knew his birthday.'

'That can be found online quite easily,' said Sam.

'I heard him lisp,' said Pearl quietly.

That shut him up. Michael looked over, his face full of pain. The blood was draining from Pearl's complexion.

It was true – I could tell. She'd scored.

'And that detail,' said Michael, 'was never released to anyone. Not the media.'

'And the mark on his back too,' Donny spoke up from his chair, sounding like he was justifying their position. 'There was that, Mum, wasn't there?'

We all turned and looked at him mainly because it was the most he'd said all afternoon.

'A leap in the dark,' Sam muttered, which confirmed to me that it was another bullseye.

Pearl turned to Michael and tapped his hand. 'I feel I will visit them again soon. You being here will resonate in my own spirit body. The connection to your son will grow stronger. He will know you are near me. Last night I suffered a migraine. It's a warning sign. A journey must be taken. Donny will alert you when it happens. Now forgive me, I am tired. I must rest. My son will see you out.'

And with that Pearl revved up and motored out of the room.

CHAPTER NINE

Within minutes we found ourselves on the steps again.

I was worried a father-son argument might erupt, so kept things short and to the point. 'We're staying at the George hotel too, Michael. Would you like to meet us there?'

Michael responded with an inauthentic but brave smile and pulled himself together. 'I could meet you in the bar?'

'Yes, that would be great,' I said and looked at Sam.

He nodded, his movements sluggish. 'Yes, Dad. Shall we regroup in a couple of hours? It's getting on. We'll be hungry by then. We can find a nice Italian.' His words were catching inside his mouth. He was incredibly weary.

Michael agreed. I offered him a lift but he said he had hired a car, so without any further ado we departed.

I directed Sam to the passenger seat. There was no way I was having him drive in this state. He didn't object. In fact he was entirely malleable.

I watched Michael pull out then I gave it a few minutes and got on the road myself.

The lane went under a bridge. I stopped at traffic lights and drummed my fingers on the steering wheel.

Sam took an audible breath then spoke. 'He had a strawberry birthmark on his right shoulder.'

It felt like a judder rippling through the car.

I didn't have to ask who he was referring to.

'Oh,' I said. 'So Pearl was right about that.'

He didn't answer. His eyes were closed. Sweat had broken out in a smear under his nose. A weird sort of moan/groan leaked from him. He sat up quickly and opened the door. Then he ran to the roadside bushes and heaved.

Christ! I thought. I bent over and rolled down the window. 'Sam! Sam! What's the matter?'

The lights turned green. 'Sam I'm going to pull up ahead.'

Someone honked their horn.

I made it a hundred metres up the road, then pulled into a lay-by. For a moment I watched him bent over, then it occurred to me he'd probably want some privacy so I turned back to the road and switched the radio on loud enough to drown out the distant sounds of retching.

After a little while the passenger door opened and Sam collapsed back into the car. The poor bloke was sweating profusely. He swallowed some water and told me to drive on.

I fired up the engine. There was no point asking him anything.

As we pulled out I gestured for him to open the glove compartment and pointed out a spare Tesco carrier. He looked at it blankly, so I said, 'Take it. Just in case.' I didn't want to risk the upholstery.

I turned the radio off and motored on.

'Are you okay?' Silly question, I know, but pertinent.

He didn't respond. Just sat there green-faced, with his hands gripping the dash, head down, looking like he had the worst hangover in the world.

The sun was disappearing behind the hills. Soon it would be completely dark. We were entering the black heart of winter. There was a chill in the air, even in the car. I turned the heating up and looked for signs to Godalming.

'I was sixteen when it happened,' said Sam suddenly.

I looked into his face and accidentally swerved the car into the middle of the road then got told off via a hoot.

'Uh huh, uh huh,' I said, trying to sound relaxed. 'Go on.' I shut my mouth and opened my ears to him.

'We were in the car,' he said.

'We?'

'Me, Mum, Dad and,' he took down a breath. 'And Jazz. Jasper.'

Ah, right. Here it came.

He gulped down air. 'He was my younger brother.'

I carefully noted his use of the past tense.

'I hadn't wanted to go,' he went on, eyes avoiding mine.

For a moment he had sounded like a whining child. The colour hadn't returned to his face and his bottom lip protruded slightly.

'Like I said,' he kept his eyes fixed on the hills in the distance and a place in his life that hurt him still. 'I was sixteen going on seventeen and stately homes weren't my thing. They aren't any teenager's thing really, are they?'

'You were going to a stately home?' I asked for clarity.

Out of the corner of my eye I saw him shake his head. 'We were on our way back from one.'

'To Essex?'

'No, we lived in North London then. Hertfordshire really.'

'Okay,' I said and mentally added the new detail to my 'Sam File'. 'You don't have to be a teenager to dislike visits to stately homes.'

He didn't smile. 'This one had a miniature railway. We'd gone for Jasper, really. He was mad about trains. Obsessed by *Thomas the Tank Engine* when he was younger. Mind you we've all been through that stage, haven't we?'

Er, no, I thought, but didn't say.

'I was in the lower sixth so of course, the last thing I wanted to do on a Sunday afternoon was get in the car with my parents and younger brother and go and ride a miniature train. But Mum and Dad insisted. They said it wouldn't be long till I went off to uni and we wouldn't have family days like this any more. So, I went. But, as you might say, Rosie, "I wasn't 'appy about it. Oh no, not at all."'

He'd articulated the last bit in a very weird cockney accent which made me wonder if I actually sounded that retarded to him. In normal circumstances I would have challenged that, but as I was continuing to develop nuance, I understood that this might not be the most appropriate time. So I shut up. But thought I might mention it later down the line. Though, to be honest with you, I did appreciate him trying to reach for some humour to lighten the mood, even when he was this upset.

He paused and tutted to himself. 'And it was all right to

begin with. We had lunch. Mum had packed a picnic and there was a re-enactment battle going on which was quite interesting. We watched it for a while. But then, we went to go and find the miniature railway and there was a massive queue. We had to line up for ages and I got annoyed about that.'

I could picture the scene easily: Michael trying to keep the peace, Sam with a schoolboy scowl, his mum and younger brother excited.

'At last it came to our turn. We piled into the carriages. But the journey only lasted about five minutes so when we got off Jazz wanted to go round again. Mum was such a pushover. We argued. I think Jazz cried.'

I could hear Sam's vocal cords straining. Some bleak agonised emotion was weighing them down. 'They went back and queued and eventually got on the last lap before it closed. Which meant we were one of the final visitors out of the car park. There was an accident on the motorway, so we had to go on a diversion on the B-roads and country lanes. Dad said he thought he knew a shortcut. These were the days before satnavs,' he said glumly. 'We got lost, of course. And all the time I was getting more and more wound up. I'd remembered some homework that I had to do and it was getting dark and I was worrying that I wouldn't have enough time to do it when we got home.'

I could feel a big 'and' coming.

'We were going down this road. I was complaining about all the time it was taking. Mum was shouting at me to be quiet. She'd seen something in the wing mirror and wanted to concentrate – a car she'd sighted at the Hall. I can't remember what she was saying about it. Neither can she.' His voice wobbled. He took a moment and mastered some internal commotion before continuing. 'I was having a go at everyone for getting us into this mess, being mean to Jazz, stressing about the teacher who was known for roasting those with late homework.' He broke off and muttered under his breath. 'Roastings. That was what I was worrying about.' Then he shook his head and carried on. 'Jasper was crying. He was only ten and getting tired and upset. By me.' He paused. 'I'm not sure how it happened. I think we started scrapping in the back. Dad had his arm round, lashing out through the gap in the seats, trying to smack us, yelling for us to "pack it in both of you". But it was all "he started it", "no, he did", "he did".' Sam had made his voice shrill. 'You know the score.'

Yep. My brother John had been a massive pain in the rectum during family day trips. And he did usually start it.

I watched Sam breathe in and then put his hands back on the dashboard, as if he were bracing himself. 'I remember a loud bang and then everything was topsy-turvy inside the car. Things falling about. I saw the ground out of the side window, upside down. Smashing, banging but no screams. That's all. I'm not even sure if it's a real memory or if I've invented it because we talked about it so much afterwards and I've internalised it.' He finished and didn't say anything for a long minute.

I kept my mouth buttoned up, held on to my questions and drove on.

When he was ready again Sam continued in a low voice, 'There was a collision. Most likely with a vehicle that had recently been sprayed red. That's pretty much all we know. Mum was thrown from the car. Dad whacked his head on the steering column and nearly exited through the windscreen. We all came round in hospital.'

'It was only when Dad regained consciousness and started asking about "the boys" that the nursing staff realised that there had been another kid in the car: Jazz.'

'You mean you didn't tell them at the scene?' I spoke without thinking and he reddened. If I could have seen the tips of his ears I knew they would be scarlet. But his hair concealed them and anyway I wasn't going to look. I was going to concentrate real hard on the road.

'It was a car crash, Rosie,' he snapped. 'None of us were conscious. Dad had to be cut out. Mum almost died from her injuries.'

Shit. 'Sorry. I didn't mean … I … yes of course …' I couldn't quite believe I'd said that. I wasn't usually so tactless. 'And so … where was Jasper?'

He remained silent for a beat, then he said, 'We don't know.'

I wanted to say, 'You don't know?' But an echo like that was the last thing he needed.

'The first people on the scene found me, Mum and Dad. I was strapped into the back seat but Jazz's side was empty.'

'Did they search the area?'

'Of course. That's how they found Mum, she had been thrown twelve metres.'

I let that settle in for a bit then thought, *shite*. 'Witnesses?'

'Only the people that found us in the ditch.'

Silence.

Then the question that just had to be asked. There was no avoiding it. 'So, what had happened to Jazz?'

Sam waited. A long time passed. I really wanted to repeat the question but I had to let the story tumble from him as he wished. I hadn't been in such a delicate position before.

Outside the air tightened. The glum sky bruised and purpled. Spatters of rain hit the windscreen. I turned on the wipers and stared ahead, following the satnav's instructions to turn right, then left, then right again. We were nearly there.

At length Sam spoke. 'Nobody knows what happened to my little brother. There was an investigation. He was filed as a Missing Person. We thought eventually that he might have been kidnapped, but there was never any ransom.' He paused. 'And there's never been a body found. We've had a number of false alarms over the years, but they haven't matched the DNA and the forensic side of that is much better these days.'

I tried to suppress a shudder of sympathy. He wouldn't like it, but – Jesus – false alarms! What he and his poor family had been through didn't bear thinking about. No wonder he didn't like to mention it. That was one MASSIVE trunk, no – garage, no – big yellow storage facility – of emotional baggage.

I think it was the shock of what he had told me

that stopped me self-censoring for a moment. 'So he just vanished?' I asked as I sighted the hotel.

This time he turned to me. I could feel his eyes on my cheek, my nose, my chin. But I couldn't turn back and meet his gaze. I indicated right and pulled into the car park.

His voice was grave, upped with a tone that was rasping around the edges. 'You and I both know that can't happen. Someone took him.'

Christ, what a story, I thought as the engine spluttered and died.

CHAPTER TEN

Over dinner it became clear that the two men had settled into some kind of truce. Jasper wasn't mentioned at all. They must have decided not to talk about him. I was relieved. I didn't want to think about it any more. It was too real. Too ghastly.

As a result, the atmosphere was lighter than it had been. Plus the food was remarkably good. We had struck lucky in one of Godalming's finest nosheries and managed to get a non-festive set menu, which wasn't too pricey. The conversation flowed well, despite a very very loud Christmas party in the corner, who spent half the night distributing their Secret Santas and the other half chasing each other round the restaurant in mankinis and comedy breasts.

Sam was a bit annoyed by the noise, though I remained silent on that count. There but for the grace of God etc.

While we waited for the bill to arrive Michael said, to make conversation, 'So Rosie, Sam tells me you have issues with the term "Essex girl".'

As opening gambits went, this was certainly bold. Or ignorant.

I was actually quite impressed.

Sam, however, shuddered. 'Er, that's why I told you, Dad. So you'd avoid it.'

'Oh,' began Michael, two dots visible in his cheeks.

But I was gallant. 'No, it's fine. Sam's right, I do have issues with it because it's a pejorative term.'

'Yes,' said Michael. 'I was surprised when Sam mentioned it. Of course I remember it from years back, but I thought it might have died out by now. These things are so faddish.'

'You'd have hoped, but no. There was a TV series that whipped it up again. Did Sam tell you about his theory about Essex girls and the Essex witches?'

'Yes, he did,' Michael nodded. 'It's awesome. What do you make of it?'

I thought about the question. 'Same as you – it's interesting. I'm coming round to the idea that the contemporary stereotype might have come out of the witch hunts. There are definite similarities. But I doubt it's the truth, *the whole truth and nothing but the truth*.'

Sam giggled and clapped his hands lightly. I was glad he was feeling better.

Michael just nodded. 'So what other reasons are there for it, or rather "she", emerging as a stereotype? What else happened? These things always have an ignition.'

'Oh,' I said, 'There was a journalist, Simon Heffer, who wrote for the *Telegraph*, and used the term "Essex Man" to account for the Tory swing in the county. He described Essex Man as young, "mildly brutish and culturally barren".' I'd talked about it so many times I knew it practically off by heart.

'Essex Man worked hard, had bought his own council house and showed off a brand new motor. Essex Man's girlfriend was blonde. She wore mini-skirts and white stilettos.'

'And that's when it happened?' Michael asked with a frown.

'Well a lot of people think that, but I know women who say it was being used way before that.'

'Oh?' he asked.

'Lots of reasons – everyone used to look down on the East End, but then mid-war and post-war the occupants moved further East. Once they got out to Essex everyone looked down on that patch instead. There's also a link to Thatcher – she used to work in Manningtree.'

'Where another witchfinder started their campaign,' Sam piped up, referring to Matthew Hopkins.

'Yes, that's right,' I said. 'And the aspirational working class, who voted for her, were seen as traitors up north. Well, that's what this bloke I met in the pub told me. Some lecturer or other.'

Michael finished his wine. 'Fascinating. I'd say it's a contender for academic research. Ironically it would be looked down upon because of the connotations.'

He was a very intelligent man, Sam's dad. Though edgy and nervy, I could see that Michael Stone had a good and keen brain. I liked him.

'What do you do, Michael?' I asked and topped up his glass.

'I'm an active lobbyist. Though part-time. Climate change legislation in the US.'

I offered the bottle to Sam, who grinned and took it. He was looking increasingly relaxed. Though he had been throwing back the booze.

'Oh,' I said, not sure what that meant or which side of the argument he was on. 'Do you believe it's happening? Climate change?'

Michael blinked in surprise then laughed. 'Actually, this is an area where belief is irrelevant. It's real. Yeah, it's happening. Unfortunately, over the past twenty years lobby groups have spent billions to influence climate change legislation. For the worse. You know – groups that stand to lose out from limits on carbon emissions – oil companies and transport etcetera.'

'But they must know what the consequences are?' I said, aware I was starting to sound incredibly naive.

'They don't care,' Michael said and necked a large swig. 'They don't think it will affect them.' He smacked his lips, savouring the merlot.

Sam put down the menu he had been browsing and said, 'What won't affect them?'

'Extinction,' said Michael and laughed grimly.

'On its way,' said Sam and nodded. 'The final course,' he waved the menu. 'Metaphorically speaking. Time to pay the bill. Sometimes I think that's probably for the better. We haven't looked after the planet very well. It's better off without humanity.'

'But we shouldn't take down all life with us,' said Michael.

God, I thought, this is fucked up. And a huge tsunami of life-sapping weariness flooded over me. 'When you put it like that, it makes everything, just everything seem so …

I don't know … Just that all our campaigning at the Witch Museum, all the protesting and pushing to get the witches' point of view across, to give voice to their stories, redress what we thought was an important historical miscarriage of justice, all the talks highlighting current witch hunts, all the exhibitions, all our railing and ranting against the stereotype of the witch, past and present, and the Essex girl … Well, what does any of it matter if mankind is going to end up a radioactive shadow on a burnt-out rock.'

'Irrelevant to interstellar visitors if there's anyone out there,' said Michael.

I sighed really heavily without meaning to.

Sam turned his gaze on me. 'All right?'

'Feeling my insignificance.'

'You're not insignificant to me,' he said, but then hiccupped. 'Sorry.'

'Nor me,' Michael added as the waitress brought the bill to the table.

'I know,' I said. 'Insignificant to the universe.'

The waitress gave me a funny look, which was rich considering the state of the mankini crowd.

'Yeah,' said Michael. 'Obliteration. It's a downer.' Then he read the bill and said, 'I'll get this. My treat.'

'Cept it didn't really feel like one any more.

CHAPTER ELEVEN

Back in my room in the George Hotel my mind swirled with images of the Grim Reaper and the mass extinction of humankind, tunnels to heaven and dead boys. Which wasn't really conducive to floating off with the fairies. Plus, I had a bad feeling – something was uncurling in my stomach, writhing like a snake down there. It could have been doom. Anxiety perhaps?

I usually read a book at this stage of insomnia but when I rummaged in my bag I found the only one I had packed was Celeste's jotter. It was almost like a security blanket sometimes. Although at others …

Still, I took it out and let my fingertips stroke its pages. The light dusty touch of the yellowing paper conjured emotions. Memories of my own, things that my dad had said about Celeste, were combining with the scenes written here to create a more vivid picture of the woman who had created me.

And not her alone.

I had read the first December entry last night. The next section would cheer me up. It was a delight. Overblown, semi-esoteric, a bit New Age cringe, it was also funny. There was a hilarious description of Bronson that always made me laugh so much I cried.

Other parts of it were perhaps a little weird for a daughter to read.

Nevertheless, it had been a bad day. I plumped up my pillows and slipped it onto my lap.

Take it away, Mum.

17th of December 1982

The Chariot

He is The Chariot rushing in on me. Helios, the Sun God in the sky – he has come. Strong and determined. Destiny is charging. I feel it.

There were so many Major Arcana in that spread. I was puzzled at first. For here I was, in the middle of nowhere – a witch museum – in a remote corner of rural Essex living a quiet existence.

Now I see the events that are unfolding before me will affect the course of my life.

It is forking, I feel, like the brook. It can go one way, or it can go the other.

A crossroads.

He, The Chariot, was a major player biding his time. And now he is here!

He has arrived.

Oh Danton, how you make me feel like a teenager. Over-sweet and soft, covered in love. No, not love. These are just rude endorphins skewing my perceptions. How silly of me to write that. I am not in love. Smitten, perhaps. In lust? Certainly.

Love is not a word that should be spoken in the first eight months. Or so. That is my rule.

Lust, however …

That firm back, still tanned from last summer, the ripple of muscles across his shoulders … so unlike any of the local lads.

I wonder if he feels it too? I'll find out tonight for sure – he is to take me out. To dinner! To 'continue our conversation'.

Didn't I say that as soon as I saw him? That I knew he wasn't an ordinary man?

And he is most definitely not.

Not physically. The dark stranger is exceptional. Slim and tall, six feet or more, he was wearing a blazer that looked like it was cut from tweed. I'm normally not a fan, but he got away with it – matched it with black jeans. Black jeans. I've never seen those before. It must be a continental thing. Perhaps he is Italian. Maybe they have them over there. He is certainly stylish. So much better than the stone-washed efforts the local casuals wear with their perms.

So, anyway, I'm getting distracted. So this is what happened – he came back! Yes!

Yesterday!

It was just as I was shutting up the lobby.

His voice was so sexy. 'Hello, I'm Danton,' he said, and he said it breathily. 'Do you remember me? I was here yesterday? This a good time to speak with you?'

It most definitely was. And I definitely DID remember him.

So most cordially, making up for Daddy's unusual ill temper, I invited him into the office. I wished I had tidied up beforehand. But I am not a woman who enjoys the domestic sphere.

Gratefully, Danton didn't appear to notice the mess. In fact he was more taken by our rose window and asked me where we had got it. I told him that I hadn't a clue and that Daddy had sourced the majority of our artefacts and he said, 'Daddy?'

And I said, 'Yes.' Then I thought it might be my accent that had caught him so I added, 'Father. Septimus. Strange.'

'But ...' he sat down heavily, looking like I had just slapped him on the forehead, eyes wide and also blinking in quick succession. His head moved slightly from side to side as he

stroked the light spread of stubble on his chin. The expression was one of total bewilderment. I liked it. Daddy, however, would have gone mad if he'd seen that five-o'clock shadow. He never ever goes unshaven. But I thought it quite spicy on this fellow. His life was far too full for anything as dull as a good clean shave.

'You look shocked,' I said and steered him in, touching his arm very gently. 'Would you like a cup of tea?'

He recovered himself and said, 'Oh yes. Perhaps. Tea would be most pleasant.'

I slipped off sexily with a Marilyn wiggle and sent him a glance over my shoulder to see if he was watching me. He wasn't. Damn. He had taken a notepad or jotter out of his pocket and was writing in it.

Whilst I lit the stove I called out, 'Is that an accent I detect there?' Which was dumb really, as it was obvious he was continental – there was more than a pinch of Mediterranean charm in his eyes and, ooh, that sultry tan. Giveaways, of course.

I heard him mutter something under his breath which may have been a foreign cuss. He was passing from bafflement to anger. When he replied to me, however, his tone was deliberately cordial. 'Yes. That is right.'

I waited for him to volunteer more information, but he didn't. So I called out, 'French?'

The answer from the office came back, 'It's compliqué. Yes, more or less.'

Which I thought was terribly enigmatic. A small shudder of delight told me I was excited to be entertaining this man of mystery in the office. Sometimes life at the Great Essex Witch Museum was fun. At other times it was deadly dreary. Humdrum routine had engulfed me lately. People are always so astonished to learn that you can get bored here but it's like any other place really. There will always be high points and low ones.

I didn't question l'homme further. Instead I turned on the radio so we could have background music. Japan's 'Nightporter' tinkled out, which really was a good omen as it's my favourite now. To me it is erotic. And it sounds like it's in a film, and being with Danton did make me feel a little self-conscious and like I was at the centre of a drama.

The kettle started to whistle, covering up the irritating middle-aged DJs pretending to be young. I made a pot and scrambled for some normal biscuits. Daddy does insist on buying job lots of broken ones to economise. I picked out the almost-whole digestives, popped a doily on a new plate, arranged the digestives, and brought out the tray.

He thanked me as I poured, then, when I had handed him the cup, he said, 'You haven't told me your name yet?'

So I did and he said, 'Marvellous. Celeste: heavenly.'

I almost burnt up with bliss.

He extended his hand. I went to shake it but he took my fingers to his lips and kissed them!

'Nice to meet you, Danton,' I said trying desperately to keep my voice on the straight and narrow.

'And you, Celeste.' He released my hand. Darn it. I was enjoying that.

I took it back a little self-consciously and said, 'We normally just do handshakes in Essex.' For a moment he was mortified, so I winked and then his mouth opened and he threw his head back and gave up a full-throated laugh. 'I like you,' he said.

Goodness, these continentals were forward. Not that I was complaining. I drank in the view. And, really, his face did look lovely at that moment: the eyes creased and twinkled. His glee was infectious. I ended up laughing too, then swallowed and had to look away.

When I felt firm enough to glance back he was taking a sip of tea, but his eyes were still fixed on me, mouth bent into a Cheshire Cat grin.

I pushed the biscuits over to him. 'Please. I'm sorry I haven't had time to make any cakes lately.' Not that I ever did. What I meant was I hadn't had a chance to go to the Spar.

He didn't want to take one but I wanted to study him in more detail, so edged the plate even closer. 'Not up to your usual standard?'

'C'est magnifique,' he said and did a good job of sounding enthusiastic, though he couldn't possibly be.

But it gave me a few seconds to contemplate this veritable treat. The nose was slightly too large for his face and dipped down at the tip towards his upper lip. Not perfect, but the right side of distinctive. Dark eyebrows, fleshy cheeks, stubble. Glossy hair the colour of Bournville chocolate. It wasn't shaped into a cool cut. There was no hint of New Romantic which was my current preferred genre of man. However, I liked the way his hair was brushed into a side parting. Although rather old-fashioned, there was a touch of Jacques Brel there. A high square forehead conferred a solid, gentlemanly appearance, which prompted me to assume he had good manners. And, as if reading my mind, he produced a packet of cigarettes and asked if I minded him smoking, which I didn't of course and I went and got the ashtray.

He offered me one. I took it, hoping it would lend me an air of sophistication. Then I asked him what he wanted to talk about.

For a minute Danton hesitated, then his eyes narrowed and he said, 'Who chose Celeste? Your mother or papa?'

I blew a smoke ring sophisticatedly. 'I don't know.'

He nodded. 'Your mother, is she from round here?'

I shook my head. 'She's not around.'

'Will she come back?'

I laughed. 'No. She's Missing. Presumed Dead. But she was born in Adder's Fork.'

He cocked his head, apparently horrified by my light tone. 'Missing?'

I didn't really want to go into it so I said, 'It was a long time ago. She was giving a séance blah blah blah, you know – walked off stage. No one saw her again.'

The effect of my words on Danton, however, was profound.

His cigarette, which was on his way to his mouth, stopped mid-air.

Damn – I was such a ditz. Living in the museum it was easy to forget some people thought the séance thing was more to do with black magic and dark occult rubbish. So I jumped in to correct him. 'She was a medium, my mother. You know, a clairaudient. A spiritualist. She worked for the good of mankind.

She tried to help people in their grief. For free. She wasn't a charlatan. Sorry – it's not a big deal to us.'

He stubbed his cigarette out with speed and removed another pen from his jacket. 'And your grandparents – her mother and father – were they of this locality?'

I hadn't expected that and so returned his answer in a manner that was unguarded. 'They were from the East End.'

'London? Always lived in the city?'

'What do you mean?'

'When did your mother's family come to the East End?'

'I'm not sure. Grandma Anne was from Ireland originally,' I said, wondering how he knew that they had come from anywhere. 'Granddad Fred was from Prague, I think.'

Danton's mouth dropped open. 'What was his name?'

'Fred,' I repeated. 'Frederick Romanov. Why?'

He made a couple of notes. 'This is remarkable. I wonder – do you know how long they were there?'

'Where?'

'Prague?'

I shook my head. 'God no. Maybe always. I'm not sure. I've never thought about it. I expect Daddy might know. Why don't you come back and speak to him?'

'Your father seems not to want to share the details of …'

But Danton was unable to finish: a knocking on the door of the office made us both start. I thought I had locked up too. It was rather annoying. But I said, 'Come in' anyway. And Terry Bridgewaters walked in carrying a toolbox. Another man trailed in after him.

Not great timing.

The second fellow was slightly older with a bushy moustache. Terry introduced him as 'Bronze'. A very athletic-looking and quite handsome chap he was. Thick brown hair and a chevron moustache that was bold and covered his full upper lip. His look was extremely Magnum P.I. which failed to pique my interest. Also I had a feeling from the way he swaggered that he quite reckoned himself a 'ladies' man'.

'Is your dad in?' Terry enquired.

My guest was watching me closely, so I conveyed the news of his absence and added, 'He's left me in charge of the place – how can I help?'

I hadn't stood up to greet them so hoped they'd get the message and bugger off post haste.

'He was hoping to speak to Bronson.' Terry nodded his head back towards the guy behind him.

Apparently, as well as sharing a full moustache, the man had something else in common with the private detective quickening the hearts of middle-aged housewives across the nation – the navy. This Bronson lad explained he'd just finished his term in the forces and, returning home now after several years in various parts of the globe, was looking for work. Apparently Daddy had mentioned to Terry that he was looking for a caretaker to help with some of the heavy lifting around the place. I wish he'd told me.

I pretended I knew all about this until Terry informed me that Daddy also wanted him and Bronson to look at a leak in the back room. Daddy had a view about turning it into some kind of lecture area or some such ridiculous idea. As if that would ever take off. Anyway, there was little I could do to avoid taking them there and showing them the leaky patch. So I made my excuses to the delightful Danton, smiling with all my mouth and told him I'd be back in just a mo.

It took us a while to get to the back, but as soon as Bronson saw the bucket positioned under the offending drip he went straight over, like a duck to water, picked it up and got straight to the business of surveying the roof. It was almost like he'd been here before. Then Terry started whistling and laying out his tools. The two guys seemed to know what they were doing so I left them to it.

It must have taken me fifteen minutes all in all. Nevertheless, when I hurried back to the office, there was no one to be seen.

I sat down rather disheartened and sank my chin onto my hands. In doing so, I noticed there was a white folded sheet of paper on the table.

A note!

I picked it up immediately and opened it. Written in a very elegant, looping hand were the wonderful words: 'Dinner? Tomorrow? I'll pick you up at six-thirty.'

That was rather presumptuous, I mused. How did he know that I wasn't otherwise engaged? Perhaps I was already taken – he didn't know, hadn't asked.

Then again, I liked a man with confidence.

And he was to pick me up, was he? That meant he'd drive. Another tick there.

He had, after all, visited Adder's Fork and seen the culinary delights on offer here. It wouldn't have taken him long to work out it wasn't quite the entertainment required to court a fine young damsel such as I.

Smart then. As well as handsome. Who was I to refuse?

CHAPTER TWELVE

I sat up, sending the journal sliding off the duvet onto the floor.

Someone was pounding on the door.

What time was it?

Thin blueish light was crawling through the gap in the curtains. Morning. Not late though.

I rubbed my eyes.

'Rosie!' Bang, bang, bang. 'Are you awake?'

Sam.

Of course, I'd fantasised about this particular scene many many times – him knocking on my door, desperate to get in.

I grunted, threw myself out of bed, settled the journal back on the bedside table, ran a brush through my hair, washed my face, sucked down some toothpaste, arranged my décolletage, and hurriedly went to the door, a kittenish smile bending my lips.

He was breathless and tense with low crunched brows. He had one arm on the door frame and leant into me. For some reason an image of him from summer – shirtless, an axe in hand – popped into my brain. That moment had been so sultry.

'You took your time,' he huffed. And didn't smile. Something was clearly up and it wasn't his libido. Sadly.

'Pearl's had an episode,' he said. 'We're going there now. If you're coming you've got five minutes to get into the foyer. Or else we'll catch you later.'

Then he was gone. Leaving me blinking with a face full of question marks.

Whatever sort of 'episode' Pearl had had Sam clearly believed it important.

Which was kind of weird after his Mr Scepticism routine yesterday. And worrying.

I looked at the shower through the en-suite door then sighed and slid on jeans.

Pearl lay on the sofa in the chintz room while Donny fanned her face.

The colour clashes had now spiralled out of control with the introduction of Pearl's floral dressing gown. It was padded and vast like a blanket, with an intricate pink and green rose pattern printed across it. No wonder she'd had a turn.

'I saw him,' Pearl wheezed, her voice weak and thin. 'Tuey. The little one outside the gates. Gathered with the other souls. He's trying to say something. I've been asking him where he is again.' She stopped and winced, then put a hand to her chest, as if the effort of speaking was bruising the inside of her ribcage. 'He was most fraught. I am still not sure if he understood the transformation he has undergone.

He felt …' she coughed into her fist, then brought it down onto her belly. 'He came to me as anxious. On the run from something. Someone. It's the Washing Up Man, he was saying. Tuey. He said, "Yella, yella, yella".' She shook her head with fatigue and frustration. Her eyebrows creased. '"Washing up – washing up". Then "he got it. All over him. He smells. You can smell him. He can smell him?", "Don't want to see the brother". What does that mean? I don't know,' she finished and dropped her chin wearily onto her bosom.

I'd started shuddering when she said 'anxious'. By the time she'd got to the word 'brother', full shivers were going up and down and up and down my backbone.

Sam gulped audibly. His father had his hand over his mouth and was rubbing it.

None of us knew what to do. But it sure as hell felt odd, us standing around the couch, looking down at Pearl delivering a message from a dead boy. One that had been abducted. By some kind of 'Washing Up Man'.

Pearl can't have been comfortable with it either.

I nudged the pouffe over so it was near her head and gestured for Michael to sit, then I crouched down and hugged my knees for balance. Sam took the hint and dropped onto the carpet where he crossed his legs and waited.

Pearl opened her eyes wide. 'Oh yes! Tuey said he smelt.'

Sam frowned and nodded but she didn't add any more.

I could hear Pearl's laboured breathing and hoped that she wouldn't have another attack.

As no one had yet answered Pearl's question as to what it all meant, I said, 'I don't know. The Washing Up Man. What is that? Someone who washes stuff? Car wash? An odd job man? Yella, I suppose means yellow? Or to yell? Could it be a "yeller"? Who yells? A newspaper seller?' I tried to think about who else might shout. A teacher perhaps? But then he'd say teacher, wouldn't he?

'Did he say anything about Jazz?' Michael sank into the soft pouffe. His knees came up as high as his chest. He was a big man.

Pearl shook her head. Her boobs trembled under the flowery print. 'No,' she said. 'But, Michael,' she put out a hand and rested it on top of his bony kneecap. 'I feel that he is there. Or he has been there. Lurking in the background, behind all the Spirit Boys. Those poor children are not where they should be: the other side of the walls. Inside the Kingdom of Light. They linger outside its reach, united by some thing, some place or some time. I don't know which for sure. But I would favour it's the man that links them to each other. And that bond, well, it's strong. It's keeping them here, I think. They can see each other, that's what they say. They have been put there. "Assembled" is the word I think Dylan used. Some of them want to move on, but they say that part of them is still here. A couple of them are becoming indistinct. As Jasper did.'

'Is that because it ...' Michael paused and tried to reword whatever it was he was going to say. 'Because it happened to him so long ago?'

But Pearl shook her head again. 'Time works differently there. It's not linear. Nor chronological.' She closed her eyes for a moment and frowned with them shut. When she opened them again her forehead stayed taut. 'On this visit the Tuey child spoke again.'

I could feel Sam unhitch from the conversation. His interest diminished if Pearl talked about other boys. This said something to me. I tried to think about it: his words voiced a rigid scepticism in what he said, but his face and expressions told another story. He *wanted* to believe. The poor bloke was having a hard time of trying to camouflage it, but I'd worked it out. Sometimes I was more perspicacious than I gave myself credit for. Of course I know I was completely dense at other times, but, now was the time to congratulate myself on this little victory.

I smiled with triumph.

Unfortunately, Pearl caught it and shook her head at me. I don't know what she assumed I was thinking, but she said, 'No, he's dead, child. And his time was not that assigned by the good Lord. Another intervened and took his life.'

I blushed. Shit. I should have monitored my expressions. My head angled to the floor so that my hair covered my cheeks. I could feel Sam's eyes on me and wondered what he made of it.

Pearl's voice was directed to Michael. 'He said "The Man" wanted him to meet the "others"...'

Through my fringe I could see her squinting her eyes tight and hard, like she was trying to focus on the very last line of an eye test chart pinned on the ceiling. 'Or it could have been "other"? Maybe "rudder"? "Buzzer"?' she said, questioning the accuracy of her own interpretation.

Yesterday Sam would have interjected, tried to pin her down, question her, back her into a corner.

Today he shut up.

But it was clear Pearl didn't have much of a clue. I hung my head for a little longer. Until the flush was over.

'I thought maybe he meant the other Spirit Boys, but how could this Washing Up Man do that? If those boys had passed into a different plane?'

The rest of our group had shut up. Possibly they were too shocked or perplexed to speak.

I tried to make sense of it. 'So, is this Washing Up Man the connection between them?'

With a weariness emphasised by her prostrate position Pearl shook her head from side to side. 'I don't know, I don't know …' Her frustration was coming across strong.

Anyone could see that she absolutely believed what she had 'seen' in her vision. I wasn't sure that I accepted the Kingdom of Light and the whole Near Death Syndrome thingummy, but I was totally assured that she did.

'I mean, if this is true, if this bloke is the link then doesn't that suggest that …' I grimaced at what I was about to say. 'I mean, is it possible that there's a serial killer on the loose that no one knows about?' Even as I said it I thought it sounded incongruous. On so many levels.

Michael stopped rubbing his lip raw. 'I had a sense that Monty had also considered this.'

Donny, who I hadn't noticed standing by the door, walked over and leant on the back of his mother's sofa. 'We're not aware of any boys going missing locally, and Mum has a feeling he's close by.'

'And fresh,' she used the term again. 'I did try to ask where he was. I did.' Now she sounded defensive. 'He didn't answer that. He said ...' she propped herself up on one elbow, enlivened by her anxiety. 'He got out. Running and running. Went back. Then something, something, "grass", "feet", "the Hunting". "Quiet", "shush". He said to fetch him. He's there.'

Donny started and let out a grunt. It was the first time I'd seen him react, so quickly. I kept my eyes on him.

'The Hunting?' Donny repeated. 'Did he say that, Mum?'

Pearl began to nod. Loosened by the movement, something shifted inside her head. Her forehead contracted into deep lines. She passed her palm over it. 'I believe he did, Donny, though I'm not sure. Never am, more's the pity. Does it mean something to you, son? I thought perhaps a symbol. Or a metaphor?'

But just then there was a ring at the door and, without answering, Donny shot off to answer it.

Pearl sank back into the cushions and closed her eyes. She readjusted her shoulders and pulled her dressing gown tight.

'Michael, be a love,' she said and waved her hand at the armchair. 'Pass over the throw on that arm.'

Michael complied, shook out the blanket then spread it over Pearl's legs. He remained standing and asked, 'Anything else?'

I wasn't sure if he meant he was at hand to make her comfortable or was nudging her back to her vision or death dream, or whatever it was she called it, to search for his son.

'That'll be Doctor Foster,' Pearl muttered, her voice losing volume.

I smirked at the nursery rhyme name and craned my neck at Sam. He hadn't reacted.

'Oh dear,' Pearl grimaced. 'I'm sorry but you'll have to go. He'll want to examine me and I shall find myself too tired to converse after that. Apologies to you all. I'm sorry I couldn't tell you no more.'

We got up. I had no wish to witness Pearl's medical examination and I don't think Sam or Michael did either because we all said our goodbyes and shuffled off towards the door pretty niftily.

Donny was coming down the narrow hallway with a man old enough to be well past retirement. Did doctors do that? Carry on till they dropped?

A trilby hat obscured the stranger's face; his winter coat, in the process of being unbuttoned, revealed a shirt and tie. In his hand he carried an old-fashioned leather bag. Doctor Foster, I presumed. He looked up as I came towards him and nodded. Tiny deep-set eyes blinked through thick glasses.

'I hope you haven't been tiring the patient,' he said. I think he was one of those people who sounded like they're telling you off whenever they said anything. Before we could answer, his lips pursed tightly and he glanced at Donny. 'What's she been saying now?' The tone was transparent – he was well irked.

It also occurred to me that this was an odd question. Whatever Pearl said was clearly nothing to do with her physical health. What did he care?

'Hello,' I said. 'Doctor Foster is it?' I held my hand out and got a whiff of dampness and talcum powder and something antiseptic, bitter and sharp as he approached. On occasion I'd come across individuals whose odour represented their innate qualities pretty accurately. The doctor ignored me and squeezed straight past. Charming. So he was one of those types then. His sour acid perfume was a warning sign.

Donny just shrugged and flattened himself against the wall, so I could pass him and his man-boobs. 'Best be going, eh?'

Doctor Foster darted a last look at us before disappearing into the flower room. He was *so* not happy to see us there.

Tough.

As he pressed past Donny, Michael thanked him for calling us.

Pearl's son shrugged and looked sheepish as if he'd done something wrong. I couldn't work it out.

I echoed more thank-yous, and squeezed myself out the end of the passage, waiting for Michael and Sam to join me on the step. They didn't say anything when they got outside, just bundled straight out and got into the car leaving me to say the final goodbye to Donny.

As I closed the door, I could see him looking after us.

On his cheeks was beginning a dark blush.

When we got back to the hotel, breakfast had finished. I had forgotten it was morning. Everything had happened quickly and engrossed me so utterly while we'd been at the Whites that I'd lost complete track of time.

We decided to venture out to a nearby café and discussed what to do next – whether to check out or stay another night. The hotel needed to know, but said they'd give us an hour to decide. They had rooms if we wanted them, but someone was scheduled into Michael Stones' twin for later that day.

Sam wasn't sure how much more we could get out of Pearl and how long we might need to wait until she saw us again. Of course Michael wanted to stay. As much as I could have done with returning, insisting that we follow up the skinned cats in Haven so I could chance it with Dorcus, I could see that Michael had not really got what he came for and it had been an exceedingly long way to travel for such a disappointing result. I felt sorry for him. Plus, we hadn't fully checked out Pearl to compile a report for Monty.

True – that could be done at the Witch Museum. But that also meant bringing Michael back with us to compare notes.

'I think it's worth staying one more night and going back to see Pearl later,' I decided. 'When she's recovered a bit. To see if she's got any more information. She might not realise it's important.'

Sam crossed his arms. 'Are we sure any of this is true? I mean, the whole thing could be fakery,' he said.

Michael nodded. His movements were cumbersome. He was labouring under the weight of a furiously busy mind. 'She said Jazz is lurking at the back. Linked to them.'

'She could be making it up,' said Sam. He had a look on his face that I had never seen before. It was kind of tragic. He was managing to look deflated and angry at the same time. His shoulders slumped forwards while his mouth twisted

– half up, half down. It wasn't flattering and I didn't like it. But there was no way I was going to tell him.

I decided to soldier on. 'Just supposing there is, somewhere, some kind of truth in it,' I hazarded. 'Don't ask me how. Sam, you were the one who told me that scepticism can be just as blinding as faith. Now, just saying Pearl picked something up, overheard information relating to Jazz. Or the Spirit Boys. I don't know where – maybe it was a doctor talking at the hospital after one of her "trips", maybe a policeman she's met somewhere along the line.' I shrugged. 'She's been unconscious in public a fair few times. Maybe she's internalised something someone has said about Jazz, or this Tuey, and incorporated it into the dreams she interprets as her journeys up to the Kingdom of Light.' I was surprised that I had his full attention. 'I actually think she's telling the truth. That she believes what she's telling us. And she seems very convinced about this Tuey. Perhaps we should be looking into that? I mean him."

There was still bitterness in his words, when Sam answered. 'Better that than Jazz. I mean he went missing over fifteen years ago. She couldn't have heard anything about him. She wasn't anywhere near where it happened!'

I decided to play Devil's advocate. 'Why, where was she? Fifteen years ago? Did she tell you?'

Sam started, 'She was probably here …' then petered out.

'Probably? You don't know that, Sam. She could have been anywhere.'

Then Michael pulled at his collar to loosen it. 'What about the timing? Donny contacted me two weeks ago through another medium who I once had dealings with.' He shot a glance at Sam and waited for his reproval.

Sam rolled his eyes. 'Why would she mention Jazz now after all these years?'

Pearl had already broached this. 'Well, her theory is that time isn't linear in this other dimension – the Kingdom. And Sam, you've suggested such a thing yourself, I'm sure you have. It's not really such an absurd idea – think of wormholes. The scientific community do. Wormholes were even predicted by the theory of relativity and you can't get much more credible than that, can you? The suggestion is that they would use the curvature of space and time to create shortcuts. Tunnels. Time tunnels! Amazing, right? So if you think about it …'

Sam interrupted with a meaningful cough to get me back on track. It worked. I came back down to earth with a bump and just enough time to remember I was talking about his vanished brother. I discarded my enthusiasm and assumed a sober tone. 'But, anyway that's not really relevant here. I'm just saying that it's a possibility. Just as the straight delineation of time is only one possibility. So going back to what Pearl has said about Jazz, and about the timing, well, another rationale could be that it's a repressed memory which has come to the fore. It might have been triggered by a recent event. Something she'd overheard that related to, I dunno, a lost boy maybe? We can't know for sure. And may never. But,' I paused and looked them both in the eye, 'just supposing that there *is* an element of truth in what she's told us …' I put my hands up. Then, don't you think it's our duty to pursue it? If not for your sake, Sam, then for your dad's.' I drew a breath down. 'And Jazz. Or this Tuey.'

No one said anything. Again.

Michael kept his eyes on the uneaten poached egg that was congealing on his plate. Sam glared at me, his nostrils flaring. There were lots of thoughts chasing each other round and round in the grey matter behind his perfectly shaped forehead.

I sat back and waited.

The man at the next table folded his newspaper and went to pay at the till. A woman with a dog started clearing the condensation from the window next to her. After catching my eye, the hipster barista with the massive beard came and asked us how our breakfast was.

Michael said vaguely, 'Fine, fine.'

I added, 'Sausages,' and gave him a thumbs up.

And still Sam said nothing.

I was beginning to wonder if I'd broken him, then at last he said, 'Oh I suppose so.'

Michael's shoulders dropped in relief.

'But, for the record,' Sam held a finger up, 'I think we'll be chasing rainbows.'

'Noted,' I said and moved quickly on. 'Right, well, we should approach this like any one of our other cases.'

'Yes we should. Proceed then, Rosie.'

My friend was back in the zone. Good.

'Okay,' I went on. 'Let's think about what Pearl has said in terms of clues. She stated that someone had referred to the "Lord of the Flies".'

Michael bent his heavy head. 'A boy she called Dylan, I believe. He was the one who had used that term. Or that was Pearl's "interpretation".' He used his fingers to put inverted commas around the last word. Then he glanced at his son to see if his outward scepticism was thawing.

'We all know that refers to the Devil,' Sam proposed, definitely less grouchy now we were discussing Pearl with more caution. 'And you don't have to be a genius to work out why a man who might have had something to do with the deaths or abductions of children, might be referred to as a devil.' He quickly added, 'If he actually did. If any of this is verifiable.'

'I don't know,' said Michael gradually and both me and Sam looked up at him. Aware of our furrowed brows, he clarified. 'I mean,' he said. 'I didn't know that term related to the Devil. I thought it was the title of a novel about boys on an island becoming feral.'

'That's right,' I said, supporting Mr Stone as much as I could. 'Kids wouldn't know the connotations with the Devil either, would they?' I paused then added, 'I only found out about that from you, back at Halloween, with the mysterious case of Ratchette Hall.'

'Case?' said Michael again. We both waved him on.

'Sam'll tell you,' I said.

His son nodded aggressively. 'Will do. But back to this – now I would gamble Pearl was familiar with the reference to Lord of the Flies.'

I consented. 'Yes, so this may be an interpretation, but at the same time, it might have been something that she's heard. Or, let's just suppose for a moment that she has heard this from one of the boys. Whatever way you look at it, then it's certainly something that warrants investigation.' I took out my notebook. 'There may be a connection to a Lord of the Flies locally. Maybe it's, I dunno ...' I looked around the café at the random clutch of people having coffee, eating and/or chatting. 'Maybe it's a local pub? There's the Devil's Dyke in Brighton, Devil's Punchbowl not far from here. The Old Nick up in town. My friend Cerise went to a Beelzebub's in Cardiff. That's a pub and a club. So, right, yes it is a possibility.' I sounded more hopeful than I was. 'We need to consider it. Sam – I'm writing your name next to it.'

'What?' he said, a little outraged, though I had no idea why. 'Me? Why?'

'You're the most knowledgeable about him – the Lord of the Flies.'

'Huh,' he said and uncrossed his arms,

'There's also this "Yella" thing. And the Washing Up Man. They mean something too,' I said and tapped my finger on the table. 'Washing Up Man – could be someone who's a washer-upper in a café, like this. Maybe a pub? Maybe he's a washer-upper in the Lord of the Flies tavern. Or something that sounds like it.'

'Well how are supposed to find that out?' Sam huffed again.

'Simple,' I said. 'We ask.'

He let a horsey snort come out of his nostrils. 'Where? There have to be a number of pubs and cafés here. I'm not sure we'll be able to go into all of them and anyway – we have no idea where they all are …'

'Mm,' I said and folded my arms. 'Hey, wouldn't it be great if there was, like, a place, where you could, like, access computers, or like, ask local people about local businesses? Maybe flick through directories or history books on the locality?'

'Yes, it would,' said Sam. I couldn't tell what emotion shaded that sentence. 'And where would we find such a place?' he pouted. Ah, I got it – arsey.

And clueless.

'Sam, if you got hold of all the energy that you're putting into being tetchy, and redirected it into some good proficient thinking, you might have worked out that there is such a thing as a library in Godalming.'

'Amazing,' said Sam.

The sarcasm finally flipped me. 'Oh for God's sake stop it now! You are really getting on my nerves, you know that. I don't know what your poor father must think.' I turned to Michael, who was leaning back away from the table as if shielding himself from the heated exchange. 'He's not usually like this,' I told him. 'There are some days when he's not an arsehole at all.'

'What?' said Sam, raising his hands to the heavens. 'It's you that's prickly! What did I say?'

'Er – the drip of sarcasm on "amazing".'

'I wasn't being sarcastic,' he said. 'I was being honest. I *am* surprised Godalming has still got a library. They're closing them all down in Essex, aren't they?'

Oh yeah, I thought, that's right.

Never mind.

I played it cool. 'Well, anyway. You come with me to the library, and Michael, I suggest you go back to the hotel, tell them we'll stay another night. Start asking about local hunting areas. That was another thing Pearl mentioned. They've got farmers round here, haven't they? They hunt.'

'Yes. I shall do that, at once,' Michael said and got to his feet. 'I'll keep you posted on developments.' Then he was out of there quicker than a bat from Meatloaf's fiery bits. It must have been the delightful atmosphere at the table.

I watched Michael disappear out the front door then fixed my eyes on Sam. 'Right. Come on then, Sweetness. Let's go and light up the library with our sunny dispositions.'

CHAPTER THIRTEEN

Turns out librarians these days aren't what they used to be, which in my book means they are nicer. Gone were the days of 'shush' and Olympic-standard glaring. Most of the staff turned out to be friendly volunteers who were passionate about books of the paper variety rather than the e-kind. Though they said they could be borrowed too. I spent a bit of time trying to get my head round that. Mostly though, it was apparent that all the staff wanted to see the library used and not closed. Which also meant there were no tuts at any of the toddlers screaming in the kids' section, no confiscations of food or sweets. In fact, a machine near the front door dispensed a variety of hot drinks, some of which were sticky and likely to be spilt willy-nilly over said premises. Yet patrons were actively encouraged to use it.

Sam and I started chatting to Clementine, a volunteer and poet. We, of course, began by asking about pub names, odd pub names, and then progressed to the devilish sort. She was quite fascinated by us, I think, and tried to probe, but we kept our answers to a minimum. She did however guide us over to some books which she felt would be of use.

There was no disapprobation when my mobile phone went off in the middle of Local Reference. No glares. Which pleased me inordinately. However, I didn't push my luck and did make a quick exit leaving Sam with Clementine, waving a slim volume of poetry that someone had self-published, and which evidently referenced several local taverns. Sam was doing his best to avoid reading it.

The air outside was crisp bordering on freezing. It hit me like a slap in the face so that I breathed in sharply just as I answered the call.

'You all right, love?' It was Auntie Babs.

'Yes, yes. The change of temperature took my breath away,' I said as I tripped down the steps and considered whether it would be safe to park my derriere on the low stone wall. It looked a bit cold.

Things had gone a little frosty with Auntie Babs over the summer too. After I found out about my secret parentage. When my biological mother, Celeste, died (in suspicious circumstances, I might add) my dad, her brother, and his wife, Maureen, who had been trying for a baby without success, stepped in and raised me as their own. Which was very nice of them really. The only problem was that they didn't tell me. I had to find out through some nutter who was trying to kill me. Not ideal.

And my favourite auntie – Babs – my mum Maureen's sister, had known all along.

I was so shocked. She'd never dropped so much as a hint or a clue. It kind of felt like a betrayal.

Of course, Babs protested that her sister had sworn her

to secrecy and that she, Auntie Babs that is, could not break a family oath whether she wanted to or not. I listened to her explanations without interruption. I think she took my silence as offence. But it wasn't any kind of indignation that was holding my tongue. It was a feeling of dismay which landed on my heart with the realisation that me and my aunt weren't blood relations at all.

I know that kind of thing happens all the time – people are adopted and brought up by their adoptive parents and everyone's very happy. Thing is – I'd spent thirty-three years of my life thinking I *was* related to Babs. That I *was* related to Mum. That we shared the same blood. I had even found physical resemblances in our eyes, the shape of our ears, Auntie B's bony elbows, Mum's knobbly knees. Shows you just how much the mind can shape the things you perceive, find meaning where there is none.

The revelation back in summer had truly pulled the rug from under my feet. It was only fair that I gave myself space to think about it and let the dust settle. And God knows there was enough of it in the Witch Museum to last a lifetime. That's not a great analogy but you get where I'm going. Time to readjust was essential for me to move on. And reconnect and process.

But I didn't tell Auntie Babs that.

Mostly because I thought it would hurt her. And there was no point any of us getting more damaged by this thing that happened such a long time ago, when I was just a wee baby. The decision to create an alternative narrative surrounding my birth was made out of love and with the best intentions.

I knew that. I just needed to weave that motivation into the way I thought about it all.

Auntie Babs was perplexed. She was completely unused to anyone being quiet or silent around her and assumed my reflective contemplation was sulking or fury. She tried to counter this by doing what she does best and offering me a range of complimentary state-of-the-art beauty treatments. Persistently. And on a daily basis. I kept gently declining, mainly because I was sorting things out in the museum. But also I wasn't yet ready for Babs in full-frontal 'Cheer Up Rosie' mode. This resulted in her turning up at the Witch Museum with her beauty kit. She'd appeared at such odd times and was so determined that on several occasions I caved in and let myself be persuaded into a variety of cosmetic procedures, just to get her off the premises. Sam had, however, put his foot down and insisted I start making appointments and keep our business to the living quarters upstairs on the first floor. Leg waxings on the till are, apparently, unprofessional.

'Just checking,' she chirped, 'that you're still on for your six o'clock pedi, darlin'? Only Sheryl, from down the road, has cancelled her bikini at four. Gawd knows why. I'm not saying nothing, but that woman grows faster than a spider plant, if you know what I mean. I'll have to start borrowing Del's motorised mower if she misses again. Anyways, the upshot is I could get to yours five-ish if that's better. Gloria said she'd lock up.'

Oh bugger, I'd forgotten. 'Auntie Babs, I'm so sorry. It slipped my mind.'

'Well, can you do it? I could stick to six if that works

better?' Her voice took on a plaintive tone that made my whole body tighten.

'No, no. It's not that, it's just, like I said, I forgot and—'

'Well don't worry. If you're busy I could come over and do a couple of hours on the till, till you're free. Oh did you hear that – on the till till you're free! I don't think I've ever said "till till" before. Have you?'

Oh dear. She was nervous. Best be careful and kind. 'Ha ha. No, I'm not sure I have. Listen, Auntie B, I'm in Surrey.'

'Surrey! Surrey? What you doing there? You gone posh on us?'

I could tell she was beginning to go hyper so took my voice down the Barry White end of the spectrum and purred, 'Oh no, not at all. I could never leave you and Essex, Auntie B, you know that. No, I'm with Sam.'

There was a pause followed by the faint scratchy sound of Bab's eyelashes fluttering. 'Oh er. At last!'

She'd picked up the wrong end of the stick and run off with it. 'Nah nothing like that,' I tried to get her back on the right track.

'Shame,' she said. 'He's a fool, that man. Quite a fool. Doesn't know what he's missing, with you, there, right under his nose.'

'Well, anyway,' I said. 'It's kind of complicated but we're looking for his brother, Jasper, who may or may not be dead.'

'Oh my good gawd,' Babs rasped. There was a jingle as she disturbed several necklaces by drawing an imaginary crucifix across her bolstered breasts. She wasn't religious, just liked the drama. 'Oh Samuel. Poor boy,' she said, completing a perfect U-turn. 'Always knew there was tragedy in his past. Knew it. I said to Del, "There's something wrong with him. Got heartbreak there. You mark my words." Some people carry it around like a cloud on a string. Don't they, Rosie?'

It was difficult to know how to come back on that. Or if she was implying anything about me. 'Yes,' I said, with hesitation. Then to stop her worrying geared up my voice a level to 'breezy'. 'So, we won't be back tonight. That's what I'm saying.'

'Roger, Roger,' said Babs. 'We'll switch it to Friday then. Can't make it tomoz. I've got fifty per cent off radio frequency facials and the whole of High Wigchuff's booked in. They do like a bargain, those Chuffers of ours. Right you are – Friday then. Be there or be square.'

'Er, well, if that's no trouble …'

'Anything for my niece. As *always*. Love to Samuel. Ciao bella.'

And she was gone. Leaving me out in the cold, wondering if I'd got anything on on Friday.

I turned and started to walk back to the library, fiddling with the diary app on my phone, so I wasn't looking when Sam galloped out the door, almost toppling me over in his haste.

His face was pasty again and his shoulders and upper body were all taut and tense.

'What's the matter?' I said. I could tell something big was up.

'Come, come and hear this.' He tugged me inside to the rather bemused-looking Clementine. 'Go on, tell her.'

She was sitting behind a computer with a box of index

cards in her hands, reading glasses pushed up onto the top of her head. 'Well, I was saying to Sam. He was telling me about Mrs White. She's quite well known in the local community. For her psychic …'

She broke off, distracted by Sam who was rotating his hand in a circle – 'Hurry up'. So rude. 'Go on, go on.'

'Sorry,' said Clementine needlessly, and adjusted her posture so she looked more attentive. Sam always seemed to make others feel compliant. I thought maybe it was his lack of self-awareness that bestowed an authority on him. Or maybe the fact he was on a mission.

Clementine put her hand over her mouth and coughed. 'And he, Sam, Mr Stone, told me why you were both looking for the Lord of the Flies …'

Sam turned to me, hair flying. 'There aren't any by the way. Pubs. Of that name. Go on.'

'And he relayed the circumstances and I happened to mention that my nephew …'

Interrupting again Sam said, 'Who is eleven.'

'Well, he and his friends have been saying there's been a man in a white van lurking around the school.'

'Oh,' I said and squinted at Sam. 'Have they reported it to the police?'

Clementine nodded, eyes bulging. 'Oh yes. Well, that is, the parents have spoken to the school.'

'And?'

'And they said they'd keep an eye out.'

'Really?' I said. 'That doesn't seem a very strong response. You hear so much about safeguarding these days.'

Clementine appeared to agree with me. 'Well, you see, none of the teachers have seen it, the van. None of the parents either. The police think it's a "meme". Apparently, there was something going round on social media, Snapchat.'

''Scuse me for not being down with the kids but what's a meme, again?' I asked.

Sam tutted. 'A virally transmitted photograph with text. Or video. It's meant to be funny. Often its puerile. This could be some kind of younger generation take on "the dirty old man".'

'But it could have started somewhere round here, or in the UK, with a real man and a real van,' I ventured to both of them. 'Couldn't it?'

Clementine shook her head. 'There's been no kids touched or, you know, abducted. Not here. Not locally. Believe me, we'd know about it here if there was.'

'Here?' I asked for clarity. 'In Godalming?'

'Well, yes,' she said. 'But look,' she pointed at the ropey carpet. 'In the library. It's a hub you see. We have to put up all the public health posters, notifications about parking suspensions, lost cat flyers, sponsored walk appeals, flu vaccine dates. See.'

She pointed to the walls by the door. They were indeed covered with hundreds of posters and leaflets. Clementine was right.

Sam's phone started ringing.

'What do you think about the man in the van?' I asked her.

She drew down her burgundy tank top over her small pot

belly. Sam stepped away to answer his phone. 'Well, I think it's a worry. But kids do make things up, don't they?'

'Yep,' I nodded and thought about Pearl. 'So do adults.'

'But none of the kids said they'd been approached?' I asked.

She shifted in her chair. 'Look, I don't really know. Like I said, it was my nephew. There's been no coverage in the local paper. It's all jumble sales and people with giant cheques. I'm sure they'd leap on a story like this if there was anything to it. It's probably nothing ...'

'What does "Washing Up Man" mean to you?'

Clementine's eyes widened. 'Pardon?'

'Washing Up Man?'

'Someone who does the washing up?'

'Yeah,' I said. 'I have no idea either.'

Sam charged back to the desk and stood in front of me, blocking my view of the poor librarian. He'd put his hand through his hair and left it sticking up on his head. His eyes were wild.

'Quick,' he said. 'We've got to go. It's Donny. He thinks he's located the Hunting.'

CHAPTER FOURTEEN

We were losing the sun. The afternoon had brought low-lying clouds down from the hills. Even though it wasn't yet three o'clock, what light remained had taken on a mauve quality. Dusk would soon be upon us, so as we approached the playing fields Sam turned on the headlights. We bumped and lurched into an unsurfaced lay-by. The car lights swept over a leaf-barren hedge and landed on Donny and Michael, who were standing to attention by the latter's hire car.

Donny blinked as the spotlight hit him. Michael's gaze held. He was finishing off a sentence and wasn't going to be deterred by our arrival. Pearl's son actually looked like a regular bloke in his winter gear. The large padded parka concealed his bulk. A fur-lined trapper hat with flaps covered his ears. Warming his hands were brown leather gloves, which were soft and had white fur cuffs, a surprisingly frivolous detail I thought at the time.

Gloves. That was a point. I checked my bag and praised the lord that I hadn't left them in the library.

Both Donny and Michael had boots on. I glanced at

my own footwear: gold cowboy boots. Possibly not the most practical. And yet certainly the most glamorous. As always.

The men's breath made clouds in the air. I sighed inside the car and didn't make any. I bet your bottom dollar I was going to get my sequins dirty today. Should have known.

It hadn't been possible to broach the subject of a quick detour to the hotel to change. Sam had jumped straight into the driving seat. His knuckles had turned white when he'd grabbed the steering wheel and they still hadn't let the blood back in.

We locked up and walked over to the two men. There were the beginnings of frost in the air. I always knew when it was on its way – it was like a white smell that crept up the insides of your nostrils: the promise of ice in tiny crystals.

Donny, Sam and I immediately shook hands, said hello and enquired after each other's good health, in excruciating but unavoidable English fashion, while Michael looked on rolling his eyes in disbelief. I went over and pecked him on the cheek. He was just as surprised by that gesture but didn't say anything or kiss me back.

'So,' he said, when we'd gone through the meeting rituals. 'Donny thinks this could be the "Hunting" that Pearl spoke of. Don't you, Donny?' which was Mr White's cue to push back his trapper hat and say, 'I'm not sure.'

Great! I thought and let go an exasperated huff. Sam put a hand on my arm, to stay me, and stamped his feet. I could also feel the cold damp coming up through the ground into my soles and so shuffled them a bit.

'What made you think that?' he said to Donny. 'The "Hunting"?'

Donny joined in the general shuffling from foot to foot. 'This place,' he said and brought his gaze up and over the hedge into the deserted playing fields. 'See the woodland over there?'

We all followed his eyes to the scrubland that grew thickly beyond the football pitch. Wisps of fog were coming up from the ground and hanging amongst the tree trunks. The air above the grass was beginning to haze.

'When I was a kid, we used to call it the Hunting Ground. We'd play games and set traps out here. Was good for hide and seek. You know,' he dropped his face for a second as if embarrassed by the memory. 'There's lots of places to hide. Some kids would come down here with air rifles too, pretending they were hunting.'

'Is it now called the Hunting?' asked Sam.

'That, I don't know,' said Donny, then added quickly. 'I don't hang around with kids, but it's worth a look.'

Michael frowned and looked over to the bare-branched trees. 'This Tuey? Do we know if he's local?'

Donny stuffed his hands in his pockets. 'Mum's only seen him of late but yes, she's indicated that he is close by.'

I thought I might as well share what we'd learnt. 'And yet, according to the local librarian there have been no reports of missing children.'

Michael flinched at the thought of it.

Sam smiled grimly. 'Well, I agree with Donny. It's worth a

shot,' said Sam. 'There is literally nothing to stop us having a look round. It's public land.'

'Um,' I said and looked at the darkening sky. 'You sure? That fog could be disorientating if it gets worse.' I didn't like the way the place was making me feel. There was an oddness here which didn't make sense. Half of the area was pretty boring. Your usual semi-rural playing fields. However, the greying trees beyond them, wrapped and teased by mist, had developed a fairy-tale quality. I could imagine Hansel and Gretel abandoned out there, in the dark all alone. Till they, of course, stumbled on the witch. Who, no doubt, was a poor old woman minding her own business until the Brothers Grimm decided to cast her as a cannibalistic old hag.

I shivered. The air was biting, but that wasn't it. Even my cynicism was unable to shift or regulate the anxiety gnawing at the edges of my abdomen, upsetting my tummy and making me want to get back into the car and turn on some parochial radio to blast the weirdness away.

'Looks like ghosts, don't it?' said Donny and pointed to haze in the forest.

When no one said anything, he cocked his head slightly upwards and held up a finger. 'No birds. No singing.'

Michael puffed his chest out. 'They sense a predator nearing.'

Was he talking about us?

I stared at the trees again and thought about how much I really really did not want to go in there.

I had been in woods recently. Witch Wood specifically. And that hadn't been a particularly convivial place. In fact,

I had stumbled over and nearly got poisoned. And hallucinated a goat-foot god. Which is something, right? And yet, this place, well it was different. Much worse. There was a threatening vibe coming off it like the mist. Danger lurked here. I could feel it.

Rosie, stop it! I took myself in hand. Really, I needed to get my imagination under control. I never used to have this much of it before I inherited the Witch Museum. Not when I was back in Benefit Fraud. Aha! I thought, that's it. To arrest this growing unease I should go back into council mode. And very easily I was able to turn my mind to my old boss and wonder what he might make of this place. And no sooner had I surveyed the asymmetric goal posts on the pitch, than my inner Derek noted, 'A civic utility should be better maintained. Those goalposts ought to be fixed and white-washed. Councils have budgets. There's no excuse for sloppiness. They must put in for a refurb. The place certainly doesn't have to worry about overheads.'

As soon as that last word passed over my brain, the couple of street lights that lined the road down which we had driven, flickered on. Street lights – good. They were no-nonsense things. Except these ones weren't. They resembled old street lamps – the kind that populated Jack the Ripper-themed nightmares. Clouds of spraying fog seeping around them were doing sod all to dispel the doom. 'Shouldn't we call the police and tell them about this? These kind of searches are more their thing, aren't they?'

Donny was staring at me. His lips formed a 'pfft'. 'No point calling the Old Bill.'

Sam started walking towards the gap in the hedge.

'What you gonna say?' Donny went on, watching him. 'That Mum had a vision whilst she was dead? That there's some "spirit boy" out in the woods what needs collecting?' He finished it with a scoff.

'Er, yes?' I offered. 'Why not? You could mention that Pearl has heard something? Or we could just say she has some information …'

But Donny shook his padded head from side to side. 'Don't you think we've tried that? Many a time, I can tell you. Mum's been banned from the local nick. Well, she was before it got closed down. The local plods were quite nice about the ban, in truth. Sensitive.' He smiled, apparently borne along by a wave of nostalgia. 'Then it was all centralised.'

Sam stopped by the gap and nodded thoughtfully. 'Same in Adder's Fork,' he said.

Donny sniffed, surrendering his fond remembrance, and dropped the smile. 'They don't listen to anything Mum says. No personal touch any more. Now the Surrey lot have got her down as an attention-seeker.'

'A nutbag?' I added without thinking.

'Exactly,' said Donny with sincerity.

Michael cleared his throat. 'Well,' he said, bringing us back to the task at hand.

Clearly no one was giving up and going home.

'We'd better get going before we lose the light completely,' Michael said, confirming my fears. 'Donny had the forethought to bring two torches so I suggest we pair up. One light each. I'll go with, er …' he surveyed the three potential choices of partner, 'Donny,' he decided. 'Sam and Rosie you take this.'

Sam grabbed a torch. I found my mobile in my bag and turned the light on. Then we set off.

Once through the hedge it was clear that my phone light was not strong enough to do any good out here in the gloaming. I pocketed it and moved closer to Sam and his big torch.

'So how do you think we should divide this up, Dad?' he asked Michael over his shoulder.

We came to a halt in the dark middle of the pitch and looked ahead. The woods spread across the field and downwards to the road on one side. On the other they went on for miles, up and over a hill. That was a lot of distance to cover. In the dark.

'Let's meet back at this point in an hour,' suggested Donny. 'We can take it from the road and then work in. You two start midway and head south.' He pointed to the dense bank of trees that seemed to stretch without any end.

'Okay?' Sam glanced at me.

I nodded without enthusiasm.

Michael and Donny peeled off towards the road. I followed Sam into the gloom.

The torch cast a wide circle of light against the trees.

Sometimes when I got deep into darkness it was rich and velvety, a magic cloak that you wanted to embrace you, like the air after a candle has been snuffed out.

This darkness wasn't like that. It was cold and full of

menace. If it wanted us, it wasn't to snuggle but to devour, bones and all.

'Lots of leaves on the floor,' said Sam and pointed the cone of light down so we could see them, rusty and glistening.

'Er, that's because it's winter, Einstein,' I said and marched over them, enjoying the crunch underfoot.

'Really? I hadn't noticed.' He replied with sarcasm. 'I meant that there are lots of *whole* leaves on the ground. Ergo, no one's been here for a while. The foliage hasn't been crushed into a mulch on the forest floor. Not yet.'

When I looked I could see he was right. There were whole leaves everywhere. 'I'm not surprised,' I said. 'It's brass monkeys. Who'd want to be out in this?'

'Cold weather wouldn't have put me off when I was a kid.' Sam pointed the beam up through the undergrowth. 'I'd still have wanted to come out to play.'

'They're all inside these days,' I said. 'On their Xboxes and PlayStations.'

We trudged on.

Sam sniffed. I could feel my nose turning red. 'Or else their parents are keeping them in. Once it gets dark.'

'Maybe.' Ferns were scratching above my knees now. I pushed a large one away and said, 'The days are short.'

'And the nights are long,' Sam said.

There was no disagreeing with that.

'Do you know what we're actually looking for?' I asked after a while, mainly to break the silence. Not that there was any actual silence – we made noise as we walked – but it was quiet.

'Not really,' Sam said, shining the light on a fallen trunk. 'Clues, I suppose.'

We changed direction to avoid the obstacle and continued deeper into the forest.

'Clues like what?'

I heard Sam sigh and turned in time to see the spray of mist come out of his mouth. 'Well, we don't know until we actually find them, do we? That's how clues work. They don't present themselves with a big neon arrow pointing to them.'

'Then anything could be a clue,' I said and scooped up a handful of twigs and leaves. They were surprisingly rigid. That frost I'd smelt earlier was creeping into the undergrowth. 'These leaves could be a clue.'

'That's right,' he said. 'Could be. We don't know.' He shone the flashlight at a trunk about twenty metres away.

I followed the beam and went over to it.

'I know we've spoken about it before,' Sam went on. 'But I do think that you should try and reach into your intuition. It's stronger than you realise.'

'Oh my God,' I said, now aware of the futility of our errand and pointed at some random branch. 'It's a clue it's a clue.' Sam didn't get it.

The torch bulb bobbed up and down as he speed-stumbled towards me.

'Where?' he said, panting when he finally caught up.

'Here.' I pointed to the tree. 'Just as much a clue as the leaves.'

'Not funny. Try to feel it. There's a power within you, I'm

sure, if only you'd let yourself feel it.' He put his hands on his hips and leant forwards, breathing out steamy air.

He looked quite fit like that so I said, 'Okey dokey. I'll feel it.' But he still thought I was taking the mick.

'All right, Bright Eyes,' he said. 'You can take the torch now.'

'Bright Eyes?'

'Yes. Is that insulting?'

'No,' I said. 'It's a rabbit from *Watership Down*.'

Sam grumbled under his breath and tossed me the torch. 'Well, I'll have to do better next time.'

So tetchy.

I caught it and shone the beam in another direction. I was getting weary. I reached into somewhere vague in my stomach (where I felt my consciousness might be) and said, 'Shall we try there?'

'As good a place as any I suppose.'

And we followed it over.

'Mmm,' I said when we reached a large tree stump covered in ivy. We inspected it. There were no clues there. 'I've got no idea which way we've come now, have you?'

As the thought dawned on him, Sam spun round. 'Ah! Good point. The car's back there isn't it?'

'I don't know,' I said, thinking my earlier Hansel and Gretel analogy might have been more prophetic than I realised at the time. 'Look, we're getting lost. We should try and find a way back. All this is doing is making us wet and cold.'

Sam hesitated for a moment then put his hand to his

forehead as if shielding himself from the light. 'Let's just give it ten minutes more.'

'Come on. We've got to have been going for an hour by now,' I said, and tugged his jacket. 'It's freezing. We're not finding anything.'

But Sam put his hands in his pockets and stood firm. 'Not yet. Five minutes more?'

'Seriously Sam, we can come back tomorrow morning. It's too dark.'

'Not just yet,' he said. His voice sounder smaller. 'I don't want to give up.'

Normally I might have been more alert to his tone, but the cold was contracting my compassion muscles. 'Okay. Suit yourself. I'm out of here. You can find your own way back.' As I had the torch I thought he would have to surrender and come with me.

But he didn't move.

So I sighed, then turned round and started marching off into the brown darkness. I had the light fixed on a cluster of grey trunks up ahead. The beam was probably higher than it should have been which meant I wasn't paying any attention to the forest floor, because suddenly – it just vanished beneath me. That is, my leading foot stepped on a fine filigree of leaves which gave way into – nothing.

I plunged downwards, throwing out my arms to grab hold of a trunk or branch or something to stop my body falling into the void, but nothing was to be had. The torch escaped my grip and pinged up into the air in a great arc, before coming back down. I registered a smash on the floor and all light went out. But I was only vaguely aware of this because my body was tumbling too. I pitched down, down, down, through twigs and roots till my head slammed into a smooth surface. The right side of my body and my bum hit a cold muddy floor. The thump, as I landed, took my breath away.

I moaned and rolled, dazed, onto my back.

I hadn't expected that.

A browny-reddy colour dominated my eyes. Purple stars danced on the inside of my lids. My head throbbed at the back.

Thoughts came in slowly.

Jumbled.

Was I upside down?

God knows what I had fallen into.

I put my fingers to the part of my neck that met my skull and rubbed it. They came away wet and warm: blood. Oh shite. I needed to get out of here.

Somewhere Sam was calling my name. I could hear him crashing across the woods. The sound was an echo in the distance, muted by all the cotton wool in my head.

'I'm here,' said a voice. Weedy and thin.

I tried to raise my head and look around.

'I'm here,' said the voice. Tiny, soft.

I twisted up right and tried to ignore the soreness in my bum and clouds in my head.

'I'm here,' cried the voice and I realised it was me.

I'd have to try harder than that to get Sam's attention.

'I'm HERE!' I yelled upwards and opened my eyes.

Dark shapes up above. Trunks glossy like phantoms. Black sky. Sharp, glittering diamonds in it.

'Where?' Sam's voice was distant. 'Keep talking,' he called.

'I'm here.' I tried to work out where exactly. 'In a hole or a dip.' A hollow with smooth sides, maybe a ditch.

'Have you got the torch?'

'No. I lost it when I fell.'

'Oh shit. I'm phoning Dad.'

'No!' I said, and took a deep breath in to steady myself. 'Come and get me first. I don't like it.' There was a smell. Horrible. Thick.

'Have you hurt yourself?'

'Yes. Back of my head.'

I heard him exhale. 'Crap. Okay. Am I getting closer?'

I couldn't tell. 'I don't know.'

'Have you got your phone?'

Ah yes, I had. I'd put it in my pocket when I was playing football earlier, I thought. Or had I? Was I playing football? No. But football was in my mind. My fingers inched into my jeans and located my mobile – good.

I looked at it in my hand and wondered who I was meant to call. 'Who am I phoning?' I asked Sam.

'Put the light on,' he instructed.

I obeyed and to my horror, found that the screen had been broken. 'Oh bugger,' I said. 'That'll cost me.'

'What will?' said a voice from above.

I looked up and saw Sam's lovely face poking over the opening in the ground, into which I had clearly toppled.

By the light of the phone I could see a tangle of roots and

twigs and mud all around, some of which looked as if it had been fashioned purposefully, like wattle, to build and conceal the cave or hole or whatever it was I had ended up in.

'My screen,' I said and began a wail.

Sam had his own phone, which he lit and shone down at me.

'Holy fuck!' he said and backed away.

Blimey. He was more upset than me about the screen. It was endearing. 'It's okay,' I tried to soothe him. 'I might be able to claim it on the Witch Museum insurance.'

'Don't,' said Sam. His face was doing that odd tight thing.

Maybe he had a point. 'No, you're right, that's not the correct insurance. I don't mind coughing up for a new ...'

'Shut up,' Sam said. And delivered the command with such authority that I found myself instantly obey.

That didn't happen very often.

'I want you to take my hand.' His vocal cords skidded over the last word. He leant over, grabbed the roots on the fringe of the hole and then stretched his other arm towards me.

I looked at it hanging there stiffly.

'Take it,' he ordered.

So I did.

And with his strength he pulled me. I levered my body up and scrambled to my feet. My head was now poking out the top. Yep, this cave or hollow had definitely been purposefully concealed.

'Right,' said my friend, squatting down on the ground, the *solid* ground. His head was only two feet higher than mine.

'Now you have to trust me, okay?' Again his voice held so much tension in it.

Sam propped his phone up on a root. The light angled down at me, illuminating the hole. Then he waggled his other hand at me. 'Take it. I'm going to try and pull you out, right?'

'Right,' I said.

'And there's just one thing I need you to do for me Rosie, okay?'

My fingers grasped his wrist. 'Yes? What is it, Sam?'

'I need you to promise you won't look down.'

And I heard the quaver in his voice and recognised, suddenly, right then, that it was fear. Fear and shock and fear. Fear.

And I understood what he was telling me.

Not to turn round.

That this was for the best.

But I couldn't help myself.

When someone says that to you, you can't, can you?

And I will wish until my dying day that I had followed Sam's instructions.

But I didn't.

I let go of his hands.

CHAPTER FIFTEEN

When I was a kid we went to this place in Western France. It was a cottage that my dad's friend had. But it was inland and in a hamlet that was quite boring. So one day Dad decided we were going to get in the car and drive a couple of hours to the nearest beach.

The day, though, was hot and the car didn't have any air-conditioning. My brother John and I spent the journey squabbling in the back seat. I think John threw up at one point too.

So when we got to the beach, I was absolutely desperate to jump in the sea. But it wasn't really the sea. Being Western France, what I waded into was the Atlantic Ocean. It was a different kettle of fish to the Thames Estuary for sure: people were out in the waves body-surfing. It looked so exciting that before anyone could stop me I had swum out past the poles and the safety flags and began to jump in the foamy water. When I finally mastered the body-surfing manoeuvre, I clocked a particularly large wave coming. I threw myself onto it and found to my great delight my body soared up over the top of the crest, and for a moment

I was gloriously borne aloft. But then it tipped and I fell, crashing down into the shallows. Instead of carrying me safely into shore, a rip caught me. The current sucked my body under the water and out to sea again, without any chance to breathe. I was tugged out gasping and swallowing, taking down water, whirling round and round like a sock in a washing machine. My forehead bashed against the rocks and my belly scraped over the sands under the waves. I was completely disorientated by the violence of the movement, unaware of which way was up or which way was down, just of being thrown around. Then another surging wave picked me up. I screamed, water filled my lungs and hurled me with force once more into shallow water, my head slamming hard this time against a slab of rock, stunning me, swirling me around under the sea. Until two strong arms thrust into the sea and began to haul me up. A pure unadulterated force, an emotion within suddenly engulfed me, galvanising me into action. Desperation came down as I gripped the arms. Then, pushing my feet into the body of the man, Dad, who was trying to save me, I climbed up, then over him, so I could get out of the water. It was sheer panic and it swept me away like a landslide.

It was something I hoped I'd never feel again.

I felt it now.

And, just like I had done all those many moons ago, I grabbed the lifeline and dug in my nails, trying to claw myself up. Away, away from this terrible sight.

For it was the most shocking thing I had ever seen.

But I shouldn't call it a 'thing'.

He must have been there for so long his body had merged into the ground, taken on its colourings; cuddy, peaty, vegetative green-brown. Like the earth had bled into him as he had bled out.

The little form was sparsely illuminated in the mechanical light. My brain translated it, at first, as an organic component, part of the cavern I had tumbled into.

Until I saw the shoes.

There was something about them that did not compute.

I experienced a brain-tremor. For there was a strip, plasticky and bright, reflecting the light from Sam's phone. Fluorescent orange flashed. It wasn't a natural colour. Not organic.

Man-made.

A shade only a kid would choose to wear on his feet.

And it suddenly dawned on me that this small brown thing was not made of earth and mud. This was human. Had been human. Had once been a human.

A little human.

Oh Christ.

My eyes boomeranged back over its length, along the prone branches, which I realised, were legs clad in fraying fabric. Denim probably, but that detail could not be discerned with accuracy. Not now, in the mobile's light, and me with no breath in my lungs but only a scream that wanted to rush out of my mouth and up into the sky and cry to the stars, 'Oh my God'.

But nothing came.

My tongue stuck fast to the back of my throat.

My gaze, though, moved on. Over the jacket with its zips and pockets, a badge with a picture of a *Star Wars* character.

To the face.

Lips pressed tight. Not in fear. Serene. No wrinkles around them. A snub nose. Cute. Little. Small. Tiny.

No eyes to speak of. Something had hopped into the hollow and found a feast in the sockets, though neglected to ravish the rest. Perhaps it had been scared off and flown away? I wondered by whom.

Across the cheeks, sallow, gaunt, a splash of what looked like brown ink, which had dried and left a flaky trail as it had drizzled to his chin then dripped off, down, catching the sides of the hollow, congealing on the floor in a mushy dark sludge.

Short hair. Silky. Don't know what colour.

Brown?

Everything was brown.

Texture like leather.

Curled up, like a prehistoric bog mummy, tucked onto a ledge.

If it weren't for the absence of eyes, I might have thought he was napping. Hands pressed together as if in prayer, brought under his head for a pillow.

A sleeping angel.

A dead child.

CHAPTER SIXTEEN

The rest happened really quickly.

I have no recollection of how I got out. There was running and breathlessness and a lot of stuff going on with my voice. Grunts. Shrieks. Yells.

I came out onto the pitch, under the snow which was coming down more thickly.

Michael and Donny running.

Shouting.

Pointing.

And then the car. *In* the car. Doors shut. Heater on.

Sam on the phone. Calling. Sitting beside me. Then gone. Donny there.

Michael and Sam in the wood.

Flashing lights.

Air freezing.

Like God wanted to ice the scene.

Preserve it.

One, two, three police cars. An ambulance. Two.

Checking my head.

'Oh no, you're not going anywhere.'

Then hospital.

Again.

Always there.

'Slight concussion.'

Then the police came.

It was nearly eleven when I got back to the hotel. Michael was in the bar talking to the barman/receptionist, who showed no signs of shutting shop, but instead was eagerly lapping up his story.

'Ah,' Michael said, and opened his arms to greet me. 'Here she comes.'

When I got to him, he gave me a loving hug, which would have surprised me if I hadn't been so tired and hollow. But I felt done in on all sides, so I returned it. And actually, I needed it. The paramedics had checked me over. I hadn't needed stitches, though I did have a cut on the back of my neck. And my back was still aching from the fall. But despite all the physical damage, and the fact I was tender, what I wanted most was human contact. I sank into his paternal embrace for a moment and felt Michael's compassion flow into me. It tasted golden.

When he released me I felt better and pulled up a stool and rested my elbows on the bar. There were only two other guests down the end of the room, finishing their beers. Other than that, the place was ours. 'Where's Sam?'

'They separated us at the station. I'm guessing he's still there. What do you want to drink? Whiskey?'

I nodded. The barman tapped the side of a bottle already

open on the counter and fetched a tumbler. 'On the rocks? With a twist?'

'Neither,' I said. 'Just double whatever you're about to pour.'

I needed something strong and sugary to block it out: whenever I closed my eyes, I saw him. The boy in the wood. Lost. Alone. The sight of him, sleeping, preserved in that hollow was imprinted on my mind. It didn't matter how I tried to dispel the image, it kept coming back again. Accompanied by a quiver full of darting questions – who was he? Why was he there? And who was experiencing the devastation that Sam and Michael and their family had gone through all those years ago with the loss of Jazz? Who was missing this child?

Just awful.

'Quickly,' I said to the barman.

He complied silently, eyes staying on mine a little longer than normal. I guessed he knew it was me who found the body. I had become an object of macabre interest.

Again.

I was getting used to it.

Actually, I wasn't. I was learning to live with the inquisitive looks and nosy glances and beginning not to take them personally. People were just interested in the ghoulish, and associating it with me. And I wasn't ghoulish. Apart from the fact I lived in a Witch Museum. And was connected with several deaths. Including those of my immediate family.

And now this one.

'When did they let you go?' I asked Michael.

He nudged the glass on the counter and delivered his lines to it. 'A couple of hours since. Had to wait for someone to drive me back here. They've kept Donny, though. Brought Pearl in too.' He bent lower to me and explained. 'Heard one of the cops talking about her. I feel bad for getting them involved.'

I didn't know what he meant. Surely they had got him, I mean us, into this? I had the impression that Donny had contacted Michael first and assumed Michael had spoken to Monty. The dear agent had then proceeded to get us involved.

'I was … I had the best of intentions, you know …' Stone senior said. I detected a weakening of his voice, a lack of tension on the vocal cords that indicated he had been relaxed by the whiskey. A lot of it. 'I just wanted to find my son!' he said and in an action that seemed to come out of nowhere, he cursed and banged his fist on the countertop.

The barman didn't flinch. He nodded and continued to polish the dimpled beer mug in his hand. ''Course you did, Mikey,' he said. 'It's understandable.'

I took the tumbler he'd poured and downed half of it enjoying the sweet-sour burn on my tongue and the warmth in my gut. There wasn't much left in the bottle.

'And the dead boy. Well, it definitely wasn't Jazz, was it.' I said. I made it sound like a statement but actually it wasn't really. No one had told me anything about the boy in the hole. I just thought that it probably wasn't the younger Stone brother. Jazz had disappeared when he was quite young. This boy, though tiny, had appeared older somehow. A teenager.

And he was clearly a fresher corpse, but I wasn't going to start telling Michael how I knew that.

Ugh. I shuddered as I thought through the words. 'A fresher corpse.' How could I even think that? So clinical. Perhaps I was in shock.

Michael seemed to be doing okay, working through his trauma with the aid of his good friend, Jack Daniels. Perhaps he had the right idea.

'No,' he said. 'Not Jazz. I saw. Not Jasper.'

I took another slug of the spirit at the same time as Michael.

He put his glass down on the counter. 'Poor lad. Didn't look like my son. But he's somebody's child.' Then he threw back the last trickle of drink.

Without being asked, the barman filled us up with the remains of the bottle, then took another from the bar and fetched himself a shot glass.

The other two drinkers brought their empties over and said, 'Goodnight Ollie,' then went up to their rooms.

The barman, Ollie, poured himself a measure.

'It's terrible,' he said. His voice was accented. East European. 'I've been here for six years and I never know anything like it. This is a quiet place. Nice people.'

Then he chucked back the shot.

Michael and I copied him.

'Do you know if any children have gone missing?' I asked.

He shook his head slowly. 'Never heard of it. Not round here.'

'You know, I used to see him,' said Michael. Both Ollie

and I let our eyes wander over. He was getting quite ruddy in the face now, trying hard to remain still though his body seemed to jerk ever so slightly, like it wanted to fall asleep but was experiencing little kicks of adrenaline. 'After he disappeared. Saw him everywhere. Holding the hands of different mums and dads. In the windows of fast food places. Libraries. Out on football pitches, riding his bike …'

I glanced uncertainly at Ollie, who was absorbing this sudden switch of subject without question. The barman finished his drink, stared at the empty glass, folded his arms and leant on the counter. When his eyes came up again they were full of pity.

My oesophagus tightened. For a moment I couldn't swallow or turn my face to the father as he mourned his son.

The room tensed. It was full of pain.

'Wasn't him, of course.' Michael tapped his head. 'The mind plays strange tricks on you when you're hostage to emotion. You know that, don't you?'

I didn't know what to say. Ollie nodded then swivelled his eyes over to the door.

Michael's followed and narrowed as he focussed. 'Ah, the prodigal son returns.'

For there was Sam, looking as knackered as I felt.

He didn't come over to us, but pulled out one of the velvet armchairs at a nearby table and leant on it.

'I need support,' he said and thumbed the back of the chair.

But I wasn't sure that he was referring to the furniture. So I got up and went over. Picking his hand up, I led him round to the front of the armchair, which he proceeded to slump into. Then I lowered myself down onto the sofa next to him and rubbed his arm. 'You look terrible,' I told him.

'Thanks,' he said without a grin. 'You're not bad yourself.'

'You wanna drink, son?' Michael called from the bar, suddenly going all American. I guessed the accent took hold when he was pissed.

Sam's head flopped forward in affirmation. He unzipped his coat and leant forward, resting his elbows on his knees. Rubbing his hands through his lovely auburn hair he let go of an enormous sigh. 'They've kept Donny in.' He sank backwards into the armchair, looking like he wanted it to eat him up whole. 'Police are scrutinising any connections he might have to the boy.'

A shiver ran through me. 'Oh. He can't have had anything to do with it, can he?'

Sam shrugged and shook his head but didn't say anything. Exhaustion was kicking in now he was relaxing ever so slightly.

Michael replied. 'Can't have,' he said as firmly as his level of inebriation would allow. 'These people are good people. Pearl and Donny got in contact because Pearl thinks she's seen Jazz. Or some of the Spirit Boys have seen him. They have something in common.' He staggered over and brought Sam's drink to the table.

Ollie followed him and settled my glass and the rest of the new bottle in the middle. 'On the house,' he said. 'I'm locking up. Shut the door when you leave.' And then he disappeared behind the bar.

Alone in the room, in various states of emotional fallout, we all stared at the bourbon like it was the only firm thing there. Michael picked it up and began sharing it out.

'We will find him,' he said as he poured. 'We have to. He needs us to.'

His words had a marked effect on his remaining son, who pitched forwards suddenly and let out a loud, anguished howl.

My hand froze, glass halfway to my lips. I had never witnessed such raw emotion. I wasn't sure what to do – to reach out, or to avert my eyes. How did he want me to react?

His features contorted. That beautiful mouth curved in profound misery, the ends firmly turned down, eyes glassy. It was an expression I had seen on a couple of occasions in other people. Intense pain. But this was finessed. This was not just bereavement. It was combined with the compromised indignity of the cynic who wanted to believe.

In a flash, I understood exactly *why* Sam had taken the path he had.

All these years, he had been trying to protect his dad – from charlatans and con-men – while investigating what he hoped might be valid empirical evidence of life outside our earth-bound zone. He wanted Jazz to have evaded annihilation. He was desperate to know, with absolute certainty, that his little brother still existed somewhere. And all that desperation, all that lack of certainty – it was killing him.

He brought his hands up to hide his expression. But just before they got there a deep shudder ran through him from the top of his head, through his arms, shoulders, chest and torso. It was like he was being physically wrenched. And I felt the pain flex and surge through the room again.

But I didn't want to be a bystander this time.

Filled with a desire to alleviate this moment for my friend, to blow some of it away, to take some of the load, I leant over and put my arms around him and pulled him to me on the sofa. And he came, responding with his body, weaving his own limbs into mine, burying his face between my neck and my shoulder. And I felt him heave and the wetness on my neck, and I rubbed his back and murmured, 'There, there. It's going to be okay,' even though I knew it wasn't.

And I could have stayed there like that all night, holding him close, patting his back, trying to take away some of the hurt he was feeling, cooing and stroking his hair.

But then Michael said, 'Come on Sonny Jim, I think we should get you to bed.'

And he came round and took one of Sam's arms and for a second I felt him resist – he wanted to stay like this too. Then he allowed his dad to haul him to his feet. I stood and slipped my arm round his waist. 'I'll help you up too.'

His face stayed down, eyes lolling at the carpet on the stairs, up onto the landing, the corridor. Michael propped him against the wall outside the room and let go of us. Then he found the key, opened the door and went in.

For a moment Sam hesitated. 'Sorry,' he said. 'I … I … you know.'

'I do,' I said, not really identifying what it was that I

professed to understand, but I reckoned whatever it was, I probably did.

'You and me, eh?' he said and, in an uncharacteristically bold move, pushed his hand through my hair.

I took a sudden breath in, excited by the turn of events. 'Yep.' I was hyper-aware of his palm resting on my cheek. I turned my face to it.

His finger traced the curve of my lips and crept over to my other cheek, and gently drew my face to his.

I was too conscious of his closeness to breathe and stared into his eyes.

Then he laughed, though it didn't sound right. It could have been bitterness, or he might have been choked. But the laugh wasn't fully there. 'What a pair,' he said and rested his forehead against mine.

Right then, I was just managing to repress the urge to get hold of him and drag him down the corridor into my double bed, slip him between the sheets and enfold him in my love.

But I didn't. Of course.

I said, 'Yeah.'

He pulled back and gave me that cute lopsided grin. 'Rosie ...'

Then a long, loud and nasal snore leaked out of the room.

The smiled left Sam's face. An expression of brief puzzlement dropped down over his features, then he stood back so I was able to see his father passed out on the bed.

'Oh yeah,' he said, dropping his shoulders as he exhaled with acute fatigue. 'Dad.' And something inside him changed. Or went back down. I think he remembered why Michael was here. Why we were standing in this corridor looking at each other. 'Tomorrow,' he said, eventually. Letting go of my gaze he turned into the room.

I watched the door close and breathed out my own sigh. Though it wasn't full of sorrow or frustration. For as Sam had pulled away I had seen the look in his eyes and a feeling stirred within: I sensed with an understanding that was deeper than intuition – something was going to happen between us soon.

I didn't know what.

But change was definitely on its way.

It just wasn't the kind that I wanted.

CHAPTER SEVENTEEN

'Snow!' I said.

The tops of the Surrey hills were white and there was a thin smattering on the ground outside the dining room. 'Since when do you get fog followed by snow?'

Michael followed my gaze out the window. 'The climate is spinning out of control. I told you.'

Great. More joy. Thanks, Michael.

I sat down at the breakfast table knocking over the salt and pepper as I plopped my bag down. 'Where's Sam?'

'Sleeping,' said his dad. 'Do you mind taking your bag off the table?'

I shrugged. Weirdo. But put it on the floor next to my boots.

Fortunately my sleep had been good and nourishing. I hadn't expected to slumber so easily but I was out like a light as soon as my head touched the pillow. The sadness that had sunk into my heart last night had contracted to a more manageable size. And I knew what to do with it. I always did. I packaged it up in a plastic container and pushed it to the back of my head to be taken out and gone through when I was in a position to contemplate and reflect. That is how I did things and it had worked for me thus far. Of course there were loads of boxes in that dark place that I'd forgotten about, gathering dust and possibly bursting at the seams, or their Tupperware seals, ready to leap upon me when I least expected it. But that wasn't my problem today. Today I was going to be focussed on Sam. And Michael. And support them. They were the ones who needed it.

I ordered coffee from the waitress. And a full English – no black pudding, but extra mushrooms please. Girl's got to keep her strength up and compassion can be quite exhausting.

Michael watched me break the egg yolk and licked his lips. 'It's been a while since I had a breakfast like that,' he said.

'Well, you can have one now.' I told him. 'It's included in the price.'

'Oh no,' he said and patted his stomach. 'Cholesterol.'

Good job a litre of whiskey is no problem in that regard, I thought but didn't say.

Amazingly Michael didn't look like he was particularly hanging. Which was, as his compatriots were fond of saying, totally awesome considering the state he was in last night.

In fact, he was sitting there grinning. 'Feel better for cutting out meat. You should think about it yourself, Rosie. You know, of course, that animal agriculture and eating meat are the biggest cause of global warming, yes?'

I chomped down on my Cumberland. 'Er …'

'Yep,' he continued. 'I know it's not welcome news but it's

true. And the production of meat is responsible for a great deal of deforestation.'

'Mmm,' I said and wiped fat from my chin with a napkin. I am a lady, right?

'Switch to a partial plant-based diet if you want to save the planet.'

I didn't like this conversation though I knew it was true. It was making me feel guilty and hot and a bit depressed again. So I said, 'Hey, have you heard from the police? Do you know if they've released Donny and Pearl yet?'

Michael broke open a bread roll and spread it with strawberry jam. 'One passed by here earlier,' he said. 'A cop.'

'Oh yes? Don't tell me – he said we can't leave town.' It was bound to happen sooner or later. A body had been discovered. We had found it. I knew the score.

But Michael shook his head. 'Nope. It was a female officer. She said that was fine. Though we should report to our local police when we get back to Adder's Fork. In case they need to follow up.'

'Oh,' I said, and tried to chew a hunk of bacon. It wasn't as tasty as I anticipated. But that was because my throat was parched. Dry, like the expanding Saharan desert, I thought glumly.

Sam appeared at my elbow and pulled out a chair. 'Scrub's going to love that,' he said evidently eavesdropping on our conversation. 'No doubt she's pegged us as supernatural ambulance-chasers.'

An image of Scooby's Mystery Mobile in hot pursuit of paramedics immediately sprinted across my inner screen.

Sometimes my mind was so literal. But anyway I smiled at him and said, 'Uh huh. You are not wrong there.'

He looked a lot less tragic than last night. Though there were remnants of the emotional extremes that had roiled through him, leaving him rudderless and at their mercy for that terrible hour: his eyes were baggy and his pride clearly bruised. A rush of tenderness swept through me. I wanted to give him a kiss and ruffle his hair and do other things to him.

'How are you feeling this morning?' I asked, my voice breaking on the last word and, as it did, I realised I had become self-conscious. Fingers crept up to my hair and patted it down in case it looked stupid and sticky-outie as it often did. Had I put lipstick on, I wondered? I had foundation and mascara but what about eyeliner? Did my eyes look like piss-holes in the Godalming snow? Oh God, there was that vulnerability again. Something I had begun to seal had erupted within me when I had held Sam in my arms last night.

This is what he did to me. That boy.

I allowed my eyes to slide over him. A skittish quality energised his movements, but then he'd had a bit of a collapse last night. It was only natural he'd feel edgy.

'I'm okay,' he said. He pushed back his hair and straightened his shoulders underneath the arran jumper he had on.

I smiled and monitored his response – was he feeling anything similar to me?

There was no chance to find out as Michael broke in. 'We

should report to the local police …' Michael repeated to himself. 'The Adder's Fork police.' It was as if the idea was just sinking in. 'Oh no,' he said with a shake of the head. 'We won't be returning to Snakes Lane for a while.'

Sam and I exchanged glances. The only emotion within them was confusion.

Michael read our expressions and reiterated. 'Snakes Lane. Adder's Fork. Your museum. We can't go back yet. No, indeed.'

'Why not?' I said. 'There's nothing to be done here. We don't know these police. They're not going to let us get involved. We're associated with their prime suspects. Were you thinking we might?'

Stone senior coughed into his fist. 'We need to find out who the poor lad was.' He sped up as if listing our tasks. 'Then we must speak to Pearl, encourage her to journey up into the celestial kingdom, find him and talk to him about where Jazz is.' His Adam's apple wobbled. Above it his face crumpled. Desperation was mixing with determination – an unsettling cocktail that I'd seen before. 'Because what if he's ….' he stumbled. 'What if he's HERE?' Now his eyes were flung wide. He jabbed his fork at the restaurant door. 'Out there. In that forest. Where the other boy …' he didn't finish. His arm dropped, face following quickly. Dark thoughts were shutting him in.

Sam stretched his hand to his arm and tapped it. 'Dad, the police are searching the area. They don't want our help. They'll do a much better job of gathering intelligence. We'd be a hindrance. And look, right now, at this moment in time they *understand* why we're here. They've looked up Jasper's file. But any messing around in their crime scene and they might decide we warrant more scrutiny.'

You could see Michael got it. He didn't want to agree, but the sensible part of himself knew his son was right.

'You're right.' He swallowed and kind of shook himself round the shoulders and neck. When his face came up again it was less stifled. 'I showed them the emails from Donny too.' His voice was losing tension. 'They didn't seem happy about them.'

'They can't think they're involved in ...?' I dropped my eyes to the table. I didn't want to use 'murder'. 'In ...' What was a word that kept emotion at bay? 'The death.'

Sam poured out a large black coffee. 'Who knows? My hunch is that, no, they weren't involved. But at the same time, Donny was the person who remembered "the Hunting". And that's where we found the boy. It's not far from their house.'

'We must see them.' Urgency was rising in Michael's voice once more. 'We need to get to the bottom of this.'

Sam gripped his arm more firmly. 'Dad, not now.'

'Then when?' Michael asked, his voice cracking.

'When they're clear and out of custody. Maybe a week? Is that okay? You can stay with us till then.' He glanced at me for approval.

I agreed quickly. 'Yes. There's plenty of room, Michael. And lots of jobs that could do with an extra pair of hands.'

'But I, I, I ... I want ... to be h, here ... for the ... investigation ...' Michael stuttered. He breathed in deeply and then paused to counter the sudden irregular rise and fall of his chest.

'I'm really not sure if there's any point,' I said as soothingly as I possibly could. 'Seriously. Sam and I have dealt with incidents …' I was going to say 'like this' but that wasn't true. 'We've dealt with some nasty crimes. And they won't let us anywhere near the scene unless they *ask* us to assist them. We will present a nuisance otherwise. We can however report to Monty, see what he thinks best. Plus, there are other leads we might pursue from the museum.'

'And, I …' Sam looked at me. There was something shining in his caramel eyes. His hand grabbed hold of mine and he sighed, 'I really, really want to go home.'

CHAPTER EIGHTEEN

'He's not what you'd call rugged though, is he?' Auntie Babs commented as she buffed the nail on my big toe.

We were debating the exact nature of Michael Stone's attraction. 'He's like Sam but bigger.'

'Only just,' she said. 'Around the waist. Softer though, I thought, didn't you, Rosie love?'

'More scattered,' I said and stretched out my other leg to the fire. Babs was blocking the heat, positioned as she was on the pouffe in front of the hearth.

I'd left the pair of them downstairs in our tiny Witch Museum kitchenette, where they were attempting to help Bronson cook. I bet the caretaker was loving that.

The more time I spent with the Stones, the more I saw that father and son shared similar gestures, as of course they would. It was fascinating to observe. The way Sam put his fingers through his hair and swept it back, I now saw, was an identical match to Michael's. He'd inherited it. And the eyes too – they were the same shape: rounded almonds, large and full of life. Though Michael's colouring in the iris was slightly different. Sam must get his amber-gold from his mum. Or maybe it was a throwback. The thick hair also clearly came from his dad, who I noted keenly, was not bald. Exactly the opposite. His barnet was lush and showed absolutely zero signs of receding.

They frowned the same way when either said 'indeed' but didn't mean anything by it – just used the word to fill the air or punctuate a silence. It made me giggle. Sam nearly caught me once, but I looked away quickly. He had also acquired his father's tall frame and broad shoulders but there the similarities ended.

Michael's skin tone was darkened by regular exposure to the Californian sun, whereas his son's was a very English cream shade. And while Sam held himself steady and firm, as a rule, though Michael was upright and straight, there was a flightiness that gnawed at the edges of his paternal authority. At times he seemed to draw in too much breath, too quickly. It gave him a hare-like, ruffled quality. Scattered.

'I don't know what you mean by that?' My auntie readjusted the cotton wool ball between my fourth and fifth toes. 'Scattered? How is he scattered?'

'Upstairs.' I pointed to my head. 'Psychologically.'

'Well, it's to be expected, ain't it? Losing a child like that – the not knowing. What do they call it these days – lack of closure. That sort of thing could send you round the twist if you let it.' A shiver ran through her and she grimaced, showing newly whitened teeth. 'I couldn't bear anything like that to happen to you or John or those kiddywinks his girlfriend has got. What's her name now?'

'Maria,' I said. 'They're engaged apparently.'

'Ohhh lovely,' she said. 'No party?'

'They haven't got much money.' I was a bit irked myself when Dad told me, but I also knew that John was lazy and they were both quite skint. Septimus had left John a nice little cash sum which I think he wanted to blow on a holiday in Vegas. But Maria had exerted her good sense and insisted they put it down as a deposit on a three-bedroom maisonette in Wanstead, down the road from Mum and Dad. With property prices being what they were, the mortgage still came in over £150K. God knows how either of them would have got on the property ladder without Granddad's legacy.

Septimus's death had changed a lot of things for a lot of people.

Profoundly.

Auntie Bab's artificially augmented boobs quivered as she exhaled. 'No. Not many have these days. John ever think about coming down Essex way? It's cheaper out here innit?'

'I don't think so. He's a London boy and likes it,' I said.

'Well you're all right down here for a bit, aintcha? Your granddad would be pleased to see you working with the old place. It's a big undertaking and you done well, love.'

'Yeah. Sam is a great help,' I said, feeling my throat contract as my tongue slipped silkily over his name.

Nothing got past Babs. She looked up for a second and checked my face. A little smile of satisfaction twisted her lips as she said, 'Yes, Sam. It's a wonder that boy's turned out as well as he has.'

She blew on my little toe. 'Fine young man, that one.

You two … have you, you know …?' she winked her heavily lashed eyelid.

'What?' I said, as defensive as ever.

'Got closer?' More winking.

Her phrasing actually demonstrated remarkable self-control despite the pantomime face-twitching that accompanied it. In fact it was verging on tactful for Babs. I told you things had been strained.

'Not *that* close,' I said. The evening before we left Godalming was still fresh in my mind. That lingering look, the sense of change on its way. 'Not *yet.* We are tight. Intimate.' I shot down her eyebrow arch. 'Not like that. But we do have something going on. There's chemistry. And it's simmering again.'

'Well you only have to look at the pair of you to see that's true. Other foot.'

I swung my right calf off of Bab's lap, took my left one out of the foot spa and replaced it on the towel she was holding. 'Yeah. A few people have said that. But …'

'But what?' she said, rubbing my heel with the cloth.

I sighed. 'Oh nothing. Just got to be organic, I guess.'

She rolled her eyes. 'I told you 'bout that, ain't I? Nothing wrong with helping things along. You want a bottle of shampoo, something classy like Bolly, a box of Thornton's and a copy of *When Harry Met Sally* on the box and I tell you – Bob's your uncle, that boy will be putty in your 'and.'

'Yeah,' I said. If only it was that easy. 'Don't think that's going to work on this one.'

'Who? You?'

'Him.'

'Why not?'

'He's not a Meg Ryan sort of bloke. In terms of films …'

'I suppose you could go for a *Die Hard* …? Bruce Willis more his thing?'

'Nah. That won't ring his bell neither.'

'Worked for me and your Uncle Del.'

Yes. Last century, in the days when the dinosaurs walked the earth and people got excited by moving pictures.

Auntie Babs bent over and plucked a small bottle out of her bag of tricks. 'So where is the tall dark stranger?'

Unprompted, a vision of Dorcus popped into my head. 'Which one?' I asked.

'Mr Stone senior?' she said and gave me another wink.

I didn't know how she'd gone from seduction techniques to enquiring after Sam's dad. Actually, I had an idea but didn't want to pursue it.

'He's helping Bronson fix up the back room, behind the Talks Area. I thought it was just storage. But Michael thinks it could be a nice garden room in the summer. He's suggesting we install a wood burner so that it can be used in winter. Reckons he could put in some long windows that can open out onto the back garden when the weather gets nice. He's very handy, turns out.'

'Well, I do like a man who's good with his hands,' she said and smiled mischievously. I didn't want to know what she was thinking. Again.

'He and Bronson have been investigating the storage areas. Turns out there's a warren of cellars underneath the museum.'

'I think I knew that,' she said and using tiny, tiny strokes, painted the varnish onto my toenails.

'Did you?' I was going to ask why she hadn't told me, but then I remembered that there was a lot she hadn't disclosed. So instead I said, 'Well I haven't seen half of it. Apparently we've got a furniture store, a dummy store and loads more artefacts, hundreds. There's a cellar where a whole batch of them have been collected and catalogued. And another store of what Sam called "Septimus's acquisitions". Haven't been through them yet. At the back of that there was a door that led into another corridor. And more rooms. Some Sam hasn't even been into. He can't find the keys to them.'

Locked rooms in the cellar with no keys, I thought, listening to myself. Could this place get more bleedin' cryptic?

'So he's downstairs then?' Babs asked again completely unimpressed by the maze we were uncovering underneath the Witch Museum. 'Michael is, is he?'

She was incorrigible. And married. Though Uncle Del was really nice, he was, to be honest, a bit boring. My mantra was the same as Lennon's – whatever gets you through the night. But even so I wasn't overly keen to witness my aunt in full-throttle mating mode, so tried to distract her.

'I like that colour,' I gestured to the bottle of nail varnish. 'What do you call it?'

'My friend, Doreen, got it from Ridley Road market. Stall there does seconds. Apparently, they want to turn it into flats.'

'The stall? How can they ...?'

'The market, you numpty.' She threw a ball of cotton wool at me. It got no higher than my kneecap. 'They want to turn it into flats.'

'Everything will get turned into flats,' I said mournfully. 'And we'll have to buy all our nail polish online. Amongst many many many many many many other things.'

'Can't buy nail varnish online,' said Auntie Babs with defiance. 'Can't see the colour properly on the screen. Where's the use of that?'

I peered at the paint coating my middle toe. 'What's that colour?'

Babs didn't look up, but said, slowly, as she moved the brush in short delicate lengths, 'Pearly Frost.'

And of course my mind went back to Pearl White. I saw her, as I had when I had first met her, gliding on her golden throne into the Flower Room. 'I wonder how Pearl's doing?' I said aloud.

''Oo?' Babs muttered over my toes.

'The lady psychic. One with Near Death Syndrome, who reckoned she was talking to the Spirit Boys,' I had relayed a concise summary of events to my aunt, which had lasted over an hour. She was inquisitive, liked to get all the details.

'Oh yes. The Spirit Boys,' she repeated. 'Them what's outside the Pearly Gates?'

'Yes,' I said and breathed in. The varnishy smell was thick in the air and made me catch my breath. 'This colour stinks.'

Babs looked up, sniffed and made a face. 'Yes, I got it too. Smells flammable.' She glanced at the fire, spluttering and dancing in the hearth. 'Perhaps we should move further away?'

I shook my head. 'Just do it quick and we can go and sit on the sofa.'

She nodded. 'Don't want you smudging my masterpiece. Masterpieces.'

'Why does it pong so much?'

'I think it's cheap. You're smelling the toluene and camphor I expect. Toluene is that sweet, strong whiff you can smell. Camphor is a bit menthol-y. Like mint.'

'Oh,' I said. 'You always did have a good nose.'

'Thank you, my love. A beautician has to. The smells are like warnings to us. When it's strong, means we need to ventilate – open a window, get the fan on.'

'Oh yeah?'

'That's right, love – toluene gives the polish that lovely smooth finish but they reckon it can cause brain damage. Mmm. And breathing difficulties, hearing loss, vomming. Camphor can cause allergies, skin irritation, dizziness and headaches. Gladys had one the other day.'

'What?' I said and jerked my foot away. 'And you're putting it on my feet!'

Babs rolled her eyes and tutted. 'This room is very big. And anyway the EU have put restrictions on them.'

'Yeah but you reckon you can smell it now?'

'Oh yes,' she said, and giggled, as if she were just connecting the dots. 'Well a little bit won't hurt will it?'

'I don't know!' I said. 'Will it?'

Babs ignored my outrage. 'Tell me how long you manage to go without chipping?' she said as she finished up.

'All right,' I said, calmed by her lack of concern.

I wiggled my tootsies. They did look very pretty, which was quite unusual: my feet had been shaped into a kind of arrow outline after decades of being crammed into pointy-toed kitten heels and cowboy boots.

Auntie Babs gave them a final once-over. 'Don't know if I'll use it in the salon, though,' she said.

'Why? The shimmer is nice.'

'I don't like the smell,' she said and went and sat down.

I looked at them again and wondered if I'd get brain damage. Maybe I already had it.

Now the lid was on, the bitter scent was dissipating.

But there was something at the back of my mind that was itching, wanting to pop forward. Something to do with what Pearl had said. But I couldn't remember what exactly. It was when she was channelling the Spirit Boys. Something had triggered a sort of sense memory in my head. It was bubbling around now.

And then I got it.

'Babs – what would you say if I mentioned Washing Up—' I was going to add 'Man', but she'd clearly been triggered.

'I'm not doing that too! The pedicure's my limit. Why ain't you got a dishwasher yet?'

'Working on it,' I said. 'But I didn't mean that. I was going to say – what smell would you think of if I said Washing Up Man?'

Auntie Babs screwed her eyes up at me. 'Man?'

'What smell?'

'What colour's the liquid?'

'Yella.' I hadn't realised that I was going to say it. But there it was, just the way Pearl had disclosed it: 'Yella, yella, yella.'

'All right,' said Auntie Babs crossly. 'Keep your hair on.'

'Yellow?' I asked myself more than Babs.

'Well if you'd slow down a minute, I can tell you,' she said. 'Lemon. Citrus. Citronellla. That sort of thing …'

'Really?' I swung my feet off the pouffe.

'Oh yes. There are some colours that have clear lines to fragrance. Orange is one, obvs. Yellow always goes with citrus – lemons.'

'That's very interesting. Where can I find these smells?'

'The most intense I'd say would be essential oils and, ooh, 'ello, love …'

The door burst open with such force, it hit the wall and bounced back again.

Sam cantered in. 'Rosie!' He was smiling. His mood had improved hugely since we returned to the museum.

'Oh,' he said, noticing my aunt sprawling at my feet. 'Sorry. Hello Babs. I forgot you were here. Rosie, can you come down? Monty's arrived.'

CHAPTER NINETEEN

'Monty Don!' shrieked Auntie Babs and threw her arms around the very smart agent.

Montgomery Walker was impeccably dressed as a rule and fantastically composed. An assault by an elaborately made-up relative of mine didn't even ruffle his feathers. Though when my aunt squeezed him, some of the air came out of his lungs and twirled the peacock feather earrings that she had on.

'Barbara,' he said, discreetly prising her hands from the top of his buttocks. 'How splendid to see you.' His smile did a good job of suggesting he was in earnest. 'How are you keeping?'

'Very well, thank you, as I'm sure you can see.' She gave her chest a little wiggle and fluttered her lashes. Oh God – Babs was shameless. I don't even know why I bothered to get embarrassed any more.

Monty took a step back. 'And how is dear old Ray Boundersby doing these days? I do think of him from time to time.'

Ah yes, I'd forgotten about that. My dear aunt had been involved in a case with Monty, back in the Smoke. In fact, now I thought about it Babs had 'volunteered' us to investigate in the first place.

'Also good,' Babs returned. Sam patted the chair next to him, a good spanking distance away from Monty's bottom. 'Ray thought he wouldn't be able to cover up all the shenanigans that had gone on in La Fleur, so he's capitalising on it instead. Changed the name to "Exploitation", made the downstairs a bar and the upstairs a private dining room, all plush but with chains and that. They all love it.' She winked at Monty.

'All?' said Sam, sliding the chair slightly to catch Bab's rapidly descending derriere.

I sent him a thumbs up – 'well caught'.

'Yep.' Babs rearranged her décolletage and tucked bits of herself back in. 'Toffs and tourists. All of them. Well up for it, they are. Personally, I wouldn't want to spend time there. Not with its history and the terrible whatnot next door with them poor girls.'

I nodded. I'd had more than my fill of La Fleur and thought Ray's new décor sounded immeasurably tasteless.

'The prices are awful 'n' all. Nowt stranger than folk, I'll say. Though, working in this place, you lot already know that, dontcha?'

It was a rhetorical question. But we all nodded in affirmation.

Months ago, I had realised there was a lot of weirdness in the world. I'd come across a great deal of it since I had inherited the museum. Of course, like attracts like and there was something in the nature of our work that clearly drew the uncommon to us and vice versa. On occasion, when my mind was wild and untethered, it felt like the museum was at the centre of a hurricane of strange phenomena, and that maybe we were sucking it towards us like a magnet. Lately, I'd even wondered if the magnetic force, if there was one, well if it was being strengthened by my presence. I know that that sounds seriously narcissistic, but even Bronson had commented on it a couple of times.

The number of strange occurrences and cases we'd looked into was apparently up. Things, he'd said, never used to be this busy. But then I'd inherited the museum and all sorts had started to crawl 'out of the woodwork'. And some of them were as dark as sin. Darker than anything I'd experienced in Benefit Fraud. Seriously, the stuff that had been going on, like what we discovered at Ray Bounderby's restaurant – well, it made fraudulent cohabitees look like choirboys. Or girls.

A shudder ran through me.

'Tea anyone?' I asked. Nothing like a cuppa to see off the chills.

Michael and Bronson appeared through the secret passageway. Bronson nodded at the agent. Michael shook hands with him warmly. It was clear that he and Monty were already acquainted.

Once everyone had sat down and been sorted with tea and biscuits Monty began.

CHAPTER TWENTY

'Right.' Monty cleared his throat. 'So, to business. Sam's filled me in on the details so far.'

I had let my lovely friend and his dad get on with writing the report summarising what had happened in Godalming. I didn't want to revisit it. The dead boy was still in my mind, on occasion emerging from the darkness. Plus, they were keen to add more context about Jazz's disappearance, and Michael had desperately needed something to occupy himself. I think the pair of them made a good job of it. Sam would undoubtedly have been thorough. The document that I glanced at was over twenty pages long. Monty certainly had a lot for his operatives to get stuck into. The involvement of Pearl brought it under his official remit apparently. Whatever that was – possibly the investigation of well strange phenomena.

'The boy's name, I gather, was Stuart Norman Fuller. Known as Stuey …' the agent explained.

Straight away Michael jolted and put his hand out to stop Monty's flow. 'My God,' he said and appealed to his son. 'Pearl said "Tuey". She said that was his name, didn't she Samuel? She did.'

It was true, I remembered it. And she'd also reported that he'd said, 'Yella, yella.' Those words again. 'Washing Up Man.' What did they mean? If anything struck me during our Godalming stay, those words did. Why? I couldn't tell you. But I was experiencing a physical reaction now as I thought about it – on the back of my neck tiny blonde hairs were prickling to attention. I should follow this vibe, I mused. See if it leads anywhere. Think on what Babs had told me about corresponding fragrances.

'Yes,' said Monty, bringing my thoughts back into the office. 'I'm aware of Pearl White's full statement to the police. And that of her son, Donald. Very interesting. We're keeping an eye on them. Now, as I was saying, Stuart was not reported missing for a good fortnight. The parents are dysfunctional. Drugs and alcohol.'

The way Monty relayed it was so matter-of-fact. I couldn't be like that. Without permission my mind reached back to that poor boy, lying there, cradled by roots and earth, unmissed. The muscles in my throat tensed. I didn't want to give in to the emotions being sparked, so I said, 'They must have wondered, surely?'

'They thought that Stuart had gone to visit his uncle in Woking. He often did. He had cousins of the same age and often spent long periods of time there as it was less chaotic and he was fed and looked after.'

Oh. It was getting worse. 'But when the uncle said he wasn't there?'

'Yes, it was he who raised the alarm. It appears that the desk sergeant assumed Stuart was a runaway and filed a missing persons report. Apparently, incidence of this is high on the estate where Stuart lived.'

Wow. My stomach flipped. A missing person.

Auntie Babs shook her head and tutted softly. 'I saw a programme on it. They reckon over a hundred thousand children run away from home every year.'

'But he was so small!' I said pointlessly. As if size had anything to do with it. And even though I tried to make it go away, drifting across my brain came the image of the boy, tucked up under the ledge looking like he was asleep.

No eyes.

I blinked. 'They should have taken that seriously.'

'He was almost fourteen,' said Monty

I shook my head. 'Younger, surely.' Little feet, little hands, little nose … Stop it!

Monty clocked the discomfort in my eyes. 'It's okay to be shocked by this, Rosie. It's an awful case. He was small because he was malnourished. Children living in poverty often are.'

The kid never stood a chance. It was a tragedy.

'Over four million nippers living in poverty now.' Babs rolled her eyes. 'That's what they said. Bleedin' disgrace. I don't pay my taxes so that the government can give it to the banks. I pay 'em so they can 'elp kids like that. It ain't right.'

'Agreed,' said Monty, then sensing the discussion might detour off towards generalised government-bashing he said. 'Tuey died from trauma to the back of the head.'

The dried spill of blood over roots. Dark patches underneath him.

'Is it consistent with a fall?'

Monty shook his head. 'No. We think a metallic instrument. Possibly a torch.'

Sam breathed in through his nose and nodded rapidly at the same time. 'It would have to be heavy to …'

I didn't want him to finish that sentence, so I coughed out my dismay.

Monty got it and interjected, 'I ran a search to see if there have been similar reports. We've had some interns running features into HOLMES, utilising different configurations.'

Bronson nodded and added, 'Sherlock.'

Sam smiled at Babs and added, 'IT system.'

Bronson nodded again and said, 'Of course.'

'Gordon Bennett!' Babs muttered under her breath. 'Robot detectives! Whatever next?'

Michael sighed and motioned for Monty to carry on. The agent complied efficiently, but his face was a picture.

'We've had matches, of course,' he told his audience. 'You keep your parameters wide and you'll get hits. And that's what we've got. Too many to mention. Sadly. But I added in details from your brief, Sam, Michael, which narrowed it down. Looked at the time spans and fed the results out to my field agents.'

'Oh yes?' said Michael and leant forwards.

'And one of them has turned something up. It's not a live case. But a couple of historic ones that may well fit into the Jasper timeline.'

'What about the recent one? Tuey?' I said, but Michael spoke over the top of me.

'Well, can we see him? Your agent?' Stone senior's body was rigid. He extended the full length of his spine.

'Of course. *She* is in the north of the country and about to go further. Tomorrow. For another case. That's why I came now. You'll need to give her this. Don't open it.' Monty passed him a sealed white envelope wrapped in a plastic wallet. 'We have to be so careful with communications and hacks. This will prove you are who you say you are. We've gone back to the good old days. You can't trust computers any more.'

'But *where* do *we* go?' said Sam.

Monty slipped him another envelope. 'Co-ordinates are in there. Don't put them into your satnav till you're on the motorway. Tracking,' he said as if we knew what that meant. 'Head north. My agent will contact you with a rendezvous point.'

'Can't you give us a lift in your helicopter?' I said. I'd been angling for a ride and I thought it might cheer me up.

'No. It's needed elsewhere, as am I. And you'll need your cars, I suspect. Take two. And don't hang around. In fact you should make tracks now. I have it on good authority there's a snowstorm on its way.'

'Oh how exciting!' said Babs and clapped her hands. 'Can I come? You never know when you might need a pedi.'

This was true but I shook my head. 'No. We need you here. Can you and Bronson sort out cover for the museum?'

I thought she'd bristle but she didn't. Instead she winked at the handyman, who nodded silently, and said, 'I'll give Trace and Vanessa a call. You get along. I'll pack you some sarnies for the road.'

CHAPTER TWENTY-ONE

We took two cars as per Monty's instructions. This time I drove on my own. Sam went with Michael. I think they had stuff to talk about.

We made a point to meet for a rest and something to eat at a services halfway up the M1 motorway.

A hunger fired Sam and Michael's eyes and made them look very much related. Same sweep of lashes, same flicks whirring within. It was strange – we were on our way to talk to an operative about disappearing boys – a horrifying prospect – and yet, there was something of an adventure in the air around us.

We stopped to stoke up on drinks, cake and pastries. The sky outside the coffee shop was smeared with sprays of bleak grey across dove white. Monty was right about the snow. I had smelt it on the way in too. The air was thick with its promise. For sure, it would fall heavy this time.

'Well,' said Michael, as we were clearing the table. 'I'm going to the shop to buy some maps and an atlas of the North.'

'Don't need them,' Sam told his dad and wiped the corners

of his mouth with a paper napkin printed with the red logo of the chain. For a second I mistook it for a bloodstain. 'Everything you need can be found on my phone.'

Michael cocked his head to one side. 'But just imagine if you can't get online, son. I think it's a good idea to have back-up, don't you?'

Sam stared at his dad. He blinked and I felt something pass between them, a challenge from the younger stag to the reigning monarch. 'It fits into your pocket.' He took his mobile out of his jeans and waggled it in front of Michael's nose.

Evidently Michael wasn't yet ready to surrender his authority to the younger generation. His mouth thinned. 'A – you can't share a phone. The screen is too small for three people to view easily. B – what if the signal drops or the battery runs out, eh? Books need neither.'

I decided to throw my hat into the ring too, for what it was worth. 'C – perspective. I prefer looking at a paper map – you get a much better sense of how far away everything is.'

Sam looked at me as if I'd just farted.

'That does it then,' said Michael. 'We're in agreement.' And he stood up and made for the central corridor and the shops.

'Thanks,' said Sam with lashings and lashings of sarcasm.

I couldn't be doing with more conflict so just followed his dad out.

While father and son began a fresh argument over atlas brands and map producers, I wandered off to the toiletries section. I was always content to browse this area and look at products: the latest developments in dermatological technology with a view to delaying the ageing process. Not that I was getting wrinkly. Even my friend Cerise had remarked upon my surprisingly smooth skin. It was remarkable when you considered how much I'd caned it in the past and all the personal earthquakes of the last year. But there you go. No accounting for folk, as Babs would say. Although at the same time I didn't know what you were meant to look like at my age really. It was difficult to get a proper gauge when you were constantly bombarded by photoshopped images of peeps who'd been filled out, slimmed down, lasered, bronzed, nipped, tucked, augmented and reduced. Plus, I'd celebrated reaching my thirty-third year in September on the twenty-first, although that might not even be the actual date of my birth. No one really knew. So much of my background, which had been fixed and firm before this year, had become very very murky.

But that was life, I guess. And I was learning that everybody had their own problems and mysteries in their pasts. Look at where I was – halfway to a meeting with a government agent who might shed light on Sam's missing younger brother.

I mean – who knew?

Really.

I was browsing through the soaps, gels, skin creams, body lotions and assorted other smellies, when a nearby display caught my eye. I never usually bothered with essential oils as they seemed a bit hippy to me. However, as my eye roamed over the bottles a word leapt out at me and I found myself recalling with stark clarity the conversation I had with dear

Auntie Babs, in the living room of the Witch Museum. As I bent closer one particular bottle seemed to catch the artificial light and wink. Lemon essential oil. I was leading with my gut as an experiment, I reminded myself, trying to reach out and pull in that illusive intuition Sam was so fond of talking about.

So I followed the idea through: if I perceived the bottle winking at me then it meant my mind was signalling that something about it was, well, in some way significant. Which meant it warranted closer attention.

I'm a nutter, I thought, but I bent over it.

Balanced on the shelf beneath, a printed description read, '100% Pure Lemon Oil (Citrus limon). Strong. Bold. Zesty-sweet tart.'

Just like yours truly, I thought and read on.

'Invigorates, refreshes and eases tension.' Exactly what we could all do with. 'Aids concentration and promotes mental detoxification. Cleanses.'

Oh yeah baby, give me some of your loving. I picked the bottle up to smell it. The cap, however, was sealed tight with plastic shrink-wrap.

'Hello. You done?' Sam was at my shoulder. 'We're finally sorted in the map department.' He sighed. 'At last. Belt and braces.' He ran his fingers along the shelf I had been looking at. 'Haven't you got enough cosmetics?'

'Cosmetics?' I said, perplexed – how could anyone mistake essential oils for make-up?

'I suppose you're going to say something about a girl can't have too many etc. etc. …' He rolled his eyes and gave the shelf one last tap. 'Well hurry up, then. Meet you back at the car. Curb your vanity for the sake of speed. If you can.'

Then he was gone, which was just as well: another moment more and I might have enhanced the convivial atmosphere further with a subtle headbutt to the middle of my curator's cute button nose.

Prick.

I let the ripple of defiance build, then when it had reached maximum capacity I let it out with some classic Anglo-Saxon, looked back at the shelf and scooped up the lemon essential oil and a handful of neighbouring bottles. Then I trotted over to the till and paid for them very slowly.

I was thinking about either explaining the difference between cosmetics and alternative healing treatments or ramming the aforementioned fripperies of my 'vanity' somewhere on Sam's body where the sun don't shine. However, when I reached my car Michael beeped and revved and Sam made a circling gesture with his hand: hurry up.

Fuck's sake.

I was tempted to flick a couple of v's at them but settled for a good glower.

Which was fairly appropriate, as when we got back on the motorway I saw we were heading straight for the storm.

CHAPTER TWENTY-TWO

By the time we had reached the rendezvous point, in the small northern city of Waketon, the storm had developed into a blizzard.

I was glad that Michael had insisted on powering up the motorway. I had wanted to stop at the next services for the loo but, to be honest, if we had we might not have made it here at all.

By the time Michael relayed the new co-ordinates to me and explained that they referred to a budget hotel, the traffic was slowing to a crawl. We came off at the next junction and began making our way into town. If the weather kept up like this, another couple of hours and the roads might become completely impassable. It was likely that we were going to get snowed in.

At the Holiday Inn the receptionist handed us a message from our 'Uncle Dan' asking us to meet him at a pub on the edge of the city centre. We dropped our bags in our rooms and headed off without delay.

Underfoot the snow crunched. We took the quickest route to the pub and trudged down dark Victorian alleys, lit by lamp posts fashioned to resemble the old iron-wrought lanterns à la Jack the Ripper again. Or perhaps they were original, never replaced, only updated. Snowflakes flew into their haloes of light, danced and then whipped away to cover the fences, trees and yards. For some reason I thought of Mr Tumnus, the Narnian faun, turned into a statue by Jadis, the evil White Witch. Though wasn't she a queen, the sole survivor of Charn, simply looking for a place to live? I sighed. Things used to be so simple before I inherited that museum.

Up ahead Michael coughed. 'It's like a Christmas card. I'd forgotten about snow.'

Sam muttered a tardy agreement.

I didn't.

It all felt a bit grim. Like grim with an extra 'm'. Fairy-tale Grimm. With all their sinister overtones.

I tucked my chin down and stuck my hands deep into my pockets. Above me, behind the white flakes, the sky was as black as sin.

Even the quiet muting of street noise, that I usually loved, felt strange. Pregnant. As if the many seasonal beasties that I had come to know – Krampus, Frau Perchta or that vicious Yule Cat – were holding their claws to their lips purring 'shhhhhh', before they jumped from white rooftops and clawed us to bits.

We turned west along a dual carriageway, with only a handful of cars braving the weather and at a crawl. A few metres ahead of us, a Volvo lay half on the pavement, broken down and abandoned to the elements.

We were walking on the side of a ring road. To my left

stood shabby tenements, to my right shops and offices. All of them in the process of turning white.

I caught up with Sam and Michael, but none of us were speaking. The gusts were picking up and smacking our faces. We angled them down and leant into the wind. My nose was running but I wasn't going to take my hands out of my pockets to wipe it, so nudged it against my collar which was stiff and icy.

And still came the snow.

We all shivered and stamped our boots as we reached our destination. I held on to the wall as we made our way up the slippery tiled steps at the front of the designated pub, Friar Tuck's. Try saying that when you've had one too many sherries.

To be honest I was wondering if the place had decided to close because of the weather. It had that neglected run-down look to the exterior. A couple of panes of glass in the two bow windows were cracked. One had a piece of brown cardboard sellotaped behind it to stop the wind whistling through the cracks. Could have been empty for years or the result of deliberate decay from a chain that wanted to run it down so it could convert from a boozer to sports bar or microbrewery. It was unloved.

But only on the outside.

Once we got through the door, the atmosphere changed. There was a feel to the place of a social or working men's club. I know they had quite a few of them up here. And the décor hadn't changed since the eighties.

But it was well populated considering the conditions outside. Most of the tables had at least one or two occupants.

Some, near a small stage in the far corner, had extended families of seven or eight gathered round. Closer to the door there were groups of office workers in suits and smart casual enjoying an end-of-week drink. Although it was also possible they had been stranded by public transport freezing to a halt.

I could see why the agent had chosen the place. It had a sense of liminality about it. A visiting speaker had used that term in a talk about ritual at the museum. According to her, it referred to the quality of 'ambiguity or disorientation' that occurs in the middle stage of a journey or rite of passage, when you are no longer one thing nor the other. When you stand at a threshold. And that felt spot on for this place and how I felt at that very moment – as if I was leaving something behind, and halfway towards beginning something else. But it was just a feeling.

The area around the pub certainly appeared to be an edgeland, caught between the domestic spheres of the council flats to its south and business to its north, neither city nor suburb. The ring road had cut it off, tried to maroon it, but people here persisted. There were both regular punters and irregular visitors from either district. No one would notice a group of strangers who had strayed in for the first time. Not on a night like tonight when travellers all over the place were seeking sanctuary in the nearest shelter.

An old bloke on the stage was singing Frank Sinatra, not particularly badly either. Ah, I noted the monitor next to him. Karaoke. That would explain the turnout, in spite of the inclement weather. I was always up for it myself. 'Love Shack' by the B-52s was a particular family favourite. My brother,

John, had lead singer, Fred Schneider, down to a T. I could go a bit of it right now, in fact. Might warm me up. But it probably wasn't the right time.

None of us spotted any solo drinkers who may or may not be the cryptic 'Uncle Dan'. I was despatched to find a table, while the other two went to the bar.

There was an empty one near a red tiled fireplace that had no fire in it so I went and spread myself out there.

The boys came back with a red wine for me, which looked dangerously opaque, two pints and a man who looked like a cross between a salesman and a trucker. He had a thick moth-eaten sheepskin coat over a grey suit. But, strangely enough, he fitted right in.

I had been expecting a woman after Monty's words, but apparently that operative had been called away.

Once Samuel had given him the envelope proving our identities, the new guy introduced himself as Gareth (not real name). He seemed particularly bland for an agent and for a second I wondered if he was actually just some random who had attached himself to our party in the hope of a bit of conversation.

However, when I introduced myself in return, he repeated my name. 'Ah yes. Rosie. Rosie Strange. You're the Essex …'

Sam's fist tensed in anticipation of my explosion. The defence and/or repositioning of my county's reluctant blonde mascot was important to me.

I headed him off. I could fight my own battles. 'For God's sake. I am more than a stereotype!'

But the agent sailed on. 'Witch,' he ended.

'Witch?' I wasn't expecting that. 'Essex witch?'

He shrugged. 'From the Essex Witch Museum?'

'Oh, I, er, well I am the owner of the museum but I wouldn't say that I'm a ...'

'No,' he said. 'Apologies. It was something that Walker implied. I shouldn't have mentioned it ... Funny that: one of my colleagues mentioned, only the other day, that our department used to have a nickname that was similar – "The Witch Centre" or sommat. From back during the War.'

I was quite interested in pursuing this tangent but Michael, who was drumming his fingers on the table, said, 'Well, well, now we're all acquainted shall we proceed directly to the matter in hand.'

I parked the couple of questions bobbing around in my head. There'd be time to trot them out later.

'Good idea,' Gareth finished. 'I've got an hour and no more. Though I can certainly hand over notes.'

'An hour!' Michael rocked back on his chair. It made a hard, squeaking noise on the wooden floor. 'That's not enough for a thorough briefing, surely.'

'Development,' Gareth said with firmness. 'UFO sightings.'

Right, because that explained everything.

Michael's demeanour changed. 'Oh right,' he said and rocked back into the table. 'Tyneside,' he whispered to the agent with wide knowing eyes.

'Correct,' Gareth stated, then, having dealt with that explanation, moved promptly on. 'Now, I hear you're connected to the boy in Godalming?'

Michael spread his fingers on the tabletop and shut up

while Sam explained the process of connection. I think they had already decided who would speak about which subject. Sam started with Michael's email from Donny about Jazz. Michael interjected and filled in the details on that particularly traumatic incident and the consequent communication. He kept it efficient and remarkably trim, all things considered. Then went on to his arrival in the UK. Sam outlined the visit to Godalming, Pearl's vision, Tuey, the 'Hunting', Stuey, the police and then Monty's latest communication.

At the end of it Gareth grimaced. 'Right.' He kept his face perfectly straight, betraying no obvious emotion – no sympathy, but no disbelief or surprise either. Which was interesting with regard to a number of things including the Near Death Syndrome. These guys were very open-minded.

I took a gulp of wine. It was viscous and a bit like jam. 'Do you know if there's any news on what happened to Stuart?'

Gareth avoided eye contact. 'Can't say.'

Can't or won't, I wondered.

He hunched his shoulders and lowered his face over the table. We all huddled in. 'There has been,' he stopped and looked left and right, 'a higher than average incidence of boys who have disappeared in this region. You're aware of this of course?'

The others seemed to be, though I hadn't heard about it. I wondered if they'd been on the phone to Monty on the way up. Slightly annoying.

Gareth produced a manila folder and laid it on the table. 'You can have this,' he said. 'But burn after use.'

'You're kidding,' I said.

He just gave me a look that was like 'Seriously?' and then slipped out a map. There were half a dozen red crosses scattered up and down it. 'We've not had much luck tracing them. Of course, there are always runaways – those who go to Leeds or down to London to discover the streets aren't paved with gold. Nearly eighty per cent of cases are resolved within twenty-four hours. The majority within a week. Two per cent of people go missing for longer. With kids, fifty per cent go missing for less than eight hours, eighty-one per cent for less than twenty-four hours, and ninety-eight per cent are found within seven days.'

'We're familiar with these statistics,' said Sam. 'Jazz was in the two per cent who aren't.'

Gareth removed expression from his face. 'And this is what our people here have turned up – stats and patterns about that two per cent. 'Cept round here, we got 3.5 per cent. More than average. Don't sound much, but it's significant. They're mostly boys. I got them to look at instances around the year 2000. Though obviously there's some gaps – files have been lost or mislaid prior to digitisation. But there are some "missings" from 1997 through to 2006 which may be of interest to you. And we had another couple last year. Still not found.'

Michael shuddered at Gareth's use of 'interest' but if the agent registered it, he wasn't letting on. The big guy drew our attention to a cross on the map. It was against a small town north of Waketon. 'This one here,' Gareth tapped it. '2002.'

'Close in chronology,' Sam muttered.

'Boy went missing from a bus stop, we think. Although there was a sighting of a young lad getting into a white van. But we don't know if it was him or if it was connected. Witness statements are hazy.'

A white van? I looked at Sam. His face didn't change. I supposed there were a lot of that type of vehicle around. But hadn't Clementine, the librarian, mentioned sightings of a similar vehicle in Godalming?

Gareth pointed to another cross that had been heavily underlined in red biro. His voice was breezy, but his brow was lined. He wasn't immune to horror – part of him was feeling it.

'Or he might have,' he said and cleared his throat. 'He might have got on the bus here,' he tapped a cluster of roads that converged in the town marked Criggthorpe. 'Could have got dropped off somewhere, en route and *then* gone missing. Bus driver couldn't remember the kid at all, so we don't know. No real CCTV then. Anyway, the alarm wasn't raised till the twenty-second of July. Two days after his last sighting.'

'What was his name?' I asked.

He poked his finger at a village north of the M1 as it began to curve west. 'Spenser Graham was thirteen. Young for his age. Sad case. His type of background is not uncommon in these cases.' And he described it.

As he spoke, my fingers began to twitch once again towards the glass. Spenser's home life was indeed, very similar to Tuey's, or Stuey as he was known – a tapestry of unintentional neglect and dysfunction brought on by addiction. You couldn't help but feel the despair in the lives that Gareth was describing. People who thought we were all born equal just didn't have a clue.

I found myself drinking quickly, gulping down the thick liquid as if it was water. We all had it in us.

Anyway, as a consequence, I finished before the others and made a point of asking them if they wanted another drink before I went to the bar.

Sam gave me a look of disdain, but I extricated myself with speed. I didn't want to hear about these cases. I probably should have made myself listen, but while Gareth had been talking a sense of foreboding had crept over me, a thump of depression, and I found myself briefly wondering what good could come of this. Were we really on to anything or were we just acting out some psychodrama on Michael's behalf?

There were a few drinkers at the bar waiting to order. As I fumbled in my handbag for my purse, my fingers knocked into the three little bottles I had purchased at the services. I'd forgotten about them. The lemon oil 'Invigorates, refreshes and eases tension' as I recalled. Well I could certainly do with some of that now. I slipped a bottle out, twisted off the top and held it to my nose. Wow that was powerful. Yep, lemon. Biting but uplifting too. Summer lawns, Greek trees, Pimms, homemade lemonade. I turned the bottle upside down on my wrist and massaged it in. The texture was thick. Almost as syrupy as the wine now churning in my stomach. I could smell the oil wicking out of the bottle, permeating the air around the bar, so fixed the top on and took out another. Citronella.

The oil from this one was slightly browner in colour. And the fragrance was different. Not like the candles you buy to put in the garden or balcony. Far more pungent. Less of a sharpness than the lemon. More complex in odour, as if it had a floral base and lighter notes over them. I touched it onto my other wrist and was so absorbed in the smelling of it that I didn't notice the barmaid standing in front of me, watching what I was doing.

'Puhwor. What's that?' she said. 'Strong perfume.'

She was at the end of middle age but dressed for youth, in a short denim skirt and tight festive jumper with flashing Christmas bell earrings. Her hair was dyed raspberry and enhanced by extensions. Didn't look too bad, I guess. Her eyes were also dressed with false lashes. The combination reminded me of a favourite auntie of my own.

'Essential oils,' I told her and offered my wrists. 'Citronella on this one. And here, that's lemon.'

She sniffed them both and backed away. 'My God,' she said. 'That right takes me back to summer. And …' she paused and thought. 'Now, who's that old bird what used to sell stuff like this at market? Always in here after trying to flog what she hadn't shifted. You know …' Seeing I had no answer she called to another staff member, roughly the same age and style, but who had blonde highlights and an equally festive wardrobe. 'Suzanne, come 'ere.'

Suzanne obeyed. 'What's up Kimmie?'

'Smell that,' instructed the first barmaid, Kimmie.

Suzanne sniffed my outstretched arms that were still prone, palms up on the bar.

'Ooh,' she said. 'What is it, Kimmie?'

'Lemon,' said the Kimmie barmaid as if she knew everything about the fragrance. 'What's the other one?'

'Citronella,' I told her.

'Citronella,' Kimmie told Suzanne.

'Citronella?' asked Suzanne.

Kimmie nodded. 'Put you in mind of anyone?'

'It do, you're right. Who was that funny old girl? Ancient. Proper blue-rinse brigade. Always damp. Smelled of dogs.'

'Dogs,' reflected Kimmie and stared at the ceiling.

'That's right. Half of mild after market on a Friday?' Suzanne asked. 'There was a tragedy wasn't there? One of her boys, the twins, got drowned or sommat?'

'Aye, that's right, Seth weren't it?' Kimmie asked herself. 'She used to come in here, didn't she? Tried to flog her potions if I recall?'

Suzanne nodded. 'Smelled like that.' She glanced at my wrists. 'The potions. Wondered if she made them strong to cover up the smell of the dogs. Funny old bird.'

'You're right,' said Kimmie. She poked her tongue out over her lips and squinted as if looking somewhere very far away. 'Old Annie MacAllister, weren't it?'

Suzanne snapped her fingers. 'You done it. That's right. Old Annie MacAllister.'

'Why does it remind you of Annie MacAllister?' I asked.

'The potions. Smelled like that stuff you got. Same combo,' said Suzanne. 'She always reckoned herself a bit of a witch.'

My antennae twitched. 'Reckoned she could do love potions too,' squeaked Suzanne. 'For a price. D'you remember Maurice from Osset? Did the fruit machines?'

'Oh yes,' said Kimmie. 'Fancied Dot from Agthorpe.'

'That's the one. Used to buy litres of the stuff. Kept Old Annie in mild for years, I reckon.'

'And it smelt like this?' I said and waved my wrists about.

'Oh no, not the love one. The jungle potion. She said it kept the mozzies off. Family recipe she reckoned. Quite effective some said.'

How damn interesting. Here we were in a place that had a history of missing boys – yuk – and someone sold this potion that smelt of these scents. All of which were associated with the colour yellow – yella yella. 'So lots of locals bought it?' I asked.

'A fair few. Some of the regulars. Bought it just to get her off their case. But there were a couple of 'em used to swear by it. A couple of brickies, folks who worked outside. There was a tree surgeon too. Used to buy it regular.' She shook her head slowly, wondering at it.

'Do you know their names?'

'Who were they now?' Suzanne put her hand to her chest. 'No, not right now. Let me think on it a few days and it'll come to me.'

We hadn't got a few days and I was impatient. 'Is there anyone here who'd know?' I looked around the bar.

'Annie would. Though she's not been in for a while now. I thought she'd carked it.' Kimmie was as tactful as my auntie. 'She had to be in her late seventies/early eighties. Sprightly as hell, mind.'

'She local?'

'The family had the pink farmhouse. Out by the old colliery. Odd sods, they were. The old man popped his clogs after the twins were born. Tobias and Seth. Poor Annie had it tough raising them two on her own. Hard work, kids are.' I nodded and glanced over at Michael. He was still deep in conversation with Gareth. Kids never stop being kids to their parents. The labour of child-rearing and caring didn't end. Not even when they vanished.

'Yes, I suppose so,' I returned, letting her know I didn't have any myself. 'Is the farmhouse nearby?'

Kimmie nodded. 'Not far out. Go east from here then take the first road that leads south …'

'Oi, I'm about to die of thirst here.' A bald man down the bar was impatient to be served. I'd monopolised them for too long.

Suzanne tutted. 'All right Tommy, coming. Keep your hair on,' she sniggered and left us.

'Look,' said Kimmie and scribbled on a beer mat. 'Holling Lane. Look it up. Now what'll you be having?'

When she went off to fetch the order, the bald man at the bar squinted at me.

'You looking for Toby?'

'Toby?' I said.

'Tobias MacAllister? The pink house?' he ventured. Then without waiting for an answer went on. 'In prison, last I heard.'

'Oh,' I said.

'Armed robbery.' Tommy continued.

Ah, perhaps I wouldn't go there after all.

Tommy read my face. 'Oh he were harmless, pet. Didn't take part in the hold-up. Got tricked into being the getaway by some ne'er-do-wells out Knottingley way. Lost control of the car. Hit an old man. Killed him. It was an accident, though. Toby were a nice enough lad before he fell in with those wrong 'uns. Bit simple, I always thought. Went down for quite a stretch.'

'But he's not likely to be there?'

'Don't think so. Armed robbery and manslaughter. That's going to be a tough sentence.'

'But Annie might be?'

'She would. She'd be there. I haven't seen her for a while, happens,' he said. 'But she'd be getting on now. Might be housebound.'

'Do you know her number?'

He laughed. 'Old girl wouldn't have no mobile phone. Not sure if she even had a landline.'

'Right,' I said and nodded as Kimmie blustered back with the drinks.

'I'll tell you who might know 'bout her, mind,' she said to Tommy. 'That doctor what was always in here.'

Tommy frowned. 'I can't recall ...'

'What was his name? Big thick glasses.' She made circles with her hands and put them over her eyes.

'Oh! I got it!' Tommy slapped his hand on the counter. 'Him, what was always on about the power of plants. Was he a real doctor anyway?'

'That's the one. He was real, I think. Had a practice, maybe still does, up on Bullring, next to Pie and Mash shop.' Kimmie grabbed a teacloth and wiped her hands on it. 'That's right. We used to laugh about him, didn't we? Because of his name – Doctor Foster. Had family down south. Somewhere like Gloucester too.'

Tommy laughed. 'But he weren't no Suranne Jones, more's the pity.'

Doctor Foster, I thought. Had family down somewhere that sounded like Gloucester. Could that be Godalming? They both begin with a 'g'. Ohhh. Coincidence? I was sure the doctor who attended Pearl had the same surname? He'd been odd and rather hostile, I thought, when I met him in the Whites' narrow hallway. Though Foster was a common name. I tried to order my thoughts. This Doctor Foster, even if he wasn't the same one, might have some of the potion, though. That could be useful. Might know who else had bought it. A tingling in my tummy suggested that this could be worth pursuing. If I was indeed listening to my gut. Which I had decided to do.

So, if I had time, I concluded, I would make myself pop into the surgery, see if there was a picture of this so-called Doctor Foster. Perhaps there'd be a resemblance. I hadn't seen Pearl's GP for long. But I could remember him, I was sure. And if there were any similarities then I could go and see him, come up with some cock 'n' bull story about my dad being an old friend of his or something. Feed the information I gleaned to Gareth. It was a plan. Sort of.

When I returned to the table, the agent was answering a volley of questions. There was no way I could get in. I'd have to wait for a pause before telling the others about my findings. Though to be honest, I knew it was a long shot. However, if Doctor Foster *was* the same person as Pearl's

GP, and *had* bought the potions, then that was something. I didn't know *what* exactly but there was a link. It was entirely possible, I thought, having more experience now with the tricks of the mind, that Pearl may have picked something up subconsciously, clues, little ticks that she had put together about this man, her doctor, and was reaching out to tell someone, us, by way of her near-death dreams.

Across the table, Sam was intense, all sweaty and flushed with alcohol. He was moving around a lot, fidgety, over-animated. A lump rose in my throat and a well of feeling opened in my stomach. I didn't want to give in to it because we were focussing on his brother. However, I realised then that I was going to try and hug him tonight. If I found Old Annie perhaps, I could purchase a love potion to speed things along.

When Gareth left, I waited for Sam and Michael to calm down so I could tell them about the doctor and the potions.

Duly the opportunity presented itself.

Concluding their discussion Michael and Sam suggested we set off tomorrow morning to see Spenser's surviving aunt in Criggthorpe. Sam suggested we should arrive around lunchtime to ensure she'd be up and about. One line of enquiry would be to try and find out if her nephew had struck up any new friendships or altered his routines at all before he disappeared. We should ask where he had gone, record the places that he had visited. No one had looked into the case with much detail since that initial flurry of investigation back in 2003 and the police hadn't been hot on obtaining CCTV or getting the sightings investigated. There had been a double murder which had redirected resources. With no body, no motive and no suspect, as in Stuey's case, it was eventually presumed he had run off. Not to London but to Leeds. Or Scotland, where his father had moved to. His face was circulated on the missing lists but that was about it. The parents also thought he might have done a runner. The mum persisted with the police until she died thirteen years ago.

I agreed that we should start in the estate where he lived. And we all settled down and decided to leave mid-morning. I wanted to mention the doctor but thought I'd start with the potions first and produced a couple of the bottles out of my handbag. 'These are essential oils. There's a woman who makes love potions and "jungle potions". Apparently, people round here referred to her as an old witch …'

My phone buzzed. It was face up on the table so I couldn't avoid seeing who the message was from. 'Oh,' I broke off. 'It's Monty.'

Both Sam and Michael looked from the bottles to my face.

'Go on. Could be important,' said Michael.

'Open it,' commanded Sam.

I pressed pause on my narrative and sighed. 'Located Big Ig,' I read out. 'Not in the country at moment. Returning next year. He has agreed that once he's back and sorted he will see you. I'll be in touch.'

'Wow,' I said, louder than I meant to.

'Oh.' The disappointment in Sam's voice was crystal clear. 'Is that all?' And his face and shoulders sagged. 'I thought it might be significant.'

I took a deep breath in and sucked in the sudden coldness at the table.

Significant?

Jesus.

'Who's Big Ig?' Michael asked.

He was, in fact, the previous head of a British Intelligence department, who was likely to have some information about the circumstances surrounding my mother's death. I'd been trying to secure an interview with him for ages. I didn't answer Michael. I was so consumed by fury my tongue was tied. Did my family history not matter then? Was my family history insignificant?

For God's sake.

'How rude,' I muttered under my breath. But neither man heard me.

Which was apt because for the first time I was realising that Sam was deaf to my needs.

And to think – I'd been on the verge of wanting to seduce him.

That could wait, for sure.

The only person that Sam cared about was Sam bloody Stone.

CHAPTER TWENTY-THREE

Another hotel. Another part of the country. Another night of whirring emotions.

Those Stones.

Okay, okay, I understood that the vanishing of Jasper Stone was a deep wound. I did, I did, I did.

I understood that Pearl's revelations, the discovery of Stuey, the discussions with Monty and Gareth – I understood that all of this was re-opening those sores, summoning up old ghosts. That it was painful and consuming.

But *my* mum had drowned.

DROWNED.

And although it had happened thirty-three years ago, it was news to me. A recent shock. It had spun my world.

And we still didn't know who was responsible for her murder.

My MUM!

For Sam to dismiss all of this with an 'Is that all?' Well, it hurt.

I couldn't get over it.

And now I couldn't stop thinking about it. Not that I really ever stopped, to be honest. Sam knew that. We'd discussed it.

He understood that I couldn't let the mystery go. He'd even helped me organise my thoughts. Together, just a couple of weeks ago, we'd even drawn up a list of known facts.

I'd listed them on the inside cover of the mustard-coloured journal of Celeste's. I could see it in my case poking out from underneath a gold lamé jumper, its mustard cover glowing. Without further ado I went and plucked it out, returned to the bed, took a sip of my wine and opened the cover.

There it was, the list. I put my finger to the first line and read:

1. Araminta de Vere stated she'd bumped Celeste's car down the bank that led into Piskey Brook.
2. However, according to her statement, the car didn't go into the brook. It hit a tree. There was 'a bang' then smoke started coming out of the bonnet. Araminta de Vere took me out and left Celeste and the man who sat beside her in the passenger seat (also unconscious).
3. Only one casualty reported: 'Celeste Strange of Adder's Fork drowned in Piskey Brook'. *Not killed from a collision with a tree.*

The section underneath was titled 'Questions'. Then another list:

a) How did Celeste get from the bank into the brook?

b) If the man in the car was Danton, why didn't he help Mum?

c) Where did he go?

I thought it likely that Big Ig might have one of those answers. As one of Monty's predecessors, he would have had some knowledge concerning what happened to the daughter of one of his operatives. I had an inkling that even Danton's visit might have sparked an alarm bell in Septimus. Perhaps he had told Ignatius of it. Whatever, my gut feeling told me that it was worth pursuing an interview with the former head of whatever government department Ignatius had overseen.

There was much to think on.

Much.

Which possibly required more time than I was giving it at the moment.

Maybe I should leave Sam and Michael to their investigation and spend my energy on my own familial mystery.

The pages before me flamed with brightness, calling me to them.

I flicked through them and began to read again:

18th of December 1982

I am happy! My heart wants to sing.

When I think back to last week when I laid this spread, it all seems so far away. Another part of my life. So much has happened since. I had never come across such a name as Danton before. Now it is all I hear. All I wish to say. I want it on my lips always.

The Empress

Just a week ago I could not conceive the reason for The Empress appearing in the spread. But there she was, crowning me, in 'aspiration', my best possible outcome. I imagine the card that appears in this position drops a hint about your situation and what may resolve it. And I was thinking, back then, when I turned her over – The Empress? My aspiration? That is not right at all. For a moment I considered the possibility she appeared for someone else, that perhaps these cards were coming out with a message for some other petitioner, perhaps a person close to me. Could she be of pertinence to

Daddy? It is unlikely but conceivable that he may have become involved with someone who displays Empress-like qualities – a nurturer, a woman who is gentle and warm. I couldn't think of anyone, but there is much about his life that I do not know. Since I was little I have understood that some things by necessity, must remain hidden. Certain aspects of his life, in fact, require silence under the Official Secrets Act. So it may have been someone relating to that part of his work which I must never know.

And yet now I have met Danton the significance of The Empress is as clear as a crystal blue sea.

For he has made me blossom. And I bloom now as I look upon the card again. Though I am not as beautiful as my mother once was, I share certain attributes. The Empress, like Mother, is a voluptuous woman with wavy hair. There she sits, in the centre of a woody glade, holding her sceptre high. Behind her the forest quivers, full of life. She looks ahead to a field of golden wheat that undulates in the soft breeze. Wheat = agriculture, fecundity, harvest, according to Great-Aunt Rozalie. She was the one who taught me the Tarot as a child.

'The Empress is a fine card, Celeste.' I can see her holding it up to me in her gnarled and bony fingers, asking me to tell her what I saw.

'A pretty lady.'

'That's good, but there's more.'

As an adult I can feel the card with my heart. And I know that this 'pretty lady' emanates peace and wisdom. You can tell from her face.

It is a card that encourages the petitioner to both give and receive pleasure. Something, according to my dear aunt, us Brits always had problems with. That was the older generation though. I don't.

On The Empress's head is a crown with twelve stars. Hint, hint. The twelve signs of the zodiac, twelve Olympian gods, twelve months, twelve animals in the Chinese years too. It's all about the cycles of life.

Look at her sitting in that 'love' chair or throne. It bears the symbol of Venus. Goddess of Love, creativity, fertility, beauty and grace.

Hah! And to think I had it down for someone else. What a laugh! Nothing could be more appropriate.

He has just left you see. And I am basking in the afterglow. Outside my window, little white flakes circle down from the snowy sky. It is cold but his warmth stays with me, trapped between the sheets.

Oh, I really did not want him to go. I have never met a man like him before: vigorous, robust, energetic and impetuous, stormy. He makes James look like a gauche schoolboy.

When we dined, Danton knew several wines on the list, and he chose well. Too well. Later we drank more than we should have done, when I invited him in for a nightcap.

We raided Daddy's bar. He liked the brandy. We both liked the brandy. I'll have to replace it now. I brought down records from my room and we danced till the small hours. And then, it must have been something I said, because he got upset, so I hugged him and, well … then it all happened. We kissed. We didn't stop kissing. We were upon each other hungrily. I tugged him up the stairs into my room and he did not resist. I laid him down in my bed and kissed every part of him. Then he kissed every part of me.

We didn't sleep till dawn.

He is lovely. And handsome and intelligent. And, and, and, and ... now he is gone. But, dear heart, he said he would be back. Soon. It is a matter of urgency, he told me in hushed breaths as I laid my head on his chest and he stroked my hair, and of such great magnitude that he must return home with the knowledge he now has.

To Brussels.

To his wife.

There. I have written it, so it is in the open now.

Yes, he has a wife.

He tells me they no longer live together. Do I believe him? Yes, of course. What's the point in not believing what he says? He made me promise not to speak of this. Or the conversations we have had. Nor of his child, Leo, who is ill. He has a disease the name of which I do not remember. Danton spoke it but I am not fluent in French.

And Leo, well, this is why he is here in England. Danton seeks something from a family. The Almas. I'm not sure what – our languages failed us at this point. Something medical. These Almas own something, I think, that may be able to help. They can heal. They have a special gift which helps them do that. Danton is desperate and hopes to help Leo in this way. Or at least prolong his life.

But time is passing. Leo's mother does not believe in medicine or somesuch. She is trying to cure Leo with prayer. Sounds like she's in a cult.

Leo is not getting better. In fact, the child gets sicker by the day. And that's why Danton left and why he must return. He has been too long away.

So noble. So honest.

But he will be back. He promises that. And I believe him. What else is there to do?

CHAPTER TWENTY-FOUR

When I woke up, I felt differently about Sam. Not in a bad way.

Deep down inside I knew he wouldn't have meant to upset me. He was perhaps just tactless. Too consumed by his own internal struggle to realise how he might have sounded. It was clear that he was focussed on his brother and that he and his father were both determined to make sense of what happened to Jazz.

It would be very true to say that, in the past, he had been thoroughly supportive of me. So it was time for me to repay the favour. And if that meant overlooking the clangers he dropped then so be it. I need to rise above it and be graceful. To draw in a touch of my biological mother's qualities.

When I drew the curtains, I was surprised to see the sun nudging over the horizon, shining low over the crisp white land like the orb in The Empress's sceptre on the card Celeste had drawn in the journal.

She had been very happy. Though, I have to say, it did feel intrusive poring over her journal. I don't think she would have imagined that, all these years later, her daughter would be reading it. But there you go. I had. And it had opened up a window into what she was like and into this Danton too – the tall dark stranger with the exotic accent. I think because I had never met her, the intimate parts weren't too bad. I wouldn't want to read anything Mum, I mean Maureen-Mum, had written about Dad, Ted-Dad. Bleah. That would be odd and a bit weird. In fact, even thinking about it just then made me shudder and I cast my eyes to the window to distract myself from the thought.

I could see snow-topped hills and fields that suggested open land and country. Which was kind of unusual considering this Holiday Inn was right in the city centre. It occurred to me Waketon wasn't very big at all. You'd have to be so high up to see the foothills of the home counties in London. Probably on the London Eye or up the Shard. And yet I was only on the fifth floor here. The countryside was on Waketon's doorstep.

Which actually gave me an idea.

We had agreed to meet in the lobby at 11a.m. But if I was quick, I could make amends for being abrupt and annoyed with the Stones last night.

Hastily I threw on some clothes, an extra jumper. Then I packed my case.

On a whim I took off my practical Ugg boots and swapped them for tan cowboys with rhinestones and gold-tipped points. They weren't gold of course but they looked pretty good and they had a bit of a grip on the sole. If the snow receded, I'd think about trainers. Though I was no longer fond of them. There had been an episode back in the summer which had made me re-evaluate that whole mode of footwear.

Cowboys it was.

I stuck my fingers through the straps and pulled them on, wrapped myself up in a thick parka with a fluffy hood.

Thinking I looked suitably attired for whatever the day might throw at me, I left the room.

Jeez – if only I'd known.

In the lobby the poor receptionist sneezed and moaned as she wiped herself down. She could have been anything from forty-five to sixty. It was difficult to tell really because of the uniform and also she looked well ropey. Her searing red nose was slightly damp, and had flakes of skin dangling around the nostrils. That was one *bad* cold.

'Could you keep my case till I get back?' I asked, ducking as she sneezed into a hanky.

She squeezed the tissue together, which made a muted cloggy noise, and then stuck it up her sleeve.

'No problem, love.' Cough, moan wheeze. 'I'll put it in Left Luggage with the rest.'

She hobbled out from behind the reception desk and put her germ-ridden hands all over my pull-along.

When she returned from the cupboard, I pointed to the road outside. 'Do I get to the Bullring up here?'

'That's right,' she said. 'Only five minutes' walk, if that.'

'Thank you,' I said. 'Looks like you could do with visiting a doctor yourself.'

'Ooh,' she said and dabbed her nose again. 'I'm getting

worse minute by minute. Sandy's in at nine, though – she'll take over. Then that's me for the day – bed, hot lemon and honey.'

'Or a hot toddy,' I said.

'Ohh,' she said. 'The thought of it, noo.'

I wished her better and left her to it.

The snow had a light thaw going on but it remained crunchy. Temperature-wise it felt a smidgen warmer than last night. Though it wasn't freezing, it was still cold. I pulled my hat low down over my eyebrows and walked up past the shops – those that were still in business. There was a lot of peeling paint and dusty windows. An air of stagnant disappointment lingered in the narrow roads. If southern high streets were on their last legs, this one was gripped in the throes of a death rattle.

It was a shame, as this high street was very much the geographical centre of things, its high-reaching Victorian architecture stately and impressive.

I came out into a sloping piazza-like square that showed more signs of bustle. Hot dog vendors readied their van, a mobile chip shop fired up its stainless steel fryers. One old man in a flat cap bending over a giant barbecue stirred his pan and sent into the air the sweet woody aroma of roasting chestnuts. A few stalls decked with Christmas decorations, cards, tinsel and wrapping paper seemed to already be doing a good trade with the early birds. And, as if we needed reminding, over by the medieval cathedral a middle-aged man with a microphone and an old-skool ghetto blaster was belting out Bing Crosby's nostalgic classic which was perfectly appropriate given the twinkling white vista of the day. I dropped a pound into his hat as I passed and wondered if I should do my bit to keep the high street going and buy some wrapping paper for the presents I had back home. Maybe. I'd think about it after I'd found the doctor's.

A signpost up ahead pointed out the cathedral and indicated that Bullring was just left, round the corner. In the other direction was a brand new shopping complex with lots of big names, which I imagined siphoned off the lifeblood from the old centre's shops.

What will we do when our high streets close, I wondered? Will we sit by our computers all day and then go to bed? Will we Skype people with a drink instead of joining them in the pub?

I always preferred shopping in actual boutiques and markets to getting online stuff. My figure, I'm privileged to say, is unique. Unfortunately, dress sizes these days have shrunk. Certainly, high street retailers take little note of the fact that fully grown women have more curves than eight-year-old girls and that some of them there curves can, at times, need some upholstery. A little bit of support in the boob area, extra uplift round the derriere – these things do not go unappreciated. Plus, big bums were in fashion at the moment – so you didn't necessarily want to minimise them. And, put it this way, I certainly wasn't backwards in pushing mine forwards. If you know what I mean. Anyway, point is, that I need to try stuff on before purchasing. I'm sick of posting online shopping back. Steve and Nicky, at the Adder's Fork corner shop were trying to get a licence for Royal Mail or something, but since the main post office shut, you had to go into Chelmsford for parcel post. And don't get me started on parking there.

I was still silently fuming about Essex traffic easing methods, or lack of, when I realised I had come to a halt in the middle of a concrete circle. Ah – this must be Bullring. Had to be circular, right? No bulls in it, mind. Only a statue of Queen Victoria looking very serious and imperial despite the traffic cone on her head and a puddle of vomit defrosting down one side of her plinth.

Beneath my feet were a pattern of spouts – some sort of street fountain which was presently frozen. Around the edges stood concrete seats, where I suppose on a pleasant sunny day you could sit down, relax and take in the sights of Paddy Power, Yorkshire Bank and a couple of estate agents.

I took stock of where I was. Behind the benches opposite was a green-painted shop. Outside it had a giant plastic pie with arms and legs and a flat cap pointing to a doorway. Kimmie had mentioned that Doctor Foster's practice was on Bullring, next to a Pie and Mash shop. My spidey senses told me that I was near the surgery. I am astute like that.

Unfortunately, however, the doctor's was shut. A sign on the door announced a number for emergency out-of-hours services and the regular times for weekday appointments. I craned my neck to see through the glass. Sometimes there are photos of the staff in the hallway. However, there was only a noticeboard with half a dozen of your usual NHS posters: 'Stop Smoking', 'Get your Flu jab' etc.

I took a photo of the phone number on the door and the website address that was listed. I'd look up the practice when we had finished in Criggthorpe. Shame I had nothing to show for my endeavours thus far.

My phone told me it was just past nine. Still two hours to kill till I met the blokes. I spied a cab rank to the north of Queen Victoria. Maybe I could get out to this pink house by the old colliery and back in time to meet them with a list of Old Annie's clients. Or would that be completely pointless?

Waketon was small. I figured it wouldn't take too much time. And Old Annie might be able to tell me about this Doctor Foster.

Yep, I made a decision. It was worth the gamble and what did I have to lose?

Within minutes I was in the back of a taxi heading for Holling Lane.

CHAPTER TWENTY-FIVE

The cabbie refused to take me all the way up the lane on account of it really not being much of a road. Not a proper one anyway. The blanket of snow was thicker here and uneven – pocked with dents and bumps, where underneath there would have been dips and puddles. In places the snow was about three feet deep so I could understand why he didn't want to risk the pristine veneer of the spanking new electric hybrid car that he had been banging on about for the past half hour.

I had been surprised on the way out, by how quickly the city gave way to the countryside. The rows and rows of houses, packed tightly in their long terraces, petered out once you got past the ring road and then the new industrial and retail estates. We had passed through a couple of suburbs, although they didn't look like suburbs. More like tiny towns in themselves. But then the cabbie had taken a B-road, and turned into a network of smaller country lanes. By the time we had reached the drop-off it felt like we were in another world.

The view over the hedges was grim and bleak. But there

was beauty in it. Here the land was wilder and more rugged than the flat countryside of Essex. Where we had sky, it was filled with hills, moors, quarries, all preserved in this crystalline state: dusted white against a sky that was losing its colour to a fast-approaching bank of clouds.

In the hedgerows, all was quiet, like the creatures who lived there had stuck out their heads and thought, 'Uh huh. Let's get back to bed – it's a nest day,' and pulled themselves back in and settled down under the birdy equivalent of a duvet. I didn't know what that might be, though. Stray feathers perhaps. Anyway, as I trudged further down the lane, I could see their point. The snow had fallen in drifts. Some came right up to my knees and over the tops of my boots. I could feel bits defrosting against the warmth of my jeans, turning them damp and cold.

Interestingly, there were no other tracks, which made me wonder rather grumpily if this sojourn into the Yorkshire wilderness was a waste of my precious time and money. If there were no tracks – there were no people. Although if Old Annie was indeed old, it was highly possible that she was sensible and wouldn't venture out on a day like today. I rubbed my nose and continued along the twisting contours of the small road, starting to wonder if I was ever going to come across signs of life. Above me a crow let out a strangulated cry. It glinted at something rustling in a ditch and dived for it. There was the yelp from an unseen small thing and the black bird disappeared behind a drift. It reappeared only seconds later with the small thing in its beak moving frantically, and took off over the hedge.

The clouds gathering to the south rumbled. I looked over and wondered if it was possible to have a storm in a snow cloud. Or perhaps this was another freakish symptom of the planet-warming apocalypse that we were staggering blindly towards. Michael would probably say so.

I rounded a kink in the road and was relieved to see a gate. Beyond it lay a small stretch of front garden and a house. Although it was pink, as either Kimmie or Suzanne had suggested, it didn't look anything like a farmhouse. Well, not my idea of a farmhouse. I'd pictured a wholesome plump building with eaves and storeys. A home with a large kitchen and boots by the back door plus a massive Aga for farmer's wives to cook their families' hearty meals. Though of course I was being sexist. I was quite sure it was also possible for farmers to serve up mung beans and health shakes and be female. So much social conditioning with this kind of thing.

But anyway, there was none of that to be had at what the sign confirmed was 'Parker's Farm'. A thoroughly dull name for a thoroughly dull house.

At the end of a garden path sat a squat sixties bungalow with a garage to its side and the roofs of outbuildings behind it. I unlatched the gate and made my way, slipping and skidding, to the front door. Should have packed some wellies.

The curtains in the front were drawn which didn't bode well. Though I thought, as my eyes left them and turned to the front door, one might have twitched. So I rang the doorbell.

A minute went by. No one came. I started to think about the warmth of the hotel and imagined Sam and Michael sitting in the bar having a cup of coffee. Michael would be ordering a latte and Sam would have his black. It was an enticing scene.

One more try.

I put my gloved finger to the bell and pressed it. Twice. Old Annie might well be deaf.

There was no answer. Okay, so this was going to be how my luck took me today. My dad would tell me I was on a 'hiding to nothing' with this one. I suppose it served me right for trying to look clever and find some clues to impress the Stone family.

I sighed and stamped the creeping cold from my feet. Then, just as I was about to either call through the letterbox one final time, or turn away, I hadn't made my mind up which, I saw a movement through the ridged glass of the front door.

A dark black fuzzy bundle appeared down the end of the hallway, then stopped.

I pressed my nose against the glass to see through the frosting.

The bundle must have clocked me, because it didn't move.

Perhaps she needed encouragement. Or to learn that I was a solitary female, not a rapist or con man or salesman or Jehovah's witness. I pulled my nose off the glass and rapped on it. 'Hello! Hello? Annie? Mrs MacAllister?'

There was a ruffling sound and more activity down the hallway, then the bundle got bigger, nearing the front door in large hefty strides. Oooh Annie must be a beefy old girl.

A pause, the scraping of several locks, then the door squeaked open.

That weren't no old lady there.

Instead I came face to face with a large shambling sort of man. A mop of nut-brown hair was threaded with grey. The badly cut fringe hung low into deep-set eyes and over the top of a bulbous nose. Mmmm. That cut and style had to be self-inflicted. I had a feeling that this man rarely hung out down the barber's.

'Hello,' I said with an amenable wrinkling of my eyes. 'I was wondering if Mrs MacAllister was in?'

The large male filled the door, full of squints and uneven looks. He cocked his head to one side and sized me up.

'Mmm,' he said, at last. 'I'm not Annie MacAllister.'

'Well, I can see that,' I said and laughed.

He didn't. In fact he looked slightly baffled. Then he shook his large shaggy head. 'That's my mother.'

'Aha!' I shifted my weight from one cold foot to another. 'Is she in? Can I talk to her?'

'No,' he said.

And that was the answer to which question? I wondered.

Best to be optimistic. 'Oooh, gone out in this weather, has she? That's brave. When will she be back?' I shivered as a cold blast of icy wind blew the lengths of my hair up over my ears.

'Back? Oh no, she won't be coming back.' The shaggy man grinned, exposing Jeremy Kyle dentistry. 'Come in for a second, pet. It's as cold as buggery out there and I can't afford to be letting all this heat out. Not with the gas being price what it is.' He shrugged. 'I come back to find they've put it on a meter. Didn't know that.' He turned and loped off down the hall.

I followed, quickly absorbed by darkness, and saw him drop his hand in a beckoning gesture. 'Shut the door will you, love? Costs a fortune.'

I did as I was bid and pushed it into place. Two automatic locks clicked down.

'They were saying, inside,' the shaggy man was mumbling, 'that it's the opposite of Robin Hood. Stealing from the poor to give to the rich – companies and shareholders and the like. They put me away, but them's the real villains.'

The bloke appeared a bit jumbled mentally. Put him away? What did he mean? Then I remembered – the bald bloke at Friar Tuck's had mentioned a son. He'd gone to prison, hadn't he? So, this could be him. I'd forgotten about that. Best to be quick here then. Straight in and out. Find out about the client list, see if this man's mother knew anything about Doctor Foster. Then bugger off and catch up with the Stones. Have a coffee to warm up and then get off to Criggthorpe to see the auntie of one of the potentially missing Spirit Boys.

'Highest rate,' the shaggy man was saying, 'when you have to buy it pre-paid, don't you know? Gas. It's daylight robbery.'

I pandered to him in the interim. 'Total rip-off,' I said as my eyes adjusted to the dimness. I was halfway up a dingy hallway with not much but a radiator, a shelf stacked with unopened mail and a carriage clock. There was mould growing from a corner of the ceiling. Plaster hung down. I think there might have even been a mushroom in there. A definite musty smell hung in the air. Everything looked like it needed a damn good clean.

'That's right,' said Shaggy Man with approval. 'A rip-off.'

I nodded.

'So,' he said and leant against a chest of drawers at the end of the hallway that was overloaded with free newspapers, circulars, flyers, leaflets, junk mail. 'What were you after Mother for?'

The warmth in the air defrosted my cheeks. I rubbed my hands together and wiggled my toes as much as possible given the fine arrow point of my boots. 'Yes, well I wanted to enquire about the lotions she makes. I was in the pub last night, the Friar Tuck. The landlady, Kimmie, said—'

'Kimmie's not the landlady,' Shaggy Man interrupted. 'There's only a landlord. Mike.'

'Sorry – I meant … this was one of the ladies serving behind the bar,' I said. 'I don't think it was a Mike.'

'Did she have red hair or brown hair or blonde hair?' Annie MacAllister's son asked.

'Red hair,' I said, then wondered if I'd got the barmaids the wrong way round. Maybe Kimmie was the one with blonde hair.

'That's Kimmie,' he confirmed. 'Unless they got new staff. Everything changes,' he said, then winked. 'Well, not everything. Some people stay the same. Don't they?'

I didn't know what he was getting at, so just said, 'That's right. But yes, Kimmie. Yes, *she* remarked that my perfume was very similar to a lemony, er,' I stopped suddenly unsure if I should use the word potion or not. Some people took offence at anything that suggested hocus pocus, and generally I thought that word did. 'A lemony mixture that your mother sold.' I could quote Kimmie, however. 'I think she called it Jungle Potion?'

'Jungle Potion?' he repeated and smiled, as something in his memory stirred. Woah – seriously – what quantity of teeth were inside that mouth? Too many for sure. And I'd never seen a set that particular shade of mustard. This was a man in need of a good whitening kit. Opened up possibilities actually. Maybe I could do a swap with him? I think Auntie Babs had some kits knocking around at her salon. A potion for me, some teeth rescue for him. It would be the tip of the iceberg with regards to MacAllister's monumental grooming needs but at least it would be a start.

Shaggy Man angled his head again. 'You got problems with the midges?' His volume went up.

I wasn't sure what he meant, so made it my turn to stare blankly.

'Mozzies.' He made a high-pitched whining noise. 'Gnats, waspies, nasty winged beasties.' Then he put his arms out either side of his body and flapped his hands. I wondered, for the first time, if he was not quite the full ticket.

'Oh right,' I said and copied his hand gesture. 'Is that what you use it for? Mozzies? Mosquitoes?'

'Aye,' he said and pushed his fringe out of his eyes. 'T' flies. We're all of a bother with 'em here on the farm. Ma reckoned there was something in us skins, me and our Sethie.'

'Sethie?' I said and tried to peer into the rooms at the end of the hall. Was there another goon in the wings?

'Me brother,' MacAllister junior said. 'But our favva, he had something in his smell too what attracts the damn peskies.'

'Oh,' I said.

'The lotion, see,' he went on. 'That's 'ow it works. Covers up your scent. It's like a trick, see. It only hides us smells. Covers them up. Cos us smells are what them bleeders like.'

'Aw,' I said. 'Got it. So, it's like going into "stealth mode". Hiding in plain sight. How clever.'

'It is,' he said and narrowed his large round eyes. 'Why you asking 'bout cream if you don't know it's for mozzies?' Now his brow wrinkled.

Good question. What would Auntie Babs say? I wondered to myself. Then bingo, I had it, 'I run a salon and I'm looking for treatments that don't include man-made chemicals. Some of them these days they've got all sorts in. You wouldn't believe some of it – parabens, sheep fat – awful. When the girls mentioned your er, lotion, I thought I'd try and track it down.'

Mr MacAllister just stared at me from under his furred brow. Maybe he didn't know what a salon was. But surely his mother would?

'Might your mother have a lotion I could buy? I'd like to get some testimonials about it. Maybe she's got a list of the people she sold it to?'

'Oh no. Doubt it. She wouldna kept a list. She weren't like that.'

Bugger I thought. 'Do you know if she sold it to a Doctor Foster?'

He shook his head. 'Can't recall.'

'Is it possible for me to see her? Does she live locally?'

His hair flopped about. 'She can't help you no more neither. She passed away two years since.'

Oh well, that put paid to that.

Damn.

It was a dead end.

'I'm sorry to hear that.' I dipped my head at Shaggy Man.

Damn. I'd have to get back onto the internet and try and contact Foster through the practice's site. Or else I'd have to phone the surgery. Oh God – then I'd have to navigate the receptionists, which was never easy nor fun. Bugger.

I sighed, trying hard to conceal my irritation. 'And there's definitely no one else who might have made something like this apart from your mum? No friends of hers she might have given the recipe to?' Might as well make sure.

Shaggy Man had picked up an envelope from the shelf and was staring at it. 'Oh, did you hear *she* made it? Did Kimmie say that, did she?' He seemed bothered by this.

Mr MacAllister looked up at me. 'No, *she* didn't make it. Wouldn't have had the patience.'

'Oh,' I said, deflating even lower. 'That's a shame.' There, that'd teach me. And I had been thinking I was on to something here. Perhaps my intuition was no different to anyone else's. I had been barking up the wrong tree. 'Where did she source it, your mum? Internet, I suppose?' I asked vaguely. At least if he gave me the name of the supplier maybe I could track them down. Though it was an Olympic-length long shot.

'Oh no!' Mr MacAllister said with a good level of energy and pride in his voice. 'This has been a family recipe since way, way back. My aunt made it. She was the herbalist in the family. All the recipes, they came from my grandmother. But Aunt Vinnie was the one what mixed them up. She had a knack for it. Ma just sold them.'

'Oh?' I said brightening. This changed things slightly. 'That's great! Does Aunt Vinnie have an address?'

'She does,' he said. 'But it won't do you any good neither. She passed over twelve month since. Sometimes it happens like that, don't it? First one then the other? Didn't go that road with me and my brother, Sethie. I wish it had, mind. He was the good one. Not me.'

'Oh right,' I said, voicing a tone that was sympathetic but distant. I did not want to get distracted down the 'dead brother' route. 'Sorry to hear that. So your Auntie Vinnie – where did she live? Do you think she might have left some stocks? I'd really like to try Jungle Potion.' Perhaps we could send a sample to Monty see if he could do some detective work.

'No, no, she didn't,' he said. 'I've not seen any. I've only got a few bottles of the stuff left meself. I've been through the house. She left it to me, you know.' He jutted out a dirty thumb and jabbed his chest proudly. 'Only surviving relation.'

'That's a shame,' I said, meaning the samples.

'Not really,' he said. 'It's worth three times as much as this.' He picked up a letter and waved it at me. 'I'm going to move into it. I'll start again. This house is falling down. Hers is much better. Worth a bomb.'

'Oh – your aunt's place? Right. Is it …?' I stopped myself from saying 'a proper farmhouse'. Instead, 'Is it a big house then?'

He shook his mop of hair about excessively and for a brief moment I thought I saw his eyes glint. But then he gave a goofy shrug and it disappeared. 'No,' he said. 'Just a bungalow – smaller than this.'

I wasn't really interested but I said, 'Smaller?' Because property's usually not smaller *and* more expensive, right? Well, not in Essex. So I said, 'Really?' and tried to look animated.

'Oh, it's not here,' he said. 'Not in Waketon. It's near you.'

That was a surprise. How did he know where I lived? 'Near me?'

'That's right,' he poked a grubby finger in my direction. 'Judging from your accent. You're a southerner, aren't you?'

'Oh,' I said. 'Yes. Essex.'

The conversation was on its way to boring. Was I now going to have the obligatory discussion about how properties were worth more down south because of the wages, about how we were all soft and Tory and la-di-dah and all the other regionally related stereotypical bollocks I'd come across whenever I ventured north of Watford. I stifled a sigh. Best to listen, look interested, bounce out a few farewells then bugger off before the snowstorm came and the cabs refused to venture beyond the comfort of the city.

'No,' he said firmly. 'Not Essex.'

'All right.' I smiled.

'Auntie Vinnie,' MacAllister continued, as if correcting me, 'lived down your way.'

Yadda yadda, I thought. Act nice and pleasant. Wind it up. 'Is that so?' I got my phone out to unlock the screen. My fingertips prickled. 'Where's that, then?'

I felt in my pocket for the cabbie's card. I'd taken one when I was paying.

'Down your way.' he repeated. 'Like I said – south.'

'That's right.' I took off one of my gloves. 'But not Essex?'

Ah! There it was! My fingers, more sensitive now the glove was off, inched around the lining of my pocket then hit a rectangular cardboard business card. I sneaked it out and waited for the right pause so I could look back down and check the number.

'Oh no,' he said. 'Further south than that.'

Quick glance – 01924 – yep. That's was the regional dialling code. This was the right card. 'Oh cool. Whereabouts?'

'Just outside godawful Godalming,' he said.

'Yeah?' I said, eyes fixed on the card.

But my throat tightened.

Down in the bony chamber of my ribs, my heart contracted longer than it should.

I was caught in an instant, unable to exhale.

And for that long moment my mind boggled. I felt my brows scrunch into a frown.

Slowly I brought my head back up. 'Godalming?' I asked.

'Godawful Godalming,' MacAllister laughed.

At first I laughed back. But it wasn't normal. Instead, the

noise coming out of my mouth sounded high, strained, a bit mad.

So I stopped.

And swallowed. 'Oh.'

I always thought that, should a situation like this arise, I would react in exactly the right way. After all, it was one of the reasons I watched so many horror films, to get the practice in. To observe the instance of realisation when our heroine suddenly learns who the baddie is. That's why I was always directing her on the screen, screaming for her to 'get the fuck out of there' or 'run!'

But she never heard me.

She just stood there like a bloody lemon.

A lemon.

Lemon.

Yellow.

Yella.

Washing up liquid.

'Ding dong,' went my brain as my memory rang a bell.

Repels flies.

Lord of the Flies.

Clang.

Disappeared in Waketon many years ago.

Then a gap.

Clang.

With no abductions.

Clang.

And this man has been to prison.

Clang.

But now he's out.

Clang.

And in Godalming.

Clang.

Where …

Stuey …

Ding, dong, bell …

Holy crap, I thought, so this is what happens to the girls in the films. For as my mind raced through all of this, my body was … 'paused'. Like someone had pressed a button and frozen me, mid-pose – mobile phone in one hand, business card in the other.

In the dimness of the narrow hall, Shaggy Man's eyes skewered me.

Something in them had changed.

I let a laboured breath escape.

'Do *you* know Godalming?' he said ever so gently.

'No,' I said. But my stupid voice cracked. My throat, you see, had become painfully dry. It gave away too much.

I took a step back stiffly towards the door and sent him what I hoped might pass for a warm smile.

Too late.

He had seen my reaction.

In some way, God knows how, maybe through some primal telepathic means, he understood that I *knew*.

A rush of chemicals exploded through my veins – an equally primitive response – and surged throughout my motionless form. Instinct was warning me I was in the presence of a predator.

At last I swallowed, breaking the paralysis, and spun round on my heel.

'Nah,' I repeated. 'Don't know it.' Please God I thought, let my casual words reassure him.

The front door was just two metres away.

I wanted to walk but I couldn't control my limbs now all the adrenaline was pouring through them. Instead I lunged towards the front door, clocking the two automatic locks.

I stretched my arms out as I ran. Fingertips connected with the button on one lock.

Click.

It opened.

Now there was just the second to try.

I reached lower towards it but as I did, I heard his footsteps pounding the lino behind me.

My fingers brushed against the brass but didn't grasp it.

Slid off it.

My phone clattered to the ground.

Ooof. The bulk of his body powered onto my back. My stomach slammed against the glass. Any more force and it might shatter. Good. I pushed back against him and jabbed my elbow into his gut, just as Sergeant Trooper had instructed, really more angry that he had got to me before I could open the door. He dropped back. Fumbled. I took the opportunity to hurl myself at the glass.

Then something woolly came over my nose.

A sweet clogging synthetic smell.

No, I was not having this. 'GET OFFFF MEEEE.' I smashed my fist into the glass pane. It did nothing but hurt.

His other hand came round the front of my parka and grasped my coat collar, pulling my torso back into his.

'No, no, no!' I protested, my voice rising as my brain struggled for a reasoned approach: self-defence – yes, they told you, that was it – I raised my knee though I was off balance and stamped hard on MacAllister's foot.

He let out a howl. One hand dropped away.

But the other stayed with the fabric pushed hard against my lips.

'Get off m …'

Dizziness came fast. My limbs dropped away.

I never completed the sentence.

CHAPTER TWENTY-SIX

Civil society is a brittle filigree based on the collective agreement of citizens to observe and adhere to certain rules. When we walk down the road, we do it on the understanding that we, and others populating our high streets and boulevards, will not run amok, smashing windows, taking what we like and stabbing each other.

When we swim in a pool, we do so with the understanding that other swimmers will not grab hold of our hair and hold our heads underwater till we gurgle our last breaths.

When we visit someone's house we do so on the understanding that the householder will not drug us, haul us out of said house and chain us up.

It just takes one person to defy this unspoken pact and the whole house of cards falls to the floor.

One minute you're thinking about snowstorms and coffee, the next … thwack … all change.

Of course, I *wasn't* thinking about any of this when I opened my eyes.

I was more concerned with why the light hurt. Even

though it wasn't very bright and didn't really illuminate much.

It was just there.

A vertical oblong of illumination. Slender. Slightly bluish. Indistinct.

Like a tube of dying neon.

Fading into oblivion.

And what indeed *was* the light doing? Standing on the floor? Over there. At the side of the door.

Which was also on its side.

Everything was entirely the wrong way round.

Or was it?

I rolled and hit my head on a hard surface. A wall.

A wall over my head? That must be a ceiling?

Hang on just a goddamn moment – no – it was me on the floor not the oblong!

I wasn't standing. I was lying.

Why was I lying? Was I tired? Had I lain down to rest?

I paused for a moment and tried to reflect.

Yes – my brain was torpid, eyelids heavy. I *was* tired.

At least that was one thing sorted out.

And it wasn't the oblong that was the wrong way up. It was me. And anyway the oblong wasn't an oblong at all. It was a slither of box-shaped light that was crawling through the bottom of the door.

The door.

Oh yes.

A door.

That rang a bell.

Somewhere in my head.

There had been lots of bells, a whole cathedral of them ringing.

No wonder it ached like it did.

I took a breath.

Now where was I? What was I doing?

Oh yes, that's right – I had been reaching for a door.

Was that correct?

I think so.

But not this one.

The door I had been reaching for was painted white. Badly, true. But it was still white. With glass. This did not have glass. And it had locks. Lots of them.

The wood on this door was unpainted. You could see the grain. It was coarse and lumpy. And scuffed. It had been re-patched and mended several times with floorboards and nails. But it didn't look like a front door. It looked like … I don't know. Not like any doors I had in my house or the museum. There were cracks in it which showed minuscule glimpses of grey light. At the bottom there were lots and lots of ominous black marks. Smears and smudges. As if little feet had kicked it repeatedly.

A flush of cortisol issued through me.

I sat up.

Damn. Shouldn't have done that so quickly.

The throbbing in my head amplified. Oh God, my brain was badly swollen.

Had I hit it?

Nah. I was more likely to be suffering from the effects of a hangover.

Although – my vision pulsed – this was a baddie indeed.

The room swam and pitched.

I put out a hand to steady myself and felt my bumpy knee.

Oh God. Something was burning my stomach lining.

I burped.

That was a mistake.

Nausea reared up and threatened to engulf me.

And just like it did when I'd overdone it on the Buttery Nipples, a familiar flush of heat rose up through my torso.

Sweat broke out in my pits and across my forehead.

I wasn't well.

My stomach buckled.

Here we go, I thought, as the undigested Holiday Inn breakfast coursed up my gullet through my mouth then emptied over the hard cement floor.

Survival instinct kicked in and I pushed myself onto my knees and continued to vomit it all out, leaning on my knuckles until the spasm died.

Christ.

This couldn't be a hangover …

No.

But my head sure was pounding.

I wiped my mouth and eased back onto what I now realised was a mattress.

My whole body was slow and lethargic.

For a moment I rested my back against the wall and groaned.

I wasn't well at all.

As my stomach climbed back down, my lungs tried to regulate my breathing the way Sergeant Trooper had taught me all those years ago when we had the training. At least it seemed like it was a long long time ago. As I was doing that, I let my vision roam across the vom and noted just beyond it a tray. A thin lightweight brown affair, the kind you got in school cafeterias.

Odd to see it there.

Odder still to realise that upon it stood a glass of water. And even more perplexing was the small saucer of pink wafer biscuits.

I sat still for a moment waiting for the room to cease its relentless orbit, then when I thought my sense of balance had more or less restored itself, I summoned enough strength to lean over and fetch the glass.

The cold liquid soothed my bile-raw throat.

Oh my God that was great.

I was, I realised, very thirsty.

But I decided not to gulp the whole glass down, just in case my stomach in its fragile state rejected it again.

So I sat back and again leant against the wall, which I realised now was very damp and very cold.

Still, I wasn't yet ready to move again. My head was groggy, though the spinning was easing.

Slowly the room settled.

The room? I thought.

What room?

Why was I in *this* room?

If indeed it was a room.

Like the door, it didn't look like any room I was familiar with. The floor beneath my feet was hard and at the same time bumpy. Uneven. Bits of gravel and dust were scattered across it, along with the odd strand of straw. The place had a draughty outdoors feel to it. The walls too were uneven, daubed with rough white wattle.

Heat was coming from somewhere. It wasn't much, but I guessed it was taking the bitterest chill out of the air. Although I was not untroubled by the coldness, I was also strangely not troubled by it. Parts of my body, you see, were colder than others. Perspiration continued to pearl upon my forehead.

I cast my eyes around and saw that over in the far corner, nestled in the thickest of shadows there was a glow. A single circle of pale amber light. A plug-in heater?

It didn't feel right. Why would you have a heater in this place? A barn? Was that what I was in? Perhaps a section of a barn, because opposite the mattress there was a wall or partition with another door. This was also closed. When I had mustered my energy, I'd go and try it. Though I kind of knew it was going to be locked.

With effort I focussed and pushed back through the miasma curdled there that was obscuring natural thought and logic. Where was I? Think, Rosie. Where have I been?

With Sam. Looking for someone. His brother.

Then nothing.

So why was I here?

I'd been looking. Looking for …? No, couldn't remember.

There had been a pub, and an agent. Gareth. That's right. Looking for Sam's brother. And the hotel and then sleep. Journal. Bullring. Ah yes, yes, yes, the doctor. No, what was it? The cab. The pink house, the man – MacAllister.

Oh shit.

The Man.

What had he done?

Had he put me here?

I tried to think, but there was nothing in my brain apart from a vague sense of simply talking to Mr MacAllister.

Shaggy Man.

He must have got me. Put me in here.

But why?

I sat back.

It would come to me.

In the meantime, I had to work out where 'here' was.

Above, the roof was vaulted, fashioned from beams and rafters. Between the cracks there were strips of sky. Not many. But enough purply grey light escaping to illuminate my prison so that, now my eyes were adjusting, I could take in my surroundings.

One side of the barn or shack had been built with concrete breeze blocks and not professionally. The bricks were messy and uneven. Splodges of cement had squeezed out during the making and not been wiped away but had solidified mid-drip. Strands of hay and dirt covered the floor. Part of the roof, where the wood had caved in had been covered, patched with corrugated iron. It was damp, with a vague bestial tinge: animals had lived here once.

Another wall, where my mattress lay, might have been part of the original structure. It was bumpy, made out of wattle and daub. Moss and a brown-coloured mould sprayed up from the bottom.

It suddenly occurred to me that I might be being monitored. I looked around for a recording device but could see none. That man had not been able to master a gas meter so it was unlikely, I supposed, that he'd be au fait with audio/video gadgets.

That was something to be grateful for, my whirring mind suggested.

I tried to still my thoughts and remember what Sergeant Cooper had told us during our training session. It wasn't clear. 'Try to remember the sounds,' she'd said of hostage situations. And more. But I couldn't remember. I should have paid more attention.

Never mind. I'd do it now.

I opened my brain and pulled out a sheet of paper. Then I made a fuzzy inventory.

1. Wind. It was shrieking around the barn getting in through cracks. Outside it whistled down through thoroughfares, perhaps the outbuildings I had seen over the top of the pink building. For I had a sense I wasn't far from the farmhouse.
2. No traffic. We had been told to listen for it. Even if there was none, it was significant. There was none.
3. Wind up high. Rustling of trees. Not near, but not far away either.

But that was it. There was nothing else.

I had a feeling it was late afternoon.

Shit. *I* was late. Sam and Michael would be waiting.

I tried to struggle up. Again the room surged.

Not a good idea.

I sat back down and felt the fabric under my bum. A threadbare mattress with a soiled duvet covering the end. At the other an aged pillow was covered in dark stains. Oh God – had my pristine hairdo been resting on that?

I felt myself gag again and told myself not to be so superficial. I needed to remain calm and focussed.

There was nothing else in the room but the tray, the biscuits, the heater, the mattress and me. Two of the walls were covered in scraps of carpet and, were they egg cartons? Why would you stick egg cartons on a wall?

Why would you drug someone?

But egg cartons?

I took another swig of water. Perhaps if I had something to eat my brain might start to work.

I picked up a stale wafer and before I realised what I was doing I'd wolfed down the lot.

That was foolish. I had no idea when I would be fed again. Probably better to make them last. And I might be sick again.

Ah well. It was done. I wasn't going to beat myself up about it. Not when there was someone not very far away who would be happy to do the job for me.

Gradually and very carefully I levered myself to my feet.

It was difficult, as I still wasn't entirely steady. But I managed in the end and was able to hobble over to the door on the interior wall. I turned the handle and pulled.

Nothing. So I turned the handle and pushed. Still nothing. It was locked. Of course. I banged my fists on it hard.

'Help!' My throat was sore, hoarse from stomach acid. 'Let me out! They'll be coming for me soon, do you hear? Let me out.'

I punched the door hard. But it did nothing but bruise my already aching hand and the effort was exhausting. No one was there.

Perhaps the other door with the boards. This was the exit to the outside, I was sure. The tiny cracks that criss-crossed it were letting in light.

I took a couple of lurching steps towards it, two metres, maybe three, but just as I was about to reach it one of my feet pulled back. It was strange. But then everything was strange. My head was feeling weird again. And now my legs were starting to disagree with my brain.

I looked down and didn't compute the scene.

There were two feet there, weren't there?

Blimey I was still woozy.

But that sight was well weird: one of my feet had lost its cowboy boot. I was pleased to see I still had a sock on, even though it was halfway down my foot. Very inelegant. I was less pleased to see a manacle clamped round my ankle.

What was that doing there? I wouldn't wear that, would I? I wasn't into steampunk. Or bondage. And there was no way I'd attach it to a rope? What the …?

I moved back and leant against the partition wall. Using it to keep me steady I managed to slide down and get into squatting position. Then, despite my best efforts, the room began to swing again. I tried to ignore it and followed the rest of the rope. It snaked across the floor then disappeared under the interior door into the next room or whatever was through there. There were no locks on this side of it. Which meant there had to be some on the outside, though because, when I tried to pull it, it still stayed firm. For fuck's sake.

I was locked into this room.

This room that was starting to rotate again. My vision was diminishing. My eyes getting heavier.

I stared at the mattress and hobbled back over, just managing to crawl onto it before I passed out.

CHAPTER TWENTY-SEVEN

I had another one of those moments where you wake up and don't know where you are, then get confused. But instead of realising that you're in a hotel or in a witch museum you remember you are in a barn.

Trapped.

Held.

Imprisoned.

Despite very slowly tumbling to this conclusion, I was too dopey to feel alarm or fear. My mind, slack though it was, registered a mild concern but was preoccupied by other issues like, what was the time?

I was facing the wall. I could see indentations and bumps above it. A plaster comb trail where someone had tried to be a bit fancy with the plasterwork then given up.

Though it was dark.

Dark outside.

And dark inside.

Yet, I could see the scrapes in the wattle and daub. There had to be some source of illumination in here.

The heater?

I began the monumental task of summoning my mental and physical strength to turn my body over to face the partition wall.

Why was I still so groggy?

It must be the middle of the night.

No heater.

I let my head flop against the edge of the mattress.

No saucer. No empty glass. One full glass.

No puddle of vomit.

Someone had been in here.

But I was thirsty. I reached out and took the tumbler then clumsily propped myself up on my elbow.

It tasted good. Clean. Unlike the rest of me. I took it all down and replaced the empty glass on the wooden tray.

After that exertion I had to rest again.

My eyelids began to sag.

A dull thread of consciousness in my brain became aware of a shuffling sound.

It was coming from the other side of the partition wall.

What was that? I thought, laconically.

The cattle lowing?

I was in a barn after all, wasn't I? Was I?

And my eyes dragged themselves towards the wall. Ah, so that was where the light was coming from. A gentle amber sledge of light was sliding under the gap between the door's ragged bottom and the concrete floor.

I thought I heard a cough but I couldn't be sure and couldn't be bothered enough to pay attention to it. Darkness was pulling me to it again.

Good.

Gloom.

Blackness.

Nothing.

Nothing.

Sleep.

Sh.

And then … awake.

Again.

Not dark now.

Not entirely.

Oh yes. Here I was back on the mattress, drool spilling out of the right side of my mouth. Soggy. Hair stuck to my face. Back here. In the barn.

But it wasn't as dark.

It was alight. Rosy. Illuminated more vividly.

I put my hand to my forehead. It ached. My brain did too. I rolled onto my back. Through the cracks in the ceiling the sky was black.

What time was it? Had I slept through one night or two?

Why was I here?

Shaggy Man.

What was he going to do with me?

I shrugged and lolled onto my side. Best not to think about that. Not just yet. My neck ached a little bit less than it had done before. I wiped the drool from my mouth and realised that the door in the partition wall was open.

The sight quickened my heart. And I guess the heightened

flow of blood must have sharpened me a bit because I was then able to sit up without too much effort.

If I leant to my left I could see inside the adjoining room. Though the light in there was so bright and golden I had to screw my eyes up and was only able to open them bit by bit so it didn't hurt.

Something in there that was radiant.

I put a hand up to shade my brow and after a few minutes was able to make out a platform in the room the other side of the door.

There were people there, on the platform. I squinted. They were sitting round a table, like they were having a meeting. It was very still. Apart from a whole load of candles, their flames dancing about in the drafts, lending the figures a sense of slight animation. But they weren't moving much at all.

I pushed myself up from the mattress. My feet and legs ached, my muscles had cramped. Senses were not a hundred per cent, still slack.

It took me a while longer to stagger to the doorway. I still had enough wits about me to slide my eyes round the frame and see if Shaggy Man was lurking. My focus was coming and going: objects, perspective, colours were blurring then sharpening then blurring again. I tried to get hold of the room, though my vision was slippery. So I waited for a moment. Nothing moved.

So no Shaggy Man, which was good.

But … wait … there were people there?

Were they praying?

A couple had their heads bent.

They looked like … wait … were they *asleep*? In their chairs?

One chair, though, was empty. Waiting for me?

And, now I saw, a step up to the platform. That was it. That was what I needed to do. Get up on the platform and shake these people awake. They could help! I couldn't overpower Shaggy Man on my own. But a group of us?

With determination I widened my eyes and tried to make them out in more detail. They were boys. But there was a taller one, I thought, next to the empty chair. In the centre. Wearing a grey jacket? A suit, was it? Well, then yes, he'd be the one to wake. Then he could help me and get me out of here.

That was it. That's what I needed to do.

I pushed my heavy body off from the frame and staggered three, four, six, eight steps to the platform, pausing to gather my breath.

The smell of the citronella mixed with another pungent aroma hit me. What was that bitter sensation? I recalled it from the salon years ago before they made Brazilian treatments safe. Something like formaldehyde. The pong was clinical, like cleaning products or air fresheners. Then it came to me – Washing Up Man.

Oh God. That's what he smelt like – washing-up liquid. This is what Stuey had been trying to communicate. It kept the flies off. He was master of them – the Lord of the Flies.

I had thought it referred to Shaggy Man, but what if it referred to the boys in here? And they, these boys, could help me.

The effort to walk was severe. My breathing was still shallow, coming in laboured bursts. But I was going to do this. I needed to wake them up and alert them to my capture. This was how I would get out.

A couple of focussed actions and I was up the step, dragging my manacled foot, pulling the rope with me.

On the platform I leant my palms against my thighs to support my upper body.

'Listen,' I called out to the man across the table. My voice rasped. I hadn't realised my throat hurt so much till I used my voice. 'This man's got me in there.' I gestured back to the dark room. 'I'm not meant to be here. You have to get help. He's tied me up.' I lifted my foot as high as it would go and pointed at the rope. 'A bleedin' manacle!'

Nothing. No response. Not even a sigh.

I tried to scan his face, which was weird and blurred, and squeezed my eyes to bring it into definition. 'Did you hear me? You have to help me do something before he gets back.'

Silence.

This was wrong.

Was he in on it too? Part of the abduction ring?

I needed to get closer, so grabbed hold of the edge of the table and clambered on to it. I could feel the rope pulling, but it hadn't yet reached its length so I slid my body over the top, pushing away the detritus. What was this? Paper plates, plastic knives and forks, serviettes? Like a tea party. A mad hatter's tea party.

Regardless, I motored on. No time to think about that

now. Slide, push, glide. Over to the main man, the largest of the group sitting there.

I moved in close but couldn't quite reach him – a sudden yank halted my progress.

'OUCH.'

Metal bit spitefully into the flesh around my ankle.

The manacle. Damn.

Its rope had drawn tight.

Pressure on my bruised tissue.

That was as far as I was getting.

But I wasn't giving up.

Instead I raised my body onto my elbows and threw my head up to look him in the face. 'Please! My name is Rosie. You need to …'

Oh fuck.

His face.

His *face*.

What was left of it.

Skin grey. Doughy in parts, papery at the sides. The lips had diminished, shrunk, contracted into a rictus grin that revealed his uneven, broken teeth.

The eyes were lifelike, but false, like the museum dummies at home. Bright and glossy, one of them had sunk into the socket and stared up, unseeing, at the roof. The other, brown, stared to the right.

Christ.

He had once been human, that I could tell, yet the spirit that had animated this young man had long since gone. He was no more. Only a shell. A cipher of a person.

A mummified corpse.

And those eyes, those eyes … As I looked into them one of them moved. Swivelled slightly to the side, and stared

straight

into

mine.

Jeeeeeeeesuz.

Was it …?

Was it alive?

A wiry thread slithered out of the socket.

Holy Mother of Christ, what fresh horror was this?

The eye seemed to bulge, its glassy pupil rotating upwards.

Beneath it the thread grew longer. The end felt around on the mushy lid, then suckered on to a section of stumpy eyelashes. A beady head, glossy black, followed. Tiny eyes. Spindly legs. Finally, a thorax emerged from under the polished glass globe. The beetle scuttled across the mummy's cheek and disappeared into his ear.

I knew I was screaming and that I shouldn't make a noise but I just couldn't stop.

My stomach flexed. Bile spewed up out of my gullet across the tabletop.

Clamping a hand over my mouth I clambered back, away from the horror show, sending the candles, the plastic plates on the table, the knives, the cups, flying. Over the table, back, back, back, away from the monstrosity, paddling on the slippery surface until it ran out and I fell off, landing with a crack on the wooden floor of the platform.

I didn't notice any pain but climbed to my knees, gripping

the ledge, forcing my legs to stop trembling and take my weight.

It was then that the full horror of the scene revealed itself.

The others, those around the table, I saw now, were in the same state as the mummified young man. Though different sizes and not so well preserved, I could see they were boys, or had been. Someone had dressed their corpses and propped them on chairs. In death they had been fashioned to play a role in this deranged tableau.

I was still screaming when I got back to my mattress.

Everything was dead.

Nobody came.

I don't know how long it took for me to calm. I don't remember much about it. My hysteria and fear must have overwhelmed me because when I finally came to my senses again I was in the dark once more.

The door was closed.

At least that was something.

I was thankful I didn't have to look upon that awful sight.

My heart was still hammering, but it was less of a gallop.

'Oh my God.'

What was going on in the amber room?

Why was it?

Jesus Christ – was Shaggy Man planning to add me to his ghastly tableau?

Couldn't. Surely not.

I made myself not think on it.

Instead, I held my mind tight and pushed it to other

areas, and the fact that I needed to GET OUT OF HERE. And as the thought possessed me I crawled over to the other door, the one patched with floorboards and nails that led outside. But I couldn't make it all the way there. The rope tightened.

I lay down and reached my hands to it over the grimy, grit-strewn floor. There was enough of a gap beneath the door to get two fingertips under. I gripped it as hard as I could and gave it a tug. It moved fractionally. I tried again. Same result.

This wasn't going to work.

I scrambled back and looked at the wall with the egg cartons.

Ah, now I remembered about them. My friend Cerise had done some backing vocals for a band once. The recording room was covered with similar stuff. It had a function, now I recalled. It soundproofed the place or reflected the sound-waves or something.

But that didn't stop me screaming in the vain hope my pleas might carry through the cracks. Through the night air.

But to who?

This place was remote.

In frustration I tried to hurl myself back at the door. But I couldn't make it. The rope held me back and instead I fell.

My hands fisted. I pounded on the floor. And I hit it and hit it and hit it.

It was solid and hard.

Soon I realised my hands were bleeding. The sense of pain was dull, though. I didn't care about it. I just wanted to get out of here.

Some part of myself began to wail but another told it not to.

I clamped a hand over my mouth to hush me and took myself back to the mattress.

'Shh,' I said gently, trying to coax a sense of coherence back into my brain. 'Take it easy. Breathe.'

So I did what I was told and took deep breaths down into my ribcage, feeling my lungs inflate.

'That's right. Slowly does it.' I told myself.

'It's difficult, though,' I replied.

'I know.'

'But,' I became firm with myself, 'you totally need to settle and get your wits back, so you can work out how the fuck to get out of here.'

'I know.'

'Okay then, so breathe.'

'I *am* breathing. But I'm scared.' I whimpered. 'I don't like this.'

'I know.'

'Separated, imprisoned, far far away from the ones I love.'

'Uh huh.'

'Not knowing whether I will live or …'

'I know.'

'Feeling that strange, crazy threat out there.'

'Yes.'

'I want my mum.'

'Then think of her.'

'Okay.'

'What did she say?'

'Say?'

'Next?'

'When?'

'In the journal?'

'Oh you mean *that* mum?'

'Yes. That one. Celeste. Come on. What did it say? You've read it so many times.'

'There was a card sketched out.'

'What was it? Now think!'

'A Christmas Card?'

'Really?'

'Yes, she talked about Christmas and that it was fun and that she saw in the New Year with her dad …'

'It wasn't a Christmas Card.'

'No, it was a tarot card. One from the spread. All of those cards, they meant something to her. And the next was …'

'Think!'

'The next was, The Hierophant.'

'Signifying what?'

'Signifying the Pope – tradition, family values, law and liberty, obedience and disobedience.'

'That's a lot.'

'It is.'

'And why was it there?'

'I don't know.'

'How did she start that entry? How? Remember, Rosie. Put your mind to it.'

'Yes, yes. She started with, with, "I have been too old."'

No. 'I have been too long …'

'Too long away, dear Diary …'

CHAPTER TWENTY-EIGHT

24th of January 1983

The Hierophant

I have been too long away, dear Diary. You must forgive me.

It has been a busy time. As Yuletide always is.

We passed the solstice and my time became busy with preparations for Christmas Day. I hadn't thought about presents but then it seemed I had to. Daddy told me we were to visit Uncle Sixus on Christmas Eve.

It meant I didn't have to cook. So I didn't put up a fight. We took the train there and didn't return till after New Year. It was cool. I was able to avoid sitting in front of the telly with the rellies on New Year's Eve and instead hit the Half Moon with Lucinda and Piers and Lucinda's new boyfriend who turned up earlier in the evening. He was quite horny but not a patch on Danton. And though I did get a few drunken propositions around midnight, I politely declined. The evening wasn't riotous, but it was sociable, and I felt like I had needed something like that. Sometimes Adder's is too quiet for me. It's a relief after the hurly burly of London. But oftentimes it is sleepy. And provincial. I won't stay here too long, methinks.

Anyway, Daddy didn't mind me going out. I did my daughterly duties and suggested that he joined us at the pub but he pointed to Uncle Sixus and Auntie Mary and announced they had guests coming for a 'grown-ups only' dinner.

I know he finds such annual celebrations rather forced. Or at least, they present rituals that he must endure with a smile hung upon his face for myself and Teddy. I suspect, however, he ruminates over Mother dear. Her absence. God knows I've wondered many times where she is. One whisky-addled moment, years ago when his guard fell away, he told me he could not give up on finding her, though he no longer thought her alive. Such a sad face, when he said those words. Such a sad sad man. I promised him I would make it my mission to find out where she was, where she went. Though he shook his head and asked me not to.

I had forgotten that night. But now, as I write this, I believe I shall consider the question once more. It is the new year, after all, and fresh resolutions are a time-honoured tradition. So yes, I jolly well will make it mine. 'Tis done. And now, I feel resolved to it, I know I will damn well find out what happened to Ethel-Rose Strange if it's the last thing I do. And Daddy will have peace at last.

Though, not sure how to start.

Teddy never says much about Mother, though he knew for her for those few years. Sometimes I am jealous of that. I can barely remember her. There is the portrait and a few holiday snaps, but not real memories to cherish. And Teddy does not like me to probe deep. He really is such a silly fish sometimes. Wouldn't come down to Uncle Sixus and Auntie Mary's. Though there is plenty of room here. One wing is completely unused. But no, Teddy and Maureen have gone to her dreadful sister, Barbara. I can just imagine what the Christmas celebrations will involve – party hats and the Hokey Cokey no doubt. I can't think on them badly as I know they are kind, but really – those people are vulgar. Still, Ted seems to like them.

I have already used some of the time spent with Lucinda and Piers to ask questions about my family. Just not Mother. No, I went further back. You see, Danton wanted to know about us. That gives me a kick. It's why I know he'll come back to me too. The night we had dinner in Chelmsford, which seems so long ago now, but that night he confided in me his conviction that Daddy knows more about the Alma Family than he is letting on. Danton wonders why he will not tell him about the Strange ancestry. I think, when we were on our main course he did tell me that he was directed to Daddy by another source, though I cannot remember who it was. A strange name. Something antique.

Danton wanted to know about our bloodline. He was quite insistent. And he wasn't interested in Daddy. Only Ethel-Rose. I was able to tell him about Aunt Rozalie and the Romanov family. That they had come to London when Rozalie was ten, Frederick, my grandfather, was eight. Mischa, the eldest, was thirteen. The parents had invested in a cigar factory.

His eyes had lit up at this news. 'Come from where?' Danton had asked. 'Do you know? Can you find out?'

'I've already told you,' I said, annoyed he hadn't hung upon my every word. 'Prague. I think. That is, Rozalie would tell me stories about the Prague Golem. So I think she must have come from there.'

His forehead had tightened over the brows. 'Were they Jewish?'

And I had shaken my head. 'Never had that impression. If she was, she wasn't orthodox. Rozalie was interested in astronomy and astrology. And she taught me the cards.'

'The cards?' A deep frown accompanied the question.

'Tarot.'

'Oh,' he said, eyes brightening once more. 'Who were her parents?'

I had a notion that the mother was Emma, but couldn't remember more. He asked me to find out, so I said I would, of course.

But when I asked, Daddy was circumspect. The Hierophant in my spread, I suspect.

Which is why I have sketched it here. And I think, perhaps, it is my father. Yes, in the main it has papal associations, and I know for a fact that Daddy has none. The Hierophant, Auntie taught me, is aligned with intuition and interpretation, which is Daddykins all over. But he, The Hierophant, also attends to the spiritual, and although my father would never deem his work so, I would. Religion, which the card embodies, suggests deep thought, knowledge and ancient sects. Someone who pays greater attention to details.

This is my father – Septimus Strange.

And the aforementioned Septimus Strange did indeed ask me why I was enquiring about my ancestry. Thinking on my feet, I told him that I was researching my genealogy. But I have a strong feeling he knew I was obfuscating. It was too much of a coincidence after Danton had turned up out of the blue and started asking him about the family.

Once I'd seen the look in his eyes, I didn't press him any further. He is shrewd and I cannot pull wool over his eyes. Instead, when I went to the pub, I got Lucinda and Piers rather pissed and asked if they knew anything. They didn't. It's the other side of the family. But they said they'd bring it up with their mum and dad. I told them to wait until we had gone. And to be subtle about it.

In the meantime, I will conduct my own investigation around Adder's. There are a lot of old-timers here, who knew Granddad and Granny and Rozalie. That's where I will start.

It quite excites me.

Everything does now.

CHAPTER TWENTY-NINE

Perhaps it was morning, though I could not tell for sure. My brain bulged against my skullcap, again. But I felt different. As if thinking about Celeste, reconstructing her diary, had cleansed my mind, straightened me out a little.

The room was brighter. It was daytime. Though it was cold. Freezing in fact. My fingers hurt from it. And the foot without the shoe, the manacled one, was numb. At the back of my mind, somewhere in a microscopic tatter of rationality clinging to my brain, I knew that the ankle that had been damaged by the rope, would be bruised and aching. But I felt nothing. And in this tiny sane place, I also understood, that this was a bad thing. Something to worry about. That I should start thinking about a plan.

Letting these faint but fresh thoughts muster me, I managed to upright myself. Though there were headspins and the usual nausea. But it wasn't too bad.

When I got myself steady and balanced I was able to look around. The black roof was letting in light through its cracks. I could see dust motes twirling in the air.

The heater was on.

But the connecting door was shut.

Perhaps I had imagined the horrors in there, I wondered. Although, at the same time, I knew I hadn't. Last night's vision had been too real, too unexpected and bizarre to make up. Those eyes were false.

One sliding out of the socket onto the embalmed cheek.

Ugh.

No, don't think on it.

But what about those others? Those gathered round the table? The young men – they too had been treated in some weird way.

My hands, before me, trembled.

I shouldn't think about it.

One thing at a time.

Take in your surroundings.

Be alert.

Look round. Look up. Look down.

On the floor I saw there was another dirty tray.

A different one.

Under the scratches and stains I could see it was decorated with a photo of three kittens in a basket. They were set beside a roaring fire, playing with a ball of red wool.

Why had he chosen that? Seemed cruel really, presenting such a warm and snug picture. When I was the opposite of cosy. It made me think briefly of Hecate and I wondered if Babs had managed to feed her. I hoped so. Sometimes Bronson was remiss. Although the Witch Museum cat did have a sure-fire way of getting what she wanted. That girl was a survivor.

Like me.

But even so, I wouldn't want to leave her for too long. She'd miss us. We'd only been away from her for a few days at any given time and now, we must have been gone for – I paused. How long? How long had I been here? A day? Two days? Three? Time held no meaning here. In this barn. In this freaking bat-crazy mortuary. Surely Sam and Michael would have missed me by now? They would be phoning around. Everyone would be alerted – the police, the airports, the coastguard.

I just had to stay alive till they found me. Shouldn't be too long.

I tried to focus and reach back into what arrangements I'd planned with them. Hadn't we agreed to meet up? The hotel. Yes, we'd said we'd regroup in the morning.

Which meant when I didn't show up, they'd start to worry. Spurred on by deep concern they would use their resources to find out where I had been. They wouldn't be fobbed off by Shaggy Man.

Sam and Michael had more sense than that. They'd suss it.

I tried to imagine what I'd do if Sam went missing.

Phone. That was it. The first thing I'd do was phone him.

I felt in the pockets of my coat.

Nothing. Not even the cabbie's receipt. Shaggy Man must have cleaned my coat out. Still, I had the other phone that Monty had given me. It was in my bag. I perked up and looked around for it, under the duvet and pillow.

There was nothing there.

He'd taken it. Of course he had.

I swallowed.

Fear was there, on the periphery of my senses.

It was growing. But it wasn't consuming me yet. Alone. In this room.

It was odd.

But at the same time I was grateful it wasn't encroaching, stupefying me, crippling my brain. Let this curious numbness stay there, I thought. Let it keep me numb.

I felt around in my head for how I was feeling. My senses remained dull.

Like being drunk.

The kind of woolly limbo you find yourself in, after too many Buttery Nipples.

And yet my mind wasn't severely encumbered. It was screwed, yes, that was true. But it wasn't as thick and clotted as it usually was when I was absolutely wrecked or totally hung-over. And, let's face it, I'd had a great deal of experience in that department.

This state was fine. I could work with it.

I had more going for me than Shaggy Man realised.

Okay, I thought, as I keeled over towards the floor. Let's use what we've got. Keen mind. Slightly blunted. But dopey body.

'Think massive hangover, Rosie,' I instructed.

Sunday mornings. Banging head. What helped?

The answer was obvious.

A fry-up. Full English with extra beans and sod the consequences for everyone else around me.

Though I didn't think Shaggy Man would be pulling out the silver service for his new guest.

However, I was becoming more centred. Sustenance was needed to speed on this process. And, actually, as wicked as he was, I observed that my captor had visited me again with just that. Food.

On top of the evil kitten tray, breakfast cereal brimmed in a bowl. Beside it a glass of water. And a cup of tea. Though it had an oily film. Still, beggars can't be choosers.

I reached for the mug.

'NOOooooooo.' A voice wailed from the shadows. 'Don't touch it.'

I recoiled, my back thrust hard against the icy wall.

Without intending to let it go there, my gaze jerked into the shadows beyond the heater.

Was there movement?

I couldn't tell. Squinting into the darkness of the corner, I tried to make out the owner of the voice. It wasn't deep. It wasn't Shaggy Man.

'Who's there?' This – my own voice – strangely alien: whispery, unused, the vowel sounds grating on dry vocal cords.

A shuffle in the darkness. Over there.

I let out a yelp.

'S'okay,' said the voice. 'I'm not hurting you.'

Knees up against my chest, heart thrashing about inside my ribcage, I chanced a peek into the shadows, unable to breath or speak.

'Don't drink the tea.' A pause. Scratching. 'It's got sleeping potion in it.'

And then, slowly, a head emerged into the halo of light cast by the heater. The face of a boy, dirty and feral. Eyes wide, hair matted. Then the body, encased in a knitted navy jumper, covered in dust and straw. So thin.

I stared at him.

He goggled me.

'Who are you?' I said at last, when I was able to master my voice.

The boy crawled in front of the fire and warmed his hands. 'He got me.'

'I can see,' I said, my voice strung tight and high.

'He got me too,' he repeated.

'What's your name?'

'Connor.' His teeth were white against his dirty face, lips plump, and extraordinarily red like roses. Matted dark, curly brown hair. Short, but came over his ears. 'What's yours?'

'Rosie.' I supressed the quiver in my voice.

Another prisoner. 'How long have you been here, Connor?'

He turned round fully and cocked his head to one side. 'I dunno.'

Shit, I thought. So I wasn't the only one. Had I disturbed Shaggy Man while he was doing … whatever he did to this boy? Or was about to? Oh God. I had to think quick. I was the adult and now I had someone else to look after. It wasn't just me. The thought was sobering. I shivered.

Connor sniffed. 'You're cold.'

I nodded.

'Come to the fire.'

I didn't do anything for a moment, then realised the good sense of it.

A couple of feet away from Connor, I held out my hands to the feeble bars. But, oh, it was good to feel heat.

'That's better,' Connor said. 'Warm yourself.'

Keeping my face pointed at the heater I swivelled my eyes sideways to inspect him. He was slight, with ragged jeans and tattered trainers that looked more like your old-fashioned plimsolls. A slight fuzz played upon his upper lip, making it difficult to guess his age.

There were a million questions I wanted to ask – why was he here? What had Shaggy Man done to him? What was the other side of the connecting door? How were we going to get out?

I didn't know where to begin.

And I didn't want to know half the answers anyway. So I said nothing.

After a while, I don't know how long, Connor said, 'So how did he get you? You're not his usual type.'

It made my innards tense and buckle – 'his usual type'. *Usual.* But I kept myself straight. 'I came here,' I said. 'I wanted some answers. Walked straight in.'

Connor made a sort of choking sound that I realised was a laugh. 'You spaz!' he said under his breath. I thought about taking issue with his terminology but decided that this was not the time or the place. No, first things first – develop rapport with fellow prisoner. And prevent creeping hysteria.

I clasped my hands together as casually as I could so Connor wouldn't see they were shaking.

Make conversation, Rosie.

'So,' I said and coughed to cover the weakness of my words. 'How did he get you?'

Connor shrugged. It seemed incongruous that he could do that given the circumstances, but he did. 'Hitch-hiking,' he said.

'Connor,' I returned without thinking. 'You shouldn't hitch-hike, you don't know who …' my voice trailed off. Such a warning was pointless now.

But Connor had got it. 'I don't know who might pick me up?' he said and laughed again, that rasping, dry sound. Incongruous. How could he even contemplate laughter in a place like this? 'Well, I've learnt my lesson now, ain't I?'

The boy had a point.

'I'm hungry,' I said.

'You can eat,' he began. 'But don't drink the tea. It's in there.'

I shuffled over and immediately began scooping grain into my mouth. My God I was hungry. It was only when I was halfway through that I realised Connor must be starving too. Mid-gulp I held out the bowl and offered it.

He shook his head. 'Nah. I'm all right. You need it more than me, it looks like.'

I wasn't sure about that but didn't require much encouragement and, after copious wolfing, finished it off with a good glug of water.

'Don't drink it all,' said Connor and put his hand out, as if to stop me.

'Why?' I removed my lips from the glass. 'Drugs?' Oh

bugger. Here I go again – I tensed waiting for my senses to dim.

But Connor said, 'No, that's okay. It's just you'll need it to get you through to the next feed.'

Good point. The boy was wise.

And once I'd finished and wiped my mouth, I leant back against the wall and put the duvet across me.

Connor watched me. I held up one end of it and said, 'Wanna get in? Just to warm up?'

The boy's eyes looked sad. He shook his head slowly.

'You don't have to come anywhere near me,' I said, conveying as much sincerity as I could without alluding to the fact that this kid's worst nightmare, somewhere outside, was indeed someone who would, very likely, come close to him.

Ugh. I shuddered again wanting to scream out at the top of my voice. But I didn't. I just said, 'It's freezing in here. Body warmth.'

'I can't,' said Connor. His voice wasn't angry or defiant, just despondent. He pointed to his leg and grappled in the darkness behind him. Light clanking sounds. Finally his hand lifted up a chain. 'Don't stretch as far as you.'

'Oh,' I said. 'Have you got a mattress?'

He shook his head. 'Just rags.'

'You want my pillow?'

He shrugged.

He was cautious.

Understandably so. I picked up the pillow, ignoring the yellow-brown stains on it, and chucked it across the room to him.

The pillow made a thunk as it hit the wall and dropped into the shadows of Connor's corner.

'Thanks,' he said.

'S'okay.' Tentatively, 'Have you been …' I nodded at the connecting door, 'in there?'

I had time to see Connor slowly bite his lip. It was an affirmation.

Oh God. The full horror of it came crashing back into my mind. Ugh – the scene, those bodies. The knowledge that Connor had seen it too was worse than depressing. It was depraved. And suddenly the awful reality of my position, of mine and Connor's, hit me like a brick to the brain. My hands sprang to my face to hide my weakness, stomach lurching to force out from my lungs a plaintive sob.

And it didn't stop. It just kept coming. Out and out and out.

The horror, the fear the grotesqueness, the danger – it all combined within me in a dark curdling scream.

I'd been doing my best to keep everything at bay, but the poor boy's face had opened up a crack, a fissure in my defence. A tsunami of emotion was sweeping me away.

I don't know when it subsided and came to its end only that at one point I fell back upon the mattress lost in its wave.

It was some time later that I became aware of the little boy cooing out words. 'Don't be afraid. It will be all right. We have to stick together and find a way out.'

At first it had no effect – I could only just hear him. Soon, though, my chest ceased its stuttering struggle and a quietness began to descend. A strange kind of peace – the realised inevitability of the convicted on the gallows, the capitulation of the drowning man who gasps in his last lungful. A curious state of mind but one that was welcome. Calm.

'Sometimes,' said Connor softly. 'He leaves the door open. When he thinks we're asleep.'

I wiped my face free of the tears and snot and tried to show him a brave smiling face.

His expression was full of curls and frowns of concern.

'Open?'

'When he thinks we're out cold, you know – from the potion. Or mibbe he forgets.'

'That's good,' I said. My eyes were swollen and feeling thick. I sniffed and tried to widen the smile. For him. For the little boy. Or young man. I couldn't guess his age.

I shouldn't have broken down like that. It was the last thing he needed. I had to be strong. I would be.

'But don't trouble yisself with it now,' he said. 'You've had a shock. Think about something good, so you can rest.'

'I don't know what.'

'I think about my mum sometimes.'

'Hmmm,' I said. 'She's never far from my mind.'

'I know how you feel,' he said. 'What's yours like?'

'I didn't know her,' I told him. 'Not for long anyway. But I've been re-reading her journal.'

'You have?' he said. 'Tell me.'

'It's a short timespan. December, Christmas. I'm up to February,' I told him. 'But it's odd. It might scare you.'

He scoffed at me again and cast his skinny hand around his corner. 'What's the worst that can happen?'

'All right,' I said.

'Tell me a story, tell me ...'

'It always starts with a card.'

CHAPTER THIRTY

20th of February 1983

Death

Death. The great equaliser. The grim reaper. Number Thirteen in the major arcana. Unlucky for some. Scary to others. Never fails to elicit a gasp from the petitioner when I draw the card.

But it is misunderstood.

This is not a bad card. It does not mean death literally.

Of course, in very few instances, it can.

It has other meanings – death is a leveller who none can avoid. It is a metaphor for the ending of things – one door closing. And we all know that when we hear the slam, another door opens. It is the end of a cycle and the beginning of another. Of course it cannot be dismissed. It foretells a major change ahead. And you may mourn what is left behind.

But, pictured in the card beyond the spectral figure on the horse, we can see the sun rising between two towers, heralding dawn. The birth of a new day. Rebirth. Ends and beginnings. And ***this*** *is the thing. This is why it came into my spread. I couldn't fathom it at first but now I can. For I am in a moment of transition. I am – wait for it – I am pregnant!*

I know it's a blessing which is mixed. Daddy, for instance, will not be pleased. And the Adders will not look kindly upon a single mother. If that is what I am to be.

Perhaps I will not. For I had a postcard from him, you see. He will arrive in London soon and wants me to meet him. No address that I could see on the card. The postmark was blurred, but the stamp was from Belgium.

And yet, and yet, I am happy. At thirty-two some would consider me 'over the hill'. I had not given much thought to motherhood. Certainly, I did not consider starting a family with James. Well, maybe in the first throes of love, our honeymoon period, when all my emotions were pumping away and I was not thinking clearly at all. But not in the middle nor at the end. No way.

And yet, here I am, and the thought of new life stirring within fills my soul with joy. Maybe this is the only way I could ever do it. With some autonomy. On my own. And sod everyone else.

Although, I also feel some trepidation. Not from Danton. Though it ails me to think so, realistically I know I may never see him again. Some men are like that. But a large part of me doesn't care. I can get through this with my beloved child. And Daddy will come round soon enough. No, I became anxious when I went into town. I had to. Obviously, I'm not visiting our local quack. Doctor Sullivan regularly holds court, in his cups, at the Seven Stars. For a double brandy or three he can divulge the most intimate secrets about his patients. We all know that. I am not about to spread my news yet. Discretion is key.

I located a drop-in clinic in Chelmsford and waited with three hopeful couples for my results. I'm sad to say, my courage for one moment did fail as I looked upon their faces. I was aware I had no husband to hold my hand and I thought I might lie and say he was on business. But I am made of stronger stuff. And the result, well, it was unexpected but not a tragedy. Though I could tell from the face of the nurse, who had looked with scorn at my naked ring finger, that contrition was required. I denied her and left with my head held high and a leaflet on 'options'.

It was when I reached the pavement and lit up a cigarette to calm my nerves that I suddenly had the oddest feeling that I was being watched. I put it down to the fact that I had been delivered of life-changing news. Sometimes that does happen.

But then at the car park I noticed a man lingering. I became aware of him snatching glances at me. He did not seem to be the usual Chelmsford type. Wearing a grey trenchcoat and trilby he loitered by the meter but did not put coins in. Nor did he smile back when I nodded his way, but turned away and did not move. I know that the forties style has come back in fashion again in alternative circles. Though I didn't get the impression he was into that scene. He was more square. No dyed hair, or make-up. Clean shaven.

When I parked up at the Witch Museum later a car drove past. Very, very slowly. I couldn't see who was in it, but as I peered into its dark windows the feeling returned to me again. With a tinge of danger.

Perhaps it is my paranoia mounting. My mind playing tricks on me. But all the same, I have decided that it will do no good for anyone to know my condition. For the time being I will conceal my pregnancy. It is best this way.

There are other things to think of. I have not yet started my investigations into Mother. And also Aunt Rozalie. I have been pointed towards Edward de Vere to seek knowledge in both regards. He knew her well. Apparently they courted. Before Daddy whisked her off her feet.

And Terry tells me his neighbour Albert might know something too. He has lived in the village all his life and was a gardener up at the manor. Terry tells me that not much escapes his eye. Though he is poorly. Cancer they say. Mr Bridgewaters thinks Albert will talk to me. But the poor man is scheduled to have an operation soon. After he has convalesced and recovered, Terry will take me to see him.

So there are many things to do. I shall not be idle!

But for now I await Danton's next communication.

I put my hands on my tiny bump of a belly and I tell my child I love it.

Things will be born of this. Not just the baby. I know it deep down in the quintessential part of me. My future has changed. Somewhere out there in the universe, the gears of Fate have shifted.

Daddy however, knowing none of this, wants my advice on the museum. He tells me I should do more, that I …

CHAPTER THIRTY-ONE

'That she what?' Connor asked.

I blinked my eyes. Daylight peeped through the cracks in the roof.

For a moment I forgot where I was, again. Then brutal reality fell upon me once more.

Connor was still in his place beside the fire, watching me with his black eyes. 'What did she tell the dad?'

My nose was running. I wiped it on the duvet. Had I been crying again?

'Rosie! Tell me.'

'Oh,' I said and rubbed my eyes. 'I don't know. The rest of the pages were torn out.'

I didn't tell him about the one left right at the back of the book with the jagged tear through it. A forgotten scrap someone had missed or overlooked.

Maybe I wanted to keep that little fragment for myself.

Connor sniffed loudly. He had changed his position while I was telling the story and was sitting cross-legged like a child at school assembly.

'Oh no. That's bollocks. Who tore them out?'

I shrugged. 'I don't know. Maybe she did. Celeste. Mother.'

'Why would she do that?'

I shrugged. 'Haste? Covering her tracks? She mentioned in an earlier entry that Danton didn't want her to talk about him. Maybe she tore the pages out because of that. Maybe he did. I know,' I went on, echoing his sentiment. 'Frustrating. But at least I have something to go on. To find the Danton man. He might be my …' I faltered unwilling to use the word 'father'.

'You'll do it. You'll find him,' Connor said, quite perkily. 'What happened to her, eh? The Celeste? Your mum?'

I swivelled round and stuck my feet off the mattress, towards the fire. They were numb and cold. 'She died. I don't want to talk about it.'

To my surprise Connor didn't let it go. 'So the card was right? It meant Death.'

'Yeah,' I said, unhappily. It did. It was such a shame. 'But it also meant birth. That was me. I was the baby.'

A memory of a photo suddenly came to me. A wrinkled and red baby with slits for eyes and scratch mittens over the hands. In a Moses basket. Caught mid-yawn. It was me, only weeks old. My mother must have taken it. Celeste and me. Me and Celeste. A moment of togetherness. I had to find it when I got back.

If I got back. Oh God.

Connor sniffed in the corner. 'My mum died too. I live with my stepdad and he don't like me.' He paused and glanced down at his hands clasped on his lap. 'Well, I used to live with him before …' he reached back and rattled his chain. 'Before here.'

'Well,' I was beginning to feel more grounded now. Connor was helping. Weirdly. He was good like that. 'This is what we need to talk about. Getting out of here.'

'Yes,' he said and nodded at me with encouragement.

'So, he leaves the door open?'

'Sometimes.' He jabbed a finger at the tray. You best pour that tea away somewhere he can't see. Then he'll think you've had it.'

Clever boy, I thought, as I splashed it over the walls in the far corner.

I replaced the mug on the ring it had left on the tray.

'I've still got this,' I said and pointed to the manacle. 'I can't go far.'

'Yeah,' he agreed. 'But it's attached to a rope. You're lucky he weren't expecting you. Had to make do. It ain't no chain, is it? Not much you can do with metal.' He clinked his own restraint. 'But rope can burn, right?'

He had a point. 'But there's nothing to burn it on,' I said, then looked at the heater.

He caught my gaze. 'That won't work. You might catch yourself on fire and then what?' Connor spoke down to me and tutted. 'We'll have to go in there.' He jerked his head to the connecting door.

'I can't. It's like some weird fucking altar,' I said. ''Scuse my French, Connor.'

He didn't acknowledge my apology. 'He lights candles.' He said. 'In there.'

I couldn't take my eyes away from the connecting door. The mere sight of it made me shudder. 'I know,' I said remembering the scene, the fake tea party.

'You need to do it for me.'

'For you?'

There was a scraping sound as again he lifted the chain that attached his small frame to the wall. 'I can't burn through this, can I? You'll have to get out and fetch help for me. It's the only way.'

I couldn't believe this. 'What? I'm not leaving you here! We both get out. Together.'

'Rosie,' he said calmly, his eyes dropping to the floor. 'It ain't going to work. Believe me, I've tried. Been pulling and pulling forever. It's cemented into the wall. There's a ring there. It's where they used to shackle horses.'

His corner was too dark, I couldn't see into it. 'But there's got to be a way to dislodge it somehow. Maybe we could get a fork – try to chip it out or something?'

He shook his head. 'We haven't got time, have we? I've tried everything. I'd be out of here if anything worked. I told you – you're lucky he run out of chain. Or we'd both be screwed you know.'

Christ, I thought. He's right.

Perhaps there was another way out. 'Maybe we could jump him and find the keys.'

Connor shrugged. 'I already thought about that. What if we jump him then find that the keys to my chain are in the house? Neither of us can get to them. Even if he's not stopping us. It's you. You have to burn through yours and get out. Get me help.'

Leave a child. Could I do that?

Perhaps.

Perhaps not.

If not, then what?

Did I really have to test my metal now?

'Shh,' said Connor suddenly and pointed to the outside door. 'He's coming.'

Oh God. 'What do I do?'

'Pretend to be asleep,' he said and scuttled into the dark. 'Play dead.'

Really? This went against all the training I'd had with Monty's people. You were meant to humanise yourself, talk about your friends and family.

Should I do that?

My gut told me that it wouldn't work with this bloke. Tobias, Shaggy Man, he was defective, possibly devoid of empathy. I mean look at what he'd done to those boys. There was no way he'd respond like other people …

Connor was right. I rolled onto the mattress and drew the rancid duvet over my shoulders. As quickly as possible I turned my head to face the wall. I didn't want to confront the monster, this weird freak who kept boys and did things to them, who had erected an altar, who …

Wet, slushy scuffling the other side of the barn door.

He was outside.

I swallowed and took down a long breath, filling my lungs. *Make it last.*

The scraping of metal locks being unbolted – one, two. That was all. Two. Remember that.

A blast of Arctic air. Like a huge freezer opening.

Muted groans of exertion.

Or was it satisfaction? Pleasure?

Stop it, Rosie. Keep breathing. Let the air out slowly.

A thud, congealed sniffs. He was inside the room now.

The soft rubbery sounds of clothing rearranged.

Clinks of metal, leather, against a belt buckle.

A rusty exhalation.

One prolonged grunt. A snuffle.

I needed to take more oxygen down. Heavy treads across the gritty floor. Crunch, crunch, crunch, crunch.

Another breath. Deeper. Louder. Nearer.

Oh God.

He was standing over me.

Two stifled phlegm-clotted sighs.

The crack of knee joints.

I held my breath.

Chinks made from glass, tin, ceramics sliding, knocking each other. Something placed on the floor.

A resonant, bassy, dirty chuckle.

Then the mattress depressed.

My body rolled slightly towards him.

Under the duvet I clenched my fists.

Play dead. Quiet.

Foul, unclean breath blew across my exposed cheek.

Behind my eyelids the light darkened.

He was bending over me. His stale mouth just inches from mine.

'That's right,' he rasped. 'Sleep little chicken.'

I kept myself from moving by squeezing my fingernails into the palms of my hands and concentrating on that pain.

A grimy finger touched my cheek.

I thought I was going to lose it, but then he sucked his lips together.

'We'll see how you go.'

His hand withdrew.

A rusty spring creaked, the mattress moved and bounced up again.

Clinking.

Footsteps retreating.

Door closing.

I breathed out.

Bolts, two, locking. Danger receding.

Blood pounded in my ears, like the sound of little fists on the door.

Bang, bang, bang, bang, bang …

CHAPTER THIRTY-TWO

'Rosie, quick! Wake up!'

Connor's voice in my head.

I rolled over. 'What is it?'

'The door is open.'

'To the outside?'

'No, silly. He's locked the front door. But only the top. He's getting sloppy. I mean the door to The Boys is open.'

'Oh.'

Connor appeared by the heater. He was squatting down, playing with a woolly thread from his jumper. 'They won't hurt you. They're finished.'

'I know,' I said. 'But it's so creepy. I don't know if I can go in there again.'

'Of course you can. The dead can't hurt you. It's the living we need to worry about.' He glanced at the connecting door with a grim smile.

'You're right,' I said.

'If you come over here, I'll hold your hand.' He rubbed his fingers together, discarding the thread, and held out his hand.

What a trooper. What a boy. I was amazed by the guts this one had.

'Well, I think you are very wise for your years,' I told him as I struggled to my feet. I was stiff and cold but decided to ignore it. There was nothing to be done: the heater wouldn't go any higher. Never mind. I stretched out my hand and Connor crawled out of the darkness. His touch was clammy and cold, his grip firm, reassuring. I smiled. 'Sometimes, though I'm the grown-up, it feels like you're looking after me.'

'Grown-up!' he said with indignation. 'I'm not a kid!'

'I know, I know. I didn't mean to offend you,' I said.

'It's all right,' he said. 'It was good that you were distracted.'

'It was?'

'Yep,' he said. 'Look – we're in.'

'Oh God,' I said, and spun round. He was right. The tableau radiated a sickly yellow glow. The tablecloth, I saw now, was made of gold foil. Red, yellow and green candles emitting various scents – citronella, mint, eucalyptus – were arranged across it. Their flames reflecting on the surface of the foil, adding to the strange colouring. Plus, there were mirrors and pictures on the wall that I hadn't noticed before. Family photographs, I suspected, but couldn't bring myself to look at. I didn't want to find myself humanising the freak.

'You should look at the boys, though,' Connor said, jerking his head towards the figures on the chairs. 'Face it out.'

I kept my eyes on him. 'I don't want to.'

'But once you see them, see that they are dead, then you'll understand they can't hurt you.'

'Rationally, I get that,' I told him. 'But it's just too repellent. What has he done to them?' I asked, though I wasn't sure I wanted to know.

'Stuffed 'em, I reckon,' said Connor matter-of-factly.

Disgust shuddered through my entire body. It was so violent, I found I had bitten my lip. 'Ugh,' I said. 'Why? Why would he do that?'

Connor shrugged and pointed to the boy in the middle. The one that was clearly positioned in the centre of it all. The mummy dressed in his Sunday best with a mop of brown hair that had been combed into a side parting and a beetle in his ear. 'That one. He's special.'

'Who is he?'

'I don't know.' Connor climbed onto the table, his chain creasing the fabric of the tablecloth. 'Don't care. Come on, let's get this done.' He stretched over and picked up a candle. 'We've not got heaps of time.'

I drifted over, transfixed by the waxy face of the mummy. I didn't want to look, but I couldn't drag my eyes off it. Off Him. Someone had tried to stop his features degenerating and sliding down his face, with a slap of greasepaint. They'd decorated his lips with red nail polish. It wasn't expertly done.

Another shudder.

I had the impression that the other figures had also been touched up in this way. But I wasn't prepared to look at them yet. Nausea was rising once more.

'Come on,' instructed Connor. 'Bring it over here.'

I lifted the rope to the candle he was holding. 'Okay, here goes.' And the flame began to scorch the fibres.

'It'll take a while,' said Connor, face down, tongue out, glaring at the rope in concentration. 'Get some of those,' he said and pointed to the edge of the platform. There was a pile of board games perched there. 'They might have bits in that can help us pick apart the rope.

'Jeez,' I said, stretching for the Monopoly. 'Just when you thought it couldn't get any weirder.' Then I removed the iron and the top hat and took them to him.

'Dig in then,' said Connor and instructed me to scrape at the blackened rope with the little pieces.

I started. It was going to be slow work.

CHAPTER THIRTY-THREE

It was still dark.

The connecting door was closed.

At last the rope connecting my manacle to the floor had been severed. I had a couple of feet of it coiled and twisted around my leg, which was unwieldy but at least I had freedom of movement. Given the utterly grim circumstances we found ourselves in I surprised myself by celebrating this minor victory with Connor by way of a high five.

We had come away from the altar tired and mentally exhausted, terrified that Shaggy Man might come in to check on us. The tension was hard to deal with.

We retired to our mattress and rags for the rest of the night and tried to sleep.

Sheer anxiety, I think, eventually knocked me out.

However, now I was awake again.

I had no sense of time. Whether it was day or night. I'd given up on working it out. All that mattered was escaping.

A new tray of food had appeared beside the bed.

I should share it with my cellmate.

'Connor?' I hissed into the darkness.

But there was no movement there.

'Connor?'

Nothing.

Oh no. What had happened while I was sleeping? Surely if there was a struggle I would have heard it? And I knew there was no way Connor would go without one.

'Connor, where are you?'

Oh God what had he done? 'Connor!'

'It's okay. I'm here. I was sleeping.'

'Thank Christ. You had me worried.'

'You've been out for the whole day. Did you drink some of the tea?'

'No, but I had all the water.'

'How did it taste?'

'Same.'

'Don't drink it any more, Rosie.'

'But I'm thirsty. And I don't feel bad. Like drunk or drugged. My brain is okay.'

'Get rid of the food,' Connor advised. 'Then lie down. Stay awake but don't talk.'

'Okay. I got that.'

'Don't talk.'

I obeyed.

As soon as I'd tucked the sandwich under my mattress I lay down.

'Throw away the tea,' Connor directed from the shadows.

Good point, I thought, and hurled the contents of the mug into the other corner. Then, as per instructions, I went back under the duvet.

'Good luck,' my cellmate whispered. 'If he leaves the door open tonight, it'll be our last time together here.'

'Please God. No offence.'

'None taken.'

So we waited. We waited so long that I wasn't sure whether I had drifted off or not and maybe missed him.

Through the cracks in the roof my eyes roved periodically over scraps of sky. They were a leaden navy colour from what I could make out. Which suggested it was night-time. Or maybe late afternoon. It had been getting dark early when I was outside. This, I realised now, my brain had configured as 'Before'. B. C. Before Captivity. Everything since I made the mistake of pressing the plastic button on the doorbell at Parker's Farm, my time in confinement – my time with Connor – it was all 'During'. D.C. I didn't know how long that had been. It bothered me that I didn't know. But not as much as wondering how long I might be here bothered me. Or what Shaggy Man intended to do.

I had tried not to let my mind stray near the options. But of course I knew there was a probability extinction was possible. My extinction. This is the word I used for it. Because it felt clinical and provoked an affinity with the dinosaurs. Which was okay, because I knew that some palaeontologists thought that birds were living dinosaurs. So some of them survived.

I couldn't let myself use the real words linked to the extinction of life. The words that you saw in newspaper headlines. I wouldn't even think them. For the act of processing them consciously would unleash a torrent of emotions and in no time at all I might be consumed by fear and rendered useless. Some people might call it denial, but I was grateful to my pragmatic mind for staying with this course of action. Or inaction. It worked to a certain degree. It helped me tame terror.

Someone muttered at the door.

All thoughts flew out the window. Or would have done if there had been one in here.

There was that shuffle.

A grunt in the familiar low earthy tone.

Goosebumps broke out over my entire body.

He was here.

I turned to the wall again and pulled the duvet over my shoulders.

The mattress squeaked.

He was quicker than before with the locks. Only one this time. Connor had been right. He was getting cocky. Sure that his prey had been subdued. Subjugated.

The word caught on my brain. Subjugation. Had he done that to me? Conquered me? Quelled both myself and Connor.

Tamed us? Crushed us?

The notion of it, of this man, this most ignoble of creatures being able to control me and this boy, inflamed a spark in my heart. Fury – now I hadn't felt that in a while. Odd. Perhaps it was the drugs that had numbed me so?

Which meant – now that I was feeling that anger – could they be wearing off?

My heart beat faster.

Cold air. Turbulent this time. Not still. The wind was up. The weather had changed.

Muted moans. Ugh, why did he do that?

Footsteps. Crunch, crunch, crunch, crunch.

The crack of bones.

A body lowering itself down onto the mattress.

This time I didn't roll towards him.

I stiffened. I couldn't help it. There was something growing inside me, something hot and dangerous that wouldn't let my muscles acquiesce so passively.

I caught a waft: citronella, formaldehyde.

He'd put the lotion on.

Stale, warm breath.

Cabbage, rotten food, alcohol, gravy, lemon.

'Here you be,' I heard him say. 'Sleepy little …'

I couldn't abide any more.

Before my brain urged me to caution or to arrest, my elbow, almost like it was operating under its own will, connected unaccountably with his face.

'Wha …?' Then, 'Arghhh.'

I flipped round and lashed out with both hands. A quick agile movement. I didn't have all of my strength yet, but the blow had caught him unawares and as such was enough to send him flailing, off balance, hands paddling, off the mattress sprawling on his back on the floor.

Both his hands went to his nose. As I leapt to my feet, one of them reached forward to grab my leg. I skipped away. The impulse to turn and stare at him was blowing up from my stomach – the sight of him there, incapacitated, was … fascinating.

Then Connor shouted, 'Fire!'

I tried to find his face in the darkness, momentarily paralysed by the word he'd cried, not processing what he meant. Then I saw the heater move an inch towards Shaggy Man.

That's right, good boy, Connor. Trooper had instructed us that we should grab anything nearby to fend off assailants. Offensive weapons can be vases, picture frames, pieces of pavement. Connor was indicating one could be a heater.

No more prompting necessary I leapt to the side and skirted round our gaoler. Now he was bending forwards on his knees, cursing. His immensity stunned me.

How could I have forgotten how big he was?

For a moment I felt fear grab me by the throat, but I pushed it off too.

I had one good foot. One good cowboy boot with a golden tip. And it was this that I swung back and brought hard into the side of his head. It wasn't a violent blow, but I aimed into his earhole with surprising accuracy. A hit like that to the inner ear had to have done some damage. Thank Christ I had good taste in footwear.

Shaggy Man sure let go a shriek. Kind of animalistic and sweet. His bulk went over close to where Connor knelt.

'No!' I yelled. He wasn't going to lay a finger on that poor kid.

At once my hands were on the heater, yanking it from the wall, holding it high above my head.

Then down hard on his temple.

It made a muffled tinny sound.

It hadn't knocked him out, but was enough to stun him.

So I picked it up again, capitalising on his shock and whacked it sideways into his cheek.

Another howl filled the room along with the faint smell of burnt hair and singed flesh.

'Go,' screamed Connor. 'Get help.'

And the door – opened. I was out, in the wet yard. Blinking against the night sky.

I paused. For just a moment, overcome by freedom.

Which way?

Scuffling behind me.

In the room he was groaning and rousing himself.

I darted to the right, down past the outside of the barn.

Cold, cold, under my feet. One foot. The other not used to moving like this. Stiff. Scraping. Not strong, not taking weight.

But I forced myself on. Dragging my stump-foot over the cobbles of the yard.

Land ahead. Snow thawing.

Rain falling. Wind screaming.

Low fence. Beyond it, trees.

I aimed for them, panting as I reached the boundary.

A commotion behind me. But not nearby. Shouting. In the distance.

I hobbled on and came to a short wire fence. Using both hands I lifted my dud foot over it.

Oof. Bang. Onto the ground.

Elbow bash.

No time to cry. Go on. Run!

Up, sliding. Slipping on mud.

Into the dark of the wood.

CHAPTER THIRTY-FOUR

Trees silhouetted. Darkness against darkness. Oddly laying shadows. Tiny rustles around me. Things in the bracken. Above, the topmost branches swirled, picked and played with by a roiling sky. Rain pelting down onto my face into my eyes. Wet hair. Icy streams.

In the distance – the man. His shouts. Quietening. Or was it the rain drowning him out?

My heart punching my chest. Stiltedly.

Stampeding through the undergrowth.

The wood was alive. Wild. Teeming with minute things that were scattering as I snapped and broke my way through the bracken.

Bang! A trunk. Silvery. Smashed right into it. Recoiled. Reached out. Caught a vine and clung on to its woody embrace. Lungs bursting. Unfit and weak. I could run no more.

Grasping my lifeline tightly, I slunk down into the undergrowth and crouched.

Everything in my body was loud. Like each organ was banging against the skin, hollering like prisoners trying to get out.

I wished I had my phone for the umpteenth time. I longed to hear Sam's voice. That low woody tone would be sweet honey to me now. How I yearned to put my arms around him now and be enfolded in his soft, strong, hard-muscled embrace. He was security, he was pleasure, he was, I realised with a sudden clarity, love.

Wow.

Love.

My God, I was going to have to tell him, be frank, let him know, when I saw him. Life was too short.

But not this short.

No way.

I wasn't going to let this crazy freaky Shaggy Man deprive me of the love of my life before it had even begun.

I tried to regain my breath.

I couldn't hear if he was near or far, just knew I had to move on.

Wresting myself up onto my feet, thoughts now reaching for Sam, I made off, again, into darkness, skidding, gliding, stumbling into puddles, falling over roots.

I was seeing more clearly now. The rain was easing off.

And there on the horizon, through the trees, was a light.

Please God let this be someone else's home.

Or could I have lost my way, gone in a circle? Was I heading back to the farm? No. That would be the worst.

But there was nothing else to head for. No other light to guide.

I aimed for it.

As I reached its perimeter fence, I saw at once this was not Parker's Farm.

It had a different feel to it. The lawn was tame and smooth.

In the vast expanse of grass I could see a brick wishing well. Snow had been cleared from the grass with a spade. There were only patches of it left now. Around and about stood comical gnomes. One sat on the wall and dropped his fishing line into the well.

I squatted to take in more details, but urgency wouldn't let me stay. Instead, compelled onwards, I lumbered across the lawn.

There was a conservatory. Through it a back door into the house.

I limped over – and banged on the glass hard. 'Hello? Please! Let me in.'

Lights from the room beyond flickered, suggesting a television was on.

I rapped again. 'Hello?' My hands hurt. I'd made them bleed somehow.

A figure at the window, cupping her eyes into the garden. A woman. Old. Seventies. Alarmed.

'Please let me in. Or call the police.'

Keys jangling. 'Hang on.' The door opened.

Oh my – the relief.

'Well, whatever are you like? I don't give to charity,' she said, a pronounced Yorkshire accent slowing the rhythm of her speech. 'But oh … are you all right, dear?'

I pushed past her, through another door, into a kitchen.

'Please,' I breathed it out. Only a whisper. Where had my voice gone? Hoarse now. 'Call the police.' So unused. Rusty.

The older woman was appalled. 'I can't go calling …'

'Have you got a mobile?' My hand lolled around. I was still unsteady. Breathless. 'I'll do it myself. 999.'

'No, love. I've got a telephone in the hallway.'

'Call it. Please NOW. There's a man over there and he's holding a boy, Connor. Young. The police – they need to get over there.'

At the mention of Connor she perked up and scuttled past me into a hall. I followed her, starting to waddle, extreme fatigue beginning take hold. The cosy warmth. I was burning up.

She lifted the phone. 'What's this all about?'

'A man. He's kept me. Kidnapped me. Parker's Farm.'

She paused, the phone in her hand. 'But that's only Tobias playing …'

'Phone them! Tell them it's Rosie Strange. Give your address.'

For a moment her eyes hardened but then she inclined her ear to the receiver. 'I don't know …' with one weedy finger she pushed her spectacles up her nose and rolled her eyes over the extent of my figure. I knew I looked a state.

Then her ears pricked. Someone down the line asked her a question. 'Police? Ambulance probably too,' she looked at me grimly. 'She says she's been kidnapped.'

I watched her, my hands gripping the door frame for strength, still panting. I knew she was old but she was SO slow. Where was the urgency? Did she even believe me?

'Yes dear,' she said into the receiver. 'That's right.'

Her eyes rolled to ceiling.

'My address?' she asked the receiver, mouth turned down at the corners as if she was insulted by the request. 'Well, it's 97 Brookmyre Lane.' She paused and put her free hand to her throat. 'B.R.O.O.K. Yes. M.Y.R.E.' Her head bopped, as the operator presumably read it back. She was stiff in the neck, I could tell. She wasn't the only one. I'd taken a knock to that part of my anatomy only days before and, now I was thawing, feeling was coming back.

My limbs were becoming increasingly weighted and now the heat of her home was softening the skin on my ankle. The exposed foot was starting to throb. I had bashed it into the frozen ground as I had run. It had been numb throughout my time in the barn room. What did that mean? I didn't want to look at it. I'd seen the state of my hands when I'd come into the kitchen. They were filthy, covered in God knows what – food, grit and splashes from the bucket I'd had to use. I must stink too. No wonder the old girl looked worried.

'Correct,' she said, at last. 'Yes, right at the end of the road, before the footpath to Blackmoor Mound.'

This was taking an age.

I tried waving a hand at her. 'Tell them my name – Rosie Strange.'

She removed the receiver from her ear and pressed it against her chest. 'They want MY name first,' she said, mildly indignant, then replaced the phone at her ear. 'Madeleine Arkwright. M.A.D…'

A hard rap at the door stopped her.

For a moment we locked eyes.

Then, incredulously, the old girl, Madeleine twisted round and began to move towards it. 'Oh, hang on,' she was saying down the phone. 'There's someone here.'

There was a shape, a shadow outside, someone big.

Someone familiar.

No. Couldn't be, could it?

'Don't,' I warned her. 'It might be …'

'But …' she began.

Then it was like a bomb had gone off.

An ear-splitting blast. Splintering wood. Something wet sprayed over my neck and face, followed by little sharp things. Bits were dropping onto the lino. Smoke.

My ears thrummed, throat and mouth full of stench and matter.

The old lady, Madeleine, was now near my feet, lying on the floor, her head at a weird angle. Wimpering. Like a wounded dog.

There was a bloody gash and a ragged patch of flesh at her shoulder. No arm.

Dust was everywhere.

Madeleine's frail tattered form convulsed and stopped moving.

I stared at the door. What was left of it.

Tobias MacAllister was filling the hole, gripping a shotgun in both hands.

At first, I couldn't move, couldn't think. Then something deep inside of myself, a voice, said 'Go! Go now!' and I spun and stumbled, hands out, towards the kitchen.

Thank God I had the presence of mind to close the door. I threw my body against it, should he try to get in. But then I thought, shotgun, he's got a shotgun. I'd seen what it had made of the front door. Instead, I heaved the bin against it then made off through the conservatory, catching the sound of the bin crashing to the floor as I exited through the door.

Now what? Left or right or into the garden?

The light from the house fell close to the wishing well. He would see me if I went out there.

I took a left and, hunching low, headed round the side of the bungalow. Every part of my body and soul, was tense. I was almost spent, using only sheer force of will to propel myself on.

As I turned the corner to the front, I sighted an external light shining over a gravel driveway. If I came out into it, he would see me for sure, but there was no way I could possibly go back, was there?

Christ – where were the police? They had to have heard the explosion down the line. Or would the blast have disconnected the call? Had it broken the phone?

I couldn't remember the state of it. My recall was becoming blurred.

Had Madeleine given them enough details? How long had it been since she'd made the call? Seconds? Minutes? It felt like years. No time to think on it. Only on. Forwards.

Limping, wracked by stark shooting pains in my foot, I crept along the side of the bungalow until I reached the corner.

Beyond the edge of the garden I could see a road, a lane.

It wasn't well lit, but further up there was another house. Its lights were coming on. If I could make it over there, then I'd be safe. Safer. Maybe they'd have their own shotgun to use against Tobias. And if they killed him, or at least disabled him, then I'd be safe. And they could call the police again. I could tell them about Connor and see if they could despatch a car to Parker's Farm. Or else no one would find him. And he was counting on me.

He was relying on *me*.

I took a breath. Then rushed out, blinking, into the light.

The end of the front garden was only metres away.

Something substantial, heavy, dropped behind me.

I shouldn't have looked back, but I did.

The front door was in ruins. Bits of jagged wood hung loose. Tobias was out, halfway to me.

'Stop,' I screamed. I shouldn't have done because it made me cough. Even so, I sucked the air down into my lungs and, half limping half sprinting, ignoring the agony in my feet and legs, I lunged forwards in the direction of the lane.

Another couple of metres. I was nearly there.

Then, suddenly, my upper half snapped back like a ricocheting bullet. Tobias had hold of my hood. I hadn't even registered that I was wearing my coat.

My hood, I was thinking, as my feet came loose.

A thick arm fastened round my waist.

My legs lifted off the ground and Tobias began to lug me backwards.

'NO!' I twisted violently and drove my nails into his hand.

His fingers unclenched and my body dropped a couple of centimetres, feet skimming the gravel on the drive. I dug the heel of my foot in.

Somewhere nearby the sound of a siren began.

Tobias must have clocked it too, because for a moment he hesitated. I seized the moment and yanked my arm out of his grip but lost balance and fell sprawling to the floor.

'No you don't,' Shaggy Man hissed and my jacket grew tight around my shoulders and I was hoicked up again. His other arm snaked back round my waist and pulled me in so tightly this time that all of the air in my lungs was forced out in a guttural 'Oof.'

'Make it easy on yourself,' he rasped in my ear. Ugh that stale breath – cabbage and decay. Beyond it the citronella, smoking wood. He lessened his grip on my waist so I could at least breathe in.

An intermittent glow was lighting the hedges in the lane, the siren's volume increasing.

'Help!' I screamed, using what air was available. Tobias slapped me across the face.

I carried on. 'Here!'

The police car swung wildly into the front garden crushing bushes and scrubs, screeching to a halt metres from us.

'Back,' said Tobias and moved his arm under my chin so he now had me gripped in a headlock. 'Steady.'

I managed to get my arms free and locked my fingers around his but he wasn't relinquishing his grip. And he was strong.

A policewoman and another man got out of the car.

Tobias paused and, keeping his arm under my head, propped my body up in front of his using me as a shield.

'Release the girl, please,' said the policeman. He was so calm.

Tobias grunted, fumbling around behind me. A cold pipe of steel came across my chest and punched the soft skin under my chin, forcing my face up.

The shotgun.

I tried to look down my nose. The policeman was coming towards us, his hands held up in surrender.

Behind him, in the lane, another van rolled into view. The doors opened and several black helmeted figures oozed from it and poured themselves silently into the land.

Tobias tensed. 'Come any further and I'll shoot her brains out.'

Both cops stopped. Behind them, the others continued to advance silently, merging with the shadows.

Another car pulled up by the van.

Tobias jerked me back another couple of feet. The barrel dug deeper into my flesh.

Oh God, I thought. This is it. This is how it ends. *Not* with a whimper but a bang.

'He's got a boy,' I yelled as loudly as I was able. 'Connor. At Parker's Farm.'

'Wah?' Tobias bared his teeth. Spittle dribbled out of his mouth and into my hair. He pinched my arm and shook me. 'She's lying.'

'I'm not. I'm not. You need to get someone over there.'

Tobias dug the nozzle so hard it broke my skin. 'Shut up, bitch.'

The policewoman put her hands up in surrender and retreated to the car. While she relayed my information into the radio, the policeman, her partner, took another tentative step towards us. He too held his hands palm up to show he had no weapon.

'Look,' he said. 'Why don't you put down the gun and we can clear this up. It's a misunderstanding, isn't it?'

But Tobias must have shaken his head.

'What's your name, then?' the policeman asked as if he was enjoying a friendly chat.

'It's Tobias,' I yelled.

Shaggy Man made a snorting noise and bridled behind me. His muscles were hard. He was smelling worse.

'Well, Tobias, my name's Bob. Why don't you let her go and we can go inside, eh? Out of the cold. Have a proper brew. Sort this out. There's no need for any of this.'

'You wouldn't understand.' Tobias's voice sounded uncertain. He shuffled both of us towards the shattered door.

'Try me,' Bob looked as sympathetic as a cold policeman in a hostage situation could.

I could feel Tobias starting to tremble. The shudders were going through my body too. 'It was my brother what made me …'

Suddenly there was movement behind Bob. A man ran into view, almost up to the policeman. The policewoman managed to intercept him, grabbing his arm and swung him back. 'Rosie,' he shouted as he wrenched her off.

Sam!

At last, I thought, here comes the cavalry. Now we can be saved.

But the policewoman blocked him with her body and shoved him back. Holding him at arm's length, she spoke into a radio on her chest.

'Who the hell is he?' Tobias gestured at Sam, taking the shotgun momentarily away from my face and pointing it at the policewoman and my dear, dear friend.

'It doesn't matter,' said the policeman.

But Tobias was getting scared. Scared and mad. 'It bloody matters to me.' He was starting to shout, and took the nozzle back to my chin.

Something in the body of his shotgun clicked.

For a moment everyone froze.

Then Sam hurtled forwards dragging the female officer with him, his arms out front, waving crazily. 'No!!' he screamed. 'Don't shoot.'

And my heart, as hard as it was beating, contracted with gratitude.

Then he said, 'He knows where my brother is.'

Where my brother is, I repeated silently in my head.

Where his brother is.

But I don't know where his brother is.

Oh, he means …

How could he?

He meant don't shoot Tobias!

And, what, leave it open for Shaggy Man to shoot … me?

As the realisation hit home, I felt my stomach slip to the

floor. The last drop of fight evaporated with the breath I blew out into the damp night air.

I guess the rest of my body must have given up too because all my muscles slackened. My legs buckled.

Unable to support my whole weight, Tobias let me slide. His right arm kept the shotgun up. The other gripped my face. With his dirty fingers he opened my mouth and shoved the barrel in.

The movement forced my head upwards. I saw Bob's face change – an understanding passed through him: endgame.

Instead of panicking, though, something else happened. Something strange: a sense of peace descended over me. And while that came down, my vision elevated. There was the peak of Bob's hat, the roof of the car, the brick of lights blinking across it, a number painted in black, the van parked behind it, men crawling like black beetles across the icy ground. I could see the top of Sam's head, Michael several feet back surrounded by uniforms, and even see myself: my body slipping, gun in mouth, making my cheek bulge, above that, Tobias, his unkempt hair spiralling out in matted tufts from his crown. The house, its square footprint, came into view, then the lane full of cars, three more sets of flashing lights, one ambulance. The trees around us moved softly, thin ends trembling in the breeze. And above their leaves, the blanket of night spread out, twinkling wonders of the stars dotting it like jewels, a dark moor, low hills in the distance, lights in the valleys between. And I felt okay, detached, as if all of this was just a scene in a play which I could turn off whenever I liked. Lightness and blackness began to enfold me.

A radio clicked into action: 'Clear shot.'

There was a crack, something whizzed past my ear.

An explosion of matter.

Then the black came back.

CHAPTER THIRTY-FIVE

The farm looked different floodlit and filled with people. There were lots of them here. Many in white suits with surgical masks over their mouths.

'You all right?' asked PC Shapworth, the policewoman from the garden. She'd stayed with me in the ambulance and later, at the hospital. And kept Sam and Michael at bay.

I didn't want to see them even though I wanted to see them.

But I was a) too dazed and b) too angry and c) too numb to deal with it. Don't worry – contradictions – I know. But that was how I felt. Full of fury and simultaneously empty. Don't ask me how that works, I'm not a psychologist. Though I had a hunch I might be seeing one in the coming weeks. Still, I was not intending to take a hard look at anything yet. I was only just about ready to do this. For Connor. But I knew it was going to be another shit show.

PC Shapworth, Debbie, treated me exactly as I wanted. She'd been kind and held my hand when they brought out Madeleine on a stretcher. The old girl was as pale as the snow thawing around us and unresponsive. Debbie assured me she wasn't dead.

It had been a relief of sorts.

Now I just had to get through this.

The slight increment in temperature meant I could see more of Parker's Farm than I had the first time I approached it. If only I hadn't come here. But I had. There was no point going over it right now. There may be lessons to learn but that would all come in the future. Right now, I had to get through the next half hour.

'You coping?' Debbie Shapworth asked me again.

Wrapping the aluminium blanket closer to me I nodded. The doctor didn't think I needed it any more, but I did. It made me shiny and hard to lose, should anyone feel the need to drug and imprison me.

I couldn't ask yet if Shaggy Man was dead. I had seen the mess of him, post bullet, and thought that there'd be no way of coming back from that. But I wasn't sure. The sense of danger had not yet withdrawn. It was still there, making me jump at loud noises, or shriek when someone large and unfamiliar approached. The doctors said I was still in shock and hadn't agreed with the police that I should return to the scene of my captivity. But I had to. I needed to make sure Connor was all right.

There was a path leading up to the bungalow and bushes in its garden. A stone birdbath lay on its side near a gutter. Muddy tracks were everywhere.

Debbie pushed my wheelchair down the side of the bungalow. My foot was bandaged. I'd managed to evade serious damage and frostbite. Apparently, I should have been grateful for the heater and the soiled duvet. That was a first.

I wasn't grateful. I never would be. Though I was pleased I wasn't going to have to have any toes lopped off. What a mess.

Dawn was breaking over the hills in the east, streaking the sky with pale ice-blues.

'Visibility is good,' I said for some unknown reason. Possibly I was trying to sound objective, unemotional, trying to keep a lid on the familiar fear that was returning as I entered the farmyard. My wheelchair bumped and jolted over the ground. Part of it close to the pink bungalow was smoothed over with concrete, but closer to the outhouses there were a number of cracks and muddy patches, each with their own white tent assembled over the top.

I put my hand on the brake and paused the chair so I could gather my strength.

Debbie stood beside me, a pained look on her face. 'He can't hurt you now,' she said.

I knew that, but all the same I didn't *feel* it, like I said.

'Take your time,' she said. 'We'll go at your pace.'

'Why are they there?' I pointed to the tents, and then brought my arm down as I noticed, beyond them, the barn. It was so unobtrusive, simple-looking. A long-neglected outhouse or shed with a pitched and tattered roof.

That was where I had been imprisoned.

Debbie wasn't looking at me. She had her eyes fixed on a hanging basket by the back door of the farmhouse. It was full of dead leaves.

'Tell me please,' I repeated with firmness. She hadn't answered my question. 'If you don't, it will be worse for my head. I'll imagine stuff.' Though what could be worse?

She knelt down so her head was level and said, 'We found a large number of human remains.'

Like I couldn't have guessed. I'd seen the mummified boys in the barn. That there were others didn't surprise me.

I leant over and retched.

Debbie waited until I'd finished then handed me a small folded tissue.

Once the cramps had subsided I wiped myself down. 'Boys?'

She nodded silently.

We moved on.

A number of people were coming and going through the barn door. It was propped open. I hadn't seen it from the outside. It was how Tobias came and went into our room. Because it was ajar you could clearly see the planks of wood nailed on the inside, and the black smears around the bottom. I hadn't kicked it, so who had left those hundreds of marks? How many had Shaggy Man kept in there?

Two men were standing just inside the doorway. One had a mobile in his hand, the other, taller, greyer, was giving him instructions. When they saw me, they both stopped speaking.

Debbie introduced us. 'This is Detective Inspector Howard and Sergeant Mason.'

The detective inspector came forward and shook my hand. He was older than the other guy. Late fifties perhaps. Well built, and boxy with a decisive manner that inspired confidence.

'Thank you for coming,' he said.

Sergeant Mason shook my hand too. He was perhaps

my age, stylishly dressed and wearing shoes, moccasins, that looked like they were probably leaking water into his socks. He didn't say anything and didn't smile but managed to convey sympathy with his eyes. 'As I understand it, Ms Strange, you were, er, detained in here. Is that right?'

As he spoke, both of them took a step into the barn, opening up my view.

Several free-standing lights had been cabled in. Illuminated to such a degree you could see detail now. And what a horror show it was in there. Filthy wasn't the word. Everything was covered in thick grime, caked with dirt, mould. Plastic markers displaying numbers littered the whole place.

There was the mattress and the soggy duvet that I was meant to be grateful for, the remainder of the long rope that had once been attached to my foot; I could see now that it snaked into the other room and through a ring concreted into the floor. Everything was just as I had left it.

I shivered.

'You all right?' Debbie asked and touched my arm.

I recoiled automatically, though I hadn't realised I would do that.

And breathe. 'I am all right.'

I willed myself to look at the back wall. The heater was on the floor where it had landed after I'd smashed it into Tobias's face. In the corner I could see the pillow that I had thrown Connor and a pile of very rusty and broken chains. I closed my eyes for a moment – please God don't let there be a body.

'Now,' said Inspector Howard. His attitude was brisk but not insensitive. 'My understanding from your statement is that the boy, who you've suggested you were imprisoned with, was chained up over there.' Howard pointed to Connor's corner which was no longer dark. It was very empty. And very grubby. 'Is that right?'

'Yes. That is correct,' I said with a tremble that betrayed my inner uncertainty. Now floodlit, the place seemed much smaller. How could I have not noticed Connor at first? I paused. I had been drugged. My senses weren't working normally. Maybe he'd been lurking in the other room. 'Have you found him yet?'

The police officers exchanged a glance. I couldn't work out what it meant.

'No, not yet,' Howard said.

Sergeant Mason moved his hand back as if beckoning me into the room.

I bit my lip. Ugh. I didn't want to go in there. But … Connor. I had to.

Debbie hovered at my shoulder and gently nudged me forwards.

'How could you not find him? He was chained up. Here,' I pointed again with emphasis at the dusty metal. 'He couldn't leave. That's why I had to make a break for it and fetch …' I stopped. Mason was opening the interconnecting door.

My lip started to tremble. There was the table, but the stuffed bodies had gone. That was something at least. More plastic markers spread across the surface. Some candles had been knocked onto their sides. 'He helped me burn through my rope – the one on my foot – with those candles. His DNA will be all over them. The whole thing was his idea.

He was clever. I was far too spun out to think straight. He's got to be here somewhere. He can't have gone far. Are you looking?'

'Of course,' Howard interjected. 'We'll find him.'

I nodded, my eyes skimming the empty chairs at the head of the table. The air was still thick with the smell of formaldehyde and citronella, rot and decay, even though the bodies had been removed. But I could still see them in my head. Their shadows would always remain. On several of the chairs you could, in fact, still see sad greasy outlines where their fluids had leaked out. 'Why did he do this? Tobias? Why would he stuff people like that?'

'The human mind is a complex world,' Howard murmured.

Sergeant Mason moved discreetly to block my view. 'We think the corpse in the middle …' he motioned to the chair where it had been propped up. I remembered my foolish plea for help, '… was his brother, Seth.'

Again, somewhere inside I think I had known this. The man at the bar, Friar Tuck's, all those years ago when I had been a normal person, he had mentioned a brother and something bad that had happened to him. A fire or a drowning. I was too tired to send my mind back to that night and retrieve the exact details.

'Looks like Tobias dug him up shortly after he was buried.'

PC Shapworth was unable to stifle a snort of disgust. It made her breathe in through her nose so she was fully assaulted by the lamentable mix of stinks present.

I watched her gag and then moved on. 'Which was when?'

'1996.'

'That's a long time ago. The body doesn't look that old. It would have decompos …' I couldn't get it out without my throat contracting. Decomposed – was the word I wanted to say. Except I didn't want to speak it out loud. It brought back hideous memories of that weird blurred face, beetles in orifices. Ugh. I needed to block that out. And quickly.

'No,' Inspector Howard continued, 'he performed some kind of DIY embalming process. Possibly before burial, possibly after. The other bodies we have retrieved from this room were also embalmed post-mortem.'

Debbie Shapworth moved her fist to her mouth and coughed into it. At least I think it was a cough. Could have been a dry heave that she was trying to camouflage in front of her superiors. But, Christ, surely it was acceptable to find this crime scene tough.

'Gross,' she said at last.

It was a very accurate statement.

Questions still boggled my mind, though. 'So why did he do that to them? And then put them there? In this …' I waved my arm to the room but kept my eyes firmly on the inspector, 'shrine?'

He answered me slowly and choosing his words with care. 'I can't say for sure. Personally, I've never seen anything like it. It's taken a lot of us by surprise.' He stood back and let his eyes roam. 'There's a lot we don't know.'

It didn't help, and I needed an answer. I said nothing, but squinted my eyes. It was an unconscious act at first but then I deepened my frown.

Howard got it. 'Okay,' he said. 'And this is only what I've

heard from other people so far. Rumours, hypotheses ...' He waved his hand as if wafting away a bad smell. 'I'd say he was trying to give his brother some company.'

'But he was dead!' I hadn't meant it to sound so full of fury. And then I remembered – Connor had said more or less the same thing.

Debbie Shapworth looked up abruptly. Sergeant Mason raised his eyebrows then dropped them and tried to look deadpan.

I'd spoken inappropriately to his superior. But they were police, they were used to far worse.

Howard seemed unaffected anyway. He took a step towards me and softened his voice. 'Maybe he wasn't to Tobias. It was his brother, his twin. The human mind, like Sergeant Mason suggested, has its own bag of strange tricks.' He looked into my eyes pointedly. 'We all have ways we develop to keep us from pain and grief. Coping methods.'

'And most of us make sure we don't impose them on others, don't chain people up and stuff them,' I said. 'Usually.'

No one spoke after that.

CHAPTER THIRTY-SIX

They uncovered eight sets of remains. Mostly boys. Though a mature male was also discovered. And a woman who had been recently buried. She was found to be MacAllister's mother, Old Annie. The police concluded she must have died at Parker's Farm and Tobias had simply decided to do a home burial.

Turns out there is no law against burying someone on private land. Though you should use an undertaker. And get permission from the council.

It amazed me just how much Tobias had got away with – there was no death certificate, no burial registration, no coffin apparently. But then again, there were far worse crimes he had carried out, without flagging up his gruesome operation to the authorities.

There were the bodies.

It was probable that the non-familial remains located in the yard matched the corpses in the shrine area. And it looked like they dated from the mid-nineties, when Seth had perished, to 2006 when Tobias had been sent down for his part in the armed robbery. Although when he'd got out, it appeared, for a while, he hadn't reoffended. Perhaps his mother had kept him on the straight and narrow. However, when she died, there was no one to restrain him. He got a job driving a van, delivering round the country. It was white, just as the eleven-year-old nephew of Clementine, the librarian, had stated. It enabled Tobias to move easily between the farm and his aunt's.

Debbie Shapworth told me that there were no further bodies in Godalming. Stuey, poor boy, was it.

The police there, on instruction from the Yorkshire CID had searched the late Vinnie Burroughs' house and grounds, which backed onto the so-called 'Hunting'. An outhouse, an old garage-cum-workshop, was discovered at the bottom of his aunt's garden. Inside there was a sleeping bag. There was a match to Stuey's DNA. In the bathroom they found embalming fluid.

Stuey, it seems, had not been violated, thank Christ. In fact, they couldn't say for sure that any of them had. Though it was suggested most had been killed by drug overdose. They weren't specific on what exactly that drug was. Said that they wouldn't have suffered. Well, that's what they told me anyway.

Stuey, however, had been slain by a blow to the back of the head. Conceivably when attempting to escape, which is why he was found where he was. He hadn't been with MacAllister long.

Debbie made it clear that it was quite possible, if I hadn't stumbled on Shaggy Man that day at Parker's Farm, he could have gone on to abduct more boys. 'So,' she said weakly, 'some good has come of … that.'

Didn't feel like it.

But it was an ongoing investigation so there was a lot they couldn't tell me.

And they still hadn't found Connor.

I wondered if he'd gone to ground. Slunk off and maybe hit Leeds. I knew his mother had passed away and he hated his stepdad so he might have managed to flee to the big city and tried his hand there. I signed up to a Missing Persons website and got updates from them. But so far – nothing.

Before I returned to the Witch Museum, I visited Madeleine in hospital. If she hadn't phoned the police then I might not be here now.

Sam came with me. He kept on trying to help out and I kept refusing. But in the end I let him accompany me to visit Madeleine because I was really anxious about seeing her. I felt terribly guilty about Tobias shooting her. If I hadn't knocked on her door … if I had turned right instead of left … if I had decided to go with Sam and his dad and not gone on my own … if, if, if.

The poor woman was confused and fearful. She didn't know who I was. The staff made me leave the huge bouquet I'd bought her in reception. I had forgotten that you couldn't take flowers into hospitals any more.

She thought Sam was her nephew. Even though her real nephew was there, keeping vigil by her side. He was older, in his fifties. Kevin, apparently. He and his wife stared at me with fury in their eyes. They didn't say a word and I didn't hang around. My presence disturbed all of them. The nurse told me Madeleine was likely to recover. But it was early days.

I left Waketon.

We went back to the Witch Museum. Bronson was there to meet us. He gave me a hug which made both of us feel awkward, then presented Tuscan roast pork with cannellini beans and blanched greens. Carmen, our friend the sculptor, had been round and brought dessert. She and our neighbour, Molly Acton, were waiting in the Stars in case we wanted company. I didn't. I did my best to eat some of the meal but as soon as I could I made my excuses and went straight to bed. I think by then I'd lost over a stone. A positive, I told myself, but actually there was no way I was doing that diet again.

The days came, the days went. My foot slowly recovered.

At some point we learnt that Jasper wasn't in either location – not in the Waketon shrine, not in the Godalming shed. Sam and Michael had given DNA samples. They were no match to any of the victims. Sam took it all philosophically and started to return to his usual self. I could see that was what kept him going – the desire to find his brother, whether dead or alive or existing somewhere in the beyond. I mean – Jazz was out there somewhere, we just hadn't found him yet.

Michael didn't change at all. He spoke to Pearl a couple of times, but the trauma of her and Donny's time in custody had interfered with her mental recall. She had no more details than those she had already given to Mr Stone and seemed reluctant to talk about the Spirit Boys. Of course, if she learnt anything else then she wouldn't hesitate to ring etc., but she thought it unlikely.

A few days before Christmas Michael went home. Unbroken. Still hopeful. Perhaps more jaded. I was vocal in my gratitude to him and Sam for (eventually) raising the alarm. It turned out that they had left the Holiday Inn at the pre-arranged time. No one had seen me at the hotel – there had been a shift change and the snotty receptionist who had taken my bag went off sick for a few days. The Stones presumed I had gone to see Big Ig, after getting the text from Monty. No one worried until Auntie Babs couldn't get hold of me for my thread vein removal. They knew I wouldn't dare to miss that. Then it was all 'I thought she was with you', 'No, she said she was with you', and so when Monty informed them Big Ig wasn't even in the country all of them started to worry. Thank God. And that's when my left luggage surfaced, which pretty much coincided with my escape from the barn.

We waved goodbye to Michael, then Sam spoke to his mum on the phone. They talked for hours.

The next day his sister phoned from Ibiza.

He had more contact with his family that winter than I think he'd experienced in the past few years.

I decided to throw out all the old curtains, moth-eaten rugs and bedding in the living quarters and replaced them with blinds, carpet and Egyptian cotton linen with a minimum 600 thread count. It seemed important to only have clean, soft, new things around me.

Sam did his best to make up for *that thing* he said, that night. He was diligent in his care. He and Bronson cooked all the meals (some better than others) and got around to doing a few of the jobs we'd left hanging when we charged off to Godalming. He let me choose what we watched on the telly for a change. Bronson made himself useful, and for a while, when the press were camped outside, he slept in the spare room.

Auntie Babs hired an agency to do a deep clean in the museum and suggested a free spray tan too. I declined, but did take her up on a haircut. Against her wishes I got her to cut away my blonde locks, then dye the rest of it to match my roots. So it was brown and styled into a bob. She suggested a makeover to help me adjust to the new shade but I wasn't in the mood.

I was in a weird one: contemplative. It wasn't usual and I could see it was freaking everyone out. So when Sam suggested we had a Christmas do at the museum I reluctantly assented.

And, do you know what? It worked.

The preparations engaged my brain in such a way that I was able to shut up memories of Waketon in an invisible box and shove it to the back of my mind, with all the other difficult issues I needed to face at some point. But not now.

Bronson and Sam were making a mess of all the decorations. I did wonder if they were doing it on purpose, but Sam assured me they weren't. Still, it was clear someone with a more enhanced sense of the aesthetic needed to step in. So I did. And it lifted my spirits. Being bossy does that for me.

In the end we had quite a marvellous 'do', despite some theatrics from our resident protestor's nephew. Sam and I got cosy under the mistletoe, and for a moment there, I really did think our luck was changing. But then Bob Acton dropped his pitchfork on the curator's foot and, well, the moment was lost.

It was some time after New Year's that Monty phoned me to give me the news that Madeleine Arkwright was going to be okay. Her operations had been successful, though she would need physiotherapy. But she would be allowed to return home in couple of months. It was good news and I think that was why I opened the back door with such a big grin on my face.

And I'm glad I did. It was late, a few hours after the museum had shut. I was expecting it to be Sam having forgotten his key or Babs dropping by to check in on me. But it was neither. It was Dorcus standing in the moonlight with a bunch of lilies in his arms.

'I won't come in,' he said. 'I just heard about your, er, incident.'

'Oh yeah,' I said, couldn't think of anything else. His eyes, round pools of infinite blackness, were drawing me in.

'I had to go away,' he said, 'so I've only just heard. But I wanted to ...' he held the bouquet out, '... I wanted to give you these.'

As our hands bumped, the hairs on my forearms prickled to attention. Not because I was scared or cold, though it was draughty out there, but because I was hyper-aware of him. And once more his touch prompted a rush of sensory memories – the hush of a bat's wing closing, a red-breasted robin's bloody beak, the spark of a cannon firing. It made me forget about everything. And I think that's why I answered the way I did.

'I thought you might need some distracting,' he said oblivious to the fact he was doing a marvellous job already. 'And there's a new fusion restaurant in Litchenfield, if you—'

'Yes,' I said, interrupting him.

'Oh,' he shook his head in pleasant surprise. 'You'll find my card in the flowers ...'

'I've already programmed it into my phone,' I said, then realised I was being too enthusiastic. 'In case I needed to speak to you about any, er, military historical researchy thingummybobs.'

'And do you?' he said, creasing his cheeks into a smile.

God, those cheekbones were to die for.

'Yes, I do.'

He nodded and backed away. A red tongue poked between his lips and moistened them. 'Maybe next week then?'

'That'll do,' I said. 'I mean maybe. I'll call you.'

And then, just like that, he was gone.

Blimey, I thought, what have I just done?

But a gal couldn't wait forever for Sam.

Life was too short.

Shaggy Man had done his worst, but there was no way I was going to let him stuff me, stuff my life.

There were things I had to reconcile and others that I would let go.

And I was going to do that.

I was going to move on.

CHAPTER THIRTY-SEVEN

Just so you're clear, I see ghosts.

Yeah.

I *know*.

I don't mean to.

But I do.

There's really no getting away from it.

I can't turn it on.

I can't turn it off.

It just happens.

And to be honest, it's no surprise really.

I've spent years attempting to be superficial. Now it turns out that I've got depths to me that other mortals haven't even dreamed of.

And me, an Essex girl.

Stick that in your dictionary definition Oxford Learner's Dictionary. Edit it in, go on. Alongside 'not intelligent, dresses badly, talks in a loud and ugly way, and is very willing to have sex'.

Yep, that's what it actually says.

Add 'sees ghosts'.

Might as well.

Though, at the same time – what are ghosts anyway?

Part of me once thought they might be memories. Fragments of people left over in your mind. Echoes.

But that's disingenuous. Truly, I now know that's not the case.

Or not *only* the case.

In fact if I'm going to be honest, and I might as well be, I guessed it long before Inspector Howard came down and put that photo on the table.

I just didn't want to admit it.

I never have.

'Is this Connor?' Howard asked.

It was a lovely picture. His bright-as-a-button smile beamed out of an untidy school uniform. Two teeth missing at the front. The tie was wonky, the neck of the jumper coming away at the shoulder and his hair much longer than I'd seen. He was a few years younger, but it was definitely him.

They'd found him, you see. The police had. Their forensics team, to be precise. He was one of the mummified boys. Way back when it happened, Tobias had watched the poor boy's family. If 'family' is what you could call it. Shaggy Man had soon learnt that if he stole Connor, the kid was unlikely to be missed.

Debbie, who'd accompanied Howard, told me there was no evidence there had been abuse. At least *nothing sexual.* Though being abducted, tied up and then drugged to death wasn't exactly nurturing, was it? That's what I'd said. She let me be hostile. She appreciated where it was coming from.

Connor Mathews had disappeared in 1999.

'So long ago?' I'd said. 'Could he have been tied up all that time?'

'But he wasn't tied up,' they nudged me gently. 'Though he *was* at the table in the barn.'

'But I saw him,' I said. 'Moving around. Talking to me.'

'He'd be around thirty now,' said Debbie.

'So,' I said. 'Who did I see?'

'There was dust on the chain,' Howard volunteered. 'The one in the barn. In the corner, where you said he had been sitting. Next to the pillow you said you threw at him. But the chain, well, it hadn't been touched for years.'

My shrink thinks I externalised a part of my self. A section of my psyche that above all wanted to survive. That wanted me to live and helped me to do so. I'd given it a form and I'd communicated with the boy that I'd made up, drawn him from scraps of what I'd seen and what I'd heard.

But I hadn't.

Sam had started talking about Apophenia but I shut him up quickly.

I'd seen Connor's ghost.

It wasn't like it hadn't happened before.

And I wasn't the only one either. Remember it was Pearl White who first heard the clue – the Washing Up Man who'd preyed upon the Spirit Boys.

One of them had talked to her.

It was hard for the police to ignore.

However, in the end, they established that there were no links between the Whites and Stuey. Thank goodness. And after a very stressful few days they were released. Some people put Pearl's 'messages' down to opportunism. Others, locals, didn't. They avoided her now. It was a shame. I don't think she deserved it but there you go. There's no judging how people will react to trauma like that.

In Stuey's former neighbourhood a campaign had started: 'Nose Out for Your Neighbours', which was all about getting people to be 'nosy' and keep an eye on each other's kids. Over a hundred people had signed up so I guess you could say that at least something good came of all the horror.

But it had been a tough time. And it wasn't over yet. I knew Inspector Howard would be back again. He'd said as much. Plus, I hadn't started my report for Monty. Agent Walker was being extremely nice about it, probably because he kicked the whole thing off by getting Michael and Sam together again. It was well intentioned, he knew there was conflict there, because of Jasper Stone, and hoped that working together might mend that relationship. Perhaps it did. It didn't really help mine, though. Still, I knew I couldn't put it off forever. I just didn't want to send my brain back to the bodies and the barn.

Grimm and grimmer.

But now I had a date with Dorcus on the horizon. Something nice and sexy to take my mind off the gloom. If we got on. Which I kind of hoped we did. But I found there was no telling with men. Sometimes they acted like they liked you, the next moment they were allowing nutters to blow your head off.

Beyond me, it really was.

'I was wondering where you had got to?' Sam's face appeared at the door of the living room. 'You look deep in thought.'

'Mmm,' I said.

'What are you thinking about?' he asked breezily and came inside. A tell-tale frown was tensing the muscles of his forehead, though he was fighting the urge to squeeze them hard.

'Shoes,' I told him.

He laughed and the tension went out of his pose. 'Of course.'

I inspected him, all worried, a strange fire burning in his eyes. I still hadn't forgiven him. But, just like the world around me, I was coming out of the darkness. The days were getting longer. Spring would soon be here. I knew that when *the incident*, as we referred to the aforementioned nutter/shotgun/death episode, occurred, my friend and curator did have a lot of things on his mind. A vanished younger brother being just one of them. I was prepared to make *some* allowances. We'd have to see how it all played out.

'You all right?' he asked and padded over to the sofa.

'What do you want? I said, though it came out unintentionally gruff.

'Well, I've had a phone call,' he wagged his mobile. 'Monty.'

'Oh yeah?' I hoped he didn't want his report.

'Big Ig is back,' he said and smiled. In his eyes those amber flints were whirring, energised by conflicting emotions – hope laced with shame.

I took it on board – he only wanted to help make amends for his lapse of judgement during *the incident* but it wasn't working for me. I'd started coming over all lethargic when I thought about the mystery of my dad. I don't know why. Perhaps the fight had gone out of me.

Hecate, who had followed him in, jumped straight on my lap and started kneading me.

'He wants us to check in on Haven.' Sam crinkled his eyes and tried to look casual.

'Oh right,' I said and then remembered – Haven. Where Dorcus lived.

As if telepathic (and quite frankly that wasn't beyond the realms of possibility), Hecate blasted me an admonishing stare.

'Sorry,' I said to her. She stuck her chin out and settled down, but continued to waft her tail under my nose by way of reprimand.

'What?' said Sam. 'Are you apologising about Big Ig?'

'Oh no,' I told him, turning back to the matter at hand. 'Oh I don't know, sometimes it just feels like Monty's dangling Big Ig like a carrot.'

'That's one mighty heavy vegetable from what I remember of him,' said Sam, then winced as a terrific crash came up from somewhere in the museum. 'Oh yes, the builders are back. With a vengeance.'

Oh God – that was all I needed. There'd be noise and dust

and teabags piling up again before you could say 'Four sugars please'. Perhaps we should duck out for a bit.

'What's in Haven? Remind me again?' I asked, attempting to recall the conversation we'd had so long ago. 'More skinned cats?'

'There's been an escalation,' Sam whispered. 'Someone's been murdered.'

But Hecate heard him and meowed. The indignant feline outcry sounded remarkably like, 'Good'.

Sam looked at her, then back to me. 'Ordeal by water.'

I frowned. 'Like the witches?'

'Got it in one,' Sam said.

I thought again about Dorcus and then a more vivid image replaced him – Celeste sinking, the waves of the brook washing over her.

'So, do you think you're ready for a new adventure?' Sam asked.

Hecate nodded and twitched her head towards the door: 'Go on.' Enough with the peer pressure.

'Well?' said Sam.

There was only ever going to be one answer to that.

'Get your car keys then,' I said.

CHAPTER THIRTY-EIGHT

... on Church Lane. I have no idea. It is altogether strange. Terry did ask months back if he would see me, I know, but the poor old man was terribly ill. Why he so fervently wishes me to grant me an audience on his death bed, and by all accounts in some great pain, is quite a mystery.

Yet go I shall. And I will listen with eagerness to all he has to tell. Maybe it is a confession – of witchcraft, sorcery or divination? My father is often called for on such occasions. I imagine that the family believe, as he is away, the duty falls to me.

Yes, that must be it. Why else would old Albert Beckinsdale insist on seeing me now?

I'll get it over and done with quickly, so I can be clear to devote my time to Danton's visit. I hope he will know who the dark men are. And why it seems they are watching me. But I'll not think on that, for it makes me frightened. I don't want that. This visit must be joyful. I should be bright and sunny and blithe when I present him with our child. My beautiful gift. My tiny, gurgling baby daughter. Such a special creature, so full of gifts. Rose will make him happy, this I know for sure. I can feel it in my heart. The future is full of hope.

Despite the cards.

ACKNOWLEDGEMENTS

Jenny Parrott and Molly Scull must be thanked first of all for their dazzling editorial brains and excellent solutions. Without you both this book would have been thoroughly evil. And Jenny, thank you for *all* your sage advice, you are a diamond. Mark Rusher and Margot Weale dish out the smarts and tell all the people about all my books, which is invaluable.

My appreciation to Francine Brody is immense. Copy-editing is the most feared stage in the birth of any book, but she manages it with finesse and wisdom and has become good friends with Rosie and her idiosyncrasies.

Continued admiration and thanks go out to the Queen and King of Oneworld, Juliet Mabey and Novin Doostdar. Thank you for letting me continue to do what I like to do and feeding me pancakes too.

Josie Moore has been such a fantastic support. Life is not always a walk in the park. Sometimes it's a frantic dash through dark and gnarled trees. Having a sister like Josie means I'm not doing it on my own. Not only is she a total gem in this regard but she is also an incredibly talented artist. Josie was able to channel the creative essence of our dear Rosie's mother and paint the marvellous tarot cards that illustrate Celeste Strange's diary.

Many thanks to my family who are such a great support. And to my friends also without whom life would be a dull affair.

And last but never least – Sean and Riley.